I could be yo[illegible]

Right. As if he'd e[illegible] to compete with the [illegible]ve forever. Besides, all his friend had wanted was for Levi to make sure Val was okay. He sincerely doubted falling for the woman had been part of his best friend's plan.

Then again…

Maybe it was time to set aside his loyalty to a dead man for a shot at something far bigger. Maybe, just maybe, this was his chance to be everything to Val, to her girls, that he couldn't have been before. Yes, it had to be her choice to move forward or not. But how could she make that choice if he didn't give her the option? And if the odds were stacked against him… tough.

Wouldn't be the first time.

* * *

Wed in the West:
New Mexico's the perfect place
to finally find true love!

A SOLDIER'S PROMISE

BY
KAREN TEMPLETON

First Published in Great Britain 2016
By Mills & Boon, an imprint of HarperCollins*Publishers*
1 London Bridge Street, London, SE1 9GF

ISBN: 978-0-263-91961-5

23-0216

Our policy is to use papers that are natural, renewable and recyclable products and made from wood grown in sustainable forests.The logging and manufacturing processes conform to the legal environmental regulations of the country of origin.

Printed and bound in Spain
by CPI, Barcelona

Karen Templeton is a recent inductee into the Romance Writers of America Hall of Fame. A three-time RITA® Award-winning author, she has written more than thirty novels for Mills & Boon and lives in New Mexico with two hideously spoiled cats. She has raised five sons and lived to tell the tale, and could not live without dark chocolate, mascara and Netflix.

To my oldest son, Christopher
Whose own service continues to bless.
Semper Fi, dude.

Chapter One

Sweat streamed down Levi Talbot's back as he sat in his pickup across the street, watching Valerie Lopez paint the window trim of a house he hadn't set foot in for… *Damn. Ten years, at least.*

She was even skinnier than he remembered, sharp shoulder blades shifting, bunching over the scoop of a white tank top that teased the waistband of her low-rise jeans. Her pale hair was still long, wadded on top of her head, pieces sticking out every which way. In a nearby play yard a dark-haired baby sat gnawing on a plastic toy, while her older sister lay on her belly on the mottled floorboards, quietly singing as she scribbled, bare feet swinging to and fro. Then the little girl shoved to her knees, thrusting the open coloring book toward her mother.

"Mama! I gave her hair like mine! See?"

Levi saw Val glance over, her smile gentle as she bent to get a better look. Chuckling softly, she fingered the girl's deep brown curls.

"A huge improvement, I'd say," she said. The child giggled, making Val smile even bigger, and Levi flinched.

How the hell was he supposed to do this? Whatever *this* was.

And why the hell had it never occurred to him he might actually have to make good on that dumb-ass promise he'd made to Tomas when they'd first enlisted?

A breeze lanced his damp shirt, making him shiver. Squinting in the bolt of sunlight glancing off the sharply angled tin roof, Levi frowned at the house, which seemed to frown right back at him. An uneasy cross between Victorian and log cabin, the house seemed to slump in on itself, like it was too tired to care anymore. Or had finally succumbed to its identity crisis. And slapping some paint over what was most likely rotting wood wasn't going to change that.

He could relate.

He waited for an SUV to pass—not much traffic on this stretch of Main Street, the last gasp of civilization before miles of nothing—before getting out of his truck, his boots crunching on asphalt chewed up even worse than usual after last winter's heavy snow. A hawk keened, annoyed, from a nearby piñon, whose branches tangled with the deep blue sky. From inside the house, a dog exploded into frenzied barking. Val and the child turned, the little girl's gaze more curious than concerned. Her mother's, however…

Yeah. Considering she hadn't exactly been a fan *before* he and Tommy had enlisted, Levi sincerely doubted that was about to change. Promise or no promise. In fact, what he saw in those blue eyes could only be described as… Well, *fierce* would work. *Pissed off* was more likely.

He stopped at the bottom step.

"Levi." Val hauled the baby out of her little cage, tucked her against her ribs. Close-up, she seemed even smaller, probably not even coming to his shoulders. He remembered, though, how her smile could light up the whole town. Not that she'd ever given him that smile. "Heard you were back."

He nodded, unsure of what came next. Hating that this puny little blonde was unnerving him more than driving supply trucks along dusty mountain roads that might or might not have been booby-trapped by the Taliban.

"Last week, yeah."

The baby grabbed hold of a hank of her mother's hair, tried to stuff it in her mouth. The older girl—seven, he thought—sidled closer; Val looped her arm around the girl's shoulders as dark eyes exactly like her father's regarded Levi with that same intense gaze. Had Val ever mentioned Levi to her daughter? Had Tommy?

"For good?" Val said.

"For now, anyway." The dog's barking grew more frantic. "So. These are your girls?"

Val shot him an are-you-nuts look, but she played along. "Yes. This is Josie," she said, giving the older girl's shoulders a quick squeeze. "And this is Risa."

Laughter in Spanish. Levi's heart knocked—Tommy had never even seen his second daughter.

"I'm sorry—"

"Don't," Val whispered, her eyes shiny.

"I couldn't get back at the time," Levi finished through a clogged throat, remembering his shock when he'd gotten the call from Tommy's dad. "I asked, but they said no."

Her face said it all: *And exactly what good would that have done?*

Along with: *You can leave now.* Except he couldn't. Because he'd made a promise. One he fully intended to keep.

Whether his best friend's widow was good with that idea or not.

* * *

Val'd figured she'd run into Levi eventually—his parents didn't live far, and there was only one halfway decent grocery store in town—but she hadn't counted on him actually seeking her out.

Of course, her rational side knew Levi Talbot wasn't responsible for her husband's death. That particular honor went to whoever had planted that roadside bomb near some godforsaken Afghani village with a name Val couldn't even pronounce. But if Levi hadn't joined the army six years ago, Val highly doubted that Tommy—who'd worshipped his best friend since high school for reasons Val had never understood—would've decided to enlist, too.

A thought that ripped open barely healed wounds all over again.

"Josie, why don't you go inside?" she quietly asked, smiling down at her daughter. At least this one might remember her daddy. Although considering how much he'd been gone…

"Mama?"

"Levi and I just need to talk alone for a sec, baby. And don't let the dog out, okay?"

Josie shot Levi a questioning look before shoving open the stubborn door and wriggling past the dog to get inside. Only after the door clicked closed did Val turn back to Levi, as muscled and tall as Tomas had been slight. All the Talbot boys were built like their father, tough and rough and full of surprising angles, like they'd been hastily hewn out of the mountains holding silent watch over sleepy Whispering Pines. Oh, yeah, Levi Talbot was one good-looking sonofagun, despite badly needing a shave and a half-grown-out buzz cut that wasn't doing him any favors—

"So you're living here now," Levi said. Carefully, like she was a horse who might spook. Val set Risa back in her play yard and handed her a toy, then crouched, gripping the top of the pen.

"Temporarily. Since Tommy's grandmother moved in with his folks, the family said we can stay as long as we need." She heard a creak behind her as he came up onto the porch.

"Big place for three people."

As in, way bigger than Val needed. Five bedrooms, three baths. Dark. Dreary. "Yeah. It is," she said, straightening in time to see Levi's gaze flick over the worn porch floorboards, the gap-toothed porch railings.

"Needs a lot of work."

Despite the situation, a smile pushed at Val's mouth. "Part of the deal was that I get it fixed up. So they can get top dollar when it goes on the market. After everything they've done for me, I couldn't exactly say no. Besides—" she almost smiled "—it would break Lita's heart if I wasn't here."

Levi's brows dipped. "They expect you to foot the bill?"

"Of course not. It's not my house, is it?"

He was staring at her. Not rudely, but intently, his muddy green eyes focused on her like lasers. Exactly like he used to do when they were younger, as though he couldn't figure her out. Or more likely, why his best friend would prefer her company to his. And damned if it didn't make her every bit as uneasy now as it did then—

"For pity's sake, Levi—why are you here?"

If her outburst threw him, he didn't let on. Although his Adam's apple definitely worked before he said, "Tommy was my closest friend, Val. I was best man at your wedding. Did you think I'd come home and not check on you?"

Risa began to fuss; Val picked her up again, pressing her lips into her curls, cool and soft against her hot face. "At least you got to come home," she murmured, then lifted her gaze to Levi's, the hurt in his eyes almost enough to make her feel like a bitch. Almost. Because there were days when her anger was about the only thing keeping her from losing it. That, and love for her daughters, she thought as Risa yawned, then plugged her thumb in her mouth and settled against Val's chest.

"And as you can see," she said, ignoring her stinging eyes, "I'm okay. So. We're good."

Levi did that staring thing again, his mouth stubborn-set, the earlier devastation in his eyes replaced by something else Val couldn't quite put a finger on but knew she didn't like.

"This place was a wreck fifteen years ago. I can only imagine what it's like now. Tommy's kids..." He paused, his nostrils flaring when he took a breath. "They deserve better than this." Another pause. "And so do you."

His words hit her. Hard. Not that people hadn't been kind since her return. But it'd been an uncomfortable kindness mostly, a ragtag collection of mumbled "sorries" and brief, awkward hugs, soon replaced by either gaping silence or a false cheeriness that made her want to scream. With Levi, though—it wasn't the same, that's all. Although it wouldn't be, would it?

"Thank you—"

"You can give me a list, if you want. Might as well start with this porch, though." He shifted his weight into the next plank over, making it squawk. "Some of these floorboards look pretty sketchy—"

"Levi."

He looked up, his brow creased. "Yeah?"

"Why?"

It was all she could think to say. Not enough, however, to provoke an answer.

"I'll be back in the morning," he said softly, then went down the steps and back across the street, where he got into a black pickup, slamming the door before taking off. Toward his parents' house, she imagined, where she'd heard via the grapevine he was staying.

Val rearranged the now sleeping baby in her arms and grabbed the wet paintbrush, then went back inside, where she dumped the brush into the chipped kitchen sink before hauling Risa upstairs to put her in her crib. This and Josie's room were the only ones she'd painted so far: a pale aqua in here, yellow in Josie's. The gouged pine floors still needed to be redone. Along with a dozen other projects that made Val's head hurt to think about.

Because the house *was* a wreck, the victim of decades of benign neglect and an old woman's failing eyesight. Yes, being so close to Tommy's parents was a blessing, and the family was being very generous in so many ways. But the idea of going through renovations on top of everything else…

All of which had sounded perfectly feasible when Angelita Lopez had promised the house to them two years ago, for when Tommy came back home.

A thought Val deliberately let linger, as though to toughen her heart. So when this one—she leaned over the crib to finger Risa's soft curls—asked about her daddy, Val would be able to speak with love, not pain. Less pain, anyway.

Risa flipped onto her back, arms splayed like she was making snow angels. A smile flickered across the baby's mouth, making Val smile in return, her heart swell. Because life, she sternly reminded herself, was about cherishing what you had, not regretting what you'd lost. About accepting the gifts that came your way. Even those that, at first glance, seemed more trouble than they were worth. Like this butt-ugly house.

Like, say, offers from the last man in the world you wanted to deal with right now—or ever—to help fix up said butt-ugly house.

Val sighed.

Back downstairs, she peeked into the cave-like living room, a hodgepodge of dull, dark wood and mismatched furniture pieces. Eyes glued to the TV screen, Josie sat cross-legged on the sofa, pointy elbows digging into scabbed bare knees. The hound stretched on the cushion beside her, dead to the world, chin and paws propped on the sofa's arm.

"Is he gone?" Josie asked.

"He is. Whatcha watching?" As if she didn't know.

"Elf."

Val smiled. "Again?"

The little girl shrugged. "I like it," she said, and Val's heart twisted. On his last leave—two Christmases ago—Tomas and Josie had watched the movie together a million times. Then Josie forgot about it…until she found the DVD when they unpacked.

"This was Daddy's favorite scene," her daughter said softly, and Val decided this was part of that toughening-up-her-heart thing. Although if a stupid movie helped her baby still feel connected to her father, she'd take it. Because Val knew those memories would fade, would be replaced by a whole life's worth of new ones. Oh, there'd be scraps left, of course, but they'd be as soft and faded as the ribbons from Val's wedding bouquet.

"Fried chicken okay for dinner?"

Josie nodded again, then pulled her knees up to her chin, her far-too-old gaze swinging to Val's.

"So that was Levi," Josie said, and Val nearly choked.

"It was. Did…Daddy talk to you about him?"

"Uh-huh," she said easily, her gaze returning to the TV. "He said if anything happened to him? Levi would take care of us."

Val could barely hear her own voice for the clanging inside her head. "When did Daddy say that?"

Josie shrugged. “Before he left. The last time. He said if he didn’t come back, Levi would make sure we were okay. Because they were best friends, that Levi always had his back. That…” The little girl frowned, as though she was trying to remember, then smiled. “That, except for you, he trusted Levi more than anyone in the world.”

Val dropped onto the edge of the craptastic armchair at right angles to the sofa, pressing her hand to her stomach as she rode out a new wave of anger. *What the hell were you* thinking, *Tommy?* To confide in Josie—who was only five at the time—rather than her…

Not to mention even suggest that he might not come back.

Val shut her eyes, breathing deeply. Funny how, with her background, Val had always considered herself a realist. Not a pessimist, exactly, but fully aware of how often things could go wrong. Tomas, though…he’d been the dreamer, the idealist, seeing silver linings where Val only saw clouds, giving her glimpses of shiny hope peeking through years of gloom and doom. No wonder she’d fallen in love with him. And consequently why, every time he left, she’d steeled herself against the possibility that he might not come home. Especially considering his particular job. “High risk” didn’t even begin to cover it.

But little girls shouldn’t have to worry about such things, or live in fear about what *might* happen. All she’d wanted—which Tomas knew—was to make a safe, secure life for her children. That her sweet, gentle husband had gone behind her back, undermining everything she’d fought so hard for—

“Mama? What’s wrong?”

How about everything?

“I… I didn’t know. About what Daddy said.”

“You mad?”

She smiled—tightly—before holding out her arms. Josie

clumsily slid off the sofa to climb on Val's lap, where Val wrapped her up tight to lay her head in her daughter's springy hair, struggling to find the peace she'd once let herself believe was finally hers.

"I'm surprised, that's all."

"That Daddy didn't tell you?"

"Uh-huh."

Josie picked at the little knotted bracelet encircling Val's wrist, the one Tomas had given her when they'd first started going together, more than a dozen years ago now. It was grimy and frayed and borderline disgusting, and Val would never take it off.

"Daddy made me promise not to say anything. He said it was our secret. But that he wanted me to know it'd be okay." She leaned back to meet Val's eyes. "With Levi."

Yeah, well, somehow Val doubted that. For a boatload of reasons so knotted up in her head she doubted she'd ever straighten them out.

But she certainly didn't need to drag her little girl into the maelstrom of emotions Levi's appearance had provoked. However...she supposed she might as well let the man fix her porch, since those rotting floorboards gave her the willies, too, and it wasn't as if she could replace them herself. And the nearby ski resort had apparently hired every contractor, carpenter and handyman in a hundred-mile radius for a massive, and long-overdue, renovation.

So. A job she could give him. Anything else, though—

Holding her daughter even more tightly, Val reminded herself, again, to be grateful for what she still had—her beautiful daughters, Tommy's doting parents, a roof over their heads, even if it wasn't exactly hers. More than she ever thought she'd have, once upon a time.

And damned if she was about to let Levi Talbot screw that up.

* * *

Levi slammed shut the gate to his old pickup and piled high what he hoped was enough lumber to fix Val's porch. Yeah, he should've taken measurements, but that would've meant hanging around, that last "Why?" of hers buzzing around inside his head like a ticked-off bee. Not that it still didn't. But yesterday, with nothing separating him and Val but a few feet of hot resentment, he couldn't deal with the question and her eyes. Those eyes—they were surreal, a pale blue like pond ice reflecting the sky. Cold as that ice, too.

At least she hadn't told him to go to hell, he thought, as he headed out of the Lowe's parking lot. Not with her mouth, anyway. He only wished Tomas had been a little clearer about what he'd meant by "Take care of them, bro."

He turned off the main road leading to the ski resort onto the dinkier one that went on to Whispering Pines. At this altitude, early mornings were chilly even in May. Would've been a peaceful drive from Taos, too, if it hadn't been for the hard rock music pulsing through the cab, his head, driving out any and all wayward thoughts. Same music he'd listen to in the Sandbox, and for the same reason—to drown out that bizarre blend of boredom and constant anxiety nobody ever admitted to. At least not out loud.

He'd thought he'd known what he was getting into, that he was prepared, only to soon discover nobody and nothing could prepare you for reality. That reality, anyway. But he'd made a commitment, and he'd kept it. One of the few things he was apparently good at. God knew he'd done more than his fair share of dumb-ass stuff growing up, but he'd never, not once, gone back on his word. And damned if he was gonna start now.

Levi tapped the steering wheel in time to the beat as the road meandered through patches of ranch land, the occasional spurt of forest, backdropped by the mountains that provided Whispering Pines and other puny little northern New Mexico towns like it, both spring runoff and something resembling a viable economy. Differences were subtle—a new fence here, a fresh coat of paint on a house there. He should've found the continuity comforting. Instead, the sameness bugged him. Same way everybody expected him to somehow fit right back in, as if he were the same goofy twenty-two-year-old who'd joined up six years ago. Not that he knew for sure yet who he was, but for sure that clueless kid wasn't it.

The village was still half asleep, the tourist traps and art galleries and chichi restaurants on Main Street not yet ready to welcome the resort patrons curious enough to come down the mountain to investigate "real" New Mexico. Almost silently, the truck navigated the gentle roller coaster that was the town's main drag, past the sheriff's office and the elementary/middle school, the 7-Eleven and the Chevron station, the corner anchored by one bank and three churches. Rosa Munoz was out in front of the Catholic church, clipping lilacs, same as she'd been doing for as long as Levi could remember. Wearing the same sweater, too, from what Levi could tell.

Long before he reached the house, he spotted Val standing on the porch in a hoodie and jeans, clutching a mug in her hands. Like maybe she was waiting for him, although common sense told him that was dumb. He backed into the driveway, the top layer of cement eroded worse than the street in front of it. The dog—a good-size hound, he now saw—bounded up when he opened the door, baying loud enough to cause an avalanche. Still seated behind the wheel, Levi glanced down at the dog, then over to Val.

"You mind calling him off?"

"Don't worry—he doesn't bite. Hasn't yet, anyway."

Shaking his head, Levi got out, pushed past the still

barking dog and headed up the driveway…straight into Val's frown. Which he ignored. By now the damn dog was jumping around, occasionally shoving his cold nose into Levi's hand. "Uh…if you got him as a guard dog, you might want to see about getting your money back."

"*I* didn't get him at all. Tommy brought him home one day from some rescue place near the base. Scrawniest puppy I'd ever seen." Levi looked up. The frown was still there, but her eyes didn't seem quite as icy as before. "I didn't have the heart to say no. To him or the dog."

Levi looked back at the beast. Who'd planted his butt on the rough ground and was waving one paw at him, like he wanted to shake. Levi obliged. "What's his name?"

"Radar."

"Because Early Warning System would've been too obvious."

Val's mouth might've twitched. "Not to mention too hard for a toddler to say." Then she clamped her mouth shut, as if regretting her humorous slip.

"Where are the girls?"

"With their grandmother. Connie and Pete live closer to the school, and she takes care of the baby while I'm at the diner—"

"The diner?"

"Annie's Café. Part-time."

"You're waitressing?"

"I'm doing whatever it takes to keep sane. And we need to get a few things straight."

Levi propped one booted foot on the bottom step as a tremor shot up his spine. "Which would be?"

Val's cheeks went pink. He guessed not from the chill in the air. "This is strictly a business arrangement. Why you're here is…immaterial. As you duly noted yesterday, the house needs a lot of work. Work I can't do."

Levi decided to put the why-he-was-here comment on hold for a moment. "Because you weigh less than the dog?"

She smirked. "Because I don't know bubkes about fixing up houses. And I gather you do."

"Enough. Although if you've got serious electrical or plumbing issues, you'll need to call in a pro. I can change out fixtures and sh—stuff, but anything more than that—"

"Got it. But I'm hiring you. Meaning I expect to be given a bill for your work—"

"Not gonna happen."

"Then you're right. It isn't."

"You don't mean that."

A moment's hesitation preceded, "Yeah. I do. And, yes, I know what I just said—"

Levi held up one hand, cutting off the conversation before it got even stupider than it already was. He remembered Tommy's mentioning Val's stubbornness from time to time. His friend found it amusing, probably because he was crazy in love with the girl. Right now, Levi was more inclined toward annoyance. Pushing back his denim jacket to cram his hands into his front pockets, he frowned.

"You really hate me that much?"

Judging from her wide eyes, he'd shocked her. Good. Took a moment before she apparently found her voice. "What I do or don't feel about you has nothing to do with it. But when there aren't clear-cut expectations, things can get…weird."

"Agreed. Except since I doubt either of us would let it, not an issue. Besides…"

Damn. He could almost hear Tomas whispering in his ear, *Dude—you gotta be up front with her.*

"Okay…when you asked 'why' yesterday, the reason I didn't answer wasn't because I didn't have an answer. It was because… I couldn't find the words. Any that sounded right, at least…"

"You're here because Tommy asked you to keep an eye on me and the girls."

Levi started. "He told you?"

"No. Josie did. Yesterday, after you left."

"Hell."

"Yeah. Still haven't wrapped my head around the fact that he said something to our kid but not me. So I already know why you're here—"

"Because I made a promise, yeah. And I know you don't like me, or trust me, or whatever, so this is every bit as awkward and uncomfortable for me as it is you. Except the longer I think about it, the more I realize none of that matters. Because what *matters* is making sure my best friend's kids aren't living someplace that's gonna fall down around their ears. That here's something I can do to maybe make things better for somebody, to honor the one person who saw through my BS when we were kids, more than even my parents, my brothers. This is about..."

He felt his throat work. "About my debt to my best friend. One I fully intend to make good on. So it might make things a little easier if you'd get on board with that. Now. You want to pay for materials, I won't object. But my labor... It's my gift, okay? Because this is about what Tommy wanted. Not you, not me—Tommy. So deal."

That got a few more moments of the staring thing before Val released a short, humorless laugh. "Wow. Guess you found your words."

"Yeah, well, don't get used to it, I just used up at least three months' worth. So are we good?"

Another pause. "Except what are you supposed to live on?"

"Never mind about that. But here." He dug the rumpled Lowe's receipt out of his pocket, handed it over. What he kept to himself, though—for the moment, anyway—was that he knew how much the family had set aside for repairs, because he'd asked Pete Lopez the night before. Not nearly enough, if his hunch was correct about the extent of the work needed. Especially if she ended up having to call in pros. "Also," he said as she looked it over, "you don't need to stick around. I brought my own lunch. And the woods over there will work fine when nature calls." Her eyes shot to his; he shrugged. "I'm used to making do."

Shaking her head, she grabbed her purse off a table on the porch, stuffed the receipt inside. "The house is open, feel free to use the facilities—"

"You're very trusting."

"Don't read too much into it—there's absolutely nothing worth stealing. Unless you have a thing for Disney princesses. In which case, knock yourself out. I'll be back around three-thirty, after I pick up the girls. The dog can stay out front as long as his water dish is filled, but don't let him out back, since there's no fence. And no, I don't get it, either, why he won't leave the front yard but heeds the call of the wild the minute he hits the back deck."

Levi swallowed his smile. "Got it."

She started down the steps, only to turn around before she reached her car, a dinged-up Toyota RAV4 with a small American flag hanging limply from the antenna. "If you do a crap job on my porch? There will be hell to pay."

"Fair enough."

With a nod, she finished the short walk to her car, stripping out of the hoodie before getting in. And Levi couldn't help noticing how the sunlight kissed her hair, her slender shoulders…the shoulders, he knew, that had borne far more burdens than they should have. Not only recently, but before, when they were still in school and he'd hear the sniggering. Like it was somehow Val's fault her mother was the way she was, that her father had left them high and dry when she was a little kid.

No, he thought as she backed out of the drive, took off,

he didn't imagine trusting had ever come easy to Valerie Oswald. With damn good reason. By comparison he and Tomas had led charmed lives, with parents who loved them, were there for them, even if Levi's had sometimes been a little more *there* than he might've liked. But it hadn't been like that for Val, who must've figured it was simply easier to keep to herself than to either live a lie or apologize for her mother. Which naturally led everyone to think she was either stuck-up or weird.

Almost everyone, anyway, Levi thought, as he yanked a large toolbox out of the truck, grabbed a crowbar to start prying up the rotten floorboards. So how could the girl who'd worked so hard to overcome her past not look at Levi without being reminded of what she'd lost?

Clearly Tommy hadn't thought that part of his plan through.

With a grunt, he wrenched up the first board and tossed it out into the yard, chuckling when the dumb dog first scampered back, then growled at the board like it was a snake.

Which pretty much said it all, didn't it?

Chapter Two

Val shoved the last of the peach pies into the commercial-size freezer, then crossed to the stainless steel sink in the gleaming kitchen to wash her hands.

"All done?" AJ Phillips, who with his wife, Annie, had run Annie's Café for thirty years, called from the other side of the checkerboard-floored room, where he was molding a half-dozen meat loaves to bake for the dinner rush. On the massive gas stove simmered cauldrons of green chile stew and posole, although the fried chicken would happen later, closer to dinnertime. In any case, the kitchen already smelled like heaven. A New Mexican's version of it, anyway.

"Yep," Val called back, shaking water off her hands before grabbing a paper towel. "A dozen."

Grinning, the bald, dark-skinned man noisily shoved the trays in the oven. "My mouth's already watering," he said, and Val laughed.

It wasn't ideal, though, having to make the pies during the afternoon lull, then freeze them to bake the next morning. But between the kids and not having a health-department-approved kitchen—yet—this was the best she could do. And since nobody was complaining, neither would she. *Take that, Marie Callender,* she thought with a slight smile as she walked back out into the dining room, where the only customer was Charley Maestas, hunched over a probably cold cup of coffee at the counter. His part pit bull mutt, sporting a blue bandanna around his neck, lay on the floor beside him, still but alert, as if he knew he wasn't supposed to be inside. Although Annie said as far as she was concerned Loco was a service dog, and that was that.

Val squeezed the older man's shoulder, his vintage denim jacket worn soft, as she passed him on her way to the ladies'. "Hey, Charley—how's it going?"

Charley grunted his acknowledgment, his hand shaking as he lifted the heavy crockery mug to his mouth. The Iraq vet wasn't homeless, although the cabin on the town's outskirts next to his old cabinetmaking shop was no palace. But his graying beard was always neatly trimmed and his clothes clean, smelling of pine needles and menthol. She knew he'd served a couple of tours overseas with the National Guard, back before she and Tomas were married, that he'd been medically discharged when an IED went off close enough to inflict some brain damage of indeterminate severity. Some days were better than others, but according to Annie the poor guy would never be able to hold down a real job again. As it was, he often had trouble simply holding on to a thought.

"Can't complain, honey." He took a sip, swallowed, then turned droopy-lidded dark eyes to hers. "You?"

Val smiled, even though seeing him nearly every day was hard on her heart. And not only because he was a constant reminder of her own loss. She remembered him as a funny, sweet man who was crazy about kids—he and his wife, who'd passed away shortly before his last tour, had been childless—with a laugh that could be heard for what seemed like miles. Seeing him like this crushed her inside. Were the sacrifices really worth it? she wondered.

"I'm doing good, thanks. But seems to me you're missing something." She reached into the glass dessert case for the last piece of blueberry pie, which she set, with a fork, in front of the older man.

"Oh. I didn't—"

"It's too messy a piece to charge for. No, seriously, it looks like my dog sat on it." She smiled at his raspy chuckle; then he sobered, staring at the pie.

"He didn't really, did he?"

"No, Charley," she said gently. "I'm just pulling your leg. Because he would've snarfed it up long before he sat on it."

Charley chuckled again, the fork trembling when he picked it up. But the flicker of light in his eyes as he looked over at her, then back at the pie—a blob of flaky crust floating in a glistening, purple puddle—made Val's heart turn over in her chest. The same as it did each time they played out this little scenario, which was pretty much every day.

"You are an angel, girl," he said softly, releasing a blissful sigh as he took his first bite. "Some guy's gonna be damned lucky to get you."

Even as her face warmed, she smiled, ignoring his last comment. She'd told him about Tomas, more than once. Wasn't his fault the information didn't stick.

"It's only a piece of pie, Charley. No biggie." With another light squeeze to his arm she went on to the ladies' room, leaning heavily on the sink to gather her wits. Because to be honest, sometimes Val thought maybe it wouldn't be so bad, not remembering the stuff that hurt.

Except then it'd be like finding out for the first time over and over, wouldn't it? As awful as it was knowing she'd never see her children's father again, she couldn't imagine reliving that initial, searing, disbelieving pain. Whether she'd know she was reliving it or not.

And there went her hyperactive brain again, she thought on a sigh as she pushed away from the sink to go potty. Over the past several hours, between waiting tables and baking, she'd been too busy to think, thank goodness. Especially about how hiring Levi Talbot had left her feeling as if she'd sold her soul. And not only because she still wasn't sure she hadn't made a pact with the devil, but because as much as she wanted to stay angry that Levi had returned unscathed while her husband hadn't returned at all, the haunted look in the devil's green eyes told her he wasn't all that unscathed. Not on the inside.

And that could be a problem.

She flushed and went to wash her hands, grimacing at her reflection in the way-too-brightly-lit mirror. Like most men, Levi would probably bluster through whatever was behind that look, or pretend it didn't matter—Tomas had been a master at it—but Val was guessing Stuff Had Happened. Bad stuff. Which poked at that damned weak spot inside her that, despite everything she'd been through, she'd never been able to toughen up, or even ignore, no matter how badly she'd wanted to. Yeah, caring could be a bitch. The only saving grace was that she imagined the dude would appreciate her sympathy even less than she wanted to feel bad for him—

The door to the tiny bathroom smacked her in the butt as Annie pushed inside. "Sorry, honey—didn't know you were in here!" Her boss vanished into the stall, calling out as she tinkled, "You know the pies sold out today, right? Except for maybe a half-dozen slices, and I doubt they'll last until five-thirty."

"So I gathered. That's great."

"You're telling me."

The toilet roared behind her employer as she emerged to wash her own hands. As usual, half of Annie's salt-and-pepper hair had escaped its topknot, floating around her sun-weathered face as she grinned. "Especially since three people bought *whole* pies. Two cherries, an apple and a lemon meringue. One person bought two," she said to Val's brief frown, then cackled. "You're famous now, girl. In fact, Pam Davis—the Congregational pastor's wife?—said, thanks to you, she's given up baking. Although if her husband ever finds out, she'll have to kill me."

"My lips are sealed," Val said, smiling and tossing her rumpled paper towel into the trash before tugging a folded-up printout from her back pocket. She smoothed it out, then showed it to the woman who'd given Val her first job when she was fifteen, cleaning up after school and making sandwiches on the weekends—a job that had given her enough money to buy something new to wear now and then, to go on school field trips. Annie wasn't the only surrogate mother figure in Val's life, but she had been the first. Nor was this the first conversation they'd had in the diner's loo. Many tears had been shed in here over the years, a good many of them onto Annie's skinny shoulder. "You think the customers would go for this? With my own tweaks, of course."

Annie shook out her readers, hanging on their glittery chain, before wriggling the earpieces through her hair. "Dulce de Leche crème? Holy crap, you bet." She plucked off the glasses and let them drop, where they bungeed off her flat chest. "I'm thinking we're gonna give that Mary-anne Hopkins a run for her money. Especially since those cupcakes of hers she swears she bakes herself? I happen to know for a fact she gets 'em from some commercial outfit in Santa Fe. God alone knows what kind of preservatives and what-all they've got in 'em. So when can you get a sample pie to me? Please say tomorrow."

Val smiled. "I'll try. Depends on how the evening goes. Josie's been balking about doing her homework, so I may have to ride herd. Spring fever, I suppose. Only one more week of school, thank goodness."

Annie's light brown eyes went soft. "How's she doing?"

"Hard to tell," Val said on a sigh. "Most of the time she seems okay, but…she's too quiet. Too serious. She used to be—" she smiled "—gigglier."

"Give her time," Annie said gently, then laid a hand on Val's arm. "And how are *you* doing?"

"Getting by. Listening to hear what's next, I suppose."

The older woman pulled her into a hug, then released her, her hands still on her shoulders. "And that's all anyone can expect. Especially so soon. Although, for what's it's worth? I think you're doing a fabulous job. Those babies are lucky to have you."

"And I'm lucky to have *you*," Val said through her tight throat, adding, as Annie batted away the comment, "No, seriously. I'm…" She took a breath. "It's good to be home."

"Lord, I never thought I'd hear that come out of your mouth."

"Neither did I, Annie. Believe me."

After another hug, and a promise to bring her boss that new pie the next morning, Val left, blinking in the bright spring sunshine flooding the small town square—the brainchild of some enterprising, and optimistic, soul from who knew how many decades before. The native pines and aspens held their own, of course, but the poor maples struggled to thrive at this altitude, and in fact had been replaced more than once over the years.

Which could also be said, Val supposed as she got in her car, parked at an angle in front of the diner, of the town's inhabitants. Outsiders loved to visit but generally found the small town stifling. There were exceptions, of course—like plants, some nonnatives adapted better than others. AJ and Annie, for instance, had landed here as newlyweds and never left. And certainly not everyone born here stayed. But most did. Or found themselves pulled back, for whatever reason. Because apparently those roots were harder to kill than the aspens that cloaked the mountainsides in a blaze of molten glory every fall.

After picking up Josie from school a few blocks away, Val continued to her in-laws' to get the baby, gratitude swelling for the hundredth time for Consuela Lopez's insistence on watching her granddaughters whenever Val needed. Even groggy, cranky ones, she thought as, with a wail of displeasure, a sweaty Risa catapulted herself from her grandmother's arms into Val's.

Underneath a colorful tunic, Connie's bosom jiggled when she laughed. "Honestly, *reynita*…your mama will think I've been pinching you!"

Shushing her screaming "little queen"—not that it worked—Val smiled. Soft and round and all about the hugs, the redhead-by-choice wouldn't have pinched an ant if it was crawling on her, let alone her adored—and only—grandchildren.

"She must've gotten too hot. It was chilly when she went down for her nap, so I put a sweater on her. But it warmed so quickly this afternoon! If I wanted hot, I'd live in Cruces!" Her mother-in-law shuddered, the typical reaction of most northern New Mexicans to the thought of living in Las Cruces, three hundred miles to the south near the Mexican border and a good twenty degrees warmer than Whispering Pines. After being stationed in the Bowels of Hell, Texas, Val could relate. "Josie," Connie now said, "go see what's out on the porch with Gramma Lita! But just look, don't touch, okay?"

At Val's raised eyebrows after her daughter scampered

off, Connie sighed. "A mother cat and her kittens. Pete found them in the Dumpster behind the store. Can you imagine? Two babies, a tuxedo and a gray tabby. Almost weaned, I'm guessing. Adorable." Then she got that look. "I don't suppose…?"

"Forget it. The dog would think I'd brought him a snack."

"Aww, Radar's such a sweetie—"

"No."

Connie shrugged, then tromped over to the fridge for one of the baby's squeezie applesauce things. "There you go, sweetie… So I hear Levi Talbot's working over at the house?"

"Jeez, Connie—" Val readjusted the schlurping Two-Ton Tessie against her hip, then glared at her mother-in-law. "A breath between thoughts would be nice."

"Can't waste time. Josie could return at any second."

"Between Angelita and the kittens? I'll be lucky if I see her again before she's twenty. And yeah. Levi's back. But how did you know?"

"He came over last night. To catch up. To talk about the house."

"He was here?" Val's mouth tightened. "And you didn't think to give me a heads-up?"

Connie took a deep breath, and Val braced herself. Six months on they both might have had more of a handle on the waterworks, but the spigots weren't rusted shut by any means. And now, when Val saw her mother-in-law's eyes glisten, her own stung in response. Then the older woman sighed.

"Look… I know you had your issues with Levi," Connie said gently, then blew a short laugh through her nose. "Heaven knows, so did we. From time to time, anyway. The Talbots are good people, and were good parents, but Levi…"

"You don't have to tell me," Val said, hoping to hell she wasn't blushing. "Believe me."

"So we didn't understand, when Tomas took up with him, of all people. But you know what? Levi was the most loyal friend Tommy ever had. Sure, the boys pulled some boneheaded stunts—and even Tomas admitted that Levi spearheaded every one of them—but as heart-stopping as those stunts were, they also broke Tommy out of his shell. So all I'm saying is…be kind to Levi—"

"Mama! Look!" Josie ran into the kitchen, a squeaking black-and-white furball clutched to her chest, a pleading look in her eyes Val knew she was gonna have a helluva time resisting. She'd seen the same look in Tommy's eyes when he brought home Radar.

The same look but different—oh, so different—she'd seen in Levi's eyes the day before. That morning. The *I need something from you* look. And to ignore that look, to pretend it didn't affect her, only made her a big old meanie, didn't it?

Clearly, the entire world was conspiring against her.

"Look what I got, Levi!"

About to nail the last new plank on the porch floor, Levi glanced over to see Josie flying toward him, a loudly mewing something—not a skunk, then—cradled under her neck. And Radar, who'd been snoozing in the grass, surged to his feet to investigate the New Thing that had invaded his territory.

"Josie! Oh, jeez… No! Wait!" Val shrieked from the driveway as she tried to get the baby out of her car seat. "We need to introduce them slowly!"

Levi bolted down the steps before the child was traumatized for life. But even as he went to grab the dog's collar he noticed Radar's wagging tail…and that he'd plopped himself down in the gravel at Josie's feet to *awoo! awoo!*

at the kitten, now clutched even more tightly in a wide-eyed, clearly terrified, Josie's arms. Levi crouched beside the dog, curling his fingers around the collar, anyway.

"He just wants to be friends," Levi said gently, his gut twisting at how much the little girl looked like her daddy. "Why don't you let him sniff the kitty? It's okay, I've got him."

"You sure?"

"We had cats and dogs all the time when I was growing up on the ranch where my daddy worked. They're not natural enemies, no matter what people think. I promise—I won't let anything bad happen."

Josie shot him a look that rattled him as much as it warmed him. To be truthful, Levi was pretty much clueless about kids. Yeah, he was an uncle three times over, but he hardly knew his nephews, having been away for the better part of the past six years. And girls? They might as well be a whole different species.

So it made his heart swell when the kid sucked in a breath, nodded, then carefully lowered the kitty so the nutso dog could check him, or her, out. At the sound of gravel crunching, Levi glanced up to see Val with the baby, clearly holding her breath. And yet, if she'd let Josie have the kitten, deep down she must've believed it'd work out, right?

That, or the woman had balls of steel.

Radar nosed the kitten, then pulled back to bay at the poor little thing before resting his snout on his front paws. Waiting.

Levi chuckled. "Put the kitten down—let 'em get acquainted."

Josie glanced over at her mama, but Val only laughed. Nice sound, that laugh. "Go ahead. Levi's got it covered."

Now why those few words sparked such a feeling of confidence, Levi had no idea. Especially since it wasn't as if he was trying to prove anything to Val or win her approval. But there was a lot to be said for feeling like you were finally doing something right.

Slowly, Josie squatted and released the kitty, who arched and hopped back a whole six inches, hissing about as loudly as you'd expect something who weighed a pound to hiss. Encouraged, Radar inched closer to nose the kitten again, sending it tumbling backward. Tiny thing was *real* pissed by now, scrambling clumsily to its feet to charge the dog, smacking him squarely on his nose. Radar, being basically dumb as a rock, figured they were best buds now; he lifted his head again to let out a joyous bay, tail wagging the entire time.

By this time they were all laughing at the goings-on, particularly Josie, who scooped up her highly annoyed new pet. "That's enough, Radar!" she said sternly, then marched up the stairs and on inside, leaving the perplexed dog to jump up and run around in circles, nose to ground, wondering where his new friend went.

Still chuckling, Levi came up to Val and the baby. He got a whiff of something sweet, then another scent that reminded him of his mother's kitchen the day before Thanksgiving.

"You got her a kitten?"

"Not exactly. My father-in-law brought them home. Little girl, kittens..." She shrugged. "Thank God Connie had already called dibs on the second one, or I'd really be in trouble. And I'd seen Radar with cats before. Dog's an idiot, and doesn't know from boundaries, but I knew it'd be okay. Hoped, anyway. And Josie needs something to focus on."

Speaking of focusing, her gaze wandered to the porch. On a little gasp, she went closer, the baby clinging to her hip. "Oh. Wow. This is...impressive."

Levi stood behind her, getting another heady whiff of domesticity. “Thanks.”

“I can’t believe you finished it so fast.”

“Wasn’t that big a deal. The foundation was still okay, only needed the boards replaced. Whoever built this originally knew what they were doing.”

“Still. It would’ve taken Tomas forever…” As if that thought had jump-started another one, her gaze jerked to his, an inch away from accusing. She hiked the baby higher on her hip, her voice soft but the anger underlying her words unmistakable. “How come you didn’t tell me you’d gone to see Connie and Pete?”

“You’re mad,” Levi said, just as softly. Her cheek pressed against her mama’s collarbone, the baby grinned up at him from around her thumb, and something squeezed inside Levi’s chest.

“I’m sure as heck not happy,” Val said, snapping him back to the moment. The baby leaned back to pat her face; Val grabbed her chubby little hand and kissed it before looking at Levi again. “If you wanted to know what the budget was, why not ask me? Why go to them?”

“First off, did you expect me *not* to go see them? And second, we got to talking about the house—”

“I have major issues with people not being up front with me, Levi. So as long as we’re…working together, no sneaking around, no hiding stuff from me. Because if it’s one thing I hate, it’s surprises. Or having to wonder what’s really going on in someone’s head.” She pulled a face. “Drives me batty.”

“It was a judgment call, okay?” he said after a moment, guessing her strong reaction had little to do with the house. “Not to bog you down with details. Like the fact that this budget isn’t going to go very far if you have to pay for labor. You’re stressed, Val,” he said when she glared at him. “More than you probably want to admit. So sue me for wanting to make things easier for you. Like I know Tommy would. Believe it or not, I'm trying my best *not* to be a jerk here."

Their gazes tangled for several moments before she sank onto the porch step, the baby still in her arms. Radar sauntered over to give kisses, and she smiled. Then sighed.

"Sorry," she mumbled.

"S'okay." Then he crossed his arms. "But you can't seriously expect me to share every single thing I'm thinking."

Another sigh preceded, "Not unless it pertains to me. Or my girls. Because I doubt either one of us really knows what the parameters are for…whatever this is. But as long as we're honest with each other, maybe it won't be quite as awkward?"

By rights, her request should've made him hugely uncomfortable. Because there was stuff lurking in his head he wasn't about to share with anyone, let alone someone in Val's situation. And yet at the same time he found her openness more of a relief than a threat. Especially considering some of the women he'd been with over the years. Might be nice, not having to work his ass off trying to figure out who this one really was.

Even if this situation was only a way to make good on his promise, since he didn't imagine Tomas would've expected it to be open-ended. Or that he and Val should become friends or anything. Besides that, she'd said her "rules" only applied to whatever affected her or the girls. Not what affected *him*.

"I suppose I can do that," he said.

Her lips curved. Barely. "So if I ask you something, you'll give me a truthful answer?"

Hell, he couldn't even answer *that* truthfully. But all he said was, "Long as you don't ask me if what you're wearing makes you look fat. 'Cause that dumb, I'm not."

He'd never noticed before the way her eyes crinkled

when she laughed. Made him feel good to make her laugh. Not that it was much of a compensation for what'd happened. But since, aside from his handyman skills, it was all he had—

"And you can ask me anything, too," she said.

"Deal." Although he wouldn't.

Because, again—that dumb, he wasn't.

Chapter Three

A short time later, Levi clacked the knocker on his oldest brother's front door, smiling at—over much excited barking—an equally excited "It's Uncle Levi!" coming from the other side. One of Zach's boys, probably. Although Josh was there, too; his twin's mud-spattered four-by-four was parked behind Zach's even dirtier Chevy pickup. Because around here, the filthiness of one's truck spoke directly to one's ballsiness. And that went for the women, too.

Speaking of ballsy…all three of them together for the first time in more than six years? *Should be interesting,* Levi mused as he took in the almost painfully cute front porch, attached to an equally adorable blue-and-white house, rosebush-choked picket fence and all. Next door stood a toned-down version, beige with black shutters, that housed Zach's veterinary practice and small-animal boarding facility. Although Levi gathered that a lot of the boarders ended up—

The door opened, and three little boys, a pair of Chihuahuas and one overly enthusiastic golden retriever all scrambled to get to Levi first.

—here.

"Guys, guys..." Laughing, Levi's fraternal twin made some lame attempt at untangling the exuberance before grabbing Levi in a back-pounding, bone-crushing man-hug. Then Josh held Levi apart, a thousand questions simmering in eyes the same murky green as Levi's, although his ten minutes' younger brother's hair was darker, straighter. Neater. Josh also stood a couple of inches shorter than Levi, a fact that had annoyed the hell out of Josh all through high school. Ten years later, though, what his twin lacked in height he'd more than made up for in rock-solid bulk. Which stood him in good stead, Levi supposed, for working with horses day in and day out.

"You look good," Josh said, grinning like crazy as he hauled his little boy up into his arms. Even a toddler, Josh'd been the sweet one, Levi the holy terror. He wondered how much that still held true.

"Thanks—"

Zach's two started messing with each other, making the dogs bark. From the kitchen, Zach called, "Cut it out! *Now!*" But not before the younger kid got in a final punch.

Ah, good times...

"Hey, Austin," Levi said over his chuckle. He'd only seen the little guy once before, as a toddler, although Josh had regularly sent pictures. "You don't remember me, huh?" The little boy shook his head, and Levi smiled. "How old are you?"

The little dude held up four fingers, then immediately tucked his hand back between him and his daddy. Who'd apparently had no issues with stepping up to bat when the boy's babymama decided to take a hike. Levi's heart cramped, thinking of Val, also the victim of a parent who hadn't stuck around.

"Wow. Big guy. Speaking of big…" Levi looked down at Zach's boys, who'd stopped wrassling with each other long enough to now give Levi matching intrigued looks. He pointed at the oldest, a gangly blond who was probably gonna spend some quality time with the orthodontist in coming years. "You're… Jeremy, right? You were this big—" Levi held his hand at hip height "—when I saw you last. But I've never met this little guy." He squatted to be eye level to his youngest nephew, redheaded and freckled and blue-eyed—like his mother, Levi thought with another cramp.

"That's Liam," Zach said, swiping his hands across his blue-jeaned butt as he came into the living room and Levi stood again. But instead of giving Levi a hug, his oldest brother extended his hand, like they were acquaintances meeting up at a business gathering. Taller than Levi, thinner, Zach had always been the most reserved of the four of them, even as a kid. But clearly he'd become even more so after his wife's death a couple of years before, the once ever-present, if quiet, spark of humor in his blue eyes faded to almost nothing behind his glasses. "Good to have you home."

"Glad to be here."

And he meant it. Even though he might not have, once upon a time, Levi realized as they crowded around Zach's beat-up dining room table for dinner, and his brothers' attempts to get spaghetti actually into their sons rather than on the table, floor and each other brought back a flood of memories…and the opportunity for reflection, since actual conversation was pointless.

Despite growing up with parents who were devoted to them and to each other, the four brothers had never been particularly close. As kids they'd all had radically different interests, temperaments, personalities. Still did, most likely. Josh was still the brawny one, and Zach had the brains. And Colin… Well, who knew about Colin, who'd fled Whispering Pines long before Levi. The idealist, their mother had said, her pride over her second born's accomplishments clearly conflicting with the pain of his rare sightings. And of course then there was Levi himself, still trying to figure out who he was, what he really wanted. How he fit into the big scheme of things.

Even so—the kids finished their meals in what seemed like two seconds flat, at which point their weary fathers released them into the wild—Levi sensed something had shifted since the last time they'd all been together. He wasn't entirely sure what. And, being guys, it was doubtful they'd actually talk about it. But like maybe whatever had kept them at such odds with each other as kids wasn't as much of an issue anymore.

"Beers?" Zach said, not even bothering to clean flung spaghetti off the front of his Henley shirt, although he did take a napkin to his glasses.

Calmly sweeping food mess from table to tiled floor—thrilling the dogs—Josh released a tired laugh. "You have to ask?"

Zach pointed to Levi, who nodded. His oldest brother disappeared, returning momentarily with three bottles of Coors, tossing two of them at his brothers before dropping back into his seat and tackling what had to be cold spaghetti. Clearly he did not care.

"This is really good, Zach," Levi said, and Zach snorted.

"Straight out of a jar, but thanks. No, mutt, that was it," he said to the retriever, sitting in rapt attention beside him. Sighing, the dog lumbered off to collapse in one of three dog beds on the other side of the room, the Chihuahuas prancing behind to snuggle up with him. The bigger dog didn't seem to mind. From the living room, somebody screamed. Josh cocked his head, waiting, lifting his beer in mock salute to his brother when there was no follow-up. Zach hoisted his in return.

"You guys look done in," Levi said, which got grunts—and exhausted grins—from both of them. Zach rubbed one eye underneath his glasses, then sagged back in his chair, his arms crossed over his chest as he chewed.

"Honestly? I can't remember *not* being tired. But it's just life, you know?" The last rays of the setting sun sliced across the table, making it hard to see his brother's eyes behind the lenses, but his smile had softened. "Either you deal with it or you go under. Speaking of which…" He leaned forward to scoop in another bite of spaghetti. "Dad says you're helping Val Lopez fix up her house?"

"Some, yeah. Although it's not her house, it's Tommy's grandmother's. The family's only letting her live there."

"For how long?" Josh asked.

Levi turned to his twin, seeing sympathy in his green eyes. Although they hadn't all hung out together much in high school—no mean feat with such a small class—Josh knew Tommy, of course. And Val. Levi doubted, however, his brother had been aware of everything, since he'd kept a pretty tight rein on his feelings. Not to mention his mouth. "As long as she needs."

"How's she doing?"

This from Zach, who knew more than anyone what it felt like to lose a spouse, especially long before you expected to.

"All right, I think." For a moment—if that—the thought flashed that his brother and Val should get together, do a miniature Brady Bunch thing with their kids. Or even Josh and Val, for that matter. Except hot on the heel of those thoughts came *Oh, hell, no.* Like a freaking sledgehammer.

"What about you guys?" he said. "How're you balancing it all?"

His brothers shrugged in unison. "Can't speak for doofus over there," Josh said, reaching for his beer, "but I don't know that I am. Doing my best, but..."

"Yeah," Zach said. "Same here. Especially juggling the child care situation. Mom helps when she can, absolutely, but since you never know when one of her clients might go into labor, that's not a sure thing. And Dad..."

Josh sighed, and Levi frowned.

"I thought he was okay?"

"Oh, he is," his twin said. "Doesn't mean he's up to herding three little boys under the age of seven. Hell, he didn't when *we* were little. No, seriously, Leev—can you remember him ever taking care of us on his own?"

"He used to take us fishing. And riding. And—"

"When we were older, yeah. Not when we were—" somebody bellowed "—this age. That honor, he left to Mom."

"So what do you do?"

Zach shrugged, his mouth pulled down at the corners. "There's a church day care, but it's only part-time. So we let 'em hang with us, when we can." He exchanged another glance with Josh. "Pawn 'em off on Gus, sometimes."

"Gus?" Levi belted a laugh. Gus Otero had been a fixture at the Vista Encantada—the ranch where he and his brothers had grown up—forever, first as a hand, then as the cook/housekeeper. Hell, the four of them had probably spent more time in Gus's kitchen than their own, and the tough old bird had never taken crap off any of them. But the man had to be nearly eighty by now.

"Don't laugh," Josh said. "I'd put my money on Gus before one of those fancy trained nannies any day. Even so..."

Josh took another gulp of his beer, then lowered his voice and said to Zach, "This isn't what either of us signed up for, is it?" A rhetorical question, apparently, since he didn't wait for a reply. Levi, however, noticed his older brother's deep frown as he stared at his bottle before Josh quickly added, "Don't get me wrong, Austin's the best thing that ever happened to me. Doesn't mean it's not a pain, trying to make the pieces fit. Or hard not to feel resentful, sometimes, that his mom didn't keep her part of the bargain."

Knowing that Josh had never been married to Austin's mother, it took Levi a moment to work up the nerve to ask, "So…it wasn't an accident?"

Josh barked out a laugh, then looked at Levi in a way he'd never done. "I know—when we were kids, you were always considered… Well, I don't want to say the *bad* one, but definitely the one more likely to get into trouble. So I did my level best not to. Then you left and maybe I didn't feel the need to compensate for your behavior anymore?" He took a swig of his beer. "And I may have gone a little nuts."

"A *little* nuts?" Zach muttered, and Josh shot him the evil eye. Then sighed.

"Okay, a lot nuts. Especially when it came to women. Not that there were dozens—"

"Which would be tricky," Zach put in, "considering where we live."

"Would you let me tell my story, for cripes' sake? Anyway. Then I met Austin's mother, and even though we were being careful…" Josh shrugged. "The thing is, though, I wasn't in love with her. Not even close. And frankly the thought of being somebody's daddy scared me to death. But the thought of Dad's reaction scared me more. So I asked her to marry me—"

"Like the good boy you always were," Zach said, half smiling.

"Shut up," Josh lobbed back, then returned his gaze to Levi. "She actually laughed. But she said she wanted to keep the baby. So we worked out this whole custody-sharing arrangement. Only…"

Josh linked his hands behind his head, his eyes on Austin, quietly building something out of blocks not ten feet away. "Only she left. Like, three years ago? Haven't heard a word from her since. And then *this* one…"

Whether because Josh's nod toward their oldest brother was met with a death glare, or because Austin came over to show off his Duplo masterpiece, Josh apparently changed his mind about whatever he was about to say. Instead he scooped his son into his lap, worry lines vanishing as he focused on his little boy. Then a minor crisis of some sort pulled Zach away from the table to tend to his crying youngest as Jeremy pled his innocence with all the fervor of a TV lawyer, leaving Levi feeling something for his brothers he'd never felt before. Admiration, maybe. Even… tenderness, if a guy was allowed to have such feelings for another dude. Let alone admit them.

For a woman, though, that was something else. Especially a woman dealing with the same issues as his brothers were. Trying to make the pieces fit, wasn't that what Josh had said?

"So how is it?" Josh said, jerking Levi out of his thoughts.

Levi frowned at his brother. Austin still sat on his lap, making soft explosion noises as he calmly, and repeatedly, smashed his creation against the tabletop. "How is what?"

"Seeing Val again." When Levi didn't answer right away, Josh chuckled. "Not exactly a secret, bro. How you felt, I mean."

So much for his brother being in the dark. "Do the others know?"

"Zach and Colin?" Josh shook his head, giving Austin's curls a quick kiss as the little boy slid off his lap and climbed into Levi's. "At that point, they didn't even want to acknowledge our existence. But you and I shared a room. Kinda hard to escape your moping."

"I did not—"

"Yeah. You did. And after Tommy and Val started going together…" Josh's head wagged. "So sad."

Levi's sigh stirred his nephew's curls, making the little boy slap his hand on top of his head, vigorously rubbing the spot like it stung.

"That tickles!"

"Sorry, dude," Levi said with a soft laugh, hoisting the slippery kid more securely onto his lap before meeting his brother's gaze again. "That was a long time ago."

"Yeah, it was. So?" When Levi didn't answer, Josh picked up his fork, dinging it softly against the side of his bowl for a moment before saying, "I have no idea what you've been through these past six years." The fork clanged back into the bowl before Josh folded his arms over his chest and met Levi's gaze again. "But I'm gonna guess it wasn't exactly a hayride. Then Tomas…" His cheeks puffed as he exhaled, shaking his head. "I'm just saying, you probably don't need any more complications right now."

Austin wriggled off Levi's lap to run back into the living room. Smiling slightly, Levi watched him for a moment, then looked back at his twin. "You're probably right," he said, taking another sip of his now-warm beer, which burned his throat as he swallowed. "Then again, who does? So what're the options? Run? Or deal? And you of all people," he said, nodding toward the living room, "should know what I'm talking about."

A long moment passed before Josh pushed out a half laugh. "Got me there," he said, then snagged Levi's gaze in his again. "Still. Be careful, okay?"

"Fully intend to," Levi said, tilting the bottle to his lips again, only to think if there was a quicker road to hell, he didn't know what it was.

That night, Val tucked Josie into the old twin bed that had once belonged to one of Tommy's aunts; the maplespindled headboard softly gleamed in the light from the bedside lamp. This was the smallest bedroom, one of three carved out of the steeply pitched attic sometime in the 1960s. But Josie had immediately laid claim to it, clearly taken with the skylight window with its unencumbered view of the night sky. Not to mention it was the perfect hideaway when, as Josie put it, her brain got too full and she needed to be alone to empty it.

Bending over to give Josie a kiss, Val smiled when a soft squeak alerted them to the kitten's arrival; a moment later the tiny thing clawed up onto the bed to snuggle against Josie's side, motor going full throttle.

Val sat on the bed's edge, reaching across her daughter to pet the kitten, who tried to nibble her fingers. She chuckled. "Looks like somebody's settling right in." Risa, bless her, had sacked out an hour ago and probably wouldn't be heard from again until the next morning. "You decide on a name yet?"

"I'm kinda waiting for her to tell me. Or him." Josie frowned. "How do you know whether it's a boy kitten or a girl kitten?"

"It'll be plain soon enough, trust me. In the meantime, maybe pick something that could go either way?"

"I guess, huh?" Radar plodded into the room to rest his muzzle on the bed, looking concerned. And confused. Because *he* had to sleep in his crate in the kitchen. The kitten all but stuck its tongue out at the dog before curling up even more tightly against Josie's hip. The little girl almost giggled, then looked up at Val with huge dark eyes.

"I like Levi. He's nice."

"He is," Val said. Sincerely even. Watching the man earlier as he patiently sorted out the dog and cat, how gentle he was with Josie, had definitely made her look at him in a different light. Maybe not a light she wanted to see him in, but nobody knew better than she that you don't always get a say in these things. So now she smiled and said, "And I think Daddy would have been glad you got to meet his best friend."

Petting the kitten, Josie frowned. "Was Levi your friend, too?"

"Not really, no," Val said, figuring it was only fair she live up to the mandate she'd given Levi. "Frankly, I thought he was kind of a goofball when we were younger. Although so was your daddy, so..."

Josie giggled again, with a little more oomph, then yawned. "Were you?"

"A goofball?" Val shook her head, then winnowed her fingers through Josie's waves. "I was much too busy being serious," she said, making a snooty face, which made Josie laugh again. One day, maybe, she'd tell her daughters about her own childhood, but that day was way off in the future. Right now it was about them, about the present, not the past. And certainly not about Val's past. "I'd like to think I've loosened up some since then, though."

"Well, I think you're just right," Josie said, and Val's chest ached. How was it possible that she somehow loved her babies more every day than she had the day before? And she prayed with all her heart that this one not lose sight of that amazing combination of sweetness and smarts and silliness that made her one incredible little kid.

"Well, I think you're just right, too," she said, giving her oldest daughter a hug and kiss. "You and Risa both."

The same as she'd believed Tomas was just right, she thought as she—and the reluctant hound—left the room, making sure the door wasn't closed all the way. Someone else who was sweet and smart and silly, who'd filled up a hole inside her she hadn't even known was there. Or at least wouldn't admit to. And she could still, even after all this time, remember when she first realized there this was someone who *got* her, someone she could trust without a moment's hesitation. She'd never doubted his love. Or believed he'd ever give her a reason to. The way he'd looked at her, with that mixture of gratitude and amazement—that had never changed. And that, she would miss for the rest of her life.

But she'd also thought she understood *him*, that they were on the same page about what they wanted, what their goals were. Except then—

Stop. Just...stop.

Pulling her hoodie closed against the evening chill, Val went back down to the cramped kitchen to make herself some hot chocolate, gather the ingredients to make this pie, the dog keeping her hopeful company. She poured milk into a mug and set it in the old microwave on the disgusting laminate counter, berating herself for letting her thoughts go down this path. Because she knew full well she'd only get sucked right back into the rabbit hole of hurt and depression she had to fight like hell not to go near, for the kids' sake.

But the nights were hard, silent and long and lonely, those thoughts whistling though her head like the wind in a cemetery.

The microwave beeped. She dumped Nesquik into the mug, swearing under her breath when half of it landed on the counter, the minor aggravation shoving her into the rabbit hole, anyway. And down she went, mad as hell but helpless to avoid it. Yes, her husband's work—work he loved and was *good* at—had been work that had saved probably countless lives. But it wasn't *fair*, that after everything she'd been through, everything she'd thought she'd finally won, that she'd had to spend so much of the past six years with her heart in her throat.

That he'd made her a widow before she was thirty.

Val shut her eyes, not only against the pain, but the frustration of not being able to get past it, to appreciate her husband's sacrifice. Dammit, everything Tomas did was for other people. Why couldn't she feel more proud of him? Why, no matter how hard she tried, couldn't she feel something more than that he'd abandoned them, broken his promise to *her*, to their children?

Hideous, selfish thoughts she didn't dare admit to anyone. Ever.

Radar nosed her hand; her eyes wet, she smiled down at that sweet face, a face she wouldn't even be looking at if Tomas hadn't rescued the dog. Much like he'd rescued Val. She couldn't imagine—didn't want to—what her life would have been like if he hadn't. She wouldn't have the girls, for one thing. Or his parents, who'd welcomed her as their own from the first time Tomas brought her home to meet them. And yet as grateful as she was for all of that—as in, her heart knew no bounds—none of it made up for what she'd lost.

For what—she took a sip of the hot chocolate, the taste cloying in her mouth—her husband's friendship with Levi Talbot had stolen from her.

And because the person she was the most honest with was herself, that was something she doubted she'd ever get over.

The haunted look in those murky green eyes notwithstanding.

Chapter Four

"That should do it," Levi said, testing the new kitchen faucet a couple of times to make sure it didn't leak. He turned to see Val standing beside him in a baggy T-shirt and even baggier jeans, arms crossed and bare mouth set, as usual. Behind her at the kitchen table Josie was drawing—the little girl tossed him a grin that punched him right in the heart—while Risa pushed and batted at things on her walker, making a helluva racket. And sprawled in the middle of the crappy linoleum floor was the dog, softly *whoop-whooping* in his sleep.

"Thanks," Val said, refusing to meet Levi's gaze. "Did you put the receipt in the can?"

"I did. And you don't have to keep asking—I'm a quicker study than you might think."

She might've smiled, but she still wouldn't look at him. So he glanced around the kitchen instead as he clunked and rattled his tools back in their metal box. In the past week, besides finishing up the porch, Levi had replaced a couple of the worst windows on the side of the house that got the most brutal winds, installed three new ceiling fans and changed out the disintegrating faucets. Except for the porch, all Band-Aid-type stuff until Val stopped dragging her feet about the more major projects. Like a sorely needed kitchen remodel. Hell, half the cabinets didn't even close anymore, and the laminate counters were completely worn through in places. However, since Val seemed loath to talk to him for more than a minute at a time, there was no telling when that—or anything else—might actually happen.

So he prodded. A skill he'd inherited from both his parents, apparently.

"You decide yet what kind of cabinets you want?"

He heard her sigh. "Keep going back and forth between white and cherry. Or maybe maple?"

"And the counters?"

"Butcher block. Or quartz." She pushed out another breath. "The family said it's up to me, but…" Levi glanced over to see her bony shoulders hitch. "What's the hurry, right?"

"Although you might as well take advantage of free labor as long as you can. Since I don't know how long I'm gonna be around."

Her brows, as pale as her hair, dipped. "I can afford to pay someone, Levi. I could afford to pay *you*. I've got my own money—"

"And you've got plenty better things to do with that money." Meaning Tommy's life insurance. As if there was any way in hell he'd take that. "Like put it away for the girls. For college or whatever. This is my gift, Val. To all of you. So let it go."

She paused. "And how long… I mean—"

"Until I'm done or you throw me out. Whichever comes first."

Pressing fingers into the base of her skull underneath her ponytail, she looked away again before offering another half-assed smile. "Well. Okay. Thanks."

"So I take it you're not throwing me out?"

"No. Not yet, anyway."

"Then we're good," he said, even though they weren't. Not by a long shot. He started toward the front door. The dog didn't even bother to get up. Lazy butt mutt. "But since we can't get going on the kitchen until you make a few decisions," he said, facing her, "I may as well start digging up those dead bushes out front on Monday. Maybe we could go over to the nursery, pick out something to replace them?"

"Oh, um…no, that's okay, I'll take the girls one afternoon. That'll save you some time, right?"

It was no skin off his nose whether they went to the nursery together or not. Especially since she was right, it would save time. But what rankled was how obvious she was being, that she didn't want to be around him.

No, what rankled was why he even gave a damn. But all he said was, "Sure, no problem," then called back down the hall, "Bye, Josie!"

"Bye, Levi! See you on Monday?"

"You bet," he said, then walked through the door, across the newly stained porch and out to his truck, feeling unaccountably pissed.

Again.

At first, Levi thought maybe her reluctance to move forward was because the house wasn't really hers. Except he eventually realized it wasn't the house she was avoiding talking *about* as much as it was him she was avoiding talking *to*. So he'd apparently imagined things thawing between them, when he'd made her laugh…when he'd thought he'd caught her looking at him like maybe he wasn't quite the slimeball she remembered.

Yeah, well, it wouldn't be the first time his imagination had played tricks on him. Not that she was snotty to him or anything, but she was cool. Careful. What he didn't get was why that bugged him. Especially since he couldn't remember the last time he'd given a rat's ass whether or not somebody approved of him. Even so, he wouldn't mind hearing that laugh again.

Being the cause of it.

Hell.

He pulled up in front of the nondescript ranch-style house his folks had been living in for the past year, a gift from Dad's old boss after his father's heart attack two years before forced him into early retirement. But the squat little house with its brown siding and white shutters seemed too small and plain to contain his parents' boisterous personalities. Too…ordinary. Heart attack or no, Levi doubted Dad would go gently into that good night. And for sure his mother never would, he thought with a soft laugh. But he supposed it would do.

His father was making sandwiches in the kitchen—bright, cheery, reasonably updated—when Levi got home, so he guessed Mom was on call. But since Billie Talbot had been a midwife ever since her boys had been old enough to fend for themselves, this was hardly the first time Dad had been left to his own devices.

Half smiling, Levi dumped his toolbox by the back door. "Dad. Really?"

Heavy white eyebrows raised, Sam Talbot turned toward Levi, a slice of bologna dangling from his fingers. He'd definitely lost weight after his scare, but the vestiges of a beer gut still hung over belted jeans. "What?"

"You could at least fire up the grill."

"Doc said I should avoid too much charbroiled meat."

"But bologna's okay?"

"It's chicken. Or turkey. One of those. Disgusting, but

at least on the approved list. Zach said you guys got together for dinner the other night?"

"We did."

"How'd it go?"

"It went fine." He chuckled at his father's side eye. "We're all grown up now, Dad. We can be around each for more than five minutes without coming to blows."

"Those boys of theirs…they're something else, aren't they?"

"They are that."

Levi was grateful for the easy, ordinary conversation, one that would've never happened a dozen years before. So unlike that excruciatingly long stretch when he and his dad never quite saw eye to eye. About anything. If Dad took one side, Levi invariably latched on to the other. In fact, he'd once heard his mother tell someone at church—laughing, at least—that Levi had been born fighting the world. *Unlike his brothers*, had been the unspoken addition to that sentence, who'd never seemed to struggle like Levi did to live up to their father's high standards.

Not that Dad had ever actually said, "Why can't you be more like them?" but Levi hadn't been blind to the frustration in those smoky-gray eyes. Problem was, he'd had no idea how to do that. Hell, at that point he hadn't clue one how to be himself—or what that even meant. Even now he wasn't entirely sure if one of the reasons—among many—he'd enlisted was to prove something to himself or his dad, but considering how much better things were between them since Levi's return, he'd achieved his goal. He and Dad might still be feeling their way with each other, but he knew his father was proud of him.

Levi opened the fridge to get a beer—light, of course, nothing else allowed in the house—spotting the defrosted, already seasoned chicken breasts sitting on a plate, right at eye level. Where, you know, even a man wouldn't miss them. "There's chicken in here, ready to go. Real chicken, I mean. Why don't I cook 'em up for us—"

"And I swear if I eat one more piece of chicken I'll start clucking."

Levi looked over at the sandwich. Piled high with the fake bologna. "But..." He sighed. "Never mind," he said, then pulled out the plate of chicken. Although frankly he'd kill for a steak. Or a hamburger. But these days the animal protein offerings at Casa Talbot were limited to things with feathers or fins. Didn't seem fair to torment his father by bringing home something the poor man couldn't have. So pan-broiled chicken it was.

For the third time this week.

"So how're things progressing with the house?" Dad asked, sitting at the table with his sandwich and a glass of low-fat milk as, with much clanging and banging, Levi wrestled the cast-iron frying pan out of the stove's bottom drawer.

"Okay." He clunked the pan onto the gas burner. "Needs a boatload of work, though."

"I can imagine. Place was falling apart thirty years ago."

"You were inside it?"

"Oh, yeah." Dad took a bite of the sandwich, made a face and grabbed his milk glass. "Pete Lopez and I used to hang out some, when we were kids. When we could, anyway, when he wasn't working for his dad at the store and I wasn't out at the ranch with mine."

As usual, Levi heard the slight regret in his father's voice, that out of four sons only one had followed in the family tradition of working at the Vista. But the ranching bug had only bitten Josh, who'd taken over as foreman after his dad's retirement. Didn't take a genius to figure out his father hated that a single wonky organ—albeit an important one—had ripped away from him the one thing, outside his wife and sons, he most loved.

"Anyway," Dad was saying, "I spent a fair amount of time in that house. Big place. But dark. Gloomy."

"And free, for as long as Val likes. It'll be nice, once it's fixed up."

He could sense his father's gaze lasering into his back. He turned to the same frown that used to scare the bejesus out of all of them when they were kids.

"How's she doing?"

Even though he doubted either of his parents knew Val all that well—she'd only been over to the house a couple of times when they were kids, after Tommy'd started seeing her but before the bubble around them had set—his father's interest didn't really surprise him. That's just the way it was in small towns. With his dad, especially, who'd tried poking around Levi's head enough, after he got back, even if Levi wasn't about to give him full access.

"On the surface?" Levi now said, not wanting to think about Val. Unable to think about much else. "As well as could be expected, I suppose. Although she doesn't seem the type to go crying on people's shoulders, in any case."

"She always did strike me as a tough little thing."

"That's one way of putting it."

His dad was quiet for a moment, then said, "Her mother passed away four, five years ago now. Did she tell you?"

Levi turned back to the stove to flip the chicken sizzling away in the scant tablespoon of olive oil he'd poured into the pan. He supposed it wasn't surprising that she hadn't. Something they had in common, maybe, not being partial to exhuming the past. Examining it, dissecting it.

"No," he said, rearranging the chicken. "But Tommy mentioned it." At the beginning, even after their military careers took them in different directions, they'd kept up—emails, texts, the occasional phone call. Less and less, though, as time went on. Oddly, Levi remembered the text, partly because of its brevity. Only that Natalie Oswald had died, nothing more. "No reason, really, for Val to bring it up, though. I gathered there was no love lost there."

"And I imagine you'd be right." His sandwich done, his father crossed his arms high on his chest, frowning. "Your mother tried to make friends with her. Val's mother, I mean."

Levi twisted around. "You're joking."

Dad snorted a soft laugh through his nose. "Nope. Because that's your mother, determined to see the good in everybody. Or at least not get caught up in the gossip, which tends to get blown out of proportion. Especially in a town this small. Anyway, after Natalie got sick and that last boyfriend of hers took off, your mom and Tommy's mother took it on themselves to go out there now and again, to make sure she had what she needed or take her to the doctor's, whatever. Since there didn't seem to be anybody else. And I know Billie felt bad for Natalie, that her daughter wasn't around. Until she got to know the woman better and realized the gossips had missed half the story."

"Half the story?"

"What'd you hear, when you guys were in school? About Val's mother?"

"Not…nice things," he said, and Dad chuckled.

"It's okay, you can say it—that she was the town tramp. Not that it was anybody's business how she conducted her personal life. And *your* mother figured, that was all there was to it. Not pretty, but hardly a punishable offense. At least in this century.

"But as time went on, your mother began to understand why the boyfriends never stuck around. Even making allowances for how sick the woman was in her last months, she never seemed to appreciate anything anybody did for her. Instead she snapped and snarled and griped about everything. And your mom finally realized the illness hadn't made her mean—that's just the way she was. So can you imagine the childhood Valerie must've had? How tough she'd *had* to be to survive? And we don't even know what some of those men her mother brought home might've been like. Tomas ever say anything to you about it?"

His gut twisting, Levi shook his head. "Nothing beyond what everyone already knew. If Val said anything to him, he kept it to himself."

"Not surprised. He was a good boy."

"Yeah. He was."

"Which makes it even worse, that Valerie should finally find some peace, only to have it snatched away from her like that." Dad pushed out a breath. "It's the tough ones—the ones who keep their feelings all wadded up inside them—who're usually hurting the most. But if that hurt doesn't find a way out…" His father got up to put his plate and glass in the dishwasher. "Things have a way of exploding."

Something about the slight change in his father's tone made Levi clench his jaw. Keeping his gaze averted, he removed the chicken pieces from the pan to lay them on a plate by the stove. "And why are you telling me this?"

"Because since you've been back," Dad said behind him, "you haven't said ten words about your deployments."

Levi turned to find his dad leaning back against the counter, his arms crossed over his chest. "You didn't ask, either."

"Didn't want to pry."

"Then what's the problem? Because let's be honest, it wasn't like we were exactly best buds before I left. Right? Maybe…I simply didn't think you'd be all that interested. Crap," he muttered, giving his head a sharp shake. "That didn't come the way I meant—"

"Sure it did. But you're wrong. I've always been interested, Levi. I *love* you, dammit. I—" He took a moment. "I always have, whether you want to believe that or not," he said quietly, and Levi's gut cramped. If Dad had ever actually said that before, he couldn't remember. Except then he said, "Yeah, even when you were being a complete knucklehead," and Levi had to smile. "So I'm asking now. What went on over there?"

Feeling as if he'd been thrown a flaming curveball, Levi looked away. "You don't want to know. Trust me."

He heard his father sigh. "Yeah, I figured that'd be your response."

"It has nothing to do with you, Dad," Levi said, facing him again. "I swear. I don't like talking about it to anybody. Anyway, it's in the past, it's over and done with—"

"The past is never *over*, son. Not as long as we remember it. And before you say anything else—if you don't want to talk to me, or your mother, that's up to you. But I'm guessing you need to talk to somebody. Maybe somebody who's in as much pain as you are."

"I'm not—"

His father held up one hand, cutting him off. "You forget—we lived through your rebel phase. Barely, but we did. The only saving grace was that for all you nearly drove your mother and me crazy with your shenanigans, we could always see a spark of something that gave us hope, that eventually you'd channel all that energy into something worthwhile. But since you've been home…" His father sighed. "It's like you're *too* steady, if that makes any sense. Whatever happened over there, you need to deal with it. And I'm guessing if Tommy were here, he'd be the one you'd talk to."

Pain stabbed. "Well, he's not, is he?"

"No. But his widow is. She hasn't been through the same hell as I'm guessing you have, but she's been through hell, nonetheless. You two might be good for each other.

Which I'm guessing was the real purpose behind Tommy's request. Because he knew if anything happened, you'd both be hurting. And that nobody would understand your hurt better than each other."

Levi gawked at his father as if he'd announced he'd chatted with Jesus. Except, damned if the truth of his words didn't whisper through the buzzing in his head. Then he pushed out a soft, humorless laugh. "Except even if I were to accept your…theory, there's another major flaw in your reasoning. Which is why would she be even remotely interested in talking to me?"

"Meaning because of the knucklehead thing?"

Levi almost smiled. "Could be."

His father was quiet for a moment—never a good sign—before he said, "So why not tell her the truth? That you tried to talk Tommy out of enlisting?"

His appetite gone, Levi grabbed the plastic wrap out of a nearby cupboard, ripping off a length of the clingy film to stretch over the chicken. His parents had only heard the one conversation, of course, right after Levi had signed up and Tomas had come over—to the old house, on the ranch—to say he'd decided to enlist, too. His eyes bright with excitement, he'd gone on and on about how the military could change his life, make Val proud of him in ways that helping out at his father's store never would. Once she got used to the idea, that was. Levi's initial reaction—aside from the irritation that, once again, his friend was playing tagalong—had been to tell Tommy he was crazy, that Val was already plenty proud of him. So, yeah, maybe he should rethink this.

Except in the days that followed Tommy only became more enthusiastic about enlisting, and Levi eventually let it go. Because ultimately it wasn't his place, or business, to talk Tommy out of anything, was it? He was a grown man capable of making his own decisions. And of handling the ramifications of those decisions. If Val wasn't exactly on the same page, what on earth did that have to do with Levi?

Even so, regret that he *hadn't* tried harder bubbled like acid to the surface of his grief over Tommy's death, nearly devastating him. Now he looked at his father, shame still eating at his gut. That he couldn't tell his father, or Val, or anyone the truth only made the sizzling worse.

"And what good would that do, Dad? Either she'd think I was only trying to cover my own butt, or—far worse—she'd believe me. And how would that make him look, that he'd gone ahead with something that *everyone* tried to talk him out of? It would only wreck her even more than she is. I know it would."

"So you'd rather let her continue to—"

"Blame me, yeah. She worshipped Tommy, Dad," Levi said through a thick throat. "He was her savior. Even if I didn't know the entire story back when they first started going together, I knew that much. Like you said, after everything she's lost… I can't take that away from her, too."

"At least he died a hero."

"Doesn't make him any less dead, does it?"

Releasing another breath, Dad slowly wagged his head. "Ten years ago we couldn't get you to take responsibility for your own actions for love nor money. Now you're taking it for something that's not even remotely your fault? No, you listen to me—when Tomas asked you to make sure Val was okay…that was guilt talking, son. *His* guilt. For his own decision. It wasn't up to you to change his mind. It never was. But now, well, you accepted the burden he dumped on you—"

"Yes, I did. For my own reasons."

Their gazes butted for a long moment before his father pointed at him. "Then if you want to make good on that promise, there's a lot more that needs fixing than that *house*. Which isn't going to happen unless you get everything out in the open. And that's my last thought on the subject," Dad said, before going out on the back deck, probably to enjoy the sun's too-brief blaze of glory before it sank behind the mountains.

Leaving Levi—again—to wrestle with the truth of his father's words. Not to mention a dilemma the size of Texas. Because which *was* the better choice? To spare the woman any more pain? Or to abide by her own demand about being honest with each other?

He sighed so hard his chest hurt. Because truthfully? There was a big part of him that wanted to turn tail and run, like he would've done when he was younger. To make up some story, any story, that'd get him out of this predicament. Except the past six years of his life had done a pretty good job of slapping him upside the head with, yeah, that whole responsibility thing. Of manning up to a challenge instead of backing down from it.

Especially when the challenge went way beyond simply making good on a promise to his best friend. Oh, no. The challenge was how to really help Val without revealing truths that would only hurt her more.

Or change that look in her eyes from anger and resentment to…

To pity.

Of course, it wasn't like he'd been pining all these years for the girl who'd never been his, the girl he'd tried like hell to stop thinking about once Tomas had confessed he was sweet on her. But the truth was, the toughness and courage that had originally attracted him to the girl had only intensified in the woman…a woman obviously doing her best not to infect her children with her own anger and grief and loss issues. Hell, Val Lopez was frickin' amazing, the kind of woman any man would be proud to call his partner.

Any man but Levi, that is.

At this rate, he thought on a rough breath, he was gonna be able to rip out those dead bushes with his bare hands.

Sweatier than a race horse, and probably stinkier, Levi glanced up to find a wild-haired Josie sitting on the porch steps, the kitten in her lap, watching him dig up that shriveled up old lilac. He was beginning to get used to the staring, as well as the way she had of saying whatever was on her mind. Actually, in some ways it was a relief, letting her take the lead in the conversation, since what he knew about how to talk to little girls you could write on a Post-it note. One of those itty-bitty ones.

Like most little girls around here, she was more likely to wear jeans and boots than some froufrou tutu or whatever. Even if her T-shirt did have some glittery hot-pink design on it. Far as he could tell, Josie was her own person, nothing like either of her parents. As someone who'd been nothing like either of his, Levi could relate.

"Hey there, Miss Josie," he said, jabbing the point of the shovel into the stubborn taproot. "How are you today?"

A heavy sigh preceded, "Bored. I miss school." The kitten abandoned her lap to jump at a fly buzzing around the porch. "Mama says I'm not supposed to bother you."

"You're not."

"You sure?"

"I'm sure."

"Okay. Whatcha doing?"

Levi scrubbed his wrist across his sweaty forehead, then plucked at the front of the soaked T-shirt plastered to his chest. Even in the spring—and even though rogue snowstorms were not out of the question—the sun was hella hot at this altitude, and the bushes had been a pain to dig out. But at least he'd been grateful to see, once he started the excavation, that the foundation seemed to be in decent enough shape, thanks to some smart waterproofing efforts in the past.

He attacked the stubborn root again. "Digging up these bushes so we can plant the new ones you and your mama bought the other day." He grinned over at the child, sitting there with her pointy little chin in her hands, her elbows digging into her knees. "Wanna help?"

She sat up straighter, beaming. "Can I?"

Levi laughed. "Sorry, honey, I was only joking." At her disappointed expression, he gently added, "The shovel's way too heavy for you to lift, let alone dig with. Besides, you'd get all dirty."

"Oh, that's okay—these are my play clothes. And I'm not some little weenie wuss. Dirt doesn't bother me. At *all*."

And with that, he definitely saw her mama in her. Even to the way she pushed her shoulders back and crossed her arms over her ribs.

"Then tell you what—when I get around to planting the new stuff, you can definitely help me. How's that?"

"Deal." She plopped her chin in her hands again. Over in a pool of shade, the sleeping dog started *whooping* in his sleep. Josie giggled, then sighed. "I don't think Mama wants me talking to you."

Levi jerked his head up. "She tell you that?"

"Nuh-uh. But I can tell. 'Cause whenever I say something about you she gets this funny look on her face. Like this." With that, she flattened her mouth and squinched up her eyes in such a dead-on imitation of her mama Levi nearly laughed aloud.

He reached over to give the damn root a mighty tug. Nope. He went back to hacking at it. "I'm not surprised. Your mama and I..." His gaze flicked to the child's, then back to his task. "We weren't exactly best buds when we were kids."

"Oh, yeah. She said."

"She did?"

"Uh-huh. She said you were a goofball."

Levi chuckled. "*Idiot* is more like it."

"That's not a nice word."

"I wasn't a very nice person. Sometimes, anyway."

"Like, how? What did you do?"

Chuckling, Levi rammed the point of the shovel under the root ball, then put all his weight on it and rocked. "Nothing a sweet little girl like you needs to know about."

"You didn't—" Josie got very quiet "—hurt people, did you? Like beat them up and stuff?"

His cheeks got tight with his grin. This kid was something else. "Of course not. I wasn't bad. Exactly. I just got in trouble a lot. Did stuff I knew I wasn't supposed to do." Or rather, that nobody else would. No, he'd never hurt anyone. As big as he'd been, he'd never had to. But he'd sure as hell put the fear of God into a few people—

"Oh. Like the time Mama told me not to stand on the chair to get something out of the cupboard, but I did it anyway, only then it fell over and I banged my head? And broke the plate I was trying to get?"

The root ball finally gave way. *Eureka.* "Yeah. Like that." The mangled clump of roots and dirt tossed aside, Levi yanked up the hem of his army-issue T-shirt to wipe the sweat out of his eyes.

"Daddy said you were the funnest person he'd ever met—"

"Josefina Maria!" Val banged back the screen door, Risa propped on her hip. "What did I tell you about bothering Levi?"

"But I'm not!" she said, scrambling to her feet, wobbling for a moment in her boots. "Levi said!"

"She wasn't, Val," Levi said calmly. "And I liked the company."

"And he said I could help him plant the new bushes, too! Didn't you, Levi?"

"I sure did," he said. Only to add at Val's thunderous look, "But only if Mama says it's okay."

"Is it, Mama? Is it?"

"We'll see," Val said, then smiled for her daughter. "Now get upstairs and straighten out your room, little girl. Which I asked you to do three hours ago, so you can stop with the eye-rolling. Go on, now."

On another heavy sigh, the child shot what could only be described as a longing look in Levi's direction before snatching up the kitten and stomping into the house, the soft-close mechanism on the new screen door not even offering the satisfaction of slamming shut behind her.

Levi picked up the shovel again to start digging up the dirt around the last bush, a rangy euonymus that'd been ugly twenty years ago.

"You can trust me around your daughters, Val," he pushed out as he rammed the shovel into the rock-hard dirt. "No matter what you think of me, or what I was like then…" He glanced up into her startled expression. "I'm not gonna hurt your kids—"

"Levi! For God's sake! I know that—"

"Or say anything to them you wouldn't want me to say. I have added a few brain cells to my collection since we were kids."

She stared at him for a moment, then lowered Risa into her little play…cage…thing, waiting until the baby was happily beating a stuffed toy with something that made a mind-numbing racket before sitting on the edge of the steps a few feet away. As usual she was wearing beat-up jeans, a hoodie, a pair of those ugly-ass rubber shoes that made her look like a damn duck. Except the hoodie was soft and clingy, and her hair was soft and shiny, and her mouth was…

Doing that pressed-tight thing her daughter had just imitated so well.

"And I can't tell you how much it ticks me off that you would even think I'd think that," she said. "I know you wouldn't hurt the kids. Or say anything. But Josie..." She glanced up, even though Levi knew the girls' bedrooms were on the other side of the house. Providing, of course, Josie was actually in her room. "I don't want her getting all these...expectations. Because of what her father said to her. And I definitely don't want—" She looked down at her hands, tightly laced together in her lap, then back at Levi. "I don't need her looking at you and seeing something that's not there. I don't need her *liking* you. Especially not in a you-could-be-my-daddy kind of way."

Because clearly her mama wasn't about to see him that way, either. Not that this was a surprise. What was a surprise was her even considering the kid might.

"So, what? You afraid I'm gonna break her heart?"

"Quite possibly."

Anger spurted through him. "So I should stop being nice to her?"

"Of course not. Just not *too* nice."

Levi blew a short, dry laugh through his nose. "First off, that was the first real conversation Josie and I have had since I started coming over, so I think we've got some wiggle room between her and me being friends and her looking to me as her new daddy—"

"You don't understand. She barely saw her father. His skill... They couldn't simply send anybody over to do that job, could they? So he was away far more than he was home. Even when he was stateside, he spent more time at the training facilities than he did with us. She adored her father, but she kept feeling like he'd been stolen from her. It didn't matter so much at first, when she was tiny. But as she got older all she wanted was for him to stay home.

To stay with her. So I'm guessing she heard in that cockamamy promise he extracted from you—"

Frowning, Levi leaned heavily on the shovel. "That I would be his replacement?"

"I doubt her thought processes would label it as such—although knowing that kid, I wouldn't put it past her. But, yeah. Dammit, Levi—she's only now getting adjusted. She even aced school last semester. But it hasn't even been seven months since Tommy died. She may act like everything's fine, but I know how fragile she still is. So the last thing I want is for her to get attached only to get hurt all over again."

Levi let Val's words bounce around in his brain for a moment or two until they lined up right in front of his eyes, like a bunch of privates ready for inspection. Not that he doubted for a moment her wanting to avoid any more pain for her daughter. What mother wouldn't? But it wasn't only *Josie's* heart she was trying to protect, was it? Whether Val herself fully realized that or not.

Like she said, it'd only been a few months. Barely time for her to come to terms with being a widow, let alone move far enough past her grief to see a future. God, it still hurt like hell every time Levi thought about how he'd never see Tomas again, so he couldn't imagine what Val was going through, how she was holding it together for the kids. Sure, he'd made other friends in the army, some of 'em close. But not like Tommy.

Same way there'd been no one like Tomas in Val's life, either.

And most likely never would be again.

"And I would never, ever intentionally hurt another living soul," Levi said over the stab of pain. "Especially a child's. No matter what I might've been like at one time." He resumed digging, deciding it was the sun making the back of his head so hot. "I'm not that person anymore. So you can tell Josie…" He glanced over, then back at the stubborn ground. "Tell her the truth, if the subject comes up. That in all likelihood, I'm not going to be around forever."

"*Is* that the truth?"

Straightening again, Levi looked at her. "It's vague enough to probably keep my butt out of court." When she sort of laughed, he added, "Look—I don't know any more than you do what's going to happen down the road. Hell, I can't even see past next week. I'm here because, well, for one thing, I had no place else to go. And for another, yeah, because of that promise. But since it wasn't like Tommy was specific about what that entailed…"

He shrugged. "All I can do, all any of us can do right now, is play this by ear. Give ourselves some space to figure out what comes next." When she looked away, her jaw tight, he said, "I totally get what your issues are with me, Val. In your position, I'm sure I'd feel the same way. So all I want," he said when her gaze shifted back to his, "is a chance to make things up to you as best I can. Since I can't exactly go back and change what happened."

"I know that," she said softly.

"But do you believe it?" he asked, and her lips stretched into a tight smile.

"Working on it."

"Then that's all I ask. In the meantime it seems to me that if the two of us work together, we ought to be able to steer one seven-year-old away from fantasyland. *Without* having to resort to not being able to talk to each other on occasion."

"You really don't have a problem with that?"

"If you mean, do I know how to interact with little girls? Not a lot, no. But—"

His throat closed up, surprising him.

"What?" Val said, her voice surprisingly gentle.

"She's Tommy's, isn't she? To get a chance to know my best friend's kid..." Unable to finish his sentence, Levi shrugged. Then he hauled in a breath and pulled himself together. "Nothing says I can't be an uncle to the girls, right?"

"As long as you're around."

"Well...yeah."

After a long moment, Val sighed. "I guess that could work. As long as we make that perfectly clear to Josie."

"I'm good with that if you are."

She nodded, then got to her feet to scoop up her youngest daughter. "But fair warning—if you really want to get to know the kids, don't be surprised if I call on you to babysit."

"You're on," Levi said, releasing a long, slow breath after she went back inside.

Karma, he thought this was called, tackling the euonymus again.

Chapter Five

Over the next few weeks, spring finally edged into summer—with only one dusting of snow to keep it real—and the house, Val noted, began to look more like a home and less like the set from *Psycho.* Somebody's home, anyway. Now that school was out, both girls spent the time Val was at the diner with their grandmother, leaving Levi—as well as Radar and Skunk, the kitten—back at the house. And Val had to admit, as Josie burst out of the car to both snatch up her cat and prattle to Levi about her day, she'd grown used to seeing him there when they returned.

And not only because of the wonders he'd worked with the house and yard, but—even harder to admit—the wonders he'd wrought with, well, all of them. Despite her initial refusal to see Levi as anything but the loser who'd led Tomas down the primrose path—and then, later, into a war zone—his quiet steadiness and impeccable work ethic, as well as a gentle sense of humor that never targeted another human being, gradually chipped away at her resentment.

Not all of it, maybe, but enough that she finally had to acknowledge this was not the old Levi. At least, not the Levi she'd turned into some kind of monster in her head.

But mostly—as she stood at the car with the baby in her arms, watching Levi patiently listen to Josie's yammering—she realized it was how he'd gotten her older daughter really laughing again that made Val's heart swell with gratitude. Even as it cowered in terror—that something was happening here she had no control over. Something that was only going to bite them all in the butt—and sooner rather than later. Yes, both she and Levi had made it clear he was there only as an honorary uncle. But his obvious horror that she would even think him capable of hurting her children had touched something deep inside her, nudging at her own still sore—and lonely—heart, making her realize her fear of *Josie's* becoming attached was the least of her worries.

As if hearing her thoughts, Levi looked over, grinning. A grin that was maybe a mite too fuzzy around the edges. A grin accompanied by a brief flicker of something in his eyes that went beyond…whatever this was.

Yeah. Loneliness was a bitch. And what Levi saw, was thinking, when he saw her, she didn't want to know. Because what came to her mind when he grinned like that, was memories. Memories of another man whose sweet smile—a smile she'd never see again, except in pictures and dreams—could turn her into a puddle.

And she'd best remember that. Because, fine, so Levi Talbot wasn't so bad after all. In fact, she might even go so far as to say he was a good man. But if every time she looked at him, she remembered…

That wasn't good at all.

Like most men, Levi had no idea what a woman might be thinking at any given moment—hell, half the time he didn't know what they were really *saying*—but he definitely knew when they *were* thinking. Because a quiet woman was a thinking woman. Although, if he focused hard enough on a woman's expression, he could usually at least pick up on whether or not he should worry. Like if you looked outside and it was cloudy, it might rain or snow. And if it wasn't, it probably wouldn't.

But right now, watching Val holding the baby? The woman could be considering what to watch on TV that night or plotting his demise. No way of telling.

Which made what he was about to suggest even more fraught with danger. Granted, he'd been thinking it over ever since he'd stumbled across that old charcoal grill in the shed, which had cleaned up better than he'd expected. But he didn't want to spook her. Or overstep some boundary she'd set up in her head. And if he had a grain of sense he'd be grateful for whatever level of détente they'd reached. Because he was really enjoying getting to know Josie—and her sister, although since Risa didn't talk, there wasn't a lot to get to know yet—and working on the house was actually feeding something inside him he hadn't known was hungry.

It felt good simply being useful. Making somebody's life a little easier, maybe. Wanting to ease someone's burden for its own sake without thinking about what he might get out of it. It also helped him forget. Or at least, not remember so hard, or so often. So he told himself, this was enough.

That hearing a little girl's laughter was enough.

That seeing Val's smile—real smiles, not those stingy little things from before—was enough.

He didn't doubt that what he was about to propose—cooking up some steaks on the grill, maybe corn on the cob—was crazy. Like they actually had the kind of relationship where he could do that.

"Hey," he said as Val came up the walk. In her arms, Risa gnawed on her own fat little fist, glistening with baby slobber. Then she grinned at Levi, showing off the two tiny bottom teeth that had only popped out the week before. Was it weird that he hadn't held her yet? That he wasn't sure why he hadn't?

"Hey, yourself," Val said back, stray wisps of hair floating around her cheeks. Since it'd gotten warmer, she'd taken to wearing it up more often than not. Levi liked it better when it was loose, of course, but *up* definitely showed off her neck and cheekbones better; so there was that. Something like profound satisfaction gleamed in her pretty blue eyes. "Sold all fifteen pies today."

"Like this is a surprise?" he said, and she rolled those eyes, then smiled, making Levi's stomach jump.

"It's gratifying is what it is. Makes me think I could actually make a go of this baking thing."

"No doubt about it." While they'd yet to share an actual meal, she had pawned off leftover pie on him from time to time. Which, out of deference to his father who couldn't have such things, Levi had personally, and happily, disposed of. Woman made damn good pie. Definitely something to add to the plus column. If he were keeping tabs, that is.

"Thanks," she said softly, and Levi thought, *Now or never, dude.*

"Um…" Heat prickled his face before he cleared his throat. "You know that old grill I found? I was wondering what you'd think about firing it up tonight? Cooking some steaks. Because if I eat one more chicken breast or piece of tilapia I'm gonna lose it. Although I bought hot dogs, too, in case Josie would rather have them…"

Val had gone completely still, staring at him. Cripes, his heart was pounding so hard his sternum hurt.

"Of course," he said, playing it cool, "if you already have dinner plans—"

"No, no." Glancing down at the baby, Val grabbed Risa's slobbery little hand, wiping it on the front of her own shirt as Levi held his breath. "I suppose..." Her gaze lifted to his again. "I could make a salad, too?"

Levi wanted to kiss her. Not that the thought hadn't crossed his mind a time or six in the last little while—complete and total inappropriateness aside—but now the impulse was from absolute relief. And, okay, because she looked absolutely frickin' adorable standing there with the baby and those strands of hair messing with her face and baby drool glistening on the front of her shirt, like she was saying, *This is my life, dammit. Deal.* But mostly relief, that he hadn't come across like an ass.

He grinned, even as he realized his heart rate hadn't gone *less* off the charts. "A salad would be great."

"I think...um...there's a bag of charcoal in the shed, too."

"I know, I saw it."

Their gazes do-si-do'd for another second or two while Levi considered the wisdom of asking her why, when he guessed she didn't grill.

"Lugged the stupid thing all the way from Texas," she said. "Silly, right? Instead of leaving it with one of the other families on the base. But..."

And he could either ignore the elephant swaying from side to side between them, or acknowledge it and move on.

"Yeah, Tommy loved his grilling," he said quietly, and she smiled. Not a happy smile, no, but more of an *I can do this* smile.

"*Obsessed* is the word I think you're looking for. But I haven't had a grilled steak since...in a long time."

"Are you sure?"

"No. But yes. It'd be…lovely. And I'm starved. Thank you."

"Okay, then. Let me zip back to my parents' and get cleaned up, grab the steaks and franks, and I'll be back around five?"

"That'll be great."

But as he drove the short distance to his folks' house, Levi couldn't help but wonder if he'd made a mistake, forcing Val to face something she'd probably worked her butt off to forget. What if his lame attempt to make her happy only made things worse?

Then again, how often had playing it safe worked before?

Yeah. That's right. Never.

She could have said no.

Except…steak.

Grilled steak, perfuming the rapidly cooling evening with smoky sweetness. Even a half hour after they'd tossed the paper plates into the garbage and shoved leftovers into the decrepit fridge, the scent still hung in the air, clinging to their clothes, the dog's fur as he happily gnawed on a sturdy bone nearby. A bittersweet scent, reminding her of the one time in her life she'd been happy. Content.

Not exactly how she'd describe what she was feeling now.

"I'll clean the grill tomorrow," Levi said, dropping into a molded plastic chair next to Val, toothpick in mouth, long legs stretched out in front of him. He'd changed from his scuzzy work clothes into a clean pair of jeans and a lightweight plaid shirt. The same boots, though—around here "cowboy" was a state of mind more than an occupation. And six-foot-something Levi did the look proud.

Damn him.

He smelled good, too. Yes, even over the aroma of charred beef.

Double damn him.

"No hurry," Val said, looking away, wrapping her hoodie more tightly around her as she shucked off her ballet flats, pulling up her knees to plant her bare feet in the chilly seat of her own chair. She glanced at the baby monitor in her hand, even though there was no need. Risa had conked out right after they'd eaten, while her older sister was doing a good job of wearing her legs to nubs chasing the kitten around the yard.

"Yeah, but the longer the gunk sits, the harder it is to get off." Levi paused. "Thanks."

"For what? You cooked."

"For *letting* me cook. For you."

Val softly laughed, even though the tightening in the pit of her stomach wasn't particularly pleasant. Or due to her full tummy. She wasn't sure why Levi was still here, but it'd be rude to ask. And to be truthful she wasn't entirely ready for him to leave, although don't ask her why. Also, the words, "You can cook for me anytime," floated behind her eyes, but she didn't dare say them out loud. For a whole bunch of reasons.

Because it'd been a long time since she'd felt this… safe, she supposed it was. And wasn't that the craziest thing ever? No, not happy, and God knew a long way from *content*, but at least as if maybe the world had stopped spinning out of control, even if for only a moment. And that's all life was about, wasn't it? Moments. Flashes of joy—if you were lucky—connected by stretches of not-so-much.

Or, like now, vestibules of what's-next?

Those were the worst—those long, unsettling periods of not knowing. So go figure how she could feel unsettled and safe at the same time.

An owl hooted nearby, the sound mournful over the soothing, off-sync chirping of a dozen crickets holed up underneath the newly laid mulch in the flower beds. The growing season was ridiculously short, up this high. And even more ridiculously iffy, with snow possible even as late as May or as early as late September.

Iffy. The perfect word to describe her existence.

"Do I dare ask what you're thinking?"

Sighing, Val set the monitor on the table beside her, then tried to burrow herself farther into the hoodie by wrapping the hem around her cold toes. It'd been ages since anyone had asked her that. Like they really cared what her answer was, anyway. Because even with Connie and Pete, it was all about keeping up appearances, wasn't it? Acting stronger than she felt, so she wouldn't bring anybody else down with her.

But it was different with Levi. Who, for one thing, she suspected probably had a pretty good BS detector. And for another…well, if he couldn't take the truth, he didn't have to hang around, did he? Wasn't as if she had anything left to lose.

"About…moments," she finally said. "Being grateful for the good ones, getting through the bad ones—"

"Mama?" Breathing hard, Josie clomped up onto the deck in her almost-too-small boots, hanging on to the loudly purring kitten. "Can I go inside and watch my movie?"

"Not the whole thing—it's getting late. But sure. Get your jammies on first, though."

"No bath?"

Smiling, Val reached over to swing an arm around Josie's waist, tug her closer. She smelled of mustard and strawberries and hot little girl, and Val wished she could bottle it. "I think we can skip tonight. And did you thank Levi for the hot dogs?"

She gave him a big snaggletoothed grin. Her front baby teeth had taken their sweet time falling out; their permanent replacements seemed in no hurry, either. "Thanks, Levi. And thanks for cookin' 'em, too."

He chuckled. "You're welcome, honey." Then Val sucked in a breath when her daughter stomped over to throw one arm around his neck and kiss his cheek before running inside.

"And which is this?" Levi asked after the patio door slid closed behind her. Frowning, Val looked over. "You were talking about moments. Good and bad. So which is this? Tonight, I mean."

Val looked down at her toes, peeking out from underneath the hoodie. She used to paint them. Weird colors, like sky blue. Maybe one day she would again. The old bracelet itched; absently, she scratched her wrist. "Truthfully? A mix of both. Because...because as nice as it is to feel *almost* normal, the night, the smell of the grill...it also reminds me of Tommy. A lot."

There. She'd said it. Out loud. To another human being—that she missed her husband.

A long pause preceded, "Wasn't my intention to cause you any more pain."

"Oh, Levi...of course not. And I do appreciate the gesture. And the food. Really. I wouldn't have agreed to it otherwise. But..."

"I know. Believe me, I know."

Val sighed. "I try to stay upbeat. For the girls' sake. For Tommy's parents. They need to know—believe—I'm okay. But there are times when I don't think I'll every truly be okay again. Not completely."

"Yeah. Sucks, doesn't it?"

She almost laughed. "Truly."

At that, Levi leaned forward, planting his feet back under him to link his hands between his knees. "I do know there's nothing I can really do to make this better. To make up for what happened. I also take full responsibility for my part in it. But as long as we're being honest…"

He faced her, the pain etched in his features clearly visible even in the paltry light over the back door. "I don't think I'll ever really be okay again, either. I loved Tommy. More than I even knew until I realized I'd never see him or talk to him again. So I felt it, too, tonight. His absence. Not that I'm comparing his and my relationship with what the two of you shared. Obviously. But I can hardly remember when he wasn't part of my life. And coming back to Whispering Pines… Dammit, I can't go down a road or into a store or by the high school that I don't think I see that big old grin of his out of the corner of my eye. Think he's gonna come around the corner in that ridiculous lowrider he drove. You remember that monstrosity?" he said, half grinning when Val laughed in spite of herself. "Man," he said, shaking his head, "that was one ugly-ass car."

As in purple. *Iridescent* purple. With painted flames. Bumping up and down Main Street like it was having convulsions. Oh, yeah, she remembered it, all right. He'd sold it, right before they moved to Texas.

Levi chuckled. "But Tommy felt like such hot stuff when he was driving it, what could I say?"

Smiling, Val swiped at a tear trickling down her cheek. "I remember the first time he picked me up in that thing. I thought I was hallucinating. But you're right—he was so proud of it."

"Not nearly as proud, though," Levi said softly, "as when you said you'd go steady with him." He looked back into the night now swallowing up the weed-wacked excuse of a yard, those flower beds, the newly planted vegetable garden tucked into a back corner. All Levi's handiwork. "Your love, Val… That was the most important thing in the world to him. And I know he loved *you* like nobody's business. Because he told me, every chance he got." He slowly shook his head. "What you guys had was pretty damn special."

Levi pushed himself to his feet, reaching down to scratch the dog's ears when he sauntered over, tail wagging. "Tommy was one lucky sonofabitch. But so were you, because there was no better human being than Tomas Lopez. Maybe your marriage didn't last as long as it should've, but do you have any idea how many people would sell their souls for those memories?"

Tears stinging her eyes, Val stood as well, her arms crossed over her rib cage. Her shoes were right by her feet, but she didn't bother to slip them on. Instead she pushed herself up to grab Levi's shoulder, pull him down enough for her to kiss him on the cheek. He looked justifiably startled.

"What was that for?"

"To say thank you."

"For dinner?"

"For...helping me to remember. The good moments. Because nothing and nobody can take those away from me, can they?"

His hands in his pockets, Levi smiled. A soft smile, his lips barely curved. "No, ma'am. They sure can't."

He grabbed his denim jacket off the back of the chair, tucking it in the crook of his elbow rather than putting it on, despite the chill in the air. "You go on inside. It's getting cold. I'll see myself out." Then, with a slight nod, he left the deck, his boots clicking against the flagstone path leading around to the front of the house. Moments later, she heard his truck start, the engine purring as he drove off.

But Val didn't go inside right away, even though she did slip her shoes back on before her feet froze. Because she needed a think, and she couldn't do that properly with *Elf*—

yet again—blasting from the TV. What Levi had done was give her permission to grieve, for as long as she needed. To hang out in the past—to *remember*, dammit—until she was ready to deal with the present. Something she now realized she hadn't fully allowed herself to do, for fear of being a wallower.

Not that she needed his—or anyone's—permission. She was a big girl. It was her call how she handled her life. Even those aspects of it she rarely let anyone see. But all the same, he'd released her from a self-imposed prison, hadn't he?

Without asking, she thought with a start, or even suggesting, that she release him from his.

Val sharply turned toward the side yard where Levi had walked away, as if half expecting to see him there. Had it really made her feel better, holding him at least partly accountable for something that had obviously been Tomas's decision, and his alone? This was the man who'd driven around in a car so loud you could see it, let alone hear it, miles away. A man who didn't care what anybody else thought, who even laughed at the taunts, the gibes. How could Val have believed that Levi held any kind of real power over her husband?

Had she really been so jealous of their friendship?

Val shut her eyes, reeling slightly, both from that realization and the one that followed hot on its heels: That Levi could have easily pointed any or all of that out tonight. Made some attempt to save his own butt, absolving himself of any responsibility for what had happened.

But he hadn't. In fact, he'd done exactly the opposite, not only still shouldering at least some of the blame, but trying to salve her still-raw wounds by reminding her that what she and Tomas had shared would always be greater than what she'd lost. By making her fall in love with her husband all over again.

And in the process smashing to smithereens whatever vestiges of resentment she'd clung to so fiercely about her husband's best friend.

Damn him, damn him, damn *him.*

Chapter Six

His mother was in the living room when Levi got home, watching some dumb reality show. Brides picking out dresses or something. She paused the DVR, though, when Levi came to the door, leaning over to pat the nearby leather recliner. God love her, she'd saved the room from death by beige by adding bright area rugs and throws and wall hangings—many of them gifts from grateful clients—not to mention a forest of houseplants huddled in front of the picture window. Nothing matched, and heaven knew the place would never win any awards, but the longer Levi was there, the more he realized *home* was far more about what a person brought to it than what they put in it.

After he obeyed Mom's unspoken command, she glanced toward the door, then whispered, "You didn't by any chance bring me a piece of that steak, did you?"

"Crap. Sorry, we got to talking and I didn't even think about it. I'll remember next time—how's that? Where's Dad?"

"In the garage. Tinkering." One dark eyebrow lifted. "So there's gonna be a next time?"

Yeah, she would latch on to that. "Figure of speech, Mom. This is Val we're talking about, remember?"

Making a sound that was more grunt than sigh, his mother relaxed against the nest of pillows she'd made in the corner of the sofa, her bare feet tucked up by her hip. For a woman in her late fifties, she was still good-looking, Levi supposed, although not in a manufactured way. She rarely wore makeup, and midwives had no use for manicures. But even though her long, thick hair—usually worn in a braid—was mostly gray now, her skin was smooth and taut over high cheekbones, and deep brown eyes behind rimless glasses always sparkled with love and life and mischief. She could also rock a pair of formfitting jeans better than most women half her age. Although no way in hell would Levi tell her that.

"So dinner went okay?"

"I suppose. Yeah." Even if things did get a little heavy there at the end.

"If you want to talk about it—"

"Thanks, but no," he said, getting to his feet again.

"Didn't mean to sound nosy."

"Like hell," he said with a smile. "It's what you do. And, yeah, Dad told me about you and Val's mother, so I can probably guess where you're coming from with this. Even so, I doubt Val'd be down with the idea of me sharing our conversations with anybody else. Even you."

The corners of Mom's mouth curved. "So you sticking around or going back out?"

"Out. To walk off dinner." He smiled. "I'd almost forgotten how good red meat was."

"And that's just mean," his mother said on a sigh, looking back at the TV. "Enjoy."

"Thanks."

But before he got to the door, she leaned over the back of the sofa. "Levi?"

"Yeah?"

"I think you are one of the bravest people I know. No, I'm serious. And I don't only mean because of your military service." She pushed up her glasses. "Which I wouldn't know about, anyway, since you keep all of that to yourself, too."

"Mom—"

She held up one hand. "I know. Grown boys aren't partial to sharing with their mamas. But I also remember how you used to feel about that young woman." Levi's face warmed as ghosts from his past shuddered between them. Like he'd expected her to forget? "I also saw how you stepped aside for Tomas, after he told you how he felt about Val." Her eyes narrowed. "Never could decide if you were being honorable or stupid, but since that was one of the few decent things you did back then, it seemed best to let it go."

"I think that's called a backhanded compliment, Mom."

"And I meant every word of it. *And* if I'm not mistaken, you're not over her. Not by a long shot."

"You're nuts," Levi said gently, smiling.

"Common side effect of raising four boys. But I'm right, aren't I?"

Levi blew a breath through his nose. "And even if that were true, I'm not Tommy. And never will be."

"Which is why you're so brave," Mom said, her smile soft. "Not to mention selfless, doing all of this with no... expectations."

His face warmed. "I'm doing it because Tommy asked—"

"Bull. You're doing it because you're a good boy. And because you've got a thing for her, but mostly because you're a good boy."

"Mom."

She laughed. "Sorry. In my head you're still that too-tall kid about to ship out who didn't completely fill out his uniform. Gonna take me a while yet to wrap my head around the man who came back. But I can tell you I'm so frickin' proud of you I could pop."

Her words should have warmed him, made him feel better. Instead, all Levi could think of was everything she didn't know about him. Oh, sure, once he was in the service he'd been obedient to a fault, to the point where his parents wouldn't have recognized him. And most of the time that discipline and order had been good things, corralling a boatload of wayward tendencies. Making him grow up, and fast. But that obedience hadn't allowed much wiggle room, either, for things like judgment calls. He'd done what was expected of him, yeah. Didn't mean he was always proud of it. Like Val had said, life was made up of moments. And unfortunately the bad ones often had a way of eclipsing the good ones.

But his mother didn't need to know that, either. So all he did was grin and say, "You'll probably be a lot happier, though, when I get out of your hair, find a place of my own." He snorted. "Not to mention a life of my own."

"Please. You've been home, what? A month? There's no hurry."

"And like you said, I'm not a kid anymore—"

"You're twenty-eight," she said gently. "And goodness, I didn't even know I wanted to be a midwife until I was in my forties. The right thing will make itself clear. It always does. So give yourself a break. It's not as if you've been sitting on your butt the last six years doing nothing, right? Now go take your walk. We'll leave the door open for you."

Once outside, Levi filled his lungs with the clear night air, then started down the unpaved drive to the road leading back into the town proper, a trek of a couple of miles that hopefully would clear his head. Bring a little peace.

The thing about mothers—his, anyway—was not only their uncanny ability to make you say stuff you instantly regretted, but that whatever *they* said was more often dead-on right than not. Part of the problem when he'd been a kid was that life never seemed to move fast enough to suit him, which living in a town the size of an apple only made worse. Nine times out of ten, he'd gotten into trouble because he was bored. And now that he was back, that old impatience reared its sorry head, that he needed to get on with it… Except he had no clue what it was he was supposed to get on with. He'd hoped joining the army would help him find his purpose, only to realize he'd only postponed the very thing he now had to figure out.

Like what on earth he was supposed to do with his life.

Not to mention his feelings for Valerie Lopez. Feelings that, after tonight, he realized weren't *less* inappropriate than they'd been back then.

The blue-black night inhaled his sigh, as if whisking it away for safekeeping in the nearby Sangre de Cristo Mountains, like a herd of slumbering dinosaurs against the moonlit sky. Levi smiled, remembering the stories he and Tommy used to make up about them, when they were kids. From miles away came the long, lonely *whoo...whooooo* of a freight train. Levi told himself it was the sound of the train making him melancholy.

Not much traffic this time of night, except for the occasional car turning into Chico's, the only place besides the Circle K open past nine. He caught the twang of an amped guitar, the distorted sound of an overloud mike, boots thundering on the wooden floor. Laughter. He briefly considered going inside, having a beer, maybe sweet-talking a pretty girl into dancing with him.

Except there was only one pretty girl Levi wanted to dance with. Although he highly doubted she'd want to dance with him. Still, he let his mind wander again, just for a moment, imagining the feel of Val's waist against his palm, her soft hair tickling his chin. The scent of flowers and baby powder overriding the tang of hops and leather and fried food.

Blowing out a sound that was half laugh, half sigh, Levi kept on down the highway, hands in his jacket pockets, as the sounds from the tavern gave way to the chirps and squeaks of assorted night critters, the crunching of his boots against gravel.

And, yeah, his thoughts, zip-zapping around his brain like hyper bats. He welcomed them, though—unlike a lot of the guys he'd served with, whose usual method of dealing with the junk inside their head was to drown it out with loud music or video games. Booze. Drugs. Being alone, being *still*? Far too scary. Levi, though, had early on decided he'd rather face the suckers head-on, and on his own terms, than having them ambush him when he least expected it. Because they always did. Nobody could run, or hide, or pretend, forever. No matter how much they might want to.

Not that he was interested in sharing, and God knew there were plenty of times he wished the memories weren't part of him. But he'd gotten pretty good at telling them to go to hell.

Whether they were interested in listening to him was something else again.

The town was asleep, silent except for the buzzing of the fluorescents in the gas station. A couple of tourist types passed, hand in hand, softly chattering as they peered into the windows of this or that gallery or gift shop. Then he heard more laughter, this time from a clump of teenagers at the far end of the block, probably on their way to somebody's house, hoping to fend off the boredom before it ate them alive. Hard to believe that'd been him and Tomas barely a dozen years ago. Some things never changed.

And yet Levi felt strangely at peace and antsy at the same time, like when you know the presents are waiting for you under the Christmas tree but you're about to pop from not knowing what they are. The idea of staying here gave him the willies; the thought of leaving for good made his chest hurt. That whatever he did was totally up to him made him slightly dizzy.

Pushing out a breath, he plopped his butt on a park bench in the town's tiny square, only to nearly jump out of his skin when he heard shuffling behind him. He wheeled around, and the figure—a man, he could now tell, leading a stiff-legged dog on a leash—jerked back, as startled as Levi. Like Levi, he wore a worn denim jacket, jeans and cowboy boots, but his wiry beard and hair—held back by a sloppily tied bandanna—were heavily shot with gray.

Squinting, the guy inched closer, into a patch of god-awful yellowish light cast by a new halogen streetlamp—somebody's idea of improvement, no doubt. The dog yawned, then sat down to have a good scratch. "You're one of Sam Talbot's sons, huh?" he said a little too loudly. "The one who went into the army? Let's see… Levi, right?"

"Uh, yeah." Then he sucked in a breath. "Charley?"

The older man released a wheezy laugh, hopefully unaware of Levi's shock. Time hadn't done the man who'd given Levi his first job when he was seventeen any favors. Although a few years younger than his father, Charley Maestas looked at least ten, fifteen years older.

"Yep. They were talking, over at Annie's, about how you were home. Figured we'd run into each other eventually." He swayed for a moment, caught his balance. "You okay?"

Levi knew what he meant. Not all vets would ask, but they all thought it.

"Yeah." Because compared with so many, he was. Then he patted the space beside him on the bench, inviting Charley to join him. The pair crept over, sighing simultaneously as they sat, Charley on the bench, the dog on the pavement by his feet. Levi reached over to pet the beast's head. His stumpy tail wagging his butt, he gave Levi's hand a quick lick, then lay down with a groan and shut his eyes, as if it was all too much.

"What's his name?"

"What? Sorry, afraid you'll have to speak up, I don't hear so good these days."

Levi leaned closer, pointing to the dog. "His name?"

"Oh. Senor Loco." Charley chuckled. "Wandered into the yard one day, decided to stay. Mostly pitty, probably, but I swear he's the most laid-back pup I ever saw." Absently scratching his beard, Charley looked down at the dog for several seconds, then crossed his arms to squint at Levi. "I remember you boys, you and Tommy Lopez. How you two would help me and Gloria out from time with the yard and all like that. Or was it…?" Now he frowned at Levi, as though he was trying to get him into focus. "You used to work for me, too, didn't you?"

"I sure did. In fact, you taught me everything I know about woodworking and carpentry."

"Did I?" Charley snorted. "Maybe you can reteach me, then. 'Cause I don't remember squat." He tapped his temple with one finger. "Have a hard time these days, making the pieces fit. And I don't only mean the wood. But let's see… Tomas… Didn't he…didn't he marry the gal who makes the pies, over at Annie's? Or am I mixing her up with somebody else?"

"No, you're good." Charley curled a hand around his ear. Levi raised his voice. "Yeah, Tommy married Valerie Oswald. Right after you left on another deployment."

"That's what I thought. That Val…she is sweeter than her pies, and that's no lie. Her smile is like the sun coming up, you know?" He sighed, shaking his head, then turned to Levi. "So how is Tommy? Heard he enlisted the same time you did."

Crap. Levi had no way of telling, of course, whether Charley really didn't know or simply didn't remember, but either way the news was probably going to shake him. "I'm sorry…nobody told you?"

On a soft moan, Charley seemed to fold into himself. "He didn't make it home?"

Levi shook his head, even as a fresh wave of pain shunted through his chest. "No," he said softly. "He died in Afghanistan. Late last year."

"How?"

"An IED smarter than he was."

The older man breathed out a swear word in Spanish, then frowned again. "You know, now that I think about it, that sounds familiar. When— What did you say his wife's name was?"

"Valerie. Val."

"Yeah, yeah…" Mustache and beard became one as Charley's mouth flattened. Reaching up, he palmed his head, massaging it. "When she started working at Annie's, I must've asked then. You know, why she'd come back. Can't seem to hang on to anything these days. I think they said it's on account of a bomb going off close by. But if I don't remember it, did it really happen?"

Figuring that was a rhetorical question, Levi let it go. Then Charley blew another sigh through his nose. "That's too bad. He was a nice boy. Tomas. A really nice boy. He used to…he used to drive that purple car around, didn't he?"

Levi chuckled. "He certainly did," he said, and Charley laughed.

"You see? Some things, I remember just fine. Well, I won't keep you. It's time Loco and me got back home, anyway, see if there's anything good on TV. If I can remember where I put the…the…" He mimed clicking a controller, his agitation growing with each squeeze of his hand. "The damn thing you use to turn the TV off and on."

"The remote?"

"That's it. The remote."

With another exhale, Charley pushed himself to his feet, startling the dog awake. Ready to get back himself, Levi stood, as well. "You still live out by the Dairy Queen?"

"Yeah. Why?"

"Just wondered how you were getting home."

"Same way we got here. On our feet. We like to walk, Loco and me. It's the one thing we can still do. Right, boy?"

The dog didn't look up, but at the sound of his name his tail pumped once or twice. Charley chuckled, then stuck out his trembling hand, which Levi took, surprised at how firm Charley's shake was. "Us vets, we gotta stick together, you know?"

Levi surprised himself by pulling his old boss into a brief hug, patting his back a couple of times before letting him go. "Absolutely. And, hey—you need anything, anything at all, you let me know," he said, adding, when it occurred to him the dude probably didn't have a phone, "You can tell Val—she'll get me a message."

It seemed to take Charley a moment to focus; then he gave his head a sharp nod. "I tell Val if I need anything—she'll tell you."

"That's right."

Charley gave him a shaky thumbs-up, then ambled off. Hands shoved in his pockets, Levi watched man and dog trudge away, feeling a frown bite into the space between his brows. Obviously he'd been getting around for years without Levi's concern or assistance. There was no reason why tonight should be the night he didn't make it home. And it would've taken Levi longer to bring back the truck than it would have for Charley to get home on his own steam. If he'd even remembered to stay put and wait in the first place…

Levi blew out a breath. It wasn't up to him to take care of the whole world.

Even if sometimes it felt like it was.

"There's somebody here asking for you," Annie whispered the next afternoon as Val wiped down the stainless steel island in the restaurant's kitchen, redolent with the aroma of two dozen freshly baked pies cooling on racks on the island.

"Who?"

"If said, you might not want to go out there."

"And if you don't, I'm sure as hell not."

"Billie Talbot. Levi's mama?"

"I know who she is, Annie." Then she froze, staring through the open door. And, yep, there sat Levi's mother at the counter, giving her a little wave. Yay.

"Told you," Annie muttered.

"Shut up," Val mumbled back, brushed most of the flour and pie crust bits off the front of her apron—not a lot she could do about the cherry stains—plastered on a smile and marched through the door to meet her destiny. Or something. In a tentlike tunic and capris, her gray hair pulled back into a flowing ponytail, Levi's mom came around to fold Val into a hug, the parachute-like fabric practically swallowing her up. The woman wasn't that much taller than Val—maybe three or four inches—but she was definitely more substantial, and for a second Val feared for her bones.

Then Billie held her back, her eyes gone all soft, and Val thought, *Please, God, no…*

"Now, honey, I'm not even gonna try to make excuses for not coming to see you before this—"

"That's okay, I'm sure you're busy—"

"Not that busy. Honestly, I've been meaning to get over here and buy one of your pies for weeks now. Especially after the way Levi goes on and on about how good they are." Like Radar on a scent, she lifted her nose toward the kitchen. "And by the smell of things, my timing's perfect." Billie grinned, the skin around her eyes crinkling. "Or are they all already spoken for?"

Relief rolled through Val. Pies she could handle.

"No, not at all. But your husband...?"

"As long as it's not deep-fried, we're good. So what've you got?"

"Well, there's fruit—apple or cherry—or custard. Or meringue. Lemon or chocolate."

"Lemon meringue would be perfect." Billie lugged her leather shoulder bag around to dig inside it, pulling out her wallet. "It's Sam's and my anniversary today," she said, handing Annie—who'd reappeared like magic—her credit card. "We stopped giving each other presents years ago, but this will be a big treat for him. After thirty-five years, you learn to appreciate the little things."

And Val figured that was that. Except, even after Annie'd processed the charge and boxed up the pie, it was clear Billie was in no hurry to leave. And Val thought, *Hell.* Maybe she had never been close to the woman, but she knew the friendship between Levi and Tomas had bonded their mothers, as well. Meaning she'd most likely been the focus of at least a couple of recent conversations.

"So you're coming out to the Vista for the Fourth, right?"

Val blinked. Not that she didn't know what Billie was talking about—the big Fourth of July barbecue and fireworks shindig Granville Blake hosted for the town every year out on the ranch where Levi had grown up.

"I hadn't really thought about it."

"Well, you should. The kids would have a blast. Your older girl, especially. In the last few years we've made it more of a potluck, although Josh will still be in charge of the fireworks. Like his daddy always did." She chuckled. "In that respect, he never grew up. But then, I don't think men every really do." Billie winked. "You could bring a couple of pies, drum up more business."

Val laughed. "And you should've been in sales, yourself."

"So you'll come?"

"I'll…think about it."

Billie smiled. "I'll take it. Along with this," she said, hoisting the boxed pie. "And you know, if you ever need a babysitter, if I'm around and Connie and Pete aren't available, please feel free. Have Levi give you my number."

And, with another hug, she was gone.

"So you gonna go?" Annie said behind her, making her jump.

Val rolled her eyes, then went to retrieve her purse, Annie dogging her heels. As a kid, Val had never gone—her mother having declared they didn't need all those people looking down on them, by which of course she meant *her*. But once Val and Tomas became an item, they'd joined the festivities every summer, until he'd enlisted and she and Josie had moved away. That and the ranch's annual Christmas party were two of the town's biggest events, outside of the rodeo every September. But the memories—of Tommy's childlike delight at the fireworks, the way he'd held her close as they'd dance afterward…

"Maybe."

"Oh, come on—it'll be fun."

"Maybe."

"You are hopeless, you know that?"

"Probably."

Annie sighed, then handed her a quart of something hot and fragrant in a to-go bag.

"What's this?"

"Green chile stew. From AJ. Because you're too skinny, he says."

Tender pork. Chunks of potato and green chile, hominy and sweet red peppers and sautéed onions, all floating in a sauce guaranteed to clear your sinuses in five seconds flat. "And if I eat all this I definitely won't be."

"Then you can share."

"Right. Josie wouldn't touch this if it was the only food in the house."

"Not talking about Josie. Or the dog."

"Annie. Really?"

"What? Now go on, so it'll still be hot by the time you get home."

Uh-huh. The stuff would still be "hot" if it was frozen solid. But Val took the offering, its scent saturating the car on the short drive home, reminding her of the Lopezes' kitchen. Of sanctuary. Love. If she could even half approximate those feelings of security for her own kids, she'd be doing good.

Once out of the car, she followed the sounds of pounding out back, where a certain sweaty, shirtless, ripped dude in baggy camo pants was repeatedly ramming a posthole digger into the uncooperative dirt in the far right corner of what would be an actual backyard. She'd never seen the tattoos before, starkly simple but exquisite, one gripping his right biceps, another more elaborate number fanning across much of his upper back.

Speaking of *hot*. The bad boy was all grown up, God help her.

Which he'd better be, since until that moment she'd never realized how much of a buffer the girls had been between them.

Radar bounded over to greet her, regaling her with a dramatic aria about his day. Laughing, Val plopped in front of the dog, careful not to jostle the bag, laughing harder when he gave her kisses. Levi straightened, breathing hard. Glistening. Grinning. Funny, how Val'd thought she didn't find pretty boys all that appealing. Just goes to show.

Then she frowned. "How'd you get him to stay in the yard?"

"Electric fence. This one's to keep other things *out*. Um…you missing somebody?"

"Connie took the girls into Taos. To, in her words, pillage Walmart."

Levi chuckled, then lifted his head. "Am I imagining things, or is that green chile stew in that bag?"

"Jeebus. Your nose is better than the dog's."

His smile broadening, Levi crossed his hands over the top of the posthole digger, muscles bunching and shifting and such as he leaned into it. The heavy breathing had slowed down some, but not the glistening. Over the past few weeks his hair had gotten significantly longer, Val realized, framing his temples in damp curls, like those little cupids painted on fancy ceilings. Nothing innocent about those dudes, either.

"I do have a keen sense of smell," he said. "In fact, I've had the scent of green chile stew in my nostrils from the moment Annie called to say you were bringing me some."

"Bringing *you*…?" Val shut her eyes. And her mouth. Her ears caught the chuckle, though.

"Aw, you're not gonna make a liar out of poor Annie, are you?"

The kidding annoyed her. Warmed her. Confused her. Made her acutely aware not only of what she missed so badly it hurt but of what was standing right in front of her. Okay, thirty feet away. But still. In her frickin' *yard*.

She sure as heck was gonna make *something* out of

Annie. Soon as she figured out what. And how the hell did she have Levi's number, anyway? Still. Never let it be said that she couldn't be a gracious hostess.

"I suppose you're hungry."

"You suppose right. Give me a sec to hose off and I'll be right in."

"Oh. We could eat out here?"

There went that devilish grin again. "No, let's eat in the kitchen."

"Whatever." Val carted the food inside, where a whole mess of samples beckoned from the beat-up kitchen counter. Slabs of stone and squares of wood, paint chips and tiles in a dozen colors, gleaming like jewels against the blah of the drab, ancient laminate. Even a half-dozen types of pulls, everything from sleek and simple bronze to whimsical, wrought-iron curlicues.

Absently she set down the bag to finger a sheet of shiny glass mosaics, like little topazes. Or there was the white brick, too. Or maybe the subway tiles…?

"Just to get your juices flowing," Levi said behind her. *Right* behind her. As in, she could smell him, all damp and male and too damn close. Yeah, her juices were flowing, all right.

"Of course, if you don't like these, we can always go to Home Depot and you can choose whatever you like. But I thought this might be easier. So you wouldn't get overwhelmed with all the choices in the store."

And that right there was far worse than how good he smelled, or the way her sad, neglected lady parts were responding to his body heat. She could—and would—ignore her hormones' screeches in her ear, the thrum of sexual awareness making her slightly dizzy. But instead of impatience—the default setting for most men, it seemed—she only heard kindness. Genuine kindness. As if he genuinely cared. And not, she didn't think, about the state of her kitchen.

Well, crap.

But she smiled, anyway, even as she kept her gaze firmly fixed on the one cabinet finish that kept pulling her back, a not-quite white that would brighten up the small space considerably. "You tired of me dragging my feet?"

"No, ma'am. But I think you are." She shut her eyes against the gentleness, the truth, as his voice downshifted into a soft rumble. "I know you don't feel ready to tackle a kitchen remodel. But you also know this kitchen sucks, right?"

When she burped a little laugh, he moved beside her, picking up the curlicue pull and holding it up in front of the cabinet door. It was adorable and completely impractical and totally her. He was covered, after a fashion, in an army-issue T-shirt. "And you deserve a pretty kitchen. So I'm giving you a little goose in the right direction."

She knew he wouldn't touch her, that she was safe. From him, anyway. From her own thoughts, not so much. Until she'd met Tomas, she hadn't known what gentleness was. That teasing didn't have to hurt. Now she was beginning to see why this man and her husband had been such good friends, and for so long.

His gaze touched hers, eyebrows slightly lifted in question. Blushing, she looked away. "Some of this stuff looks expensive."

"Nope. Even if you chose the granite, or these pulls—" he waggled the curlicue "—you'd still be under budget. And there's another surprise—when I talked to Annie, she mentioned as how she and AJ were thinking of upgrading the restaurant's range. It's old, but she said it works just fine—"

"Are you kidding? It works perfectly. I've been doing most of my baking in it. And AJ keeps it immaculate—"

"So she said it's yours, if you want. It'd mean reworking the lower cabinets some, but I can do that—"

"Wait. They're giving me that range?"

"But only on the condition you get your butt in gear about the remodel." When Val blew out a sigh, Levi set down the pull, then slipped his hands in his pockets. "What's going through your head?"

"That there's way too many pushy people in my life?"

On a soft laugh, Levi dug into the bag for the stew, loosened the top and set it in the microwave. Sighing again, Val pulled a pair of bowls from the cupboard, wrestled open a battered drawer for a couple of spoons, a ladle. Then she remembered.

"Your mom came into the restaurant earlier."

"What? Why?"

"To buy a pie for your folks' anniversary dinner tonight."

"That's tonight? Damn, I guess it is." His forehead crunched. "My brothers and I should probably have done something for them, huh?"

The microwave dinged. Val carefully pulled out the container and set it on the old pine table taking up half the floor space, then grabbed two bottles of water from the fridge and a package of fresh tortillas.

"Sounded like she had things well in hand," Val said as Levi sat across from her and opened the container, releasing a spicy-scented burst of steam. He reached for her bowl, filling it before his. "Like, you know, they wanted to be alone?"

She almost laughed at the slight blush that bloomed in Levi's cheeks before the look he gave her stopped the laugh cold. "That near miss with Dad's heart scared the bejesus out of them both. So I imagine so. What kind of pie did she get?"

"Lemon meringue."

"Then at least if he goes, he'll go happy." A huge spoonful of the stew disappeared into his mouth before he said, "Your lemon meringue pie is the best I've ever had, no lie."

"You've also been eating army food for the past six years," Val said gently, adding, when his eyes shot to hers, "Tomas wouldn't talk about much, when he was home. But he bitched about the food constantly."

Levi stilled, then reached for a tortilla, which he slowly ripped into two before dunking a ragged edge in the stew. "Sometimes it wasn't so bad. When we weren't out in the field, anyway. Not particularly healthy, but if it stopped the hunger, we were good." He shoved the stew-soaked tortilla into his mouth. "Eating…it became all about filling your belly. Keeping yourself alive. Enjoyment ran a distant third."

"So I gathered."

Tension crackled between them for several seconds before Levi asked, not looking at her, "Did Tommy say much else? About his experiences, I mean."

She shook her head. "When he wasn't there, he *really* wasn't there. He didn't want to think about it, let alone talk about it."

"Yeah, that pretty much sums it up."

"But that's not really possible, is it? To not think about it?"

Another several seconds passed before Levi said, very softly, "I ran into Charley Maestas last night."

In other words, *Do not go there.*

So much for honesty.

Chapter Seven

Judging from how Val's eyes narrowed, Levi guessed his attempt at switching the subject hadn't gone over too well. But all she did was take a bite of her stew and say, "You did? Where?"

"In town. When I was out for a walk." He paused. "Does anyone actually look out for him?"

"I think we all do," she said, leaning back in her chair and fidgeting with her ponytail, which had slipped over her shoulder. One of her few nervous habits, Levi had noticed. Just like he'd noticed how she still wore that ratty old friendship bracelet Tommy'd given her way back when. "But we have to be sneaky about how we help him so we don't wound his pride. Like the way Annie and I pretend he's doing us a favor by eating the 'leftovers.'" Her mouth pulled flat for a moment before she sat up again, spooned in more stew. "The poor guy's already lost so much—his dignity is all he has left."

Something she could probably say about herself, Levi thought.

"I remember when he came back from Iraq that last time."

Val hesitated, then said, very softly, "And yet you enlisted, anyway."

Levi felt one side of his mouth kick up. "Weirdly, it was partly because of Charley that I did. I almost felt… I don't know. Like I wanted to pay homage to him. To finish what he started, maybe. Although there's no *finishing* any of it, is there? Not really. But what did I know back then?"

"And why else did you join?" When he frowned, she said, "You said *partly* because of Charley."

Levi paused, realizing that, once again, he didn't dare be entirely honest. "Because… I felt like I needed answers?" At her silence, he released a sigh. "I was doing okay, working with that cabinetmaker up in Questa, but… I can't explain it. Except that I felt incomplete."

"And did you find those answers?"

Too late, he realized she'd snagged his gaze in hers, the spoon in a death grip in her fingers. She was the one still looking for answers, about why her husband had voluntarily left her and their daughter to go fight a war she obviously believed wasn't his to fight. Answers he couldn't give her.

"Not really, no," he said. "Doesn't mean other people don't, though. Everybody has their own reason for enlisting. For serving. Take Charley," he said, gently steering the conversation back into more neutral territory. He hoped. "He didn't have to volunteer to deploy, especially at his age. But the Guard helped get a lot of our people home, you know."

"True. But—"

"And I'll bet Charley would say, if he was one of the drivers who helped get our soldiers safely out of there, his sacrifice was worth it. I knew Charley pretty well, remember. And I'm sure glory was the last thing on his mind. Getting the job done, however, probably wasn't."

Her gaze bored into his again. "Just like Tommy?"

"Just like Tommy," Levi said, as the stew bubbled in his gut. "Word was that he was damned good at what he did. Bomb disposal takes more than nerves of steel. It takes extraordinary skill—"

"Well aware of that, Levi."

He leaned closer to wrap his hand around hers, his heart aching at the pain in her eyes. "His work saved a helluva lot of lives, Val."

"Except his," she said, then puffed out a sigh. "I think about him every time I see Charley, you know. And I wonder, was any of it worth…that."

Another question he couldn't answer. If she'd even listen to him, anyway. Or anyone. So all he said was, "I know. Believe me."

Val looked at their linked hands. "Do you?" she said, then grimaced, her free hand fisting beside her bowl. "Of course you do, you were there, too… I'm sorry. I'm not always very rational these days."

"Understandable," Levi said, then let go. He bit off another chunk of tortilla. "So, I take it Charley lives alone? Or would you rather we not talk about him?"

"No, that's fine. And it's not like I can exactly escape the reminders, is it? Tommy's parents, the town…"

"Me," Levi said, and she pushed out a short laugh.

"Especially you. But the benefits of being home far outweigh, well, the other stuff. Family…it's something I never really had until Tommy came into my life. And I'd put out my right eye rather than take that away from the girls. I think it's the same for Charley. Yes, he lives alone. But he's not totally isolated. His neighbors ask him to help with little things, like keeping an eye out for the mail, stuff like that. So they can keep an eye on *him*."

"The memory thing, though." Levi shook his head. Like Val said, was it worth it? Lost limbs, memories, *lives*...

"I know. Breaks my heart. But apparently it hasn't gotten worse over the last few years. At least that." She sat back again, stretching out her arms on either side of her bowl, her fingers splaying as she frowned. Her wedding ring—a slim silver-and-turquoise band—was clearly too big, now. Levi wondered how she kept it on. "There might be services that would help, maybe in Santa Fe or Albuquerque. But since he couldn't possibly live there..." She shrugged, then folded her arms across her ribs, tucking her hands away. "Frankly, I think he's better off here, where at least he's with people who care. Where nobody will let him go homeless."

His chest aching, Levi thought about the women he'd dated, to use the term loosely. Before he joined the army he'd never really had a serious girlfriend. Because, for one thing, slim pickings. And for another... Well, that reason was sitting three feet away from him. And to be honest while he was in the service "dating" was more about occasional stress relief than working toward anything even remotely resembling forever. Not something he was particularly proud of, especially considering his parents' example. But at least he'd always been up front with any girl he took to bed, and if anyone ever had an issue with it, they never said anything. Not to him, anyway.

Except the life you choose when you're in your early twenties and not sure you're going to see your early thirties—and Levi had never been blind to the fact that going into a war zone could very well mean not coming *out*—wasn't necessarily the life you wanted when adulthood finally grabbed you by the throat and said, *You. Now.* Back then, he wasn't looking for compassion, or kindness, or anything much beyond looking and smelling good. But listening to Val now, hearing her voice shake as she talked about Charley, watching her eyes fill…

If only, he thought with a spurt of irritation that actually hurt.

"What about you?" he said, and puzzled eyes met his. "There's, you know, programs to help, um, surviving spouses?"

"Oh. Yeah. I was in one, for a while. Online." She shrugged. "I'm sure they're lifesavers for a lot of people, but some stuff I think a person has to work through alone, you know?"

Yeah. He did.

He got up from the table, holding out his hand for her bowl.

"You done?"

She nodded. "Thanks."

He carried their bowls over to the chewed-up ceramic sink, washed them out and set them into the drainer set over a towel on the counter.

"We are so getting you a dishwasher," he muttered, drying his hands on another towel, and she softly laughed.

"I never had one growing up. And the one in our apartment near the base kept going on the fritz. So no big deal?"

Something in her voice—a flatness, maybe—made him turn. Made him even madder, as though he couldn't figure out how to come up with a conversational topic that wouldn't upset her. Still seated, she was frowning slightly at her hands, folded in front of her on the table. A good, solid table Levi would love to get his hands on, bring it back to life.

Same as he'd like to do with her. With both him and her, frankly.

As if he had any idea how to do that.

"Val?"

She inhaled sharply, then gave him a bright smile. "Sorry. Slipped away for a moment. What were we talking about?"

"Dishwashers. As in, you're getting one whether you want it or not."

"Except…it wouldn't be for me, would it?" She got up as well, stretching her arms over her head before folding them across her stomach as she walked to the patio door. "I'm only borrowing the place, after all."

Like I've done with everything else.

The thought slugged Levi in the gut as hard as if she'd said the words out loud…that everything good in her life had been transient, a blip of happiness punctuating a long, long stretch of simply struggling not to go under. Not that he could hear a trace of self-pity in her voice, but he did hear resignation, that this was simply her lot in life. And on the heels of that thought came another—that, with the possible exception of his mother, Val was the strongest woman he'd ever met.

They heard the front door open, the pounding footsteps of an excited seven-year-old. A second later a grinning Josie burst into the kitchen with no less than three stuffed Walmart bags.

A second *before* Levi might've pulled Val into his arms. So, whew. Because for damn sure it wasn't *Levi's* arms Val wanted wrapped around her. Sure, he could build fences and replacing rotting porch floorboards and replace dying bushes…but he couldn't replace the only thing that mattered.

And he'd best remember that.

Honestly. There were enough pink and purple and turquoise duds piled on the kitchen table to outfit every second-grader in the state.

"You didn't have to do this, Connie," Val said, even

as, on the other side of the open patio door, she heard her oldest daughter jibber-jabbing away to Levi as he worked, as though unable to get her thoughts out of her head fast enough. "Really."

"Hey. I've been waiting a long time to buy little-girl clothes." On her lap, Risa let out a squeal, just because, then gave Val a slobbery grin. "So let an old woman live. Right, *reynita*?"

"Bah?" Risa said, pointing out the door. Her only "word" so far, but an amazingly versatile one.

"That's right, that's Uncle Levi," Connie said, her dark gaze sliding to Val. Full of meaning. Which was absurd since it wasn't as if her mother-in-law had caught them *doing* anything. "And somebody needs her diaper changed. Don't you, sweetie?"

Val stood, arms outstretched, but Connie shook her head, hefting herself—and the stinky, grinning baby—to her feet. "Nope, I've got this. You just sit here and admire the view."

"Really, Connie?"

Chuckling, her mother-in-law shuffled out of the room, and Val sighed. Because the woman was nothing if not perceptive. Meaning Val guessed she'd definitely picked up on something when she'd come in earlier.

A moment, Val was guessing.

A moment where she'd let down her guard, letting in verboten thoughts that kept creeping up on her no matter how often she told them to take a hike…a moment where she could feel Levi's mental pull like an actual physical thing. Or that could have been the loneliness talking. Hers, anyway. What was really going on inside his head, she had no idea. Partly because he clearly wasn't about to tell her, partly because she didn't want to know. Because *if* she knew, if he ever did open up to her…

The words *really, really bad* came to mind.

"There ya go, one much sweeter-smelling little girl," Connie said, returning to set Risa down on the not-exactly-pristine kitchen floor. Instantly the kid was on her hands and knees, flashing her frilled booty as she made fast tracks toward the only cupboard without a lock, where Val kept an assortment of things the kid could clang and bang to her heart's delight.

"So," Connie said, gathering her purse. "I assume you and the girls are going to the big doin's up at the ranch on the Fourth?"

"You're the second person to ask me that today." A half-dozen plastic containers tumbled onto the floor. Risa squealed and clapped her hands. "And the answer is I don't know."

"And you do not want the girls to be the only children in town who aren't there."

"So why don't you and Pete take them?"

"I think you know the answer to that."

Her eyes suddenly stinging, Val faced the open door, watching a giggling Josie with Levi, who was laughing, as well. Not from a strained politeness, the way a lot of adults might, but the kind of laugh guaranteed to get everybody around him laughing, too.

She remembered that laugh. Remembered, too, how often it led to shenanigans. Shenanigans that—in the early days, at least—had often involved Tommy. A laugh that still spelled trouble, but these days of an entirely different variety.

"And eight years ago, on the Fourth," Val said softly, "your son asked me to marry him, right before they started the fireworks."

"I remember."

Val sighed. "You know, I made a conscious decision to come back to Whispering Pines. It's where the girls belong, close to you and Pete. That doesn't mean I didn't have a lot of mixed feelings about it. Still do, even though I'm glad I'm here. The memories..."

Her mouth tight, she shook her head. "Mostly I can deal with them. But the ranch, on the Fourth." Her eyes burned.

On a soft moan, Connie wrapped her arm around Val's waist. "Which is exactly why you need to go. Not only for the girls' sake, but for yours—"

"I know, but—"

"Tommy's not coming back, honey," she said gently. "And no amount of wishing or praying or grieving's gonna change that... Oh, dear Lord," Connie said when Levi broke into some bizarre by-the-light-of-the-moon dance with the posthole digger, making Josie shriek with laughter and Connie chuckle. "That's exactly what he did with Tommy, you know."

"Levi danced for him?"

Her mother-in-law laughed again. "No. Brought him out of himself. Made Tommy more than he thought he could be." She paused. "And I'm thinking you need to let him dance for you, too."

"Connie, do not go there—"

"And where would that be? To maybe someplace where a young man might keep a young woman warm at night? From being lonely?"

"I can't believe you said that," Val said, pushing out a stingy little laugh. "And anyway, you do realize Levi's only here because of some dumb-ass promise he made to Tommy? Do I think he's changed? Maybe. But that doesn't mean..." She blew out a breath. "Jeez, Connie—it hasn't even been a year yet—"

"And opportunities don't always happen when we *think* we're ready, but when we *are* ready."

"That doesn't even make sense."

"Little about life does. And I'm giving notice—if you don't show up at the ranch? I will personally come and drag your skinny little ass there myself. Yeah, chew on that for a minute, missy."

Then her mother-in-law hustled her own not-so-skinny ass out of there, and Val blew out a long, long breath. Because Val wouldn't put it past Connie to make good on her threat.

All in the name of love, of course.

"Josie? Come on in, honey, before you talk the poor man's ear off!"

Levi glanced up as Josie let out a groaned "Aww..." before slogging off to obey her mama's call. And something to the set of Val's mouth, her posture, set off all kinds of alarms. His work done, anyway, Levi returned the digger to the shed, the dog keeping tabs to make sure he did it properly. Then, mopping off sweat with an old towel, he trekked back to the porch, where Val held Risa on her hip, her gaze fixed on him the way a woman does when she's trying to figure you out. Figure something out, anyway.

She gave the girl a quick one-armed hug, then said, "Take all those clothes Grandma bought to your room. We'll sort 'em out together after dinner."

"Did she show you what I wanna wear to the fireworks show?"

Levi saw Val's gaze shoot to the girl's. "No. But later, okay? Now git—go do what I said."

"She wasn't bothering me, Val," Levi said quietly after Josie huffed into the house. "Really." Frankly, he was getting pretty tired of repeating himself. In fact, the more he was around the kid, the more he *liked* being around her. Josie was the funniest thing going—although no surprise there, considering her dad's vehicle of choice. So he wished Val would get over whatever her issues were with him and her daughter, and simply let things be whatever they were going to be.

And he could only imagine the hell there'd be to pay if he actually said that out loud.

Val's mouth pulled flat. "And I said—"

"I know what you said. Although something tells me if she was thinking of terms of me being more than *Uncle* Levi, I'd know it. Josie doesn't strike me as somebody who plays her cards close to her chest."

At that, the tightness seemed to ease a little. "This is true—"

"Bah?" the baby said, pointing at Levi with a slimy finger.

Levi smiled. "Uncle Levi," he said, pressing a hand to his chest.

"Bah!" Risa squealed, clapping her hands and wriggling her nose, before hurtling herself out of Val's arms and toward Levi.

"Whoa, kiddo!" Levi said, laughing, catching the kid before she landed on her noggin.

His heart skipped a beat when she immediately settled against his damp chest with a satisfied, "Bah."

"Oh, jeez… I'm way too smelly to be holding a baby."

"That's okay. Give her time, and she'll smell a lot worse than you ever could."

Levi's gaze flicked to Val's. And, yep, two telltale red splotches gave her away. Calling her on it, though, would be highly ungentlemanly. He grinned for the slobbery baby, then bounced her until she belly laughed, making Levi laugh almost as hard.

"So…" Grinning, he turned to Val. "You all going out to the ranch for the Fourth?"

At that, the splotches practically glowed. Wasn't until he caught the pain, however, sharp as broken glass in those bright blue eyes, that he realized how deeply he'd put his foot in it. Because too late he remembered Tomas practically knocking down his door that Fourth of July all those years ago, his own eyes bright, his smile about to split his face in two.

"She said yes, bro! Holy hell, we're gonna get married!"

"Damn, Val… I'm sorry—"

"Why?" She reached for the baby, tucking Risa's soft curls under her chin. The way she mothered her girls… Man, that tugged at something deep inside Levi he didn't know could be tugged. Making him want things he'd had no idea he'd wanted. "Since clearly nobody else gives a rat's ass how I might feel about it."

Levi plowed his hands into his fatigues' pockets. "Well, I do. No, I forgot for a moment, and I really am sorry about that. But you know what? You don't want to go, just tell everybody else to back off. Whether you do or not, or why, is nobody's business but yours."

"But the girls…"

"Their grandparents can take 'em. Or mine. Or me, for that matter, if you trust me that far. But don't you dare let anybody push you around. Because believe me—I know how that goes."

It took a second for Levi's words to register. And more than the words, what was behind them. Because, once again, he was giving her permission to do what she felt was best for her. Instead of *telling* her what was best for her.

Pointing out, actually, that she didn't need anyone's permission to do—or not do—anything.

"Thank you," she said.

He looked surprised. "What for?"

"For backing me up."

"You mean, like friends are supposed to?"

She almost smiled. "Yeah."

He glanced away, squinting in the late-day sunlight clinging to the mountaintops, cloaking the yard—and the man in front of her—in a peachy gold, bronzing his damp skin, his curls. The T-shirt hugging his broad chest and shoulders. She hadn't realized how late it'd gotten.

Levi looked back, his eyes landing on the babbling baby slapping Val's chest. He smiled, then dug his keys out of his pocket.

"I'll be back tomorrow to set those posts. Josh said he'd come over to help string the fence, since he's got more experience than me. But as far as the kitchen goes…" His chest expanded with the force of his breath. "It occurs to me I was probably one of those people pushing you to make decisions before you were ready. If so, I apologize. God knows I never liked being pushed, so for me to do the same thing to you…" He shook his head. "So no rush. It's not like I'm going anywhere."

Then, with a nod, he walked around front to his truck, singing softly to himself. Wasn't until after she heard the roar of the truck's engine as he pulled away that his last words sank in, that he wasn't going anywhere. Words she should have found as reassuring as what he'd said about not letting other people push her around.

Instead, she felt as if the rug had been yanked out from underneath her all over again. Because the idea of him sticking around…

Bah.

Chapter Eight

"Mama!"

Val looked at her daughter, hands on hips as she stood in the master bedroom's doorway, shaking her head.

"What?"

Hands went out, all dramatic-like. "That's what you wear, like, every *day*. This is a *party*! You need to look *pretty*!"

Gee, thanks, kid, Val thought, as Risa—wobbling on her brand-new sparkly pink sneakers, fistfuls of hobnail bedspread clutched in her vice-like grip—screeched at the kitten trying to take a nap in the center of the bed. Val glanced at the baby, then the mildly pissed cat—whom Josie had finally named Skunk, of all things—before frowning at herself in the banged-up cheval mirror that'd seen who knew how many reflections over the years. Personally, she didn't see what was wrong with the outfit—jeans, a tank top, a cropped denim jacket for when it cooled off, later on. Dangly earrings. Because, hey. Like Josie said—*party.*

And the only pair of cowboy boots she owned, harking back from before she was married—the first thing she'd purchased with her own money. Deep red leather with, appropriately enough for the occasion, two blue and ivory stripes along the sides and matching stars across the instep.

Because, yes, she was going to the damn fireworks display out on the damn ranch. Not because anybody, or everybody, had bullied her into it, but because, dammit, the weenie wuss routine was not gonna cut it. Although she hadn't counted on being given a fashion critique by a seven-year-old. Who, Val had to admit, looked totes adorbs in a frilly little flowered dress and embroidered denim jacket and her own cowboy boots. New ones—because her feet *would* keep growing—that Connie had bought for her.

The cat yawned. The baby laughed. Val sighed. "And what would you suggest I wear?"

"A *dress*. Duh."

Now the dog wandered in, giving first Val, then Risa, a sniff before curling up into a ball under the window and immediately passing out.

"You do realize most of the women will be in jeans, right?"

"All I'm saying is that you can do better." And with that, her daughter marched to the piddly closet, rifled through Val's even more piddly wardrobe and pulled out the only dress she owned. From the *very* back of the closet. A dress she'd never worn. Never had the chance.

She knew she should've gotten rid of the damn thing.

"And you, young lady, were snooping."

Kid didn't even have the courtesy to look guilty. "You never said I couldn't," she said matter-of-factly, flipping the dress around like a saleswoman determined to score. The skirt softly flared, beckoning. "This is *so* pretty."

Yes, it was. A rare indulgence, ordered online on a whim. Although at least it had been half-off, so not a terrible indulgence. And Val remembered, when she unwrapped it, her moan at how soft the fabric was. How, after she slipped it on, she'd felt as if she were lying in a field of wildflowers, blues and purples, reds and deep pinks and white… How feminine the deep V neckline and cinched waist and floaty skirt had made her feel.

How she'd imagined the look on Tommy's face when he saw her in it.

Val held her breath, waiting for the ache. The sting of tears. Something.

But…nothing. Not right now, anyway.

"Please try it on, Mama?"

Yeah, back in the Land of the Pushy People, all righty. But how could she say no to her snoopy little girl, who'd plopped down on the old stuffed chair in the corner of the room with her chunky little sister on her lap, calmly explaining to the baby that kitties didn't much like being screeched at. So Val toed off the boots and wriggled out of her jeans, her hair going all staticky when she tugged off the top—Josie giggled—then slipped on the dress. It floated over her body, weightlessly settling around her bony hips and ribs. *Like a lover's sigh,* she thought, her cheeks warming.

"Ohmigosh! You're so *beautiful*! Like a princess!"

The spell broken, Val laughed. "Not hardly," she said, running a comb through her hair before tugging the boots back on.

"You're gonna wear boots? With that dress?"

"Why not?" Val pointed to her daughter's feet. "You are."

"But I'm a kid."

You were never a kid, Val thought, then said, "Well, too bad. Because tonight I'm wearing cowboy boots with my dress. And this," she added, slipping the jacket back on and admiring her shabby chic country self in the mirror. It'd been a long time since she'd worn her hair loose, too. She hadn't even realized how long it'd gotten, nearly to her waist in places. If she had a grain of sense she'd either put it up or at least braid it, but…no. Go big or go home and all that.

Grunting, Josie stood and came up beside her, the baby straddling her hip. Kid was a lot stronger than she looked. Like Val was herself, she thought before pulling them both close. One blonde, two brunettes, three rockin' chicks. "Do the Lopez girls rule, or what?"

Josie grinned, giving Val a glimpse of what she was going to look like in a few years. Also, heart palpitations. "Everybody there is so going to be looking at you!"

Yeah. *Just* what she wanted.

In the mirror, she saw Josie frown. "What are you doing?"

"It's a little chilly, don't you think?" she said, fastening most of the jacket's silver buttons, and her daughter released a you-are-hopeless sigh.

His cowboy hat angled against the sinking sun and a longneck dangling from his fingers, Levi propped the heel of one boot up against the massive gnarled trunk of a geriatric cottonwood, watching. Waiting. The air was already beginning to cool in the near-constant breeze rustling the bright green leaves, sending puffs of "cotton" floating across the front yard. More dirt than grass, pretty much like he remembered, but what grass there was was lush in the deep late-day shade.

From a half-dozen grills brought in for the occasion—and overseen by an equal number of people Levi didn't know—barbecue smoke tangoed with the cottony wisps, the scent reminding him of when he'd cooked up those steaks for Val and him a while back. The sun wouldn't set for a while, taking the wind with it. But once it did, it'd be a perfect night for fireworks. For other things, too, if one were inclined to let one's mind drift, like the smoke, in that direction.

Not that he was.

Never mind that, from the moment he'd heard Val and the kids were coming, he hadn't taken his eyes off the patch of pasture nearest the house, now chock-full of pickups and SUVs. None of 'em hers.

All around him folks milled about, yakking and laughing. Whispering Pines didn't seem so tiny once you got half the population jockeying for positions at the twenty-five-foot-long food table. And no wonder, considering the endless variety of dishes and casseroles on display, from pulled pork to steaming enchiladas, fried chicken and huge vats of spicy pinto beans, salads and rolls and every kind of dessert you could imagine.

And if the culinary delights weren't enough, the hacienda's massive flagstone porch took almost obscene advantage of the incredible view of the Sangre de Cristos, canopied by an endless sky with what people told him was a blazing tangle of purples and oranges and turquoises.

He took a swig of the beer, thinking how weird it was that this had been home for the first eighteen years of his life. How badly he'd wanted to escape. But whatever issues Levi might've had with wanting a different life from his father's, he doubted there was a more beautiful spot on earth. He smiled again, remembering that dinky two-bedroom house in town he and Tomas moved into after graduation, living the mighty fine bachelor life as only a pair of clueless nineteen-year-olds could.

Until Tomas and Val got married, anyway.

Good old Gus wandered over to stand under the tree with Levi, crossing his short arms high over his beach ball belly. Somebody's dog flounced over, carrying a stick in its mouth. Levi obliged.

"Seems like more people come every year, don' it?" the housekeeper said, his heavy northern New Mexican Spanish accent losing more end consonants as time went on. "Good thing I wen' back and bought more hamburger buns. Not to mention hamburgers."

At one time, the ranch had been all about steaks on the hoof. These days, however, it was a much leaner—and smaller—operation, the property's resources now devoted to breeding and training champion quarter horses. Even so, for a hundred years, maybe more, town and ranch had been inextricably connected, because Granville Blake—and his predecessors—had seen to it that they were.

Still focused on the makeshift parking lot, Levi smiled. "I remember when you and my mother did most of the cooking yourselves."

Gus snorted. "Those days, I don' miss. It was your mother, though, who put the bee in Mr. Gran's bonnet about turning it into a potluck. Except for the grilling, of course. They getting on okay?" he said, nodding at Levi's parents, chatting with Zach as he tried to keep tabs on two hyperexcited little boys. He hadn't seen his brothers much since that dinner—because even in small towns, folks got busy. But they talked. Texted. It was good.

"They are," Levi said, finally answering Gus's question. "I heard Dad's even riding again?"

"Yep, was out last week, in fact…"

But Levi barely heard Gus's comment, his gaze fixed on a certain old Toyota RAV4 that'd just pulled into the field. And behind that, the same Explorer Tomas learned to drive in more than fifteen years ago. A minute later, everyone disembarked from both vehicles, including Tommy's grandmother, her black dress shapeless as a garbage bag and nearly as shiny. Smiling, Pete Lopez tucked the old woman's hand in the crook of his arm before starting toward the house. Connie strapped Risa into a stroller, only to then fuss nonstop as the damn thing bumped and lurched over the uneven pasture.

But it was Val—hauling a half-dozen pie boxes as Josie bounced around, beside, in front of her, constantly yammering—who stole Levi's breath. The breeze snatched at her loose hair, filmy gold in the slanted sun, then at the hem of her dress, at total odds with the beat-up boots, her worn denim jacket. Then she looked up, her gaze catching in Levi's, and…

Damn.

Beside him, he heard Gus's low chuckle. "Gal looks like she could use some help," he said, walking away.

She wasn't the only one, Levi thought as he started toward the family, annoyed he couldn't reach her fast enough, half wanting to turn tail and get the hell out of there. Yes, even after all that waiting—

"Levi!" Her outfit similar to her mother's, Josie ran over, skinny arms and legs going in a dozen different directions. The arms stopped windmilling long enough to wrap around Levi's waist, allowing him a whiff of baby shampoo when her head briefly pressed into his stomach. Then she leaned back, grinning, and he thought no fireworks on earth could possibly rival the glittering in those dark eyes. Not to mention the explosions going on inside his head, at how this kid simply liked him for him. No judgment, no expectations.

She grinned, showing off the ridged beginnings of big-girl front teeth. "This is gonna be so much fun, huh?"

"That's the plan," he said, and she giggled. And for a moment, Tomas was right here, all that unbridled joy expressed in this elf-child with the sparkling eyes. His heart turning over in his chest, Levi hauled her into his arms, where she threw hers around his neck and kissed his cheek.

Hell. Yep, he was head over heels in love. And damned if those protective feelings didn't kick in, hard.

"See that man over there in the blue shirt?" he whispered into her curls. "With the bolo tie?"

"Uh-huh."

"That's Gus. He knew your daddy really well. Why don't you go on over, and he'll hook you up with the best food on the table."

Josie looked back at Val, who nodded.

"Okay," she said, sliding down Levi's leg as he lowered her to the ground before she took off. By now the others had caught up, Tomas's grandmother snagging his wrist in cool, trembling fingers before pulling him aside. A thousand wrinkles shifted when she smiled, although he caught the censure, too, in those dark eyes.

"You've been a bad boy," Angelita said in Spanish, her soft white curls like the old-fashioned spun-glass angel hair she'd put on her Christmas tree when Tommy and him were kids. "Not coming to see me." Then she wagged one of those skinny fingers at him, saying in English, "I should strip you of your honorary grandson status."

"And you'd have every right. I'm sorry—"

Lita winked. "And I'm sure you have better things to do than spend time with an old woman, no?" Her gaze slid to Val, crouched in front of the stroller as she tried to calm a fussy Risa, before coming to rest back on Levi. "I miss my Tomas so much," she said with a long sigh, and Levi gently tugged her to his side, like she used to do with him when he was a kid. Of course, she used to swat him, too, when he'd been naughty. Because sometimes love hurts, she used to say.

Wasn't that the truth?

"We all do," he said.

She sighed again, then motioned for him to lean down so she could kiss his cheek, only to make a face.

"You need to shave," she said, then toddled off to rejoin

the family…and Levi finally met Val's questioning gaze. And, oh, yeah, reached for the pies.

"Let me get those for you—"

"No, I'm good—"

"For godssake, Val," Connie said, grunting as she shoved the stroller over another bump on the ground. "Let the man help you!"

Levi grinned. Casually. Like his heart wasn't about to hammer right out of his chest, for reasons only partly influenced by how hot Val looked in that crazy getup. "You heard the woman. Hand 'em over."

With an eye-roll worthy of her daughter, Val complied. Only to then cross her arms as if she had no idea what to do with her hands. "Just so you know," she said so only he could hear, "I'm not here because anybody bullied me into it."

"Didn't think you were." He paused, partly to gather his thoughts, partly to get a stronger bead on her scent, something musky and flowery that had rattled those thoughts to begin with. "But I'm glad you are." He glanced down at her, walking beside him, her arms all tight against her ribs and a frown dug into her forehead, and he wished like hell he could make it better. "For Josie's sake, if nothing else. But for yours, too."

She didn't say anything for a second. Then, looking straight ahead, she said, "Why for me?"

"Same reason I'm here, I suppose. To nudge us both back to feeling normal again."

Another pause. "Thought you said that wasn't even possible."

"I think we owe it to Tommy to at least try, right?" They'd reached the veranda by now, where Levi shifted things around on the table's dessert end to make room for the pies. Trying not to read too much into her silence, he opened the first box, nearly falling over from the heady scent. "What are these?"

"Fruit, mostly," she said after a moment. "Since I knew they'd keep until dinner was over."

She let him finish setting the pies out on the table. Apple. Blueberry. Cherry. Peach, he thought. More than one person stopped to admire them, make Val promise to save them a slice. Smiling, she said she'd do her best, her voice as warm and friendly as usual but definitely subdued. Not that Levi blamed her. As hard as this was for him, it had to be a hundred times worse for her.

"Thanks," she said when the crowd thinned.

"No problem," Levi said, shoving the empty boxes underneath the table.

"No, I mean…"

Val huffed a breath, making him look at her. She'd unfolded her arms, only to stick her hands in her jacket pockets. Between the getup and the way the light played over her sharp features, she looked eighteen again. No, younger. Before Tommy, when she used to pile on defiance like some girls layered on makeup. And he realized it had been that defiance that had first snagged him all those years ago. Made him want to do something, anything, to mitigate whatever had put it there.

Still did.

She glanced out at all the people shuffling around in the yard, then back at him. "I mean, thanks for being okay with talking about Tommy."

"Why wouldn't I be?"

One side of her mouth lifted. Levi told himself the way her hair was floating around her shoulders wasn't distracting as hell. "Because everybody else… I don't know. I can't decide if they're afraid they'll lose it or I will."

As far as chinks went, it was pretty slim. But he'd take it.

"His folks…?"

"The one exception," she said, averting her gaze again to skim her fingers on the edge of the table. "Even so, I can tell there's times when we're holding back. On both sides. You know what I was saying, about being honest?" A breath left her lungs. "I think the world of Tommy's parents. And I know I wouldn't've gotten through this without them. But…"

"But they're not exactly objective."

Another tiny smile pushed at her mouth. "How can I say everything I'm really thinking without causing them more pain?"

Levi glanced across the yard, where the Lopezes had staked out a claim underneath that old cottonwood, Connie spreading a blanket on the ground for them and the kids, Pete setting up a lawn chair for Tomas's grandma. The old lady leaned forward, smiling at Risa in her stroller, right as Connie looked over and caught Levi's gaze in hers. And he could see in her expression exactly what they were all thinking—that Tomas wasn't here. More to the point, that he *should* be. A lump rose in Levi's throat.

"And you think they don't know what's going on in your head? Whether you say it out loud or not? Tommy will always be part of our lives, Val," he said softly, nodding at Connie, who smiled back before returning her attention to her husband. Levi faced Val again. "So anytime you want to talk about him—or anything else, actually—I'm more than happy to listen."

At least that got a laugh out of her. "You better be careful or they'll revoke your membership in the Dude's Club."

He shrugged. "After listening to my army buddies bitch for hours on end, I'll take my chances. Now. How's about we get some grub before the locusts eat it all up—"

"The same goes, you know." Levi frowned down at her. The corners of her mouth lifted. Barely. "If you need an ear, I mean…" Her gaze darted away as she sucked in a breath. "Crap. What's he doing here?"

"Who?"

"Charley." She nodded toward the old vet making his way toward the table. "Annie said he came a couple of years ago, got totally freaked out by the fireworks. So she's been taking the cookout to him, afterward. How on earth did he even get here?"

Levi glanced down the table, where a grinning Charley was spooning baked beans onto his plate. His showing up wasn't even a question—the dude had his ways. But his guess was that the old soldier didn't remember about the fireworks. Or the effect they had on him. A lot of guys with PTSD didn't, until something happened to trigger the flashbacks. Levi had been one of the "lucky" ones, as far as that went—although he'd been close enough to a few explosions to scare the crap out of him when they'd happened, there hadn't been any real lasting effects. None that he could tell, anyway. Yeah, he had his issues, but fear of loud noises wasn't one of them.

"Maybe he's not planning on staying."

"Maybe. But…"

The concern in her voice twisted something inside him. "You're quite the mama hen, aren't you?" he said, and a short laugh bubbled from her chest, followed by a sigh.

"Everybody needs to know somebody cares about 'em," she said, still watching Charley. Then her eyes lifted to Levi's. "Don't you think?"

"Absolutely," he said quietly, then gave her shoulder a quick squeeze. "Go on back to your family. I'll keep an eye on him."

"You sure?"

At the incredulousness in her voice, his gaze sank to its knees in hers, smack-dab into a mixture of strength and pain and soul-deep kindness that shook him to his core. He smiled. “It’s no big deal, Val—”

“Not to you, maybe. To him, though…”

“Hey,” he said. “That man saved my butt, back when more than a few people wondered if it could be saved. The least I can do now is return the favor. And speaking of saving…” He pointed to the cherry pie. “That one.” Then he started toward his old boss, thinking this was definitely not how he’d seen the evening panning out. But that slightly confused, if grateful, look on Val’s face was definitely worth a slight change of plans.

And even that was more than he deserved.

It was something like Tommy would’ve done, Val mused some time later, the way Levi had given up part of himself to make sure somebody else was safe, taken care of.

Of course, between the crowd and needing to stick close to her chicks, she’d lost track of Levi and Charley shortly after that. But she’d occasionally catch glimpses of that beat-up old cowboy hat—yes, she could tell Levi’s beat-up old cowboy hat apart from all the others, she had special powers like that—and since there hadn’t been any set-tos that she was aware of, she assumed all had been well.

For Charley, anyway. Because as great as the food had been, and as hard as she’d smiled watching the girls’ eyes and mouths go wide at the fireworks display, the more fun everyone else had, the wider the hole in her heart seemed to get.

A hole that, even if only for a moment, a tall man in a beat-up old cowboy hat had filled, like when he’d swung her daughter up into his arms, or volunteered to watch over a fellow vet who only half remembered who Levi—or anyone else—was.

A hole she had no business even thinking about letting anyone else fill. Because she'd learned her lesson about that, hadn't she—?

"You okay, *querida*?"

At her father-in-law's gentle voice, Val smiled. He'd temporarily commandeered Lita's lawn chair while Connie escorted the old woman to one of the nearby porta-potties. Now, on her knees as she gathered up everyone's paper plates and cups from dinner, Val smiled up at him. She imagined this is what Tommy would have looked like at fifty, handsome and silver haired, a little stockier than he should be. But with a smile that would have still melted her heart. Even though she understood her resistance, looking back it seemed silly how long it'd taken for her to accept Pedro Lopez as a real father figure in her life. As if this lovely man could hurt a fly. And she couldn't ask for a better grandfather to her girls.

"I'm fine," she said, looking up at the blue-black sky, pinpricked with a million stars softly glimmering through leftover tendrils of fireworks smoke. "I'm glad we came."

And she was, the hole in her heart notwithstanding. Because she'd faced down more than a few demons tonight, hadn't she? Okay, maybe she hadn't exactly vanquished them, but at least she wasn't off sucking her thumb in a corner, either. So she'd take that as a win.

"Good," Pete said, getting to his feet and hitching his belt underneath his belly, and Val smiled, knowing that was the end to the conversation.

If not the end to her swirling thoughts.

Way on the other side of the house, from the massive old barn that'd been original to the place a hundred years ago, came the screech of an amplifier system cranking up, a twang or two of an electric guitar. Because for some people the party wasn't anywhere near over. For *some* people, there was still dancing to be done, boot-scootin' and two-steppin', and hot-stuff cowboys kissing pretty girls—

"Everybody ready to go?" she said, standing so abruptly she stumbled. That'd been the plan, after all, getting the kids home and to bed after the fireworks. As it was Risa had conked out a half hour ago, and poor Josie, usually sawing logs by nine, was lurching around like a zombie.

"Oh, we're taking the girls back to our place," Connie said. "So you can stay and hang out with the other young people."

"And why would I do that?" Val said, thinking, *Other young people?* True, she had a ways to go before she collected Social Security, but compared with the *real* "young people" making tracks toward the barn, she felt like a long-buried pueblo artifact, brittle and dusty and faded.

"Because," Connie said, giving her a nudge as she folded up the blanket they'd been sitting on, "looks to me like somebody's come back for you."

"What?"

Val followed Connie's gaze. And sure enough, there was Levi, striding toward them, hatless and determined and grinning like a fool.

Of course, nothing said Levi's intentions—whatever those might be—even remotely lined up with Connie's active imagination. Or that Val couldn't plead exhaustion and worm her way out of whatever that look in his eyes—yeah, he was close enough now to see a definite glint to go along with the grin—meant. Because, really, hadn't she done enough demon banishing for one night?

Another electrified twang sliced through the cool, still, gunpowder-scented night, and Levi stopped a few feet away, his hands in his pockets, that stupid grin on his face, and Connie giggled.

And clear as day, she heard a voice in her head say,

Be honest—you wanna leave because you're tired? Or because you're scared?

You know, those damn demons could shut the hell up anytime now. Jeebus.

Chapter Nine

Levi still wasn't entirely sure what had prompted him to return after taking Charley home. What he'd expected to happen. For all he'd known the Lopezes would've been long gone, especially with two little girls and an old woman in tow.

He took the fact that they'd been still there as a sign. Of what, he wasn't sure. His own idiocy, most likely.

Because it wasn't like this was ever gonna go anywhere. Then again, he thought as the stomping and electrified music from the barn sucked Val and him in like moths to a flame, maybe that's what made it easier—knowing there were no expectations. Except, he hoped, seeing more of those smiles. Hearing that laugh. Easing something inside the woman walking beside him, her hands jammed in her jacket pockets, he'd never be able to fully ease inside himself. Of course, could be she was simply pissed that her in-laws had swooped off with her children like a pair of benevolent hawks, not even giving her a chance to protest.

"You mad?" he said, figuring he might as well get it out in the open instead of letting it fester for the rest of the evening.

Predictably enough, she sighed. "Not real fond of being ambushed."

"That what you think I'm doing?"

"I have no idea what you're doing. Connie and Pete, though…that's something else."

"You can leave anytime you like, you know."

"Heh. And did you notice Connie took my car? Because, she said, she didn't want to have to move the car seats." Her mouth screwed up. "Kind of a long walk back to town. So, yeah, I'm mad. But not at you."

"You sure about that?"

A beat or two passed before she shrugged. "All I want, all I've ever wanted, is to make my own choices. Within reason, I mean. Sure, there's times when your *only* choice is to deal with the crap life tosses at you, but you should at least have the opportunity to make your own decisions about how you deal with that crap, you know? I mean, jeez—I went from nobody giving a damn about me to people caring too much. A little balance would be nice."

Levi chuckled. "No such thing in a small town."

She sighed again, then shouted over the music, the general mayhem as they got closer to the barn. "I suppose you're right." Then she glanced over. "So what happened with Charley? He okay?"

Now who's caring too much? he wanted to say. But he wasn't that stupid. Somebody'd gotten a bonfire going, out in the dirt. The light flickered in her eyes, across her face. Val wasn't all soft and pretty in a conventional sense, but she had one of those faces you couldn't take your eyes off. He couldn't, anyway. And he was surprised to realize that if her hand had been where he could reach it, he would've taken it. Which was probably why it wasn't.

Nodding, Levi pushed his denim jacket aside to shove his own hands in his pockets. "Oh, yeah. He knew about the fireworks, but I couldn't talk him out of staying. So I steered us far enough away that I hoped it wouldn't be a problem. And he was good." He shrugged. "Maybe because he knew they were coming, so it wasn't a surprise... Where you going?"

Val'd hung a right toward the bonfire. Which felt pretty nice, actually, as the temperature dropped. She stood with her feet apart, hands stuffed in pockets. When he came up beside her, she said, "So it's not a problem for you?"

The genuine concern in her voice rippled through him. "Not like it is for some people," he said softly, focused on the writhing flames.

He felt her gaze on the side of his face, her unasked questions piercing his skull. Finally he lowered his eyes to hers, figuring he may as well answer one or two of them. "I'm okay, Val. Mostly, anyway. But when I was asked if I wanted to re-up, I had no trouble saying no."

She frowned again into the fire. "And that's all you're going to say, I take it."

"For now."

After a moment, she nodded, then sucked in a breath. "So. I guess we should do this," she said, backing away and heading toward the barn. Levi followed, grinning in spite of himself at the Western version of Cinderella's ball inside. God knew New Mexico wasn't entirely tumbleweeds and cowboy boots—in fact, most of it wasn't—but Whispering Pines had always taken great pride in its unapologetic Western vibes. And nowhere more than the Vista's Fourth of July bash.

The grin morphed into a chuckle. What the town lacked in size—or, let's face it, culture—was more than made up for in blatant over-the-topness. If nothing else, people around here knew how to have fun. Or at least how to make the most out of whatever fun there was to be had. Not that Levi could dance worth spit, but then, most of the people out there strutting their stuff couldn't, either.

At last, he had a reason to offer Val his hand. "Wanna dance?" he shouted, his smile dying at her expression when he glanced over—sadness, anger, determination, all balled up into something that broke his heart. He pushed his hand back into his pocket.

"Hey. You don't want to do this, I'm happy to take you home—"

"What I want," she said, chin jutting, "is a beer. Maybe two. *Then* I'll dance."

Okay, this wasn't good. Small as Val was, she probably had the tolerance of a gnat. Levi also guessed, judging from the weird light in her eyes—although that might've been from the lanterns strung up all over the barn—it'd been a while since she'd had to find out. "You sure?"

"About the dancing?"

"No. The drinking."

She huffed a sigh. "Oh, Lord…not you, too?"

"Me, too, what?"

"Telling me what I can or cannot do." That fierce little gaze zinged to his. "Not driving, no kids to take care of… If I want a beer, I can damn well have a beer."

"Yes, you can. Except you don't drink, do you?" When she glared at him again, he said, "Just pointing out the obvious."

Val looked back inside, at all those people having a grand old time, and Levi saw everything she was thinking right on her face. So it was no surprise when she said, "This is something I need to do. But no way am I gonna get through it without a little help. So come on."

She reached over to yank his hand out of his pocket and pulled him onto the makeshift dance floor, with a pit stop at one of the metal washtubs filled with ice and Coors. And behind the washtub, a stony-faced responsible adult, there to ensure that (1) no one under legit drinking age partook of the offerings, and (2) that no one *of* legit drinking age partook of more than they could handle. Or—

"He's driving," Val said, jerking a thumb in his direction before grabbing one of the beers.

—they were with a designated driver. Although one of the sheriff's deputies was probably out in the makeshift parking lot, anyway, making sure nobody got behind the wheel who shouldn't.

So he let her have her beer…and then another one, figuring this was one of those times when it's best to let the woman do things her own way, clean up the mess later. Yes, even if those messes were actual messes. After dealing with it plenty in the army, a little gal puke was hardly gonna put him off. Sure, maybe she thought she was relying on some liquid in an amber bottle to get her through this, but he was the one she was with. And not, say, one of any number of obviously willing candidates he'd been shooting death glares at for the past half hour. So, yeah.

Over the next little while, Levi discovered two things: That Valerie Lopez did indeed get drunk faster than a frat dude in a drinking game, and that she was the cutest drunk he'd ever seen. And God knew he'd seen his fair share of drunk women. Not all that much fun, truth be told. The slurring and hanging all over him and whatnot. But Val was not a slurrer. Or a hanger-on-er. Her eyes did sparkle more, though. And she actually giggled from time to time—

"Oooh" came out on a whooshed, hops-scented breath when the band started up with a line dance. They'd been sitting on a hay bale—well, she'd been sitting, perched atop the thing like a little kid, her short legs dangling—and now she clumsily clunked to the wooden floor and grabbed Levi's hand, this time tugging him into the crowd with a smile that arrowed right to his heart. Even if it wasn't for him.

Of course, the minute Levi got out on the floor he remembered that his feet had minds of their own. Tommy had been good at this stuff, he remembered. Not him. He could fake a two-step well enough, but this actually required some coordination. But damned if he didn't get caught up in the music and laughter, in watching Val's face glow in a way he hadn't seen in…well. A very long time. Yeah, she was drunk off her cute little ass, and she was probably going to wake up with one whopper of a headache. But right now, she was having a helluva good time. And who was he to begrudge her that?

Then, like somebody'd pulled a plug, the music slowed, and she was in his arms, all soft and sweet smelling and not exactly steady on her pins. Which, after they'd been swaying for a couple of minutes, her forehead pressed into his sternum, she even admitted, with a cute little hiccup.

"I might be a little…" She burped. "Dizzy."

Levi peered down at her, his breath teasing her hair, her scent teasing his…everything. "You gonna be sick?"

Still glued to his chest, she shook her head. Carefully. "Uh-uh. Long as I don't look up, anyway." She hiccupped again.

Chuckling, he slipped a hand to her waist and steered her toward the door. "Let's get you some fresh air, wild woman."

"'Kay."

They'd no sooner gotten outside when they ran into Gus, who clucked at Val like an old hen. "Somebody looks like she needs to go home—"

"No!" She gave her head a sharp shake, only to grab it like it might fly off her neck before peering back at the barn. "Not yet," she said softly, tears cresting in her eyes.

"I'll be good, I promise. Just don't make me go home yet. Please."

Gus snorted. "Go on up to the house, the back door's open. Coffee's in the cupboard to the right of the sink, right over the maker."

However, by the time they made the short trek to the house, the chilly night air had apparently cleared her head. At least enough that she appeared sober, although Levi seriously doubted she would've passed a Breathalyzer test.

"Gotta pee," she said the second they got inside, and he directed her to the hall bath right off the kitchen. Which, as he walked in, looked nearly the same as Levi remembered—dark wood cabinets, terra-cotta floors, brilliantly colored Mexican tile backsplash and counters. Off-white appliances, except for the dark blue six-burner stove. A hodge-podge of traditional New Mexican and 1990s cutting edge.

Behind him, Val's boot heels softly clopped against the tiled floor.

"Ooh…pretty."

He turned. "This your first time in the house?"

"Tommy never came without you, remember?"

And by an unspoken understanding, the three of them had never been together. Not here, anyway.

While Levi went about putting on a pot of coffee, Val leaned over the counter to inspect the tiles, hands fisted in her pockets. Then she straightened, looking around. "Actually, this is how I always pictured my own kitchen."

"Outdated by thirty years?"

She laughed. "Homey. With a history. And those tiles…" She reached out to skim her fingers across the bold hand-painted pattern. "I really love these. Like, more than I love chocolate. Which says a lot, believe me."

Levi leaned one hip against the counter edge, listening to the drip and hiss of the coffee trickling into the old-school carafe. "At least that's one mystery solved."

Val looked over, a slight crease between her brows. "Mystery?"

"Now I know why you've been dragging your feet about finishing the kitchen."

She blew a short laugh through her nose. "Maybe. Not that all those samples you showed me aren't pretty, but yeah. They're not…me."

When the pot was full, Levi poured two mugs and brought them over to the same six-foot-long pine table where he and his brothers often ended up doing their homework, usually under Gus's supervision, once their mother started delivering babies. "So let's rethink things," he said, sliding onto one of the benches. "It's not like we can't find a place or six that sells Mexican tiles around here."

"And—again—I can't exactly put my personal touch on a space I'm only babysitting, can I?"

Stirring sugar into his coffee, Levi looked up to see her still staring at the tiles with a wistful expression that tore him to pieces. Because once again, she didn't have free rein to make her own choice. Even about some stupid tiles. But before he could figure out what to say, she climbed over the bench to sit beside him, dumping three spoonsful of sugar into her own coffee.

"Thanks. And I don't mean for this." She jabbed her spoon toward the dark swirling liquid. "I mean for…indulging me, I suppose. Tonight. Although I may never live it down around town."

Levi smiled. "All anyone saw—if they even noticed, it was pretty crowded in there—was a gal having fun. Hardly a hanging offense." She snorted. "But you're welcome. I'm glad…" He frowned at his own coffee. "I'm glad you felt you could trust me enough to do that. That I wouldn't take advantage of you. Or something."

She actually laughed. "Seriously, Levi? You're surprised that I trust you?"

"Uh…yeah? I mean, considering our history and all. Right?"

She squeezed shut her eyes, then opened them again to blow out a breath. "Well, I do. Trust you."

He took a moment. "This is a new development, I take it?"

Her mouth twisted. "New…ish. You've been a good friend, Levi. And I don't have a lot of those. So thank you."

Levi stared at his hands, curled around the steaming mug, almost incapable of processing her sincerity. "You have no idea," he finally said, "how honored that makes me feel."

She took a sip of her coffee, then set down the mug, going very still. "Same goes," she said softly. "In fact… I owe you an apology."

"Now I know you're drunk," he said, and she laughed. But it was a sad sound, battering his heart all over again.

"Still drunk enough to let down the wall, maybe. But not so drunk that I don't know what I'm saying." Her eyes lifted to his. "You probably know I blamed you all these years for Tommy's going into the army."

"Kinda got that impression, yeah. But—"

"No, let me finish before the caffeine kicks in and I lose my nerve. All my life, people have left. Made promises they didn't keep. My parents, especially. Then Tommy showed up, and I thought—finally. Someone who'll actually stick around. So when he decided to enlist, I couldn't believe it. And I didn't want to believe it of him. That he'd leave me, just like everybody else. So since the thought of laying the blame at his feet nearly killed me, I shifted it to you."

"Since you already didn't like me and all."

One side of her mouth lifted. "You were definitely convenient. And then you came back, and…" She shrugged. "I wanted to be angry. I *needed* to be angry."

Without thinking, Levi reached for her hand. Which she let him take. "Except…" She exhaled. "Hanging on to a lie doesn't make it true. It only makes you look like an idiot." She stared at their linked hands. "Maybe your enlisting put the idea in Tommy's head to do the same thing, but it was his choice. A choice I doubt I'll ever completely understand, but blaming you for it…" She lifted her eyes to his. "That was wrong. And I apologize."

His brain locking up again, Levi let go of her hand to tug her to his side, his chest constricting when she laid her head on his shoulder. And it simply felt…right. For them, for this moment. Because he didn't have a whole lot of friends, either. And he could do far worse than having this woman fill that position.

"I could've done more, though," he said into her hair, "to talk him out of it—"

"No, Levi. You couldn't have. This was the dude who bought that god-awful purple car, remember? Jeez, Levi—the man gave up sex to serve his country."

"Um… I take it the coffee hasn't fully kicked in yet?"

"We were married, Levi. We had sex. *Good* sex. When he was around. Not gonna lie, I miss that." Yeah, definitely the beer still talking. Had to be. "But it was something Tommy felt he had to do," she went on. "And because of that choice, a lot of lives were saved." She pulled away, taking her warmth with her. "One of those things nobody warns you about falling for an honorable dude—"

"Thought I heard voices," said a gruff voice from the doorway, pushing both of them to their feet. A moment later Granville Blake came into the room, leaning heavily on a three-pronged cane. Levi started—the last time he'd seen his father's old employer the man had been as fit as any of his much younger hands, tall and proud and black haired, with light-colored eyes that could—and did—pierce straight through a person. And if it hadn't been for those eyes, Levi wouldn't have recognized him.

"Gus told me you were here." Stiffly, Granville walked toward them, his hand extended. "Welcome home, son."

Levi clasped the older man's hand, his chest constricting at how frail it felt. "Thank you, sir. I don't think you know Valerie Lopez? She married my friend Tomas."

"Ooh..." Granville's gaze turned to Val. "I'm so sorry, honey. *So* sorry. Yes, I remember Tomas quite well. Fine young man." Leaning heavily on the cane, he gave Val a sympathetic smile. "You getting on okay?"

"Yes. Thank you—"

"Wait. Valerie...your maiden name was Oswald, wasn't it?"

"It was, yes."

Granville sucked in a long breath, every line in his face deepening. "Knew your mother. Not well, but..." He cleared his throat, a slight flush sweeping across his pallid cheeks. "I was sorry to hear of her passing. Real sorry."

Even an idiot could've heard the subtext screaming underneath those words. And for damn sure Val obviously did. This time her "Thank you" was mumbled before she said, "It's getting late, I should really be getting back. But the party was great—thanks so much for hosting it..."

After a few more words with Granville, they left. The festivities were winding down, the only sounds the occasional slam of a truck door, tires bumping over dirt. A bellow of good-old-boy laughter. From a nearby barn, a horse nickered, the sound suspended in the chilled night air that cloaked them as they walked back to Levi's truck, Val with her arms pretzeled over her ribs.

"God, I could so use another beer right now."

"No, you couldn't."

"He slept with my mother, Levi." The darkness snatched at her words. Her anger.

"You don't know that."

"Don't I?"

"Okay," Levi said, knowing arguing would be pointless. Especially with a woman as ticked off as this one was. "But he's been a widower for a long time—"

"And we *all* know what my mother was. So no big deal, right?" Then she stopped dead in her tracks to lift her face to the clear, star-pricked black sky. His hands fisted in his jacket pockets, Levi had no idea what to do, what she wanted or needed from him. If anything. Except, maybe, simply his presence. Clearly his lot in life, he thought with a slight smile.

"Val?"

A breeze plucked at her hair, silver in the moonlight. "Why should I even care? Especially since it obviously happened years ago. When I wasn't even around. But damn…" A harsh laugh pushed from her lungs. "Sometimes I think the woman hooked up with every breathing male in a hundred-mile radius."

Unfortunately, he couldn't exactly refute her assumption. So instead he waited until she took his hand, then continued on to the truck. "And maybe, for a little while, she was able to offer a lonely man some solace."

"Solace? Clearly you never knew my mother."

"No, but I knew Granville Blake. And I remember when his wife died. How hard he took it."

Val was quiet for a moment. "They never had any kids?"

"One. A daughter. A little younger than Josh and me. Granville sent her to DC to live with her aunt and uncle when she was fourteen, fifteen, something like that."

"Why?" She sounded appalled.

"I have no idea. I know—it seemed crazy to us, too, that he'd send away his only child. Far as I know she hasn't been back in years. I'm guessing what you saw tonight was a lot of regret." He looked over at her. "So you might not want to take out your frustration on him."

"It's not him I'm frustrated with," she sighed out. "Obviously. And what my mother did after I left was her business. It just kicked a lot of memories back to life. That's all."

"You must've hated her."

On a sound that was half laugh, half sigh, Val picked her way across a network of braided cottonwood roots to plant her butt on a chewed-up swing that'd been dangling from that old tree for as long as Levi could remember. He feared for her safety, even though he doubted her weight even registered on the sturdy branch. He followed to stand in front of her, his thumbs hooked in the front pockets of his jeans.

"I'm guessing you're still not ready to go home?"

She gave him an almost apologetic smile. "It's funny. It's not as if there's anything there I'm trying to avoid. Except, maybe…" Her lips pursed. "The quiet."

"I can understand that."

"So you don't mind?"

"Not at all."

Tilting back her head, Val curled her fingers high on the ropes, looking up through a million heart-shaped leaves shivering in the gentle breeze, ghostly in the scant light reaching them from the house, the barns. "To answer your question…no, I didn't hate my mother. Although sometimes I think it would've been easier if I had. And God knows, I wanted to. Horrible as that sounds. But what I wanted more, was to simply feel important to her. To feel—" her gaze met his again, eerily clear in the shadowed light "—like I mattered. To her, to anybody. Seeing as how my father clearly didn't care, either."

Oddly, he knew she wasn't looking for pity. In fact,

she probably would've slugged him if he'd offered it. But he still felt compelled to say, "It must've been hard, when he left."

Val halfheartedly shoved off the ground; the swing wobbled, like it wasn't sure what it was supposed to do, before settling into a gentle rocking motion. "I was only five, so I don't remember much about it. Or him, for that matter. Except for a couple of vague impressions."

"Good, bad…?"

She shrugged. "Neither. Although not sure what difference that makes, since he's never tried to make contact."

"Not even once?"

"Nope. Although since my parents weren't married, maybe he never felt any real obligation…?"

"Plenty of men father children with women they're not married to, Val. Has nothing to do with how they feel about their kids."

"Not in this case. Frankly I've always wondered why he stuck around as long as he did. But whatever. Between that and my mother's always looking at me like she didn't understand why I was there…" Her fingers tightened around the ropes. "Nothing like being made to feel like a mistake nobody could figure out how to fix. So when Tommy came into my life…" She shrugged, her eyes glittering in the moonlight.

"He did make you feel like you mattered."

She smiled. "And then some. And that took guts, you know? In a town this small, hooking up with someone like me."

Anger spiking through him, Levi leaned against the tree's massive trunk. "You weren't your mother, Val."

"Tell that to the kids—and their parents—who judged me." Her mouth twisted. "Or assumed I was *exactly* like my mother."

Something hard and cold fisted in Levi's chest. The

sneers and snide comments had been bad enough. The close-minded judging. But something in her voice told him that hadn't been the end of it. "Who?"

Her eyes flashed to his, startled. Then she shook her head. "Not important."

"Like hell."

Sighing, she leaned her temple against her hand, fisted around the rope. "It wasn't anybody you would've known—he didn't live here. And this was before Tomas. I was lucky, if you can call it that. I got away before the worst happened."

He could barely breathe. "How old were you?"

"Thirteen? Fourteen?"

"Good God, Val. Did Tommy know?"

"No."

"Why the hell not?"

"Because for years I was too…ashamed? Confused? I honestly don't know. Then I guess I thought, why rehash, relive, whatever, something I wanted to forget? It was enough that Tommy'd rescued me from what he did know about." She smiled. "That he loved me, baggage and all. And I will always love him for that. For seeing past all the stuff the other boys couldn't. Or wouldn't."

Through a wad of impossibly tangled thoughts, Levi waited out a surge of something he couldn't even define. Irritation, maybe, that he hadn't known? "But you're telling me now."

A slight smile touched her lips. "Yeah."

"Why?"

"Because…dunno. It's not so scary anymore?"

"The memory? Or the idea of telling someone?"

"Not sure. Both?"

"I'm so sorry—"

"For something that had nothing to do with you? Why? I never even told my mother," she said before he could answer her question. "Can you believe it? God, if my girls ever thought they couldn't tell me about *any*thing…" Her eyes glittered. "It would gut me, Levi. Absolutely *gut* me."

"I doubt you have anything to worry about on that score," he said, which got a little smile, even as he thought about how much he'd kept from his parents when he was younger. That undoubtedly there'd be times her girls would rather put their eyes out rather than share with their mother. But best not to go there. Instead, he veered onto a side road with, "Did you know my mother helped take care of yours, after she got sick?"

Val shook her head. "Natalie and I…well. We didn't have a whole lot to say to each other at that point."

"Did you even know?"

"No. And, yes, that's the truth."

"Did you think I wouldn't believe you?"

Her mouth thinned. "No matter what our relationship was—or wasn't—we were all each other had at that point. I can only imagine what some people must've thought, that I wasn't here to take care of her."

"And those people can go screw themselves," he said, and she almost laughed. "If she didn't tell you, I think that lets you off the hook. And seriously—according to my mother, yours was a bitch on wheels. Sorry—"

"No, sounds about right. There was a reason—several, actually—I stayed as far out of her radar as…" She yawned. "As possible. She knew about Josie, but…"

"The kid didn't need to be around that. And you were right to protect her." He hesitated. "Not to mention yourself. Her needs were met, as well as she'd let anybody meet them. And while God knows I may not have figured out much about life yet, I do know one thing—we're not responsible for anybody else's screwups. Our own, yeah. But not anyone else's. Damn, Val…"

He shoved his hands in his pockets again, not quite believing what he was about to say. But knowing he'd explode if he didn't. "You know the thing I most remember about you, from when we were kids?" Eyes glued to his, she shook her head. "Your dignity. The way you'd hold up your head high when you had to know the other kids were talking about you. Even though you were obviously going through a hell that nobody else had a clue about. Not really. But damned if you were going to let anybody else see it. Or let it poison you. And you could have, you know. And the way you cared about other people, even then…" He swallowed as he felt heat blaze across his face. Thank God it was dark. "There's a reason Tommy fell as hard as he did. Because you…you were something else. You still are."

Val stared at him for several seconds, which did nothing to help the blazing-face thing, then slowly smiled. "Holy crap, Levi," she said softly. "I…" She glanced away, pushing out a small laugh, before facing him again. "Wow…" Another yawn attacked, this one epic. She covered her mouth, then gripped the rope again. "I don't know what to say."

"Why do you have to say anything? It's true. But I think it's time we get you home before you fall off that swing."

She yawned again, then pushed out a tired laugh. "You might have a point."

A point she proved long before they got back to Whispering Pines, when, despite the coffee, she conked out in the car. She didn't exactly wake up when they reached her house, either, although she came to enough to murmur, "Where are we?" when he opened the passenger-side door. From inside, Radar went into overdrive, baying his fool head off.

"Your house."

Her eyes drifted shut again. "Not my house."

Levi reached inside, scooped her into his arms. She didn't protest. In fact, she looped her arms around his neck and snuggled right against his chest, and he thought, *Oh, hell.* "But that's definitely your dog."

Her head wagged again, her hair tickling his chin. "Not my dog, either," she mumbled. "Tommy's."

Beginning to see a pattern here, Levi carted her up the porch steps. She weighed, like, nothing. Behind the door, the dog went crazy. "How about the cat?"

"Josie's."

"Well, hell, woman..." He shifted to dig the keys out of her purse, unlock the door. "What *is* yours?"

"These," she said, lifting one foot. But not her head. "Boots are *allll* mine."

Chuckling over the sting to his heart, he carted her inside, kneeing aside the frantic dog before carrying her upstairs to her room. She was sawing logs again before he'd even lowered her to the bed. Carefully, he removed the boots, then dislodged a very miffed kitten to tug a fluffy throw off the chair, which he gently tucked around Val's delicate shoulders.

Then he stood back, half smiling as Skunk hopped up to curl into the space in front of her stomach and the dog climbed up to smash himself against her back, and he thought, *Me.*

I could be yours.

Right. As if he'd ever in a million years be able to compete with the guy she'd just said she'd love forever, for having the cojones to do what Levi hadn't. Besides, all Tomas had wanted was for Levi to make sure she was okay. He sincerely doubted falling for the woman had been part of his best friend's plan.

Then again...

Levi leaned over to place a soft kiss on Val's even softer cheek, then straightened, his hands in his pockets. A smile flickered across her lips, not unlike Risa's when she was dreaming, and Levi's heart started hammering in his chest.

Because there was no getting around it—for the first time in his life, he was in love.

As in, drowning.

So maybe it was time he find those cojones, setting aside his loyalty to a dead man for a shot at something far bigger. Maybe, just maybe, this was his chance to be everything to Val, to her girls, he *couldn't* have been before. Yes, it had to be her choice to move forward or not. But how could she make that choice if he didn't give her the option? And if the odds were stacked against him… tough. Wouldn't be the first time.

However, it was the first time that defying those odds made him feel as if he'd gotten hold of some bad booze. Hell, laying his life on the line was nothing compared with the prospect of offering his *heart*.

A floorboard squawked as Levi tiptoed out of the room, imagining his brothers laughing their fool heads off.

Chapter Ten

The sun was blasting through the open window when Val woke with a start the next morning, dry-mouthed and fuzzy-brained. To make matters worse, that fuzzy brain had way too much information to process at once, including, but not limited to, (1) she was still fully dressed; (2) her daughters were giggling like mad downstairs; and (3) since she could hear Levi as well, she was guessing he was the cause of the giggling.

Great.

She kneed the kitten aside—bad move, ouch—to peel off the throw so she could get to the bathroom before her bladder exploded, at which point a quick glance in the mottled mirror over the 1980s-era sink made her remember why she rarely wore makeup. Because raccoon eyes were not her friends. Also, if she was going to look—and feel—like a prime candidate for the walk of shame, shouldn't she at least have something to be ashamed *of*?

Something close to a chuckle burped from her chest. Oh, the irony.

Then it hit her, everything Levi had said, about…back then. About her being dignified and all that—a thought that brought a smile, considering at the moment she was about as dignified as roadkill. Add to that the look in his eyes, intense and searing and mad as hell, for her sake. The feel of him, holding her when they danced, when he carried her into the house, warm and solid and protective and, heaven help her, *alive.*

So alive.

Because, no, she hadn't been that drunk. Or sleepy.

Blood surged to her face, bringing her hand to her red-hot cheeks. Because only once before, had a man said or done anything to make her feel…special. Worthy.

As if she mattered.

And that man—the second one, not the first—was downstairs, right this very minute, making her children laugh. Also pancakes, if her nose was to be believed.

Val squeezed shut her hairy eyes. Granted, not hating him—anymore—was a good thing. As was forgiving him. Or rather, realizing she had nothing to forgive him for. But *liking* him…?

Being *attracted* to him…?

"Mama?"

Still leaning on the cultured marble sink—because she wasn't entirely sure she wouldn't fall over if she didn't—Val smiled in the mirror for her oldest child, all perky and adorable and grinning.

"Good morning, cutie," she said, and said child scurried over to wrap her arms around Val's waist. And then frown at her.

"You look funny. Are you sick?"

The thought crossed Val's feeble mind that this would be a great opportunity for an object lesson on the consequences of alcohol overindulgence. Except adolescence would come soon enough; why knock herself off the pedestal a minute before the kid would, anyway?

So all she said was, "I'm fine, sweetie. Just slept too hard is all." As in, like the dead, but let's not go there.

"Why are you still dressed?" Josie said, because *there* was exactly where a seven-year-old was going to go.

"I was too tired to undress." And somehow she left the question mark off the end of that sentence.

"Oh. Okay. Anyway… Levi's making pancakes."

"So I gathered." Wait. "When did Grandma drop you off?"

"A little while ago. Levi was already here. He said he spent the night."

"To *Grandma*?"

"Uh-huh. She got a real weird look on her face. And then she smiled. Like this." Josie demonstrated, giving Val the eeriest sensation of what her baby girl would look like in fifty years. And again, she was swamped with the unfairness of it all, that now her mother-in-law was probably thinking…

Sweet baby Jesus.

"So are you coming downstairs?"

"Not looking like this, I'm not. Give me ten minutes, okay?"

"Okay." Josie started to scamper away—honestly, the kid never walked if she could run, skip or hop—only to turn back around and say, "Levi makes really, really good pancakes."

Of course he did.

As promised, ten minutes later, showered and clothed and more or less in her right mind, Val ventured downstairs—carefully—where the dog rushed her, a blur of canine joy, only to rush back to Him Who Had the Food. Josie was at the kitchen table, prattling away about…something, while this big, sweet, handsome man held her baby against his hip as if he'd been doing this for years, giving Risa a step-by-step tutorial on how to flip pancakes as the kid gnawed on her own, happily getting soggy, crummy slobber all over Levi's shoulder.

Things were less bizarre when she *was* drunk.

"Mama's here!" Josie cried, and Risa clapped her gooey hands. Levi looked over, grinning, and for a second Val thought how easy it would be to buy into whatever Levi was selling. Although since he probably had no idea what that was, or that he was even selling it, she'd best be keeping her slightly hungover wits about her.

Especially since loneliness and grief—fading, yes, but by no means done with—blended with chronic disappointment made for really crappy soil to grow anything in. At least, anything that wasn't bound to eventually shrivel up and die.

"Mornin', Cinderella." Val grimaced, and he chuckled, and her hungover hormones got all shivery. "Coffee's on. Kids are fed. Would've made bacon but there wasn't any. And what's up with that?"

"Take it up with the food fairy," Val muttered, then gawked at the piled-high plate on the stove. "Exactly how many of those do you expect me to eat?"

"Figured you'd be hungry after last night," he said, not even trying to keep the innuendo out of his voice, and she was sorely tempted to grab the spatula from his hand and beat him over the head with it. However, having neither the energy to carry through nor the wherewithal to explain to Miss Big Eyes, she settled for sitting at the table and letting Levi wait on her.

Josie jumped up to run outside, taking the reluctant dog with her, and Levi lowered the babbling baby into her high chair.

"You have to strap her in—"

"Got it."

"And make sure her fingers are out of the way before you snap on the tray—" He shot her a *Seriously?* look, and she pressed her lips together.

"Okay, I'll shut up now."

"You do that," he said, handing the baby another pancake before setting a humongous plate of the same in front of Val, along with syrup and butter. And coffee, bless him. And damned if her eyes didn't go all stingy.

"What?" he said, sliding into the seat across from her.

Shaking her head, she smeared soft butter between each layer, then drowned the pancakes in syrup before the butter had fully melted, making little yellow islands in a glistening, gooey amber sea. The weird thing was, it wasn't as if nobody had ever made breakfast for her. Connie had, all the time, when she and the girls had lived with her and Pete. But before then, that honor had fallen to Tommy, initially when they were first married, then when he'd be home on leave. Because after everything she'd been through, he'd said, she deserved to be pampered.

But there was no need to mention that now. Really. Because maybe there was such a thing as being too honest. Levi needed to be appreciated for his own sake and his own deeds. Not because he reminded her of Tommy.

And certainly not because she was feeling especially… needy. Did she dream he'd kissed her on the cheek last night? Or had that really happened?

So she skirted his concern entirely by asking, "Why on earth did you stay?"

Chewing around a huge bite of pancakes, he shrugged. "Didn't like the idea of you being alone in the house at night."

"Never mind that I always am." He shrugged again, and she sighed. "You do realize that Connie probably jumped to all manner of conclusions."

"Since I was still sacked out on the sofa when she arrived, maybe not so much."

"Oh."

"Yeah. Oh. So no worries, sweet cheeks, your virtue is still untarnished."

She threw her coffee spoon at him. Risa squealed, delighted, clapping her hands as a chuckling Levi easily caught the spoon before handing it to the baby, then leaned over to touch his forehead to hers. Tears sprang to Val's eyes; she quickly blinked them away, chuckling when the baby lifted the spoon, triumphant.

"Bah?"

"Bah," Levi said, straightening. Grinning her evil baby grin, Risa curled in on herself, her prize clutched to her chest, and Levi laughed. Val smiled.

"You're really good with her. With both of them."

Straightening, he gave her an almost sheepish smile as the baby gleefully banged the spoon on her high chair tray. "I know. Surprised the heck out of me, too."

She took a bite of pancakes. They were freaking perfect. "You ever think about having kids of your own?"

"Before a few weeks ago?" Something bloomed in his eyes. Something she didn't want to think about too hard. "No."

Val lifted her coffee mug to her mouth, hoping her cheeks didn't look as red as they felt. "I'm so sorry you had to sleep on the sofa, it really sucks—"

"Considering I didn't exactly spend the last six years on a Sleep Number bed, I was good. You going into work today?"

"Yeah," she said, glancing at the kitchen clock. "Soon, actually. Since I couldn't bake yesterday, I have to go in early to get some pies done for the lunch rush. Which means I need to get the kids back to Connie's—"

"No worries, I've got 'em."

She blinked at him. "What? Why?"

"Why not?" He polished off his breakfast, stood to clear their plates.

"Because what do you know about taking care of a baby?"

He pointed to the obviously happy infant currently auditioning for lead drummer in a rock band, then carried the dishes to the sink. "You don't think I can handle it?"

"I…" She frowned. "Can you?"

"Yes," he said over the running water as he washed the dishes. "And if things get too crazy, I can always call Connie. She said," he said when Val opened her mouth to protest.

"Why?" she repeated, and Levi looked out the kitchen window for a long moment before turning back to her. And while she couldn't have defined what she saw in his eyes if her life depended on it, whatever it was reached right inside her and wrapped around her heart. And squeezed. Hard.

"Even if Tommy hadn't asked me to look out for you and the girls," he said, "I'd like to believe I would've, anyway. And now that I'm here…" He smiled down at the sticky-faced baby shrieking at the kitten who'd come into the kitchen, before meeting Val's gaze again. "I owe this much to him, to be whatever you all need me to be in your lives." His gaze touched hers. "And I do mean *whatever* you need me to be."

And what if I don't want you to do that?

The thought sliced through her like a samurai blade. Which it undoubtedly would have Levi, too, if she'd had it in her to give voice to it. But she was hardly going to slap the man's kindness in the face, was she? He meant well; she knew that. And it wasn't as if she wasn't grateful, because she was. Heart-achingly so. That didn't mean she wasn't also scared out of her gourd of losing everything she'd fought so hard for over the last little while, to trust her own decisions about what was best for her and the girls. Because if it was one thing she'd learned, it was that the only person she could truly count on was herself.

But now was not the time to lay all that out there, both because she needed to get her butt to work and because she'd put out her own eye before hurting Levi. So all she did was smile and say, "And I appreciate that. I really do," even as the hollowness of her own words made her inwardly wince. She got up from the table, scouring her hands down the backside of her jeans. "Lord, I didn't realize how late it was."

She jumped when Levi laid a hand on her shoulder, his touch so warm, so steady, searing through the thin fabric of her blouse. "Hey. I didn't mean to upset you—"

"You didn't—"

"And you're a lousy liar," he said, and her face flamed. And not only about being caught out. Because those hormones had sobered right up, boy, reminding her of that which she sorely missed. Including, apparently, her sanity.

Because oh, dear *Lord,* did she want to kiss him. Or have him kiss her. Whichever, whatever, didn't matter. Worse, though—since she clearly had a masochistic streak a mile wide—it was killing her not to ask him what he really wanted from her. With her.

Because if she did, then he'd have to answer. And whatever the answer was she already knew she'd have no idea what to do with it.

Because then she'd have to decide what she really wanted from *him.*

With him.

"Thanks for watching the kids," she mumbled, giving Risa a quick nuzzle and kiss before scurrying away, like the flustered coward she was.

* * *

Josie was lying on her back in the backyard, the sun hot on her closed eyelids, when suddenly it got darker.

"What on earth are you doing, little girl?"

The laughter in Levi's voice made her giggle before she opened her eyes to find him standing over her with Risa in his arms. He was so big, like a giant. *A lot bigger than Daddy,* she thought. Although truthfully she was remembering Daddy less and less these days. A thought that made her heart hurt.

"I like to lie in the sun and think about stuff."

"Sounds reasonable," Levi said, sitting beside her. He set Risa in the grass, although she immediately started crawling away. It was crazy, how fast she was on her hands and knees. But Radar, who'd been asleep beside Josie, jumped up and got in front of the baby, making sure she didn't go too far. Josie hugged her knees, her forehead squished.

"Where's Mama?"

"She went to work. So I'm staying with you guys until she gets back. If that's okay with you?"

"Oh. Yeah, sure." Josie picked off a piece of little plant with itty-bitty purple flowers on it. Mama said it was a weed, but it was still pretty. "Thank you for breakfast."

"You're welcome. Hey," Levi said, gently bumping shoulders. "What's going on?"

"Just thinking about Daddy."

"Ah."

She squinted up at Levi in the bright sun. "Do you mind if I talk about him?"

"Not at all. Why should I?"

"Because he was your best friend?"

"All the more reason to talk about him, right?"

"Yeah, that would be my take on it," she said on a sigh, wondering why Levi sounded like he was trying not to laugh. "But if I talk about him to Mama or Gramma, they go all weird on me. I mean, I can see they're trying not to, but that only makes it weirder. You know?"

"I do."

"So how come it doesn't bother you?"

Levi got real quiet, then said, "Because when I look at you and Risa, it's like your dad is right here. And that helps me not miss him so much."

"Huh." Josie thought about that for a moment. "So how come Mama and Gramma don't feel like that?"

"Couldn't tell you. Although I guess…it's all about perspective."

"What's that?"

"How a person looks at things. Not with their eyes, but with their minds. Your mom and your grandmother… maybe they only see what they're missing. I see what I *had*. The crazy times your dad and I used to have together. I'm not saying it doesn't hurt, knowing we won't ever be able to have any more of those crazy times, but remembering them…" He smiled. "It makes me feel very…rich."

"But what if you don't have those memories? Or at least, not a lot of them. And Risa…" She nodded at her sister, gurgling at the dog as she patted his back. "She never even met Daddy. So she *can't* remember him."

Levi leaned back on his elbow, his own forehead all crinkly. "I see your point."

"Yeah. Sucks."

He smiled again, then looked over at her. His eyes… They always made her feel safe. As if she didn't have to be afraid when he was around. "You know if there's any pictures of your dad?"

She thought. "I know Gramma has this big book with some. I'm not sure about Mom, though. Maybe on her phone?"

"And there's probably some on people's computers, too,"

Levi said. "So how's about we print out some of those pictures, then make an album for Risa? Then your mom and I, and your grandparents, could write down our memories of him to go along with the pictures. That way, your dad won't be forgotten."

"Really? We could do that?"

"Absolutely." Then Levi got a funny look on his face. "I know I said it'd be for Risa—and you, of course—but it might also be a good way to help your mom and your grandparents deal with your dad not being here anymore. To help them remember the good times." He grinned. "How funny your dad was. And how much he liked to *have* fun."

Josie wrapped her arms around her legs to lean her chin on her knees, thinking this over. "So if we do this, it might help Mama stop being so sad all the time?"

"Couldn't hurt to try, right?"

No, Josie thought. She didn't suppose it would. Then she made a face.

"Ew, Risa—you stink *so* bad!"

Levi laughed, and her baby sister grinned, her chin all shiny with drool. For somebody so cute, she sure could be gross. Then Levi got to his feet, swinging the baby up against his side, as if it didn't even bother him how yucky she smelled. "Oh, yeah, somebody definitely needs her pants changed," he said, then held out his hand to Josie. "Then let's go over to your grandma's, see about getting some of those pictures."

And Josie put her hand in his, and you know what? For the moment, things felt pretty okay. In fact, once they got inside and Levi took the baby upstairs to change her diaper, Josie went over to the DVD player and took out *Elf*. She'd watched it so much she could practically say all the words along with the characters. And she still loved it. But she thought maybe she didn't need it to remember Daddy anymore. Especially now that Levi was around.

Smiling, she carefully put the DVD back into its case and then on the shelf under the TV, where it would be safe.

It'd been slower than usual, which Val supposed wasn't all that surprising for the day after the Fourth. Even so, yesterday's shindig had netted her—and the diner—a few new customers, so the day wasn't a total loss. But by three the place was dead. Except for Charley, of course, in his usual spot at the end of the counter.

Val slid a piece of chocolate cream pie in front of him, warmth flooding her when his face lit up.

"For me?"

"Nobody else."

"She's spoiling you something rotten," Annie said good-naturedly as she swiped down the counter. Charley grinned around a mouthful of rich chocolate and whipped cream.

"And don't I know it."

"And what you probably don't know," Annie said to Val, "is that I had somebody from the ski resort in today asking if we—well, you—sold in bulk."

"The resort?"

"Yep. Apparently word's gotten out that we sell the best pies in northern New Mexico. So they want a piece of the action. Well, more than a piece. The gal said they could probably move several dozen whole pies a day during peak season."

"You're kidding?"

"Nope. And before you go off on some rant about loyalty or whatever…you'd be an idiot to turn up your nose at the opportunity. Unless you want to waitress for me the rest of your life? Yeah, that's what I thought. So, here." Annie dug into her pocket and handed Val a business card. "There's her number. Call her."

"And how on earth would I handle that kind of volume?"

"You give the idea to the universe, let the universe figure it out. Oh, customer..." Annie smiled for the slight graying man who'd come in clutching a brown cowboy hat in his hands. "Go on and take a seat anywhere. Want some coffee?"

"No, actually I'm looking for someone." Bandy-legged and slightly barrel-chested, the man had "rodeo rider" written all over him. Or one of the clowns maybe. In any case, Val'd never seen him before. Until pale blue eyes shot to hers, as a shy, almost frightened smile creased the man's sun-beaten face...and Val's heart shot into her throat.

"Valerie Ann?" the man said softly, gnarled fingers now strangling the hat's brim. "You probably don't recognize me—"

"No. I do," she said, impossible though that might seem.

The man's smile softened. Grew.

And once again, her world went sideways.

Chapter Eleven

Val couldn't remember when she'd determined that treating other people better than she'd been treated was her ticket out of her lousy childhood. Not that she hadn't had issues with people, for various reasons—like, say, Levi—but even as a kid she realized that returning cursing for cursing did nobody any favors. Especially herself. Maybe she had no control over the events of her life, but how she reacted to those events was entirely up to her. Mostly, anyway.

A fact she now reminded herself of as she sat in a back booth with her father, who looked every bit as awkward as she felt. God knows her first impulse had been to run, but something—Annie, most likely—had held her back. And thus far she couldn't decide whether being in shock made the encounter easier or harder. She only prayed it would be over soon.

She'd texted Levi to make sure it was okay if she was late. She didn't say why. Although what did it say about her sorry state of mind, that she half wished he was here with her, all calm and steady and rocklike? And right there was the problem, wasn't it?

"Why?" she now said, glaring at her hands folded in front of her on the table. Refusing to meet her father's eyes. Because no way was she getting sucked in. No. Damn. Way.

"Why am I here?" he asked. "Or why did I leave?"

At least he had the courage to come straight to the point. Meaning she needed to find enough to look at the man. "Take your pick."

"You have every right to be pissed off—"

"That's not even a question," she said, refusing to flinch at the guilt darkening his gaze.

He scrubbed his hand across his whiskery face, looking...worn-out. It occurred to Val she had no idea how old he actually was. Or even his last name, actually. "Surprising you like this probably wasn't the best move, but since I didn't know how else to contact you...it was one of those spur-of-the-moment things, you know? I was on my way north for a rodeo and... I can't explain it. It was like something pushed me back here, and then I found myself asking if anybody knew you. Guy up the street, he pointed me in the right direction." He smiled, revealing a missing incisor. "And here you are—"

"Right where I've been most of my life." Except for the years she'd been in Texas, when Tommy was in the service. But this man didn't need to know that. "So you could've put in an appearance anytime. And not only because 'something' prompted you to see if I was around, like some old high school classmate you decided to look up."

"Your mother...she didn't tell you? About what happened between us?"

"Natalie never mentioned you at all after you left."

Her father released a resigned sigh. "No surprise there,

I guess." His forehead creased. "You call her by her first name?"

"It worked for us." Val paused. "Do you even know she passed away?"

"No." A brief startled look was almost instantly replaced with what Val could only surmise was relief. "When?"

"Few years back. Cancer."

"I'm sorry to hear that—"

"Somehow I doubt it. Since you don't seem particularly bothered that she didn't talk about you."

"Considering how badly I screwed up? Why would she? I didn't… You need to know, Valerie, I didn't leave of my own accord. Your mother kicked me out." He cleared his throat. "Because she found out I was cheating on her."

Val almost laughed. "Oh, jeez—"

"I was a twenty-four-year-old asshole, Valerie. What the hell did I know about responsibility?"

Twenty-*four*? Which would have made him…nineteen when she was born. Seven years younger than her mother. Holy hell.

"That why you're not listed on my birth certificate?"

His mouth turned down at the corners. "That wasn't my choice—believe me."

Val sagged back in the booth, her arms crossed. "Are you even sure…?"

"That I'm your dad? Yeah. I took you into Albuquerque when you were a baby, had a paternity test done."

"Wow. Were they even that common back then?"

"Not like they are now, no. And, boy, was your mother mad when the test results landed in our mailbox. But…" His scruffy cheeks puffed when he released a breath. "I just wanted to be sure. Like you said."

To get away from the storm inside her head, Val looked out the window. At some point the absurdity of the encounter was going to hit her between the eyes, but for now shock numbed the anger. Somewhat, anyway.

"I found a picture," she said quietly, facing him again, "when I came back to clear out my mother's things. Of the two of you, with me as a toddler. Your name was on the back. Your first name, anyway. Otherwise I wouldn't have even known that much. The photo was mixed in with some other papers. I doubt she even remembered it was there—"

"It's McAdams."

"Pardon?"

"My last name. McAdams."

Val took a moment to process this before her forehead knotted. "You were really that young?"

Her father leaned sideways to pull his wallet out of his back pocket, which he flipped open to show her his driver's license. His hand shook, she noticed. Not badly, but way too much for a man only in his late forties. Craig Andrew McAdams, it said. The picture was recent. He wasn't smiling.

"I wasn't ready to be a father, to be honest," he said quietly, shifting again to replace the wallet. "But when Nat told me she was pregnant, I figured I should at least try. Shoot, I even offered to marry her. She was having none of it. Actually she wasn't even all that hot on us moving in together. And considering how bad things were between us, I should've probably listened to her."

"So you cheated on her."

His mouth tightened. "It was an impossible situation. We weren't getting along—at all—but there you were, and…" He shrugged, his eyes watering. "Like I said. I screwed up. With her, with you…everybody. But I did love you. And for more than five years, I gave it my best shot, I swear. As much as the sorry piece of crap I was understood how to do that."

"Only not enough to ever make contact again."

Craig glanced down at his scarred hands, then back at her. "There was more. I might've...been involved in a few things I shouldn't've been. Your mother used that as leverage."

"Things?"

"Drugs," he said, and Val shut her eyes, feeling as if she'd just stepped into an episode of *Breaking Bad*. "The cheating, I think Nat might've gotten over. Onetime thing, meant nothing. We'd had a fight..." He waved away the rest of the thought. "But the other stuff... I guess everybody has their line in the sand. That was hers. She said if I tried to contact you, she'd sic the cops on me. So my hands were tied. For what it's worth, I'm clean now. Have been for years."

"Glad to hear it."

Craig grimaced. "But by the time I'd gotten my head on straight, so much time had passed, I figured you'd probably forgotten me. Or didn't care."

"You're right. I didn't. Care, I mean." Or so she'd convinced herself.

"And the other?"

Val hesitated, glancing out the window before meeting his hopeful gaze again. "I didn't exactly remember you. How could I—I was so little when you left? But I never forgot you, either. Doesn't mean, however, that I'm even remotely interested in resurrecting a relationship you killed."

Her stomach quaking, Val pushed herself out of the booth. "Blame my mother all you want—and believe me, I understand where you're coming from on that—but everything happened as a consequence of decisions *you* made. And sorry, but excuses don't cut it. Because I was young, too, when I got married, had my first daughter. And trust me—nothing in heaven or on earth could've convinced me to abandon her. Yeah, you had a lot of crap to work through, I got it. But once you did..."

She swallowed past the knot in her throat. "You knew what my mother was like, but you never even tried to find out if I was okay. On what planet is that *loving* me? So thanks, but no thanks."

Several seconds passed before her father pushed out a heavy sigh. "So I guess checking to see if you're okay now doesn't really count?"

She thought of Levi, everything he'd done for her and the girls in the name of making sure they were okay, and her heart twisted in her chest. "What do you think?"

"It was a long shot," her father said quietly, then stood as well, grabbing his hat off the seat. "You're married, then? I mean, if I can at least ask that much?"

Oh, dear God—could this conversation get any worse? Val took a moment to steady her breathing. "Was. My husband…was killed. In Afghanistan. Last year."

What looked like genuine sympathy flooded faded eyes. "Oh, honey, I'm so sorry." Val nodded, unable to speak. "And you said, um, you have a daughter?"

"Two, actually. Josie is seven, Risa isn't a year yet."

"So you're raising them on your own?"

"Not entirely, no," she said and left it there.

Silence jittered between them for several seconds before her father dug his wallet out again, this time extracting a ratty-looking business card, which he handed to her. Along with his name and cell phone number was a picture of him in rodeo clown getup. Under other circumstances, Val might've smiled.

"What with everything you've been through," Craig said softly, "the last thing you needed was me butting back into your life right now. I'm more sorry about that than I can say. And God knows I don't deserve anything from you. Especially forgiveness. Because you're right. What happened between your mother and me was a long time ago, and at some point I should've at least tried to make things right between *you* and me. That I didn't…there's no excuse for that. So I'm just grateful…" He cleared his throat. "That at least I got to see you again. Talk to you for a minute. But you keep that card," he said, tapping it. "And if, at some point, it seems right to tell those girls of yours about me…"

He screwed his hat back on his head. "You were the sweetest little girl," he said, his mouth tilted in a soft smile. "And I bet your daughters are, too. Well…" He hesitated, then nodded. "You take care, sweetheart. Okay?"

Then he walked away, nodding at Charley before he left. Frozen to the spot, Val watched through the window as her father got into his pickup and drove off. And she wondered, briefly, if it would've been worse, when she was little, to actually see him go, rather than waking up to discover he'd already gone.

Because she hadn't been entirely truthful about not remembering him. Not how he looked or sounded, maybe, but even now images played through, of sitting in his lap, of him carrying her piggyback. Of being hugged and kissed good-night.

Of feeling safe.

Annie slipped an arm around her waist. "How you doing, honey?"

"I have no idea," Val said, then left before she made more of a fool of herself than she already had. But the drive back to the house wasn't nearly long enough to sort out the million and one thoughts in her head. Except for two things that had become crystal clear in the space of the last few hours. One, that once again, a man was offering to plug up that hole in her heart.

And two, that she'd be ten kinds of fool to let him do that.

Levi and Josie were cleaning up the kitchen table when he heard the front door open. A moment later, Val appeared, looking as though she'd just had a run-in with the devil himself. Levi's heart bolted into his throat as Josie looked up, grinning, apparently oblivious to the wretched look on her mother's face.

"Me and Levi are making an album for Risa all about Daddy. With pictures and everything. So we won't forget him. Come look!"

"Really?" Val said, her smile brittle even as she pulled the girl to her side, gently shuffling some of the photos laid out on the table with her other hand. Not that there was much to look at yet. But Connie had given them a whole bunch of pics from when Tommy had been a kid, so Levi and Josie had spent the past hour or so sorting through them, choosing which ones to put in the album. "What on earth made you think of doing this?"

"It was Levi's idea. And we're all gonna write stuff to go with the pictures. Him and me and Gramma and Grampa. And you, if you want. Gramma says she's got this special paper, it'll last for years and years. Cool, huh? Oh, and Levi said we can print pictures off the phone, too. Right?" She flashed him another grin, then picked up a photo of Tommy from when they were in high school. "This one's my favorite." Her forehead crinkled. "You remember how he used to smile like that?"

Val cleared her throat, her eyes shiny. "I sure do, sweetie," she said, then pulled her daughter closer to kiss the top of her head. Same as he'd seen her do a thousand times. But not like this. Not as though the only thing keeping her from losing it was the feel of her child in her arms—

"Mama! You're squishing me!"

"Sorry, baby," Val said with a slight laugh, then let go, shifting her watery gaze to Levi. "Thank you."

His face warmed. "I know I probably should've asked you first—"

"Not at all. This..." She glanced at the pictures again, then smiled for her daughter. "I'm only sorry I didn't come up with it myself," she said, and Josie giggled right as the doorbell rang. The kid jumped up from the chair.

"That's probably Luisa from school. She asked earlier if I could go over to her house to play until dinnertime. She lives right down the street, so is it okay?"

"Of course. Go on—have fun."

A minute later, the door slammed again, and Val dropped into the chair Josie'd been sitting in, her head in her hands, looking like all the air'd been sucked out of her. Levi's chest cramped.

"I just thought the album would be a good way for Josie to work through some of the stuff about her dad—"

"The album's a great idea," she breathed out, lifting her head but not looking at him.

"Val?"

"Is Risa asleep?"

Levi handed over the monitor; Val's expression as she looked at the tiny image of the sleeping baby nearly did him in. "She went down an hour ago. Josie says she usually sleeps until almost five?"

"Yeah." Her gaze shifted to the window. "My father showed up at the diner."

"Your...? You're kidding?"

"Nope." She pushed out a tight little laugh. "Surprise."

"And...not a good one, I take it."

"What do you think?"

What he thought was that the woman needed another shock like a hole in the head. Also, that she was holding in her emotions so tightly she was probably close to erupting. He held out his hand. "Come here."

Val frowned at his hand, then got up to wrench open the patio door and walk out onto the deck, clutching the monitor as Radar bounded up to her like she'd been gone for three years. Levi followed, not even trying to guess what was going on in her head as she lowered herself to the deck's steps, letting the dog lather her face in kisses for several seconds before gently pushing him away. Behind them, a storm softly rumbled on the plains, probably headed in their direction. *In more ways than one,* Levi guessed as Val picked up a stray branch and threw it for the dog.

He sat beside her, apprehension knifing through him. Because whatever she was about to say, he was pretty sure he wasn't going to like it.

Val hauled in a breath, inhaling Levi's scent, that calm strength that was the very reason why she had to get these thoughts out of her head. Because she at least owed him that much.

"As I was sitting in Annie's," she finally said, "listening to my father tell me how sorry he was for basically abandoning me, a lot of old junk roared back to the surface. Junk I thought I'd sorted through years ago. Apparently not."

Radar sauntered back, prize clamped between his jowls. Levi tugged the stick free, tossed it again. This time the dumb dog plopped down in the grass to gnaw on it.

"What kind of junk?" Levi said quietly. Patiently. Val hugged her knees, as if to steel herself against his kindness.

"If my mother ever held and cuddled me, I don't remember. I do vaguely remember my father being affectionate, but of course he left. And after that...well, there was that dirtbag who felt me up, but that doesn't count."

"I should hope not."

She pushed out a dry laugh, then sighed. "Tommy was the first guy I ever trusted, you know? First *person*, actually. That I could remember, anyway. And suddenly I was *happy*. Up to that point I'd survived, sure. Made the best of things and all that. But with Tommy… I felt as though I'd awakened from a bad dream. And, man, was reality sweet."

A rain-scented breeze shuddered the leaves, making a loose piece of hair tickle her nose; she shoved it behind her ear. "But we were so young when we got married. And I was so naive. So…underdone. But after all those years of deprivation—emotional, physical, all of it—I finally felt it was okay to let myself feel, well, *safe*, I suppose."

"Isn't that how it's supposed to work?"

"Maybe for some people, but…"

"Not only for some people, Val. For everybody."

His anger on her behalf made her smile. "Only…" A sigh escaped her lungs. "Only because Tommy was everything I'd never had, everything I thought I needed, I totally missed that I wasn't everything to *him*. And even worse…" She somehow met Levi's concerned gaze. "The problem was his love didn't make me less needy. It made me *more*."

"For crying out loud, Val, cut yourself some slack. You said yourself you guys were so young—"

"Which would be my point. It doesn't take a degree in psychology to figure out I just transferred that need for what I was missing to Tommy. Except looking to other people—even people who brought you out of hell—to make you whole and safe and loved…it's a trap. Yes, it is," she said when he glanced away, shaking his head. "I don't dare let myself turn back into that needy teenager, Levi. Cripes, even as I watched my father take off a little bit ago, all I wanted was for him to hold me. As if that would somehow make everything okay."

Thunder rumbled. The wind picked up, hard enough to loosen a few leaves. The dog abandoned the stick to chase them, barking.

"And why are you telling me this, Val?"

Oh, dear God… What she heard in those few words nearly shredded her. "Because," she said, her eyes stinging, "I walked in the house, and there you were, working on that album with my little girl, and I saw how happy she was…and the m-more you do for us the m-more I feel—" The rest of the sentence lodged in her throat. She swallowed it down. "And *then* you say all this stuff about being anything I need you to be, and…*dammit*. Everything I've worked so hard for this past little while… No!" Her hands flew up. *"Don't touch me!"*

Levi backed off, but Val couldn't bring herself to look at him, see the hurt in his eyes. And she felt like crap warmed over. Especially when he said, very softly, "You do realize you're not making a whole lot of sense, right?"

She nearly laughed, even as she wiped her eyes. Then she sighed. "What I'm trying to say is, I'm still that needy girl who just wants…connection."

Several seconds passed before he said, on a long breath, "I see."

"Do you?"

"We are talking about sex, right?" She nodded. "Then I get it." He scrubbed a hand across his face, then linked it with his other one between his knees. "But what *you* don't get…" He frowned into her eyes. "Is that what I'm feeling? It's is about a helluva lot more than that."

"Levi…don't…"

"Don't what? Let you know what I'm thinking? How I really feel? Hey, you want honesty, here it is. Hell, yeah, I want to make love to you. *With* you. But that's not all I want. Not by a long shot. I don't only want you in my bed, Val—I want you in my *life*. Because I'm *in love with you*. Yeah. Deal. God knows that's not at all what I expected to happen when I came back. But it did, so it's way past time I own it, you know? What you do with that information…" He glanced out at the yard, then back at her. "That's up to you."

Her heart hammering, Val looked away. Away from

those eyes so full of promises. Promises she didn't have the courage to accept. A tear trickled down her cheek.

"I can't be what you want, Levi," she said softly. "What you deserve. Not that..." Oh, Lord. "Not that I don't want to, but I can't."

"Why?" he said gently, and she thought her heart would shatter.

"Because until I saw my father a little bit ago, I didn't realize how far I still have to go. How much growing I still need to do. For the girls' sake, especially. And even being around you... I'm terrified of getting sucked in again, into believing you'd keep me safe. Because that doesn't last, does it? It's...illusion."

He was quiet for a long moment, then blew out a breath. "And there's nothing I can say to convince you—"

"Of what?" she said, making herself meet his gaze. "That you won't change your mind down the road? That you won't *die on me*?"

A couple of fat raindrops splatted in the dirt in front of them. Another few seconds passed before Levi stood, then pushed out a dry, humorless laugh. "And here my biggest worry was you'd think of me as a substitute for Tommy."

"Oh, for God's sake..." Val shoved to her feet, as well. "This isn't about you. Or Tommy. Or anybody else, including my dysfunctional parents. It's about me getting my head on straight. I'm *scared*, Levi. Petrified, actually. And if I can't go into something freely, *happily*, then..." Her eyes filled. "How fair would that be to you?"

Levi held her gaze for another long moment before, with a nod, he walked off the deck. Except, when he reached the yard, he turned, frowning. A second later he climbed the steps again to winnow his fingers through her hair and lower his mouth to hers, probably tasting in her kiss all the fear and doubt and desire and confusion she'd balled up into one holy mess. Then he broke the kiss to tuck her against his chest, where his heartbeat slammed against her ear.

"In the interest of full disclosure?" he whispered, his cheek in her hair. "You're the only woman I've ever loved."

Then he left, and Val collapsed in a blubbering heap on the deck, barely aware of Radar's worried nudges as he circled her, whining.

Chapter Twelve

Along with shorter days and chillier nights, August brought with it one of the soggiest monsoon seasons in recent memory—the main topic of conversation in a town close enough to the forest to fully appreciate the blessings of a wet summer. Much to be said for not having to worry about your house burning down. Or choking on fire smoke. This was also the month for shopping trips for school supplies and new clothes and gearing up for Josie's birthday in September. How was it possible Val's little girl was almost eight?

The lunch rush had been even more rushed than usual, although Val wasn't complaining. Keeping busy was also a blessing. As were her girls. What was hard were the nights, after the girls were in bed and the house was dead quiet, and the dog and cat were her only company. She told herself the normalcy, the predictability and constancy, was what she wanted. What she needed to heal. That this was the choice she'd made and she was good with it. Relieved, even.

Until she'd be sitting on her sofa, trying to watch TV, and the memory of that kiss would assault her like a missile in some video game, and then she wasn't so sure.

Or, like now, when the crowd finally cleared enough for her to slip Charley his piece of pie—the gal up at the resort was still bugging her to sell to them, but since Val hadn't yet figured out how that'd work she kept putting her off—and she looked up to see Levi come through the door, toting a small cooler and a plastic shopping bag and grinning that grin of his that, let's face it, made everything quiver. Lord, spare her from the quivering. Worse, spare her from liking the man.

From missing him.

"Hey," he said softly, making a slow but deliberate beeline for her as a million *What the hells?* exploded in her brain.

"Um…hey?" she said back, ignoring the quivering. It wasn't as if she hadn't seen him at all since that conversation—and that kiss—but catching glimpses of him around town now and again was a whole lot different than his being practically a fixture in her house. Yeah, maybe the new Val knew she'd done the right thing, but the old Val—the whiny, needy Val—was sure she'd lost her mind.

She caught Annie giving her the eye—because she knew enough of the whole sordid tale to do that—before her boss turned her I-love-everybody grin on Levi.

"Hey, there, handsome. Sit anywhere you like—"

"Just came to see Val."

"Then she can sit with you. Yes, she can," she said to Val, and Levi chuckled.

"Now, Annie—you know she doesn't like to be pushed."

"Like that's gonna stop me? Ha!" Annie's saggy chins pleated when she lowered her head to glare at Val. "You wanna keep your job, girl?" She pointed to the booth. "Sit your skinny butt down and talk to the nice man."

Muttering, "A forest fire's got nothing on that woman," Val obeyed, only to smile at Levi's laugh.

"Man, I've missed that mouth," he said, clearly not realizing what he'd said as he plunked the cooler between them, stuffing the bag in the corner of the booth. Only then he met her gaze and winked, and she blushed and realized he'd probably never said anything by mistake in his life.

"What's in the cooler?" she said casually. As if it hadn't been weeks since they'd really seen each other, let alone had a normal conversation. As if her heart wasn't about to explode out of her chest. "Or maybe I shouldn't ask."

"Not a head, if that's what you're worried about. No, Josh and I went fishing this morning up at the ranch, caught a whole mess of trout. Thought you might like some. Don't worry, they're all cleaned, all you have to do is cook 'em up—" Then he frowned. "Do you even like trout?"

"Me? I love it. Josie probably won't touch it, but that only means more for me, right?" She hesitated. "Thank you."

"You're welcome. And it's all packed in ice. It'll be good for hours yet." Then he sucked in a breath. "So. How are you?"

What *was* the man about? "Good. You?"

His mouth tilted in a lazy grin. "You know, one of the problems with honest people is that they can't lie worth spit."

"Not to mention not knowing when to *leave* things lie." She swallowed. "Nothing's changed, Levi."

The smile softened. "Didn't figure it had. How're the kids?"

Val tucked her hands under the counter so he wouldn't

see how much they were shaking. "Um…they're great. Risa's trying so hard to walk—"

"You're kidding? Isn't that kind of young?"

"Eleven months. Not really. And Josie's gearing up for her birthday next month." Her cheeks heated. "She wants you to come."

"Wouldn't miss it." His eyes narrowed. "Unless Mama has an issue with that?"

Despite her flaming face—and sitting right next to the window, it wasn't as if he couldn't see—Val smiled and said, "Of course not—why would I?"

As it was, Josie asked nearly every day why they hadn't seen Levi, and when would they, and was there something wrong? And all Val could say was that he'd been busy, but she was sure they'd see him soon. Somehow, she doubted Josie was buying it.

"I have some news," Levi said quietly, jerking her back to the present.

"Oh?"

"Yeah. I've enrolled over at New Mexico Highlands for the next semester."

"What?" Was it surprising, how genuinely pleased she was? "That's wonderful! What in?"

He glanced at Charley reading a Louis L'Amour novel as he ate his pie, then back at Val before leaning over and lowering his voice. "Being around Charley, remembering my time in the service… I want to help. Somehow. Because I know what they've been through, right?" He straightened. "But I need to know *how* to help them. Besides just listening, I mean. And since Uncle Sam's good with paying my tuition…" He shrugged, then sighed. "Although it's been ten years since I did homework. And I wasn't exactly the best student. So it's kind of scary, frankly."

Val's eyes stung. "You'll do fine. Ohmigosh, I am so proud of you," she said softly, and the look on his face…

Oh, dear God. She could feel her resolve dissolving like sidewalk chalk in the rain. So good thing, then, he wouldn't be around much.

"You'll be living on campus, then?"

He frowned slightly. "Why? It's less than an hour from here."

"Not if you actually obey the speed limit, it isn't," she said, and he chuckled.

"I'm only on campus a couple days a week, two of my classes are online. So I'm not going anywhere."

"You're…staying in Whispering Pines."

The frown deepening, he looked at his folded hands, then back at her. "You know, when I got back home, I didn't know what the hell I wanted. What I was supposed to do with my life. So, yeah, I toyed with the idea of looking for something—although God knows what—'out there.' Turns out everything I need is right here. So… I bought a house."

"You what?" Clearly he wasn't giving her a chance to think too hard about that "everything I need" business. "Where?"

"That little adobe that went up for sale a couple of months ago, not far from Tommy's folks. Needs work, but I'm more than game."

Val knew the place. One of the rare real adobe homes in town. Cozy, was Realtor-speak for it. Lots of trees. Big yard. And "needs work" was a gross understatement.

"I wasn't, um, aware you were looking to buy a house."

His lips curved. "Meaning, how was I *able* to buy a house."

She blushed. "Well…yeah."

Levi glanced out the window for a moment, then back at her. "When our grandmother passed, years ago, she left each of us kids little nest eggs we couldn't touch until we were eighteen. Mr. Blake helped my father invest the money for us, in high-yield funds. What the others did with theirs, I have no idea. But I left mine alone. One of the few smart things I did back then, actually. Then I figured I might as well toss in a good chunk of my army wages, since it wasn't like I needed to spend them on much else. So the nest egg grew." He paused. "And I paid cash for the house."

"Wow. You have grown up."

Levi chuckled, then snapped his fingers. "Damn, don't know where my head is…" He reached for the bag, which he handed to her. "Happened to see this when I was out with Zach and his boys—thought immediately of you. Didn't have a clue about the size though, so I hope it's okay."

Giving him a puzzled look, Val removed the T-shirt from the bag and unfolded it, her eyes watering when she read what was on front.

I'm stronger than I thought.

The shirt was some hideous noncolor, and, yes, it was big enough to fit Levi, but…damn.

"Thank you," she whispered, fingering the lettering, then meeting his gaze. And his grin cracked her heart.

"You're welcome. Because it's true. Always has been." Then he got up, nudging the cooler toward her. "Enjoy the fish. Oh…and if you get a chance, maybe you could come by the house sometime, give me some ideas about what to do with it?"

"Me? You're the one with all the mad skills."

"Yeah, but I'm color-blind. Partially, anyway."

"You're kidding?"

"Nope. So's my dad. Josh dodged that particular bullet, but only because we're not identical. Anyway. Let me know when Josie's party is. I'll be there."

Val stayed in the booth after he left, clutching the soft shirt to her chest and staring at the cooler as if it were a crystal ball. Until Annie passed by and swatted her shoulder. "Customers," she said, and Val shook herself out of her stupor and got to her feet, only to run smack into Annie when she turned. "Also," her boss said, "you're an idiot."

"Love you, too," Val said, stuffing Levi's gifts under the counter before tromping over to table five to take their order, refusing to admit Annie might be right.

Josh's almost black brows practically collided as he glowered at the kitchen. Not that Levi blamed him. In the past week he'd done some painting and ripped up the tatty gold carpet, still flummoxed that people would cover the pretty pine floors. But the kitchen—while big and sunny—made the one in Tommy's grandmother's house look top of the line in comparison.

"Would somebody please tell me," his brother said, "how in the *hell* baby-poop green made it into the top ten colors of 1973?"

"Is that what color it is?" Levi said, reaching into the wobbly old fridge for a beer, handing one to his brother. "Green?"

"In a manner of speaking." Shuddering, Josh popped the tab before his eyes cut to Levi. "Val has no idea you bought the house with her in mind, does she?"

"Do I *look* like a man with a death wish?"

"You tell me. The woman rejected you, Levi—"

"What she rejected was a whole lotta crap from her past." He took a sip of his own beer. "Considering the mess *I* was? I can hardly blame her for that, can I?"

"I don't know, bro. Wouldn't it be better to just move on?"

"And why would I do that? When I'm right where I want to be?"

"Hoping some woman's gonna change her mind? Yeah, good luck with that."

He tilted the beer to his brother. "Hope's what makes the world go round. Look," he said when Josh shook his head, "the way I see it, my options are give up, press on or wait it out. So number three it is."

"I still think you're off your rocker."

"And you're entitled to your opinion. Doesn't mean I have to pay it any mind." Not that his brother was entirely wrong. Since even if he could eventually convince her he'd never walk out on her, he couldn't exactly guarantee he'd never die.

However. First things first.

One hand in his jeans' pocket, Levi shifted his weight against the counter. "Maybe I didn't go into the army for the best reasons, but it sure as hell made me grow. Learned more about myself in those six years than I had in the whole twenty-two before. Yeah, I still had—have—some fine-tuning to do, but by the time I got out I was at least beginning to get a handle on who I was, even if I still wasn't sure what I was supposed to *do*. Val never got that chance. She went from a borderline abusive situation into an early marriage, then became a mother soon after that…"

Frowning at the beer can, Levi huffed out a sigh. "The way I see it, this is her time to figure out who *she* is. What she really wants. So it's up to me to figure out the balance between being there for her and the girls and not getting in her face."

Josh crossed his arms. "Do you even know how she feels about you?"

He smirked. "Hell, I'm not even sure she knows how *she* feels about me. Not entirely. But I do know she's scared."

"Of what?"

"Best as I can figure out? Of letting herself be happy. Or at least, of trusting that it'll last."

"That's crazy."

"After what she's been through? Not as much as you might think."

"And do *you* really think she's worth the risk?"

"Do I honestly know if I'm doing the right thing? Not hardly. Maybe I am barking up the wrong tree. Except you know what? Once before, I gave up because…well, because I'd convinced myself I wasn't what she'd needed. Stakes are a helluva lot higher now. But what kind of choice am I giving her if I remove myself entirely from the equation? Kinda hard to convince her she can count on me if I'm not around to prove it. So I have to be patient."

"And I'm guessing she doesn't know about that, does she? That you had a thing for her way back when?"

"No."

"You think maybe you should tell her?"

"Why?"

His brother frowned at him for several seconds before blowing out a sigh. "I still don't get—"

"You don't see what I see, Josh. Yeah, she's doing a pretty hard-core battle with one big-ass bogeyman right now, but when she's not…" His jaw clenching, Levi glanced toward the kitchen window, then back at his brother. "You should see her with her kids. Tommy's parents. Hear how she worries about Charley. Woman's got a heart way too big for that little body. And if I could somehow get that heart to stop hurting…" He shrugged.

"And what if that never happens?"

Levi thought of that kiss. The look in her eyes when the kiss was over. When she spotted him in the diner the other day. Then again, he hadn't heard a peep from her since then. But the only way to be patient was to, you know, actually *be patient*.

"Then at least I'll know I tried," he said softly, before pushing himself away from the counter and out into the dining room, where all four walls were covered in nasty, peeling, Southwest geometric wallpaper that had nothing whatsoever to do with the baby-poop kitchen. He was guessing, anyway. "You any good at stripping wallpaper?"

"I have no idea."

"That makes two of us, then," Levi said, reaching up to tug at a curling corner. A whopping three inches came off in his hand.

"Let me guess," Josh said. "This is gonna take longer than you figured."

"Yeah, but it'll be worth it in the end."

"You hope," his brother muttered, and Levi was pretty sure they weren't talking about wallpaper anymore.

After a week, Val realized if she waited any longer to return the cooler she'd come across as either a lamebrain or a coward. Although at least taking the girls with her would prevent random pheromone/hormone interminglings between her and Levi. Or so she thought. Because soon as he opened his door—shirtless, damn him—she realized… nope. Not by a long shot.

Especially when he gave her—and the girls, let's be fair—one of those smiles that said there was nobody else he'd rather see.

"On our way to Connie and Pete's for dinner," Val said, her pulse banging in her throat. "Figured I might as well return the cooler while we're out."

"But you can come in for a minute? At least see the place?" This said while reaching for a babbly Risa with one hand, taking the cooler with the other.

"Um…sure. For a minute."

Mugging for the baby, Levi stood aside to let them in. Place looked like a bomb had gone off.

"Excuse the mess," he said, heading toward what she assumed was the kitchen. "Charley was over today helping me with the demo. We made real progress." He clunked the cooler on top of the counter. Which, along with the rest of the kitchen—except for the chewed-up dark cabinets—was kind of a slime green. "Although I don't suppose it looks like that to the casual observer. But the wall between the living and dining room? Had to go."

Still holding the baby, Levi smiled down at Josie, her forehead crimped as she surveyed the kitchen. The *huge* kitchen. With a *huge* window. And a skylight—

"Hey, kiddo. How's school?"

Her daughter grinned up at him. Her beaver-esque front teeth had finally finished their descent. Although at least they were straight. "It's only been a couple of days. But it's good. Second grade *rocks*. Mama says you're coming to my birthday?"

Levi turned that smile on Val, making her shiver underneath her sleeveless top, before focusing again on Josie. "I sure am. I remember when I turned eight, thinking *finally* I wasn't a little kid anymore."

"I know, right?" Then she slung her arms around Levi's waist to press her cheek into his stomach, her eyes squeezing shut. "I miss you, Levi."

Cupping the back of Josie's head with his free hand, Levi quietly said, "Miss you, too, little bit."

Just kill her now.

"Why don't you go check out the backyard?" he then said. "The previous owners left one of those play fort things."

"Cool!" Josie said, taking off through the French doors—*French doors!*—before Val even had a chance to yell at her to be careful.

"I already made sure it was safe," Levi said. "So my monkey nephews don't bust their heads or anything—"

"Bah!" Risa said, struggling to get out of Levi's arms.

"Nope, floor's not clean," Levi said, getting a firmer grip before pulling a box of graham crackers from a nearby cabinet. "This okay?"

"Go for it."

He handed the baby a quarter of a cracker; she happily settled in the crook of his elbow, gnawing. Somehow, Val tore away her gaze. "This kitchen sure is…green."

"See, I thought it was brown. So there you go."

"Some of that stuff you showed me for the other house would look good in here, I think."

"Actually, I was thinking of those Mexican tiles you liked. But you'd have to help me pick them so I don't end up with a bunch of weird colors."

"If it's only you living here, not sure what difference it would make. Unless you're thinking of resale value."

He got very quiet. The kind of quiet that makes a girl's heart pound. And makes her turn to watch her child playing outside. "Didn't buy the place to flip it," he said behind her. "Not planning on being the only one living here, either. Not forever, anyway. But in the meantime, seems to me this could be a real good setup for your pie business."

Val whipped around. Levi calmly handed the baby another piece of cracker.

"What?"

"Part of the reason I bought the house. Because of the kitchen. And don't worry, I already checked—got a list, in fact, of what we need to do in order to get it approved. Not easy, but definitely doable. Best news is, there's no limit on how much you can sell." He pointed to a space beside the sink. "Or how easy cleanup'll be with the top-of-the-line dishwasher that'll be right there. There's even plenty of room for AJ's stove, if you want. Or double ovens. Whatever would work best for you."

In the center of the room—right where, say, a good-size island might go—sat a pathetic Formica table and a couple of mismatched chairs. Onto one of these Val now sank, her emotions more tangled than Josie's hair after a restless night.

"Val? Look at me."

She finally did, sure that thunderbolts must be shooting out of her eyes.

"All I'm offering," he said gently, "is my kitchen. Since it seems a shame to waste such a big space on me maybe boiling a hot dog now and then. Making some toast—"

"Levi, I don't need—"

"You need a kitchen. I can give you a kitchen. Heck, maybe that's the only thing I can give you, to say…thanks."

"For what?"

He glanced out the window over the sink, then turned back to her. "You know the real reason Tommy joined the army?"

"Yes. Because he wanted me to feel proud of him."

"Yeah, but…it was more than that. Because he wanted to feel like he mattered, too. Like he had a purpose. I couldn't talk him out of it, no. But he told me that if *you'd* said no, he wouldn't've gone."

Her eyes filled. "And what right did I have to do that?"

Still holding the baby, Levi came closer to crouch in front of her; still gumming her cracker, the baby threw herself into Val's arms. "The truth?" he said gently. "You had every right. I'm not sure he ever knew how scared you were. Because you never let him see it, did you?"

Unable to speak, she wagged her head again. Levi smiled. "Of the two of you," he said softly, "I'm gonna say you were the braver one. So don't tell me you don't deserve something for that."

What the hell makes you think you deserve *anything, little girl? Like you're somebody special. Like you're better than your mama? Well, here's a news flash—you're not…*

Nausea roiled as the words oozed through her, oily and hot. Words she'd thought couldn't affect her anymore. As though trying to shake herself free from her mother's voice, Val shifted the baby to heave herself out of the chair.

"Meaning a kitchen?" she said, realizing looking at Levi made the nausea worse.

"Meaning a *future*," he said, standing as well to slug his fingers into his pockets. "One of your own making, finally. And maybe a little peace to go along with it?"

Peace? As if. Because when Val looked into those eyes, sure as hell *peaceful* was the last thing she felt.

Because sure as hell he was still offering a lot more than a kitchen.

And sure as hell she still wasn't sure which frightened her more—turning that offer down, or accepting it.

No, what scared the bejesus out of her was how much she *wanted* to accept it.

"Can I think about it?" she said, annoyed at how small her voice sounded.

"Absolutely. No rush." Levi touched her shoulder, forcing her to meet his gaze. "And no pressure, I swear. Totally up to you."

Nodding, she opened the glass-paned door, called Josie. "We're leaving, sweetie."

The kid came bouncing inside, out of breath and grinning. "C'n I come here again?"

"Anytime you like," Levi said.

Of course he would walk them outside, watching while Val strapped Risa into her stroller, then as they walked away, a hopping/skipping/bouncing Josie wriggling around to give him a last wave when they reached the sidewalk. Val, however, refused to look back, to see all those questions she couldn't answer in those kind, sexy eyes.

She was pretty sure she'd never be able to breathe properly again.

Levi slammed his hand against the gross laminate counter with enough force to make the coffeemaker rattle. *Idiot.*

Not that he hadn't meant what he'd said. All of it. But clearly he'd jumped the gun, hoping the past few weeks would've given her a little more perspective, stupidly taking encouragement from what he'd seen in her eyes, heard in her voice a week ago in the diner. Only, what he'd seen just now—leaking out from the edges of her bravado—was a woman every bit as stressed and rattled as any soldier returning from deployment. Or still in the middle of it, actually.

And dammit, he'd known better than to poke the bear of her stress, even in the guise of being helpful. Of *loving* her, of wanting to fix whatever was broken, *because* he loved her. Except judging from the look on her face, that fact that she hadn't even said goodbye…he'd blown it.

Releasing a harsh, lung-stinging breath, Levi could practically hear Josh's *told you so.*

Chapter Thirteen

"Okay," Connie said, stretching plastic wrap over the leftover enchiladas before sliding them into the fridge. "What's up?"

Val pushed out a sound that sounded more like a strangled cat than a laugh. "Why do you—"

"Because you barely touched your dinner. So unless you've been lying to me all these years about how much you love my enchiladas…" One eyebrow lifted.

Fortunately—or unfortunately, Val wasn't sure which—the girls were in the family room with their papa, watching some kids' movie. And Tommy's grandmother had excused herself to sit outside and watch the sunset, as she did every night. Leaving Val alone with her mother-in-law.

Who knew full well how much Val loved her enchiladas.

But before she could figure out what to say, Connie said, "So what's going on with you and Levi these days?"

Val stuck the last glass in the dishwasher, loaded it.

Turned it on. Stood for a moment, listening to the whoosh of water filling the machine.

Thought about that kitchen.

The half-naked man standing in the middle of it, holding her child, offering her…

So much.

Then Connie touched her arm and, yeah. Waterworks.

Muttering in Spanish, the older woman steered Val into the living room, a pristine testimonial to Southwest kitsch, making Val sit on the peach-and-aqua-patterned couch.

"Well?"

Val blew her nose. Sniffed. "Apparently a major reason Levi bought the house was so I could use the kitchen. For my pies."

"Gee, that'd make me cry, too."

She sniffed again. Skunk's sister jumped up on her lap, purring. "Yeah, well, this isn't only about his kitchen."

"Didn't figure it was," Connie said, clearly amused. "And does Levi know how you feel?"

"I didn't say—"

"*Querida.* Seriously?"

Groaning, Val sank back into the sofa's cushions, thinking about how, for so long, this had been her safe place when her own home hadn't been. That it didn't feel even remotely safe now. Especially when Connie said, "What are you so afraid of, sweetheart?"

The baby cat's fur was so soft, so soothing, under her fingers as Val stroked her, gathering her courage. Then she looked over at Connie, the patience and love she saw in her mother-in-law's eyes making hers sting. "Everybody thinks I was so…noble, I guess you'd call it. The proud military wife and all that. But the thing is, I hated it. Hated being left to raise Josie on my own, hated that… that Tommy yanked the *one* thing I'd wanted my entire life out from under m-me. And most of all, I hated that I felt so…so selfish. Like my m-mother."

"Oh, honey…" Connie practically jumped out of her chair to sit beside Val, wrapping an arm around her shoulders and squeezing, hard. "First off, do not ever let me hear you compare yourself to your mother again, you hear me? God rest her soul, but that woman's got some serious atoning to do wherever she is now. And second…" She sat back to gently stroke Val's hair away from her face. "If you really didn't want Tommy to go, why didn't you say something?"

"Because that *would* have been selfish—"

"Then call me selfish, too, because I felt exactly the same way. Sure, I was proud of him. Doesn't mean I wasn't mad as hell when he died. At him, at the army, at the bastard who planted that bomb. And I'm not seeing me getting over that anytime soon. But I'm not sure I understand what any of that has to do with you and Levi."

"Because maybe I *don't* deserve happiness. Maybe nobody *deserves* it, maybe happiness is totally random, this elusive thing that happens to some people and not others. I don't know. Here I've barely gotten my balance back after Tommy—"

"And you're scared of losing again."

Val took a moment, absorbing. Accepting the last piece of truth she hadn't wanted to face. "I don't think I could stand it. Not again. And Josie…"

"You're afraid Levi's going to leave you?"

"No." Val almost smiled. "*No.* But…stuff happens, doesn't it?"

"I see. So you've decided to let evil win?"

Val frowned at her mother-in-law. "I think it's more that I've decided to not give it that chance."

"And if that isn't the biggest load of crap I've ever heard, I don't know what is. Yeah, you're right. Happiness can be elusive. Seems like it, anyway. Which is why we've got to grab it when we find it, and then hang on with everything we've got. Doesn't matter how long the ride lasts, what matters is enjoying the hell out of it while we're on it. Because guess what? You do deserve to be happy. Just like everybody else on the planet. And would you deprive the girls of *their* shot at happiness? Of a *father*?"

"Dammit, Connie—do not guilt me—"

"So I'm guessing you don't know the whole story."

"What whole story?"

"That Levi loved you first."

"Excuse me?"

"Then you really had no idea that Levi had more or less appointed himself your guardian angel when you guys were still in school? That when he heard the other kids talking smack about you, he'd sometimes…intervene. That his mother got called to the principal's office more than once on your account."

"On my—"

"So Levi got something of a reputation as a hothead, even though I don't think he ever actually hurt anybody. Scared the pants off 'em a few times, though. But the thing is…if it hadn't been for Levi, I'm not sure Tommy would've given you a second look."

Her head was spinning. "And Tommy never…?"

Connie chuckled. "Sixteen-year-old boys aren't exactly known for their critical thinking skills. And Tommy told *us* that Levi said he was only sticking up for you because it was the right thing to do."

"Then why would you think there was anything more to it than that? It wasn't like Levi didn't have other girlfriends—"

"If you can call them that. And only after you and Tommy started going together. Not to mention Levi never put his butt on the line like that for anybody else. Think back, *querida*. Am I right?"

So she thought. And…hell. The woman was right. At this rate Val's head was going to explode.

Not to mention her heart.

"So Tommy really never knew?"

"That his best friend got out of his way to give him a chance with you? I really don't think he did."

"But why?"

"My guess? Because Levi believed being with him would've had exactly the opposite effect from what he was trying to defend you from. What with that hothead business and everything." Connie reached for her hand, holding it in both of hers. "But the result was…it gave us *you*." The older woman's eyes glittered. "The best daughter we could've asked for. Is it any wonder why we love Levi almost as much as we loved our own boy?"

Val slumped back against the sofa cushions, the sudden move dislodging the kitten, who gave her back paw a fast lick before streaking out of the room.

"Sweetheart," Connie said softly, "you're the one always on about choices. So don't you think you should have all the information possible to help you make those choices?"

Yeah, she knew that was gonna come back to chomp her on the butt someday. Her gaze slid to Connie's.

"So why didn't you tell me this sooner?"

"Because I was hoping you and Levi would've worked this out by now. Since you haven't…" Connie shrugged. "And so help me, God, do not tell me you feel like you'd be cheating on Tommy."

Despite her exploding head, Val had to laugh. "No. Well, okay, a little, maybe. But…"

She told her the condensed version of what she'd said to Levi, about how little physical affection she'd gotten as a child. And where that had led, with Tommy. And now, with Levi…

"I mean…am I just repeating history? How do I even know if this is real?"

"Man, you are one messed-up *chica*—you know that?"

"You're only now figuring this out?"

Connie chuckled. "Listen to me. What you had with Tommy, that was real. And I think you know it. Yes, despite all the garbage from your childhood. So why wouldn't this be real with Levi?"

"Because I'm one messed-up *chica*?"

"And what does that say about that young man, that in spite of that he hasn't given up on you? Not this time, anyway. Okay, so he had issues when he was younger. Issues that in large part stemmed from how he felt about *you*. Issues that made him the good man he is now. Do you really want to throw that away just because you're scared of what *might* happen? Is that what you want for your daughters, to be afraid to trust their hearts— *Dios mio*, what was that?"

What that was, was a very loud sneeze from a very small person.

Who, Val was guessing, had just gotten an earful.

Crap.

"Josie?" Mama called. "Get your little behind out here!"

Abuelita, who'd been hiding out in the hallway with Josie, held out her hand for Josie to take before slowly leading her into the living room. At the beginning, Josie'd only meant to come see what Mama and Gramma were doing, since Grampa had fallen asleep with the baby on his chest, and it was kind of a dumb movie, anyway. But something about their voices had made her stop, even though she knew she wasn't supposed to listen without them knowing she was there. Not that she understood everything they were saying, but she got most of it. All she knew, was that it sucked, almost never seeing Levi anymore, and that Mama was back to being sad all the time. And you know what? Josie was really, really tired of all the gloom and doom, like Mama would say. Seriously—

Mama's mouth dropped open. "Lita! You, too?"

"You should listen to Consuela," Abuelita said to Mama, like she didn't see how surprised she was. Or care, maybe. "Because I know you are not a fool." Still holding on real tight to Josie's hand, Abuelita bent over to lay her other hand on Mama's cheek. "What you are, little one, is brave. So brave." Abuelita smiled. "Like a warrior."

"That's right," Josie said, even though her knees were shaking a little. Mama didn't get mad a whole lot, but when she did…watch out. "You are." But instead of fussing at her, Mama's eyes got all wet.

"Oh, baby…" She pulled Josie into her lap, wrapping her up tight in her arms from behind as Abuelita kinda fell on the sofa to put her arm around Mama's shoulders. Across from them, Gramma looked like she was holding her breath.

"Blessings and fear," Josie heard Abuelita say, "are like light and darkness. They cannot live in the same place." Josie liked the sound of that, even if she didn't completely understand it. "So, *preciosa*," her great-grandmother said, "which will you choose?"

Mama got very still, holding Josie close. And it was like Josie could feel something change, in the room. In Mama. Especially when she blew out a breath that tickled Josie's curls.

"So, Lita," Mama said, very softly. "If I didn't want to stay in the house…?"

Abuelita laughed. "It was only there to use as long as you needed it. If you don't anymore…"

"But I never did finish up the kitchen—"

"That's what contractors are for," Gramma said, winking at Josie. Then she smiled at Mama. "Go, honey. Grab your future. Now. Before you chicken out."

"As if you'd let me."

"You got that right," Abuelita said, and all the grown-ups laughed.

Then everybody got real quiet for a long time, until Mama said, "Okay," on a great big breath, then gently slid Josie off her lap. Only then she turned her around and looked deep into her eyes, so it was like they were the only two people in the room. "Do you really like Levi, baby?"

"Are you kidding?" Josie said, wondering where on earth *that* question had come from. "I love him. He makes me feel...safe."

"Oh, yeah?" Mama said, her eyes getting all watery again.

"Yeah. And good." She giggled. "He's so funny."

Mama smiled. "Yes, he is. But he's not Daddy, you know."

Josie frowned. "Of course he isn't. He's Levi. Isn't that good enough?"

Blinking like a million times as she brushed curls off Josie's shoulder, Mama nodded. "Absolutely." Then she turned to Gramma. "The kids...?"

"Like you have to ask. Go, for God's sake." But after Mama picked up her purse and stuff, Josie thought of something.

"Mama?"

She turned back around. "Yeah, baby?"

"You know Daddy wants us to be happy, right?"

"Oh, jeez..." Mama grabbed Josie in a hug so hard it almost hurt, then held her face in her soft hands. "You have any idea how much I love you?"

Josie grinned. "Maybe," she said, and Mama laughed.

Then she was gone, and Josie let out a great big breath. Because this time, she was *sure* everything was going to be okay.

She could feel it in her heart.

* * *

A surprise thunderstorm had released its fury barely five minutes before Levi opened his door to a soaking-wet Val, her hair, clothes, everything, clinging like seaweed to her skin.

"I hope to hell you're alone," she said before he could find his voice, "because otherwise this could be awkward."

"Uh…" Slowly, his lips curved, even as his heart started beating like crazy. "Yeah."

"Good," she said, walking into his arms, rain pummeling the porch roof as he kissed her, over and over, half-afraid to stop. Like if he did he'd discover this was only a dream. Still, she had to be freezing in that clammy shirt.

So, in between mumbled explanations about the kids being with the Lopezes and her having stopped at the house to let the dog out and change, so she didn't have any place else she needed to be, he tugged her into the bedroom where he'd gotten a fire going in the kiva fireplace, tucked into the far corner. An air mattress, an old dresser… It wasn't much. But right now, the two of them and a fire and a mattress—it was enough.

Actually, what it was, was heaven.

Wasn't until he grabbed the shirt's hem that he realized what she was wearing. Damn thing hung to the middle of her thighs. "You're right—this is way too big."

"I'm thinking I might have to grow into it," she said, smiling, before she shivered, making her nipples poke at the damp fabric. With that, he tugged the soggy thing up and over her head, tossing it to one side, catching just enough of a glimpse of small, perfect breasts to get him hard before he wrapped her up in a towel he'd tossed on the mattress earlier. Then he kissed her again, one of those long, deep, kinda messy ones that went on forever, and she moaned and wrapped her hands around his neck to stand on tiptoe, and he remembered what she'd said, about liking sex, and he thought, *Well, all right.*

But…

"You sure?"

"Didn't come over to look at paint swatches. And, yes, I'm protected," she said, and like *that* they were both naked and on the bed, pretty much feasting on each other, the heat from the fire licking her dry as he licked her wet all over again.

"Oh, yes," she breathed, eyes closed, clutching the sheets. Toes probably curled, too, but he was too busy to check. Then he took things up a notch, and she laughed, and arched, and cried out—begged, actually—her hands now all tangled in his hair as he teased her some more, smiling to himself at her cute little noises, the change in her breathing as she got closer—

Then thunder cracked, loud enough to rattle the windows, and she shrieked, startled. Laughing, Levi shifted positions.

"Damn," she said, "now we have to start over."

"Not a problem," he said, placing a kiss on that delectable spot where neck meets shoulder. She shivered. And sighed. Especially when he started south again. Belly button. Hip bone. Lower. "Trust me," he said between kisses, "it'll be all the better for waiting."

"But you—"

"You complaining?"

"No, but—"

He hiked himself back up to palm her breast, flicking one thumb over that adorable little nipple. Her breathing hitched. He chuckled. "What can I say? I'm a giver. Now hush and let me give."

"Jeez, *fine*," she said, her eyes drifting closed, and the next few minutes were filled with a symphony of rain and thunder, the hiss and crackle of the fire, her moans and gasps and soft, sweet laughter…and then her cries as she sailed over the edge. But before the cries had even died out she'd flipped him on his back and taken him inside her, her messed-up, half-dry hair curtaining her shoulders, her breasts, glowing gold in the firelight.

Her lips, all puffy and red, curved slightly as she splayed warm, soft hands on his chest. "Hey. I'm a giver, too," she said, which was when Levi realized the glow was actually coming from someplace inside her. His eyes burning, he touched her hair, moving it off her shoulder to expose one breast. The nipple perked up, inviting. He tugged her closer, accepting.

"You kicked fear's ass?" he whispered around it.

"Working on it," she said, and he laid back down to hook her gaze in his, soft in the firelight. He threaded his fingers through her hair, afraid to say the words. Tears collected in the corners of her eyes.

"Same here," she murmured, bending to kiss him.

For a long time afterward they lay in silence underneath his comforter, wrapped in each other's arms and listening to their breathing, the dying fire's muffled hisses, the *plop-plop-plop* from dripping *canales* jutting out from the house's flat roof.

"I thought," Levi finally said, "when you left—"

"I know."

"So what happened?"

She softly laughed. "I was ganged up on."

"By?"

"Three generations of Lopez women. Lita. Connie. My own daughter." She softly chuckled. "I didn't stand a chance." Only then she sighed.

"That sounds ominous."

Val hitched onto one elbow to meet Levi's gaze, shivering a little when he stroked her bare back. "I'm here because I want to be—"

"Glad to hear it—"

"No, wait…" She palmed his chest, feeling his heart beat. "I'm still sorting through a *lot* of junk in my head."

His gaze gentling so much it hurt, Levi sifted trembling fingers through her hair. "It'd be weird if you weren't. But we can work through it together. Okay?"

Nodding, she lay back down, reveling in his scent, his feel. His solidity. "You know the real reason I didn't try to stop Tommy from going into the army?" Her hand knotted on Levi's chest. "I was scared to death if I didn't let him go, I'd lose him, anyway. His love, I mean."

A second or two passed before Levi said, "That wouldn't've happened."

"You don't know that. And for sure I didn't. Not then. And even now…" She listened to that steady heartbeat under her ear, drawing strength from it. "All my life," she said quietly, "I thought if I could somehow be whoever somebody wanted me to be, say whatever they wanted to hear, they wouldn't leave. And not only did that not work…" She waited out the sting of tears. "The only person I really lost was myself. *Not* a legacy I want to leave to my girls."

Levi wrapped her up more tightly, kissed her temple. "Good for you," he whispered, and she smiled, only to sigh again.

"Yeah, well, I'm a work in progress. Maybe in some ways I *am* stronger than I thought I was, but it's always going to be a struggle for me to find that balance, I guess, between supporting someone else and sticking up for myself. For *my* needs."

"And that right there is why I love you."

"Because I'm screwed up?"

That got a soft laugh. "Hell, who isn't? But not everyone has the cojones to admit it. Let alone—" his chest rose with his breath "—to *face* their fears. As far as legacies go, that's a pretty damned good one. However, since we're on the subject..."

At the change in his tone, Val shifted to meet his gaze. Still gentle but dead serious. "What I said, about Tommy being grateful for your support, was absolutely true. At the beginning, anyway. What I didn't say was that as time went on I think he began to question his decision. Only by then he didn't feel he could back out and save face."

"Save face? With whom?"

"You. So, see, he was as conflicted as you were. And he felt guilty as hell about it. Something even my dad picked up on."

Her brow puckered, Val watched the fire for several seconds, barely feeling Levi stroking her hair, her shoulder. "And since we weren't honest with each other..."

"Exactly."

Tears welled in her eyes. "So you think that's why he made you promise?"

"Maybe."

On a soft groan, Val sat up, tugging the comforter up over her breasts and wrapping her arms around her knees. "This has to be the strangest post-sex conversation ever."

Behind her, Levi quietly chuckled. "I somehow doubt that."

"Yeah, well, it's about to get stranger." She looked back over her shoulder at him. "Connie said you had a thing for me when we were in school. That you never told Tommy."

His fingers bumped down her spine. "I wasn't right for you, Val. Not then."

"So it's true?"

He nodded, and she laughed.

"What's so funny?"

"As it happens, I had a little crush on you, too. Before Tommy, obviously."

"You're kidding?"

"Nope. Until I realized you were way too much like the creeps my mother hooked up with."

"Oh, that's low," he said, then sighed. "Although not far from the truth."

"Actually," she said quietly, "it's about as far from the truth as it gets, apparently. Since according to Tommy's mother you regularly defended my honor."

His expression was priceless. "She told you that?"

"Yep. Oh, and then there's the small issue of you stepping aside for your best friend. What a jerk. Seriously."

Then she looked away again, hugging her knees more tightly. Several beats passed before Levi said, very softly, "Hey. You okay?"

She pushed out a little laugh. "I want to be—how's that? I really do want to move past the fear. Past…the past."

Levi sat up beside her, big and solid and *good*. "And I'd say you're well on your way," he whispered, kissing her shoulder. "You're safe now, honey. You can't lose me, not as long as I have breath. No matter what you say, or do, or think. Because there's no way I'm stepping aside this time, for anything or anybody. And I won't let you lose yourself."

She blinked back tears. "Promise?"

"Promise. Because what I saw back then was only a glimpse of who you are now. A woman who…" He swallowed. "A woman I'd be so damn proud to have by my side, I can't even tell you."

"Well, hell," she said.

"Yeah. Deal."

Way in the distance, the train whistle blew. Val snuggled closer, smiling when Levi draped an arm around her shoulders. Then his fingers closed around her left wrist. Oh, right.

"Where—"

"In my jewelry case. With my wedding ring." Which she'd taken off weeks ago, before it *fell* off. "Although I might let Josie put the bracelet in the album. If she wants to."

After a moment, she angled her head to look up at him again. "So why did you enlist?"

That got a soft laugh. "Your brain definitely works in strange ways."

"Believe it or not, there was a thread. The bracelet… Tommy…the army…you. Well?"

"I told you—"

"I know. But it keeps coming to me—" she kissed his hand "—that there's something more."

His fingers traced back and forth across her skin. "Because I was running away."

"From?"

He hesitated, then said, "Seeing how happy you and Tommy were."

"Oh, Levi…" Her heart cramped. "Really?"

"Crazy, right?"

"Probably," she said gently, leaning into him again. "Not to mention drastic."

"I needed to take my head someplace different," he said quietly. "Someplace I couldn't…" A breath left his lungs. "Wouldn't be tempted to think about you. As tempted, anyway. About what I'd let go. And, yes, I know what I said, every bit of which I believed at the time. Still do, to some extent. Didn't mean I didn't regret the hell out of it." He stroked her jaw, making her shiver. "I'd convinced myself I'd forgotten you. Biggest lie I've ever told myself. Because I've loved you since I was sixteen years old."

Enough to let her go, she thought, her eyes stinging.

Just as he'd loved both her *and* Tommy enough to get himself out of the way so they could find each other, when *each other* was exactly what they'd needed at the time. No matter what came later.

"And you had no idea what you were really getting into, did you? With the army, I mean."

He got very quiet again. "Not really, no."

"Was it hell?"

"Sometimes."

"Will you tell me about it someday?"

After a moment, he nodded. "Yes."

"Promise?"

"I'll try—how's that? Although…it wasn't all bad. I learned I had a lot more to offer than I thought. Like that I really get off on helping people."

"Ya think?"

He chuckled, then sighed. "I know *I* can't make you happy, Val. Or get rid of the fear for you. Only you can figure out how to do that. But I sure as hell want to be there when you do. Which I know you will, because you are one awesome lady."

"Oh, Levi…" Her eyes burning, Val palmed his cheek. "And you are one awesome dude." She smiled. "Well, now, anyway. According to Connie, it was touch and go for a while there."

Laughing, he shifted them so she was flat on her back again, kneeing her legs apart. About a million hormones released happy little sighs. "No doubt my parents would agree with you on that."

"Maybe we should stop talking about our parents now."

"Good point," he said and kissed her. And it was very good.

As in, off the charts.

Then she framed his face in her hands, smiling into his eyes. "You do realize the only other man I ever did this with, I married?"

His chuckle rumbled through all sorts of interesting places. "One helluva gauntlet you just threw down there."

"Yep. I want you in my life, too, Levi. And I know..." She swallowed. "I know Tommy would've wanted me to be happy. To be afraid of that—of taking chances—isn't exactly honoring the man who was all about taking chances, is it?"

"No," Levi said softly. "It isn't. One thing, though..." His face went all stern. "Whatever choices we make, about anything, we make together. None of this suffer in silence crap. Unless the other person willingly concedes to the other. Like, say, on wall colors. 'Cause even if I could see them, I probably wouldn't care." When she laughed, he said, "And if you don't like the house? Consider it sold. We can pick out something together."

Her eyes pricked. "But you love it—"

"More than you? Not a chance. Sweetheart," he said so gently she teared up all over again, "the only thing that matters to me about the house, *any* house, is whether you and the girls are in it with me. That it's someplace where the past can't hurt you anymore. Although that would be tricky, since it's gonna have to get through me first."

Aching for him, Val linked her hands around the back of his neck. "And would that be you picking up that gauntlet?"

His gaze softened. "Shoot, I caught that thing before it even hit the ground. I know this is crazy, but...marry me, Val. Whenever you're ready—no rush. But even before that, let me be whatever I can be for you. For those little girls. Because I love them every bit as much as I love you—"

"Yes," she whispered. "To all of it. Because I love you, too, you big goof."

The look in his eyes slayed her. "Say that again."

"I love you." She touched her forehead to his. "I *love* you."

Smiling, he kissed her nose. "Thank you."

"Anytime."

Then he grinned, that same wicked grin that used to make her roll her eyes, that always meant he was up to no good. Now, however, what she saw behind that grin was a man who knew what he was about…a man who would love her girls every bit as much as Tommy had. And who would never let them forget their father. How could she *not* love this man? How could she not trust him?

Or more to the point, trust that being with him would make her the best *herself* she could be?

"So," Levi said, his hand sliding down over her waist, her hip, "should we seal the deal?"

"Sounds like a plan," she said, smiling, embracing her future with her whole heart.

Epilogue

"Josie! Stay where we can see you! And don't get too close to the water!"

Not much more than a speck in the distance, the girl waved to them from the riverbank as Radar barked his own reply. Levi smiled—what with the water being friskier than usual after the latest storm, he couldn't half blame Val for the mama bear routine. But still. They weren't talking the Amazon.

"You sure this is the spot?" Strapped to his back, Risa babbled away. To what, God only knew.

"Enough." Val glanced up at the small mobile home park, at the half-dozen dingy trailers hugging the bluff. The second stop on their little field trip on this cloudy morning. She squinted out toward the river, then pointed, her eyes lighting up. "That's it—that's the outcropping."

Pushing through a clot of overgrown salt cedars hugging the river's edge, Val stopped a yard or so from the water. Above them, a mature cottonwood lazily embraced the patchy sky, glowing against the somber clouds. He knew it was supposed to be green, but since he didn't really know what *green* was, he had no choice but to accept its beauty as he saw it. And that was just fine with him.

"My mother wasn't exactly a big fan of nature," Val said quietly over the gurgling river, hugging closed a heavy-weight hoodie. "But I remember her bringing me here in the evenings during the summer, when I was little. Especially after my father left. And she'd go out there—" she nodded toward the flat rocks several yards out from the shore "—and just…stand there, looking up at the sky."

"Praying?"

"I somehow doubt it. But I think she found peace. As much as she could, anyway."

"You want me to wait here?"

"Please? Keep an eye on Josie?"

"Sure."

Carefully, she navigated the slippery rocks until she came to the biggest, flattest one. Then she took a moment, her eyes closed, before opening the small cardboard box to dump the ashes into the swirling current, and Levi's chest cramped.

The past week had been a whirlwind of planning and talking and, yes, lovemaking…and more talking. So much talking, sorting through their thoughts and feelings as much as their things. Much to his relief, Josie had been thrilled at the idea of Levi's becoming her stepdaddy, although she hadn't yet decided what she should call him. He'd reassured her it was completely up to her. So far, Dad seemed to be winning. Since, she'd said, she was already too big for "daddy," and anyway, that's what she'd called Tommy, so…

He doubted she had any idea how pleased he was.

And he and Val had decided to forgo a big wedding in favor of a quick—and cheaper—one, to be held out at the ranch in the next month or so, before it got too cold. Instead they decided to concentrate on fixing up the house, getting the kitchen up to snuff so she could have her pie business in full swing by the start of ski season. Honestly, he didn't think he'd ever met a more focused human being…or, now, a happier one. Except, perhaps, for himself.

But after dinner the other night at Lita's house—which, with her blessing, would go on the market as soon as she and girls moved in with him after the wedding—Val had said that as much as she was all about looking forward, she still needed to tidy up a few things from her past.

So they'd started by taking the girls to see where she'd grown up. The lot was surprisingly pretty, surrounded by pines and aspens with a pretty decent mountain view. None of the disintegrating mobile homes were occupied, though, and a For Sale sign proclaimed the owner's intention. Levi imagined he'd get a pretty penny for the lot.

Val had walked up to the trailer through foot-high weeds, looking up at it as she laid her hand on the pock-marked siding. There'd been no discernible expression on her face, except maybe of relief. As though the memories had finally lost their hold over her.

He'd no idea, either, she'd had her mother's ashes. He could only imagine how freeing that must've been, too, finally letting them go. But what Val said—and what had touched him so deeply—was that, actually, it was her *mother* she was freeing, from all the hurt and negative thoughts Val had been carting around inside her own head for so long.

She came back up onto the bank with the empty carton, folded flat.

"Any plans for that?"

"Dunno." She frowned at it, then smiled. "It's biodegradable, though, so…maybe shred it, use it as mulch for a rosebush at the house?"

"Sounds good."

Josie and the dog ran toward them, both panting. "Can we get lunch now? I'm *starving*."

Val chuckled. "In a minute, baby. Okay?"

"'Kay," the kid said, flashing a grin at Levi as she bounded off again, arms flailing, and he loved her so much it hurt. Releasing a breathy laugh, Val looked out at the water, determinedly chugging south. "Thought I'd call my father a little later."

"You don't have to do everything at once, you know. There's no rush."

"No, it feels right. And I want him to meet you. And his granddaughters."

"You sure?"

She paused, then said, "Whether he'll ever be a real part of my life again, I have no idea. But I'd like him to know that you are." Her eyes lifted to his, the light in their pale depths turning him inside out. "Thank you for not giving up on me. On us."

Levi wrapped an arm around her shoulders, pulling her close. "Wasn't even a possibility."

And it hadn't been, he realized, from the moment he'd seen her again. Because that purpose he'd been looking for? She and the girls were it. His whole reason for returning to Whispering Pines. And definitely his reason for staying there, he thought as Josie ran back and he hauled her up into his arms.

"Levi! For heaven's sake," Val said, laughing. "You've already carrying the baby!"

"It's okay," he said, grinning into Josie's eyes. "I can handle it."

Linking her hands behind his neck, Josie grinned back at him, then leaned close to whisper, "You kept your promise, huh? To Daddy?"

His eyes stinging, Levi kissed the top of her head.

"You bet," he whispered back just as the clouds parted. And call him crazy, but Levi could have sworn he felt his friend's smile in the sunbeam that washed over them—

"Ohmigosh, Levi! Look! Across the river!"

Levi squinted at where Val was pointing, catching a glimpse of a bright purple lowrider bumping along the road on the other side, playing peekaboo with the trees.

Laughing, his arms—and heart—full, Levi looked up at the sky and winked.

* * * * *

'So, do you always go to bed so early?' The moment she had the words out a deep blush bloomed on her cheeks and her lips twisted into a small wince.

Amused at her embarrassment, he couldn't resist saying, 'Only when I have good cause to.'

Her eyes popped open and heat infused her cheeks.

For a moment they just stared at one another, and the atmosphere immediately grew thick with awareness. Two strangers… alone in a house. She was wearing his clothes.

A spark of something happening between them had his pulse firing for the first time in years. And warning bells rang in his ears. She was his neighbour. He was not into relationships. Period. He was no good at them. He had a long day ahead of him. He needed to walk away.

SWEPT INTO THE RICH MAN'S WORLD

BY
KATRINA CUDMORE

First Published in Great Britain 2016
By Mills & Boon, an imprint of HarperCollins*Publishers*
1 London Bridge Street, London, SE1 9GF

ISBN: 978-0-263-91961-5

23-0216

Our policy is to use papers that are natural, renewable and recyclable products and made from wood grown in sustainable forests.The logging and manufacturing processes conform to the legal environmental regulations of the country of origin.

Printed and bound in Spain
by CPI, Barcelona

A city-loving book addict, peony obsessive **Katrina Cudmore** lives in Cork, Ireland, with her husband, four active children and a very daft dog. A psychology graduate, with a MSc in Human Resources, Katrina spent many years working in multinational companies and can't believe she is lucky enough now to have a job that involves daydreaming about love and handsome men!

You can visit Katrina at www.katrinacudmore.com.

This book is dedicated to my mum.
I miss you with all my heart.

CHAPTER ONE

'HELLO? IS ANYONE HOME?'

Her lungs on fire, Aideen Ryan desperately heaved in some air as she waited for someone to answer her knock and call. She had run in the dark through gale-force winds and rain to get to Ashbrooke House: the only place that could give her shelter from the storm currently pounding the entire Atlantic coastline of Ireland.

Ashbrooke House, stately home of billionaire Patrick Fitzsimon. A man who, given the impenetrable walls that surrounded his vast estate and his über-wealthy lifestyle, was unlikely to welcome her intrusion.

She straightened her rain jacket and ran a hand through her hair. *Oh, for crying out loud.* Her hair was a tangled mess. Soaked to the skull and resembling a frizz bomb… She really hoped it wouldn't be Patrick Fitzsimon who answered the door. Not the suave, gorgeous man she had seen in countless magazines. A man who stared at the camera with such serious intensity and intelligence that she had held her breath in alarm, worried for a few crazy seconds that he could see her spying on him.

The only sightings anyone ever made of him locally was when he was helicoptered in and out of the estate. Intrigued, she had looked him up. But just because she'd been unable to resist checking out her neighbour, one of the world's 'top ten most eligible billionaire bachelors', it didn't alter the fact that she was determined to keep her life a man-free zone.

A nearby tree branch creaked loudly as a ferocious gust of wind and rain swept up from the sea. How was her poor cottage faring in the storm without her? And how on earth was her business going to survive this?

Pushing down her spiralling panic, she took hold of the brass knocker and rapped it against the imposing door again, the metal vibrating against her skin.

'Hello? Please…I need help. Is anyone home?'

Please, please, let one of his staff answer.

But the vast house remained in silence, while beyond the columned entrance porch sheets of rain swept across the often written about formal gardens of Ashbrooke.

And then slow realisation dawned. Although outside lighting had showcased the perfect symmetry and beauty of the Palladian house as she had run up the driveway, not a single interior light had shone through the large sash windows.

In her panic, that simple fact had failed to register with her…until now.

What if nobody was at home?

But that didn't make sense. A house this size had to have an army of staff. The classically inspired villa had a three-storey central block, connected by colonnades to two vast wings. The house was enormous—even bigger than the pictures suggested.

Somebody simply *had* to be home. They probably just couldn't hear her above the storm. She needed to knock louder.

She grabbed hold of the knocker again, but just as

she raised it high to pound it down on the door the door swung open. As she flew forward with it all she could see was a tanned, muscular six-pack vanishing beneath a grey sweatshirt, its owner in the midst of quickly dressing. But not before she headbutted that glorious vision of masculine perfection.

It was like colliding against steel. As she ricocheted backwards she heard a loud grunt. Then hands gripped her upper arms and yanked her back from slamming bottom first on to the ground. The momentum pulled her back towards that hard body, and this time her forehead landed heavily on the person's chest with a thud.

For a moment neither of them moved, and her already spinning head became lost in a giddy sensation of warmth, the safe embrace of another human being, the deep, masculine scent of a man…

She couldn't tell who sprang away first, but as embarrassment barrelled through her, her eyes dropped down to bare feet and dark grey sweatpants before travelling back up over a long, lean, muscular body. Dark stubble lined a sculpted jawline. Taking a deep swallow, she looked up into eyes that were the light blue of an early-morning Irish spring sky. How often had she tried without success to replicate that colour in her designs?

Patrick Fitzsimon.

Those beautiful blue eyes narrowed. 'What the—?'

'I'm sorry I woke you, but my home's been flooded and everything I own is probably floating to America at this stage. I tried to drive into Mooncoyne but the road is flooded. My car got stuck. I was so glad your gates were open…I thought they would be locked, like they usually are. I honestly didn't know what I was going to do if they were locked.'

He held up a hand in the universal *stop* position. 'Okay. Slow down. Let's start again. Explain to me who you are.'

Oh, why did she jabber so much when she was nervous? And, for crying out loud, did she *have* to blush so brightly that she could light up a small house?

Pushing her hand out towards him, she said, 'I'm Aideen Ryan. I'm your neighbour. I live in Fuchsia Cottage…down by the edge of the lough.'

He gave a quick nod of recognition, but then he drew his arms across his impossibly wide chest and his gaze narrowed even more. 'What is it you need, exactly?'

Humiliation burnt in her chest at having to ask for help from a stranger, but she looked into his cool blue eyes and blurted out what had to be said. 'I need a place to stay tonight.'

His mouth twisted unhappily. For a moment she feared he was about to close the door on her.

But instead he took a backward step and said, 'Come inside.'

At best, it was a very reluctant invitation.

The door closed behind them with a solid clunk. Without uttering a word, he left her standing alone in the vast entrance hall. Her body started to shake as her wet clothes clung to her limbs. Her teeth chattered in the vast space and, to her ears, seemed to echo off the dome-shaped ceiling, from which hung the largest crystal chandelier she'd ever seen.

Why couldn't she have a normal neighbour? Why did hers have to be a billionaire who lived in a palace at the end of a mile-long driveway? She hated having to ask for help. From anyone. But having to ask for help from a megarich gorgeous man made her feel as though the universe was having a good laugh at her expense.

When he returned, he passed her a yellow and white striped towel without comment. Accepting it gratefully, she patted her hands and face. For a moment their eyes met.

Her heart stuttered as his gaze assessed her, his generous mouth flattened into a grimace, his long legs planted wide apart, his body rigid. Her breath caught. She felt intimidated by the intensity of his stare, his size, his silent unsmiling presence. She lowered her gaze and concentrated on twisting the towel through her hair, her eyes closing as an unaccountable nervousness overtook her.

'So where's your car?'

'I tried to drive into Mooncoyne but the river had burst its banks at Foley's Bridge. It's the same on your estate—the bridge on your drive is impassable, too.'

He shook his head in confusion. 'So how did you get here?'

'I climbed on to the bridge wall and crawled along it… My car is still on the other side.'

Just great. Not only had he been woken from a jet-lagged sleep, but now he realised he was dealing with a crazy woman. This was all he needed.

'Are you serious? Are you telling me you climbed over a flooded river in gale-force winds? Have you lost your mind?'

For a moment a wounded look flashed in her cocoa-brown eyes, but then she stared defiantly back at him.

'The sea was about to flood my cottage. I called the emergency services but they are swamped with the flooding throughout Mooncoyne. And anyway they can't reach here—Foley's Bridge is impassable even to them. You're my only neighbour. There was no other place I could come to for shelter.' Throwing her head back, she took a deep breath before she continued, a tremor in her voice. 'I did contemplate staying in my car overnight, but frankly I was more concerned about hypothermia than climbing along a bridge wall.'

Okay, so she had a point. But it had still been a crazy risk to take.

He inhaled a deep breath. For the first time ever he wished his staff resided in the house. If she'd been here, his housekeeper, Maureen, would happily have taken this dishevelled woman in hand. And he could have got some much-needed sleep.

He had awoken to her knocking jet-lagged and perplexed as to how anyone had got past his security. All of Ashbrooke's thousand-acre parkland was ring-fenced by a twenty-foot stone wall, built at the same time as the house in the eighteenth century. The impenetrable wall and the electronic front gates kept the outside world away.

Well, they were *supposed* to.

He would be having words with his estate manager in the morning. But right now he had a stranger dripping water down on to his polished limestone floor. He had an urgent teleconference in less than four hours with Hong Kong. To be followed up with a day of endless other teleconferences to wrap up his biggest acquisition ever. The acquisition, however, was still mired in legal and technical difficulties. Difficulties his teams should have sorted out weeks ago. The arrival of his neighbour at this time of night was the last thing he needed.

He glanced at her again. She gave him a brief uncertain smile. And he did a double take. Beneath that mass of wild, out-of-control hair she was beautiful.

Full Cupid's bow lips, clear rosy skin, thick arched

eyebrows and the most expressive eyes he had ever seen, framed by long dark eyelashes. Not the striking, almost hard supermodel beauty of some of his exes. She was… really pretty.

But then with a twinge of guilt he realised that she was shivering, and that she had noticeably paled in the past few minutes.

'You need to get out of those wet clothes and have a shower.'

A glimmer of heat showed on her cheeks and she shuffled uneasily. 'I don't have any spare clothes. I didn't pack any. I only had time to get some office equipment and files out…the things I had to save.'

Oh, great. Well, he didn't have any spare women's clothes hanging around here. He had never brought any of his dates to Ashbrooke. This was his sanctuary. And it had become even more so in the past few years as his ever-growing business demanded his absolute concentration.

Deep down he knew he should say some words of comfort to her. But he was no good in these situations, at saying the right thing. God knew his history with his own sister, Orla, proved that. His skill in life was making money. It clearly wasn't having effective personal relationships.

The thought of how he had failed not only Orla but also his mum and dad left a bitter taste in his mouth as his eyes moved up to meet his neighbour's. Two pools of wary brown met him. He could provide this woman with practical help. But nothing more.

'Pass me your jacket and I'll show you to a guest bedroom. I'll find you some clothes to wear while you shower.'

Her hands trembled as she shrugged off her pink and red floral rain jacket. Beneath it she wore a red and white striped cotton top, a short denim miniskirt, black wool tights and Converse trainers. Not exactly clothing suitable for being outdoors in the midst of an Atlantic storm.

The wet clothes clung to her skin. Despite himself he let his gaze trail down the soft curves of her body, gliding over the gentle slope of her breasts, narrow waist and along the long length of her legs.

When he looked up she gave a shrug. 'I didn't have time to get changed.'

She must have mistaken his stare of appreciation for incredulity. Good. He certainly didn't want her getting any other ideas.

He took her coat and in silence they walked up the stairs.

He glanced briefly at his watch. He would show her to her room and then go and get some sleep. He needed to be at the top of his game tomorrow, to unravel this mess his acquisition teams seemed incapable of sorting out.

She followed him up a cantilevered stone staircase. Despite her longing to get changed out of her rain-soaked clothes—not least her trainers, which squelched with every step—she couldn't help but stop and stare at the opulent rococo plasterwork that curved along the walls of the staircase. Exquisite delicate masks and scallop shells rendered in porcelain-like plaster had her longing to reach out and touch the silent angelic faces, which seemed to follow her steps with knowing smiles.

It was one of the most stunning rooms she had ever seen…if you could call a hallway a room. Good Lord, if the entrance hall was like this what was the rest of the house like? *Talk about making a girl feel inadequate...*

Ahead of her he continued to climb the stairs, his tall, broad frame causing an unwanted flip in her stomach. He was big, dark, and handsome beyond belief. And you didn't need to be Sherlock Holmes to figure out that he wasn't too keen on having her here.

Well, she wasn't too keen on being here herself. She'd much prefer to be at home, snuggled up in her own bed. Having to face the displeasure of a billionaire who, given his monumental success at such a young age, was probably hard-nosed and cold-hearted, was not exactly her idea of a fun night.

Upstairs, he led her down a never-ending corridor in silence. She had an insane urge to talk, to kill the tension that seemed to simmer silently between them.

'Your helicopter often passes over my cottage. Do you travel a lot?'

'When required.'

Okay, so it hadn't been the most interesting or insightful of questions, but he could have given a little more detail in the way of an answer. It wouldn't kill him to make a little small talk with her, would it?

He stopped and opened a door, and signalled for her to enter first. As she passed he studied her with a coolness that gave nothing away. She found herself giving him an involuntary smile. But when his face remained impassive, apart from the slight narrowing of his eyes, she felt rather silly.

His cool attitude pinged in her brain like a wake-up call. She was here out of necessity, not because she wanted to be, and he shouldn't be making her feel so uneasy. She straightened her back with resolve and pride and marched further into the room. First thing tomorrow morning she was out of here.

But she hadn't gone far when her steps faltered. 'Oh, wow, this bedroom is stunning...and it's *huge!* A family of six could easily sleep in that bed.'

An imposing oversized bed sat in the middle of the room, surrounded by sofas and occasional chairs covered in glazed cotton in varying tones of sage-green. An antique desk and a vanity table sat either side of the white marble fireplace.

He didn't acknowledge her words of admiration but instead made for the door. 'I'll go and get you some clothes to change into.'

When he was gone she pulled a face. Did she really have to sound so gushing? Right—from here on in she was playing it cool with Patrick Fitzsimon.

Two doors led to a bathroom and a dressing room. In the bathroom she eyed the shower longingly. She didn't suppose he would be too impressed to return to find her already in the locked bathroom, the shower running, making herself at home...

This was all so horribly awkward. Barging in on a very reluctant neighbour at this time of night...

But then a giggle escaped as she imagined his expression if he returned to a closed bathroom door and, beyond it, the sound of her voice belting out a show tune inside the running shower.

Her laughter died, though, when she walked back out into the bedroom to be confronted with the exact frown she had imagined. As she reddened he threw her a stark look.

'Is something the matter?'

'No…it's just that my wet shoes are making the sound of a sickly duck whenever I walk.'

Oh, for crying out loud. So much for playing it cool. Where had *that* come from?

He looked at her as though he was concerned about her sanity. With a quick shake of his head he placed the bundle in his hands on to one of the fireside chairs. 'Have a shower and get changed. You'll need to wash and dry your clothes for when you leave in the morning. There's a laundry room at the end of this corridor—please use that.'

With that, he turned away. His back was still turned to her when she heard him say goodnight.

'Is it okay if I get myself a drink after I shower?'

He slowed at her question and for a fraction too long he paused, a new tension radiating across his broad shoulders.

When he turned she shrugged and gave an apologetic smile. 'I could really do with something to warm me up. If you tell me how to get to the kitchen, I'll pop down there after.'

Cue a deepening of his grimace. Just for a moment she wondered how gorgeous he must be when he smiled, because he was pretty impressive even when grimacing. *If* he ever smiled, that was.

'Turn left outside the bedroom door and you will find another set of stairs a little further along that will take you down to the west wing. The kitchen is the fifth door on the left.'

He twisted away and was gone before she could voice her thanks.

She exhaled heavily. Was he this abrasive with everyone, or was it her in particular?

God knew she had met plenty of curt people in her

line of business, but there was something about Patrick Fitzsimon that completely threw her. In his company she felt as though an invisible wall separated them. She got on with most people—she was good at putting them at ease. But with him she got the distinct feeling that getting on with people was pretty low on his agenda.

On the bed, she unfurled his bundle: soft grey cotton pyjama bottoms and a pale blue shirt, wrapped around a toothbrush and toothpaste.

Her heart did a funny little shimmy at the thought of wearing his clothes, and before she knew what she was doing she brought them to her nose. Her eyes closed as she inhaled the intoxicating smell of fresh laundry, but there was no hint of the scent she had inhaled earlier when she'd fallen against him. Salt and grass…and a deep, hot, masculine scent that had her swallowing a sigh in remembrance. For a few crazy seconds earlier she had wanted to wrap her arms around his waist. Take shelter against his hardness for ever.

She threw her eyes upwards. What was she doing? The man was as cold as ice.

Anyway, it didn't matter. After tomorrow she would probably never see him again. And she was not interested in men right now anyway. Her hard-won independence was too precious. From here on in she wanted to live a life in which she was in charge of her own destiny. Where *she* called the shots.

One night and she was out of here. Back to her work and back to nights in, eating pizza and watching box sets on her own. Which she was perfectly happy with, thank you very much.

CHAPTER TWO

SIXTEEN BEDROOMS, EIGHT reception rooms. A ballroom that could cater to over three hundred guests. Two libraries and countless other rooms he rarely visited. And yet he resented the idea of having to share this vast house with someone. He knew it made no sense. It was almost midnight. She would be gone within hours. But, after spending the past few years immersed in the solitude of his work, having to share his home even for one night was an alien and uncomfortable prospect.

Two years ago, after yet another bewildering argument with his sister, he had come to the realisation that he should focus on what he was good at, what he could control: his work. He had been exhausted and frustrated by Orla's constant battle of wills with him, and it had been almost a relief to turn away from the fraught world of relationships to the uncomplicated black and white world of work.

He hadn't needed Orla to tell him he was inept at handling relationships, though she happily did so on a regular basis, because he'd seen it in the pain etched on her face when she didn't realise he was watching her.

He still didn't know what had gone wrong. Where *he* had gone wrong. They had once been so close. After his mum had died he had been so scared and lonely he had thought his heart would break. But the smiling, gurgling Orla had saved him.

And then his father had died when Orla was sixteen, and almost overnight she had changed. She had gone from being happy-go-lucky to sullen and non-communicative, and their once unbreakable bond had been broken.

The scrape of a tree branch against the kitchen window pane brought him back to the present with a jolt.

He put the tea canister next to the already boiled kettle. Then he wrote his house guest a quick note, telling her to help herself to anything she needed. All the while he was hearing his father's incredulous voice in his head, scolding him for his inhospitality. And once again he was reminded of how different he was from his father.

Note finished, he knew he should walk away before she came down. But the image of her standing in his entrance hall, a raindrop running down over the deep crevice of her full lips, held him. Lips he had had an insane urge to taste…

His instant attraction to her had to be down to the fact that he had been without a steady bedmate for quite some time. A lifetime for a guy who had once never been able to resist the lure of a beautiful woman. But two years ago his appetite for his usual short, frivolous affairs had disappeared. And a serious relationship was off the cards. Permanently.

And, anyway, she was his neighbour. If—and it was a big *if*—he ever was to start casually dating again, it certainly wouldn't be on his own doorstep.

He turned at a soft knock on the door.

Standing at the entrance to the vast kitchen, she gave him a wary smile.

He should have gone when he could. Now he would be forced to make small talk.

She had rolled up the cuffs of his pyjama bottoms and shirt and her feet were bare. He got the briefest glimpse of a delicate shin bone, which caused a tightening in his belly in a way it never should. Her hair, though still wet, was now tamed and fell like a heavy dark curtain down her back. For a moment his eyes caught on how she had left the top two buttons of the shirt undone, and although he could only see a small triangle of flesh his pulse quickened.

He didn't want to be feeling any of this. He crumpled the note he had left her into the palm of his hand. 'The kettle is boiled. Please help yourself to anything you need.'

'Thank you.' As he went to walk to the door she added, 'I didn't say it earlier, but thank you for giving me shelter for the night—and I'm sorry if I woke you up.'

She blushed when she'd finished, and wound her arms about her waist, eyeing him cautiously. There was something about her standing there in his clothes, waiting for his response, that got to him.

He felt compelled to hold out an olive branch. 'In the morning I will arrange for my estate manager to drive you home.'

She shook her head firmly. 'I'll walk. It's not far to the bridge.'

'Fine.'

It was time for him to go and get some sleep. But something was holding him back. Perhaps it was his thoughts of Orla, and how he would like someone to treat *her* if she was in a similar predicament.

With a heavy sigh he said, 'How about we start again?'

Her head tilted to the side and she bit her lip, unsure.

He walked over to her and held out his hand and said words that, in truth, he didn't entirely mean. 'Welcome to Ashbrooke.'

Her hand was ice-cold. Instinctively he coiled his own around the soft, delicate skin as gently as he could.

'You're cold.'

Her head popped up from where she had been staring at their enclosed hands and when she spoke there was a tremble in her voice that matched the one in her hand. 'I know. The shower helped a little, but I was wet to the bone. I've never seen a storm like it before.'

He crossed over to the cloakroom, situated just off the kitchen, and grabbed one of the heavy fleeces he used for horse riding.

Back in the kitchen, he handed her the fleece.

'Thank you. I…' Her voice trailed off and her gaze wandered behind him before her mouth broke into a wide glorious smile. 'Oh—hello, you two.'

He twisted around to find the source of her affection. His two golden Labs had left their beds in the cloakroom and now ambled towards her, tails wagging at the prospect of having someone else to love them.

Both immediately went to her and bumped their heads against her leg. She leant over and rubbed them vigorously. In the process of her doing so her shirt fell forward and he got a brief glimpse of the smooth swell of her breasts. She was not wearing a bra.

Blood pounded in his ears. It was definitely time for bed.

'They're gorgeous. What are their names?'

'Mustard and Mayo.'

Raising an eyebrow, she gave him a quick grin. 'Interesting choice of names.'

A sputter of pleasure fired through him at the teasing in her voice. And he experienced a crazy urge to keep this brief moment of ease between them going. But that didn't make sense, so instead he said curtly, 'Remind me of your name again?'

Her eyes grew wide and her cheeks reddened. With a low groan she threw her hands up in the air. 'I *knew* it. I woke you up, didn't I?'

He folded his arms. 'Maybe I'm just terrible at remembering people's names?'

Her eyes narrowed shrewdly. 'I doubt that very much.' And then she added, 'So, do you always go to bed so early?'

The moment she had the words out an even deeper blush bloomed on her cheeks and her lips twisted into a small wince.

Something fired in his blood. 'Only when I have good cause to.'

Her mouth fell open.

For a moment they just stared at one another, and the atmosphere immediately grew thick with awareness. Two strangers, alone in a house. She was wearing his clothes. The spark of something happening between them had his pulse firing for the first time in years. And warning bells rang in his ears. She was his neighbour. He was not into relationships. Period. He was no good at them. He had a long day ahead of him. He needed to walk away.

A coil of heat grew in Aideen's belly.

Propped against an antique wing-backed chair, in the low light of the kitchen, Patrick looked at her with an edgy darkness. She stood close by, her back to the island unit. She dropped her gaze to the small sprigs of flowers on the material covering the chair, instantly recognising the signature motif of a luxurious French textile manufacturer. Everything in this house was expensive, out of her league. Including its owner.

She should talk, but her pulse was beating way too quickly for her to formulate a sensible sentence. He went to stand up, and his movement prompted her to blurt out, 'Aideen Ryan… My name is Aideen Ryan.'

Rather reluctantly he held out his hand. 'And I'm Patrick Fitzsimon.'

Thrown by the way her heart fluttered once again at the touch of his hand, she said without thinking, 'Oh, I know that.'

'Really?'

For a moment she debated whether she could bluster her way out of the situation, but one look into his razor-sharp eyes told her she would be wasting her time. 'Every time I drove by I was intrigued as to who lived here, so I looked you up one day.'

His expression tightened.

She realised she must sound like some billionaire groupie or, worse, a gold digger, and blurted out, 'We *are* the only houses out here on the headland. I wanted to know who my only neighbour was. There was nothing else to it.'

After a torturous few seconds during which he considered her answer, he said, 'I'll ask my estate manager to drop down to you tomorrow. He can give you his contact details. That way if you ever need any help you can contact him directly.'

For a few seconds she smiled at him gratefully, but

then humiliation licked at her bones. He was putting a filter between them. But then what did she expect? Patrick Fitzsimon lived in the moneyed world of the super-rich. He wasn't interested in his neighbours.

'Thanks, but I'm able to cope on my own.'

He stood up straight and scowled at her. 'I didn't say you weren't.'

She gave a tight laugh, memories of her ex taunting her. 'Well, you're not like a lot of men, then…'

The scowl darkened even more. 'That's a bit of a sweeping statement, isn't it? I was only trying to be helpful.'

The last sentence had been practically growled. He looked really angry with her, and she couldn't help but think she had hit a raw nerve.

She inhaled a deep breath and said, 'I'm sorry…I'm a bit battle-scarred at the moment.'

He stared at her in surprise and, praying he wouldn't ask her what she meant, she said quickly, 'I don't know about you, but I could do with a cup of tea. Will you join me?'

He looked as taken aback by her invitation as she was. Did she *really* want to spend more time with this taciturn man? But after the night she'd had, and three months of living alone, the truth was she was starved for company.

He looked down at his watch and when he looked up again frowned at her in thought. 'I'll stay five minutes.'

Could he have said it with any *less* enthusiasm? He looked edgy. As though he wanted to escape.

He walked towards the countertop where the kettle stood. 'Take a seat at the table. If you prefer, I also have hot chocolate or brandy.'

'Thanks, but I'd love tea.'

Instead of going to the table she walked to the picture window in the glass extension at the side of the kitchen. The faint flashing light from the lighthouse out on the end of the headland was the only sight in the darkness of the stormy night.

'Do you think my cottage will be okay?'

He didn't answer immediately. Instead he walked over to her side and he, too, looked out of the window towards the lighthouse. In the reflection of the window she could see that he stood four, maybe five inches taller than her, his huge frame dwarfing hers.

'I called the emergency services when you were in the shower. I really don't know what will happen to your cottage. The timing of the storm surge was terrible—right at the same time as high tide. I thought the worst of the storms was over, but April can be an unpredictable month.' He turned slightly towards her. 'I know you must be worried—it's your home—but you're safe. That's all that matters.'

His words surprised her, and she had to swallow against the lump of emotion that formed in her throat. He didn't try to pretend everything would be okay, didn't lie to her, but he didn't dismiss how she was feeling either.

She gave him a grateful smile, but he looked away from her with a frown.

He moved away from the window, back towards the table, and said in a now tight voice, 'Your tea is ready.'

For a while she looked down at the mug tentatively, two forces battling within her. The need to be self-reliant was vying with her need to talk to someone—even someone as closed-off as Patrick Fitzsimon. To hear a little reassurance that things would be okay. And then she just blurted it out, the tension in her body easing fractionally as the words tumbled out.

'It's not just my cottage, though. My studio is there. I have some urgent work I have to complete. I missed a deadline today and I have another commissioned piece I need to deliver next week.'

His silence and his frown told her she had said too much, and her insides curled with embarrassment. The man was a billionaire. Her problems must seem trivial to him.

She twisted her mug on the table, knowing he was studying her but unable to meet his gaze.

'I'm sorry to hear that. I didn't realise. What is it that you do?'

'I'm a textile designer.'

He nodded, and his eyes held hers briefly before he looked away. 'Try not to think about work until tomorrow. You might be worrying for no reason… And even in the worst of situations there's always a solution.'

'Hopefully you're right.'

'Do you have anyone who can help you tomorrow?'

She shook her head. 'I haven't got to know people locally yet, and my family live in Dublin. Most of my friends are either there or in London.'

Realising she still hadn't touched her tea, she sipped it. In her nervousness she pulled the mug away too quickly and had to lick a falling drip of tea from her bottom lip.

Her heart somersaulted as she saw his eyes were trained on her mouth, something darkening in their intensity. Then very slowly his gaze moved up to capture hers. Awareness fluttered through her.

'I heard someone had bought Fuchsia Cottage late last year—why did you move here to Mooncoyne?'

He asked the question in an almost accusatory tone, as though he almost wished she hadn't.

'I saw the cottage and the studio online and I fell in love with them straight away. The cottage is adorable, and the studio space is incredible. It's perfect for my work.' Forcing herself to smile, she said, 'Unfortunately I hadn't bargained on the cottage and studio flooding. The auctioneer assured me it wouldn't.'

He gave a brief shrug of understanding. 'You weren't tempted to go back to your family in Dublin?'

'Have you seen the price of property in Dublin? I know it's not as bad as London, but it's still crazy.' Then, remembering who she was talking to, she felt her insides twist and a feeling of foolishness grip her. Clearing her throat, she asked, 'Has Ashbrooke always been in your family?'

He looked at her incredulously, as though her question was ridiculous. 'No…absolutely not. I grew up in a modest house. My family weren't wealthy.'

Taken aback by the defensive tone of his voice, she blurted out exactly what was on her mind. 'So how did all of this happen?'

He studied her with a blistering glance, his mouth a thin line of unhappiness. In the end he said curtly, 'I was lucky. I saw the opportunities available in mobile applications ahead of the curve. I developed some music streaming apps that were bought by some of the big internet providers. Afterwards I had the capital to invest in other applications and software start-ups.'

She couldn't help but shake her head and give him a mock sceptical look. 'Oh, come on—that wasn't luck.'

'Meaning…?'

'Look, I ran my own business for five years. I know

success is down to hard work, taking risks, and being constantly on the ball. Making smart business decisions…I reckon luck has very little to do with it.'

'All true. But sometimes you get a good roll of the dice—sometimes you don't. It's about getting back up when things go wrong, knowing there's always a solution to a problem.'

His words were said with such certainty they unlocked something inside her.

For a good few minutes she toyed with her mug. The need to speak, to *tell* him, was building up in her like a pressure cooker. Part of her felt ridiculous, thinking of telling a billionaire of her failings, but another part wanted to. Why, she wasn't sure. Maybe it was the freedom of confessing to a stranger? To a person she wouldn't see after tomorrow? Perhaps it was not being able to talk to her family and friends about it because she had got it all so wrong.

'I lost my business last year,' she said in a rush.

Non-judgemental eyes met hers, and he said in a tone she hadn't heard from him before, 'What happened?'

Taken aback by the softening in him, she hesitated. Her pulse began to pound. Suddenly her throat felt bone-dry. 'Oh, it's a long story, but I made some very poor business decisions.'

'But you're back? Trying again.'

He said it with such certainty, as though that was all that mattered, and she couldn't help but smile. Something lifted inside her at the knowledge he was right. Yes, she was trying again—trying hard. Just hearing him say it made her realise how true it was.

'Yes, I am.'

His serious, intelligent gaze remained locked on hers. 'What are your plans for the future?'

His question caused a flutter of anxiety and her hands clenched on the mug. She shuffled in her seat. For some reason she wanted to get this right. She wanted his approval.

She inhaled a deep breath and said, 'To build a new label, re-establish my reputation.' She cringed at the wobble in her voice; it was just that she was so desperate to rebuild the career she loved so much.

He leant across the table and fixed his gaze on her. It was unnerving to be captivated by those blue eyes. By the sheer size and strength of him as his arms rested on the table, his broad shoulders angled towards her.

'There's no shame in failing, Aideen.'

Heat barrelled through her and she leant back in her chair, away from him. 'Really?' She pushed her mug to the side. 'What would *you* know about failing?'

His jaw hardened, and when he spoke his low voice was harsh with something she couldn't identify.

'Trust me—I have failed many times in my life. I'm far from perfect.'

She looked at him sceptically. He looked pretty perfect to her. From his financial stability and security and his film-star looks to this beautiful house, everything *was* perfect…even his spotless kitchen.

He stood and grabbed both mugs. With his back to her he said, 'I think it's time we went to bed.'

Once again he was annoyed with her. She should leave it. Go to bed, as he had suggested. But curiosity got the better of her. 'Why are you here in Mooncoyne? Why not somewhere like New York or London?'

He turned and folded his arms, leant against the counter. 'I met the previous owner of Ashbrooke, Lord Balfe, at a dinner party in London and we became good friends. He invited me to stay here and I fell in love with the house and the estate. Lord Balfe couldn't afford the upkeep any longer, and he was looking to sell the estate to someone who felt as passionate as he did about conserving it. So I agreed to buy it.' His unwavering eyes held hers and he said matter-of-factly, 'My business was growing ever more demanding. I knew I needed to live somewhere quiet in order to focus on it. This estate seemed the perfect place. And also Mooncoyne reminded me of the small fishing village where I grew up in County Antrim.'

So *that* was why he had traces of a soft, melodic Northern Irish brogue. 'Do your family still live there?'

Another quick look at his watch. He flicked his gaze back up to her. He looked as though he wasn't going to answer, but then he took her by surprise and said, 'No, my mum died when I was a boy and my dad passed away a number of years ago.'

For a moment their eyes locked and incomprehensively she felt tears form at the back of hers. 'I'm sorry.'

Blue eyes held hers and her pulse quickened at the intimacy of looking into a stranger's eyes for more than a polite second or two. Not being able to look away…not wanting to look away.

Then his hands gripped the countertop and he dipped his head for a moment before he looked back up and spoke. 'It happens. I have a younger sister, Orla, who lives in Madrid.'

'Do you see her often?'

His mouth twisted unhappily. 'Occasionally.'

His tone told her to back off. Tension filled the room.

She hated an unhappy atmosphere. And she didn't want to cause him any offence.

So, in a bid to make amends and lighten the tension, she said what she had been thinking all night. 'You've a spectacularly beautiful home.'

He gave a brief nod of acknowledgement. 'Thank you. I'm very proud of the work we've done here over the past few years.'

'How many staff do you employ?'

'I've cleaning and housekeeping staff who come in every day. Out on the estate my estate manager, William, employs twenty-two staff between the stables and the farm.'

'No housekeeper…even a butler?'

His mouth lifted ever so slightly. If she had blinked she would have missed it.

'Sorry to disappoint you but I like my privacy. And I can cook for myself, do up my own buttons, tie my own shoelaces…'

She knew she was pushing it, but decided to push her luck as curiosity got the better of her. 'A girlfriend?' She tried to ignore the unexpected stab of jealousy that came with the thought that there might be a special woman in his life.

Something dark flashed in his eyes and he quietly answered. 'No—no girlfriend.'

She tried to fill the silence that followed. 'So nobody but you lives in the house?'

'No. Now, I think it's time for bed.'

So they were all alone tonight. It shouldn't matter, but for some reason heat grew in her belly at that thought. This was a huge place for one man to live in alone.

Though she stood in preparation for leaving the

kitchen she didn't move away from the table. Instead she said, 'Wow. Don't you get lonely?'

'I prefer to live on my own. I don't have time for relationships.' He studied her sombrely. 'Why? Do *you* get lonely?'

Taken aback, she answered, 'I'm too busy. I can—'

A tightness in her chest stopped her mid-sentence. Maybe she *had* been lonely these past few months, and had been denying it all along in her determination to get her business back up and running again.

She shrugged and looked at him with a half smile. 'I must admit it's nice to talk to someone face to face for a change, rather than on the phone or over the internet. I seem to spend all my days on the phone at the moment, calling prospective clients.' With a sigh of exasperation she added, 'I really should go and visit them. It would save me a lot of time being put on hold.'

'Why don't you?'

She felt herself blush. 'Most of my clients are based in Paris, and it's on my list of priorities to visit them.' She couldn't admit that financially she wasn't in a position to travel there, so instead she said, 'But, to be honest, part of me is embarrassed. I haven't seen any of them since I lost my business. I suppose my pride has taken a dent.'

'Go back out there and be proud that you're back and fighting. *I'm* going to Paris next week…' He didn't finish the sentence and a look of annoyance flashed across his face. His tone now cooler, he said, 'You have a long day ahead of you tomorrow. I'll walk you back to your room.'

He called to the dogs and led them back to their beds in the cloakroom.

As they approached the bottom of the stairs she gave him a smile and offered him her hand. 'Thank you for tonight.' A surprising lump of something had formed in her throat, and her voice was croaky when she finally managed to continue to speak. 'Thank you for taking me in. I plan on leaving early tomorrow, so in case I don't see you then, it was nice to meet you.'

Tension seemed to bounce off the surrounding walls and she felt dizzy when his hand took hers. 'I wake before dawn, so the security alarm will be disabled after that.' With a quick nod he added, 'Take care of yourself.'

He walked away, back towards the main entrance hall.

She walked up the stairs slowly, her head spinning. What on earth had possessed her to tell him so much? And why on earth did the thought that she might never see him again make her feel sad? The man obviously didn't want her in his house.

As she lay in bed the memory of his incredible blue eyes and quiet but assured presence left her twisting and tumbling and wishing the hours away so she could leave for home. Where she could lose herself in her work again.

And when sleep finally started to pull her into oblivion her tired mind replayed on a loop his deep voice saying, 'You're safe. That's all that matters.' Words he would probably say to anyone. But when he had said them to her, he had looked at her with such intensity it had felt as though he was tattooing them on her heart.

CHAPTER THREE

PATRICK TORE ALONG the bridle path that cut through the woods, pushing his horse harder and harder. Soft ground underfoot, branches whizzing by, the flash of vivid, almost purple patches of bluebells, calm cool air beating against his skin…

When they reached the edge of the woods they raced through the parkland's glistening green grass. They leapt time and time again over the ditches separating the fields. Adrenaline pumped in both man and mare.

They followed the ancient pathway that hugged the coast and galloped in the steps of the medieval pilgrims who had come to Mooncoyne abbey.

The rising sun slatted its thick rays of sunlight through the window openings and he pulled the horse to a halt by the entrance. He dismounted and walked into the nave.

He hadn't managed to get back to sleep again last night. Instead he had lain awake, wondering how his conversation with Aideen Ryan had become so personal so quickly. It had unsettled him. That wasn't how he operated. He didn't open up to anyone.

For crying out loud, he had almost suggested to her that she travel with him to Paris. His guess was that it wasn't just pride standing in her way of going, but also financial difficulties. In the end he had ended the conversation, been glad when she'd made her own way to bed, because he hadn't been able to handle how good it was to talk to someone else, to actually *connect* with them.

And, despite himself, he was deeply attracted to her.

All of which was dangerous.

He threw his head back and stared up into the endless depths of the blue sky.

Hadn't he already proved he wasn't capable of having effective relationships? He had a string of exes who had been beautiful but superficial. A sister who wouldn't talk to him. And a nephew or niece he would never get to know.

The baby would be born in the next month. He should be there. Supporting Orla. At least she was willing to accept his financial support. If she had refused to do so then he really would have been out of his mind, worrying about how she was going to cope.

His call to Hong Kong earlier had gone well. If he kept up the pressure for the remainder of the day, with the rest of his acquisition teams, then the deal would go through later tonight. It would be strange for it all to be over. For months he had worked day and night to see it happen.

A strange emptiness sat in his chest. What would he do once the project was over?

The slow tendrils of an idea had formed in his mind but he kept pushing them away. But as he walked through the ruins of the abbey the idea came back, stronger and more insistent this time.

He should help Aideen. It was what any good neighbour would do. It was what his father would have done.

But would he be crazy to do it? Last night he had lowered his guard around her. He couldn't allow that again. If he was to help then it would have to be done on a strictly business basis. He could help her re-establish her business, mentor her if required. He knew what it was like to throw your heart and soul into a business. And he knew only too well the pain of failure.

He would help her. And it would all be professional and uncomplicated.

The memory of a deep voice snaked through Aideen's brain. She gave a small sigh, smiled to herself, and stretched out on the bed.

But then her eyes popped open and she looked around, disorientated. Small shafts of daylight sneaked under drawn curtains.

Slowly she remembered where she was. And what she had to face today.

Dreaming about Patrick Fitzsimon was the last thing she should be doing.

The cottage. Deadlines.

For a few seconds she pulled the duvet up over her head. Maybe she could just stay here in this warm and dark cocoon for a few days.

With a groan she pushed back the cover. Time to rise and shine. And face what the day had to bring.

Anyway, it couldn't be any worse than being forced out of the business she'd once created. She had survived the past year, so she would survive this.

She pulled the curtains apart and winced as daylight flooded the room.

The view out of her window was breathtaking. Below her, formal box gardens led down to a gigantic fountain that sprayed a sprout of water so vigorously upwards it was as though it was trying to defy gravity. Rose gardens lay beyond the fountain, and then a long rolling meadow, rich in rain-drenched emerald green grass, ran all the way down to the faraway sea.

Though the sun was still low in the sky the light was dazzling, thanks to a startlingly clear blue sky.

Had last night's storm been in her imagination? How could such furious weather be followed by such a beautiful day?

She could almost convince herself maybe her cottage hadn't flooded. That the weather was a good omen. But she had seen the ferocity of the sea. There was no way her cottage had got away with avoiding that angry swell.

When she had come to view the property she had fallen in love with the old cottage and its outbuildings, arranged around a courtyard garden. Fuchsia had dangled from the hedgerows and fading old roses had tumbled from its walls. It had seemed the perfect solution then.

But now her income was sparser and more sporadic than she had projected, and sometimes she wondered whether she could make this work. That was one of the worst consequences of losing her business: the vulnerability and constant questioning of whether she was doing the right thing, making the right decisions.

But a burning passion for her work along with a heavy dose of pride got her through most days. She would sacrifice everything to make this business a success.

Her heart was a different matter, though. It felt bruised. To think that once upon a time she had thought her ex had loved her…

Pressing the edges of her palms against her eyes, she drew in a deep breath.

A quick shower, an even quicker coffee, and she would

head home to start sorting out whatever was waiting for her.

She mightn't even see Patrick. Which would be a *good* thing, right?

Heading to the bathroom, she sighed. Just who was she trying to kid?

The truth was giddiness was fizzing through her veins at the prospect of seeing his tall, muscular body, the darkness of his hair, and his lightly tanned skin which emphasised the celestial blue of his eyes.

Showered and dressed, she was about to open the bedroom door when she spotted a note pushed under it. Picking it up, she read the brief words.

Aideen,
I will drive you back to your cottage. Help yourself to breakfast in the kitchen. I will meet you in the main entrance hall at nine.
Patrick

It was a generous offer, but she needed to face the cottage on her own. It was her responsibility. She had taken up enough of his time as it was.

And then she studied the note again as an uncomfortable truth dawned on her. Was he offering to take her as a way of ensuring that she left? Humiliation burnt on her cheeks.

She checked the time on her phone. It was not yet eight o'clock. She would get changed and then go reassure him that she was leaving and was perfectly capable of making her own way home.

Thirty minutes later she had searched for him throughout the house but there was no sign of him. Her search in this exquisite house, as she'd gasped at the beauty of the baroque ballroom, with its frescoed ceiling, mirrored walls, and golden chandeliers, had brought home how different their lives were.

She was writing a note for him in the kitchen when the cloakroom door swung open.

Over off-white jodhpurs and black riding boots he was wearing a loose pale green shirt, the top three buttons open to reveal a masculine smattering of dark hair. His skin glistened with a sheen of perspiration.

He came to a stop when he spotted her at the table.

'Good morning.' He moved across the kitchen in long strides while adding, 'Help yourself to breakfast. I'll have a quick shower and be ready by nine.'

His manner was brusque, and she was left with no doubt that he just wanted to get the business of taking her home over and done with. Embarrassment coiled its way around her insides and she wanted to curl up into a protective ball against his rejection.

But instead she gave him a sunny smile. 'Thank you for the offer, but there's really no need for you to drive me. I've taken up enough of your time.' He turned to her with a frown and she added, as way of explanation, 'I'll collect my car down by the bridge. I could do with a walk anyway.'

'I'm coming.'

Didn't he trust her? Was he always this insistent?

'No, honestly—you've done enough.'

He leant against the island unit at the centre of the kitchen. 'Aideen, there's no point in arguing. I've made up my mind.'

His cool composure set her teeth on edge. 'I want to go to the cottage by myself.'

'Why?'

Oh, for crying out loud. 'Because I can manage. The cottage is my responsibility. And I have no doubt that you are an extremely busy man. I can't take up any more of your time.'

'I'm taking you. End of story.'

She was leaving. Why wasn't that enough for him? She gave a small laugh and said jokingly, 'You don't have to personally escort me off the estate, you know.'

He obviously didn't enjoy her joke as annoyance flared on his face. 'Do you really think that is why I want to drive you to the cottage? That I want to make sure you leave?'

Thrown by his anger, she challenged him back. 'What other reason could you possibly have?'

His blue gaze held hers for a long time, and then, with a deep inhalation, he said in a quiet voice, 'Why can't you just accept that I want to help you?'

He moved beside the table and hunkered down beside her. Heat coursed through her veins at having his powerful body so close by, at seeing the movement of the hard muscles of his thighs beneath the thin fabric of the jodhpurs, the beauty of his lightly tanned hand and forearm which rested on the table beside her.

He didn't speak again until she met his determined gaze. 'Let me help you.'

Why wasn't he listening to her? She was able to look after herself—she didn't need any help.

'I appreciate the offer, but I can manage by myself.'

He stood, his jaw working, and eyed her unhappily. 'As you wish.'

With that, he strode out of the kitchen without a backward glance.

* * *

For the second time in less than twelve hours Aideen knocked at Patrick's front door. If she'd hated to ask for help the first time around then it was ten times worse now. Talk about having to eat humble pie…

As she waited for her knock to be answered she looked back towards her car. Thankfully it had started immediately, and although the floor was a little damp, the files and office equipment piled on to the back seat and in the boot had escaped the storm and flood waters.

Unlike her cottage.

She needed to think straight, but her mind was ping-ponging all over the place. Work. Deadlines. Insurance claims. Where would she even start in finding a reputable builder to carry out the necessary repairs?

She turned to the sound of the door opening.

A middle-aged woman stood there, a puzzled look on her face. As though she was surprised to find someone standing at the door. 'Can I help you?'

'Can I speak to Patrick, please?'

The woman looked totally taken aback. To assure her that she wasn't some random stranger, Aideen quickly added, 'I'm Aideen Ryan. I live in Fuchsia Cottage, down by the lough. Your estate manager was at the front gates, repairing them after last night's storm. Patrick had told him how my cottage flooded last night and he let me in when I said I needed to talk to Patrick again.'

'Oh, you poor thing. Of course—come in. Sure, half the village is flooded. I never saw anything like it in my life.'

The woman led her to a large reception room off the entrance hall, chatting all the way.

'You took me by surprise. We don't tend to get many

visitors. Make yourself comfortable and I'll let Patrick know you're here.'

It took Patrick so long to arrive that for a while she worried that he was refusing to see her. He marched into the room, his brow furrowed. He was wearing a light blue formal shirt, open at the neck, fine navy wool trousers and expensive tan-coloured shoes. It all screamed expensive Italian designer and he looked every inch the successful billionaire that he was.

She gave him a crooked smile. 'I'm back.'

His frown didn't budge an inch. 'So I see.'

She took a deep breath. She had to focus on work. A little bit of humility had never killed anyone. 'My cottage is uninhabitable. The insurance company is sending out an assessor tomorrow. I tried to go to Mooncoyne, but Foley's Bridge is still impassable.' Trying not to wince at his deepening frown, she said in a rush, 'I was wondering if it would be possible for me to work from here… until the flooding subsides.'

His head tilted forward and he pinned her with a look.

'It's just that I have a commission I need to complete by the end of today and I need access to the internet.'

'What condition is the cottage in?'

Her stomach lurched, but she clenched her fists and forced herself to speak. 'There's still floodwater in both the cottage and the studio. Most of my furniture and all the fitted furniture will probably need to be replaced. At a guess, and after speaking to the insurance company, I'll be out of the cottage for at least a month.'

She was feigning calmness about the whole situation but she wasn't fooling him. The storm damage was exactly as he had anticipated. He clenched his teeth in frustration.

Why had she been so stubborn in refusing his offer to go with her? He'd had some spare time then. Now he had back-to-back meetings scheduled for the rest of the day.

He would give her fifteen minutes. Get her to see the sense of his plan. And then he would get back to wrapping up this acquisition.

'How about all your personal belongings? Are they okay?'

'All of my clothes survived, but not my shoes—unfortunately.' A sad, crooked smile broke on her mouth before she added in bewilderment, with a catch in her voice, 'I mean, *shoes*! They are the least of my worries… but I loved them so much.'

'Where are you going to live?'

'I'm not sure… I called the Harbour View Hotel but they're completely booked out tonight, and apparently all the bed and breakfasts in a ten-mile radius are the same because of people having to evacuate. I'll probably have to stay in one of the hotels in Ballymore.'

There was no way she was going to manage the renovations from twenty miles away and work on her commissions at the same time.

'It's going to be difficult for you to manage the repairs from Ballymore. I'll get William, my estate manager, to project-manage the renovations for you.'

She stared at him in disbelief. 'Why on earth would you do that?'

'Because you need to concentrate on your business—not spend your days driving all over the countryside and chasing builders.'

'I appreciate the offer, but I need to manage the renovations by myself.'

'Why?'

Tiredly, she rubbed her palms over her face and looked at him imploringly. 'Let me ask you the same question. Why? Why are you doing this?'

Taking a step closer, he stared down at her. Boy, was she obstinate. 'Maybe I just want to help you. Nothing more.'

'I can't accept your help.'

'Why not?'

'Because…'

This woman was impossible. *Why* wouldn't she accept his help? She was as bad as Orla.

He gave an exasperated sigh. 'Aideen, will you stop being a pain and just agree to letting William sort out the renovations…? It's not a big deal. And I don't know about you, but I have better things to be doing than standing here arguing about my motives.'

Not a big deal to him, perhaps, but it was to her. She needed to rebuild her life by herself, on her own terms.

Bewildered, she said, 'You don't even know me.'

'So? You're my neighbour. That's a good enough reason for me to want to help.'

He made it all sound so simple. And for a moment she wanted to believe him. But then a siren of warning sounded in her brain. She needed to be in control of her own life. 'I don't want to sound ungrateful, and I do appreciate your offer, but I have to manage the renovations by myself.'

'And what if your business suffers as a result?'

She flinched at the truth of his words. Ballymore was twenty miles away, on twisting roads. Trying to manage the renovations and run her business from a hotel room was going to be a nightmare.

Frustration at the whole situation had her arguing back. 'I'll manage.'

His mouth tensed at the anger in her voice and he considered her through narrowed eyes. 'You *are* stubborn, aren't you?'

'So it has been said in the past,' she muttered.

On an exasperated exhalation he folded his arms. 'Your business has to be your number one priority. William will sort out the renovations. You will move in here until the cottage is ready, and on Sunday you will come to Paris with me.'

A bolt of pain radiated through his jawline as he clamped his teeth together. Hard. For a few seconds he wondered at the words he had so casually tossed out. Disquiet rumbled in his stomach. Was he about to walk into a minefield of complications by inviting this woman into his life? But in an instant he killed that doubt. This was the right thing to do. She needed his help. Even if the horror in her eyes told him that she wasn't ready to accept it yet.

Stupefied, Aideen stared at him for the longest while, waiting for him to give the tiniest indication that he was joking. But his mouth didn't twitch…his eyes didn't soften.

She gave a laugh of disbelief. 'Are you being serious?'

'Yes. I have meetings in Paris all of next week. You said yourself that you should be out meeting clients. Well, now is your opportunity. I have a chateau close to Paris we can use.'

'But I would be intruding.'

'Look, you've seen the size of Ashbrooke. My chateau outside Paris is large, too. You can set up a temporary studio there for the week. We can keep out of each other's way.'

Shaking her head, she folded her arms across her chest. 'You said last night you like living on your own… and so do I. It won't work.'

'We'll lead our own lives. I'm simply offering you a bed and a place to work—both here and in Paris. You come and go as you please. My chauffeur will be available to you whenever you need him. It doesn't have to be more complicated than that.'

'But *why*?'

'What is it with you and your questions? Why don't you believe that I'm just trying to be a good neighbour? That it's the right thing to do? I admire your tenacity and I want to support you in rebuilding your business. I think you need help even if you are too stubborn to admit it yourself.'

Taken aback by the powerful intensity of his words, she wavered a little. 'I'd pay you back.'

Taking a deep breath, he said with exasperation, 'I don't want your money. Can't you just accept it as a neighbourly gesture?'

'I'll be paying rent.'

He held up his hands. 'Fine. You can pay me once your insurance money comes through. Now I need to get back to work. I'll show you to the library, where you can work today. Use the same bedroom as last night to sleep in.' Out in the corridor, he added, 'You met my housekeeper, Maureen, earlier. Speak to her if you need anything. I'll get William to call in to see you and together you can discuss the renovation plans.'

She followed him to the library. Was she crazy to agree to this? But it was the only sensible option open to her. Wasn't it she who had said she would do anything to make her business a success? Just how hard would it be to move into his house for a month? She would have the space she needed and she would be close by the cottage to keep an eye on the renovations. And she did need to go to Paris.

It was a no-brainer, really. But could she really cope with living under the same roof as him? When there was this strange push-and-pull thing going on between them…attraction vying with wariness?

But it wasn't as if he was welcoming her with open arms anyway. He was a busy man who travelled the world. She mightn't see him for most of the time she was his guest.

A little while later, she was about to go about unpacking her car when she glanced around to see him watching her with a dark intensity.

How long would it take for him to regret asking her to stay? If he wasn't already doing so…?

CHAPTER FOUR

MONDAY MORNING. THEY HAD flown to Paris the day before, and today he had a number of client and in-house meetings before him. The acquisition had gone through on Friday evening.

He had set Aideen up with a temporary studio space in the library of the chateau, and she planned on spending the day organising meetings with clients.

He jogged past the walled garden in the grounds of the chateau and then broke into a sprint. He had dined out last night with his French management team. Glad to have an excuse to leave the chateau and her offer to cook them dinner.

They had both worked on the plane over yesterday afternoon, but he had found his gaze repeatedly wandering towards her, intrigued by how absorbed she had been in her work. With her hair swept up into a messy bun she had stared at her laptop screen, her long fingers tapping the delicate column of her neck in thought. And he had wondered what it would be like to have those fingers run against his skin.

After that, the thought of sharing dinner alone with her had set alarm bells off in his brain. He had to keep his distance.

Taking the steps of the garden two at a time, he ran across the stone terrace that traversed the entire length of the back of the sixteenth-century chateau. He entered the house and walked towards the kitchen. Was that *baking* he smelt?

An explosion of household goods were scattered across the surface of the island. The shells of juiced oranges, an upturned egg carton, an open milk bottle teetering precariously on the edge of the unit. Behind them, a trail of baking tins and bowls was scattered along the kitchen counter.

He turned to the sound of footsteps out in the corridor. Aideen walked towards him, a huge bunch of multicoloured tulips in her arms, a carton of eggs in her hand, rosy-cheeked and bright-eyed, a wide smile on her face. Her hair, thick glossy waves of soft chestnut curls, fell down her back.

'Oh, you're back.' She flashed him a quick smile before her gaze darted guiltily to the chaos behind him. 'I thought you would be out for a while yet.'

'What's happened to the kitchen?'

'I'm making breakfast. I hope you don't mind.'

Actually, he did. He wanted his kitchen clean and tidy, as it usually was. Not this mess.

She sidestepped him and began to search through the kitchen cupboards.

He gritted his teeth and tried to resist the urge to start clearing up the mess himself. His stomach, however, had very different thoughts as it rumbled at the delicious sweet smells of baking.

She plopped the tulips in a vase she had found in a cupboard and placed it on the kitchen table. 'I met your gardener earlier, and he gave me the use of his bike to cycle down to the village so that I could go to the *boulangerie*. But then I ran out of eggs, so I had to go again. The cycle down is easy but, boy, the hill back up is tricky. The countryside here is beautiful, and the village is so pretty. When I came back he gave me these flowers from the garden—aren't they stunning?'

The tulips did look good, but something about their cheery presence in the kitchen niggled him…they were just too *homely*.

For a few seconds she looked at him expectantly. When he didn't respond she smiled at him uncertainly, before rolling up the sleeves of her pink and white striped shirt.

'I'll tidy up here and then put some breakfast on. In honour of being in France, I'm going to make us *oeufs en cocotte*.'

He looked at her, bewildered. And slowly it dawned on him that she was expecting them to have breakfast *together*.

For a few brief seconds he was tempted to give in to the tantalising aroma of fresh baking filling the room. But a glimpse of her white lace bra as she bent over to swoop up the errant milk cap from the floor had him coming back to reality with a bang.

This wasn't what her stay was supposed to be about. A bed and an office… Not seeing too much of her. *That* was what he had signed up for. Not this cosy domesticity. Not some breakfast routine that could quickly become a habit. Not feeling desire for a woman first thing in the morning.

'I don't eat breakfast.'

It was almost the truth. He usually just grabbed some toast and coffee and took it to his office, eager to start work.

She was going about gathering up all the empty packaging on the island unit and paused briefly to give him a quick look. 'But that's crazy. After exercising you should eat.'

His spine stiffened and his jaw muscles tightened. Irritated, he grabbed a mug from the cupboard and went about making himself a coffee. 'I'm not hungry.'

At the sink, she rinsed out a cloth before she turned and caught his gaze. 'Have *something*. I wanted to thank you for having me here. For the flight over…the accommodation. I have some croissants and a baguette I bought in the *boulangerie* earlier warming in the oven.' She stopped and grimaced before admitting, 'My first attempt at *oeufs en cocotte* didn't quite work out, so I had to pop out for more eggs, but I'll have them ready in ten minutes.'

For a moment he almost wavered. 'I appreciate the gesture, but I'll stick to my usual coffee.'

With a disappointed sigh she added, 'If you won't eat, at least let me make the coffee for you.'

He threw his hands up in surrender. 'If you insist—two shots of espresso.'

'I've set the table out in the courtyard. If you would like to go out and sit there I'll bring you out the coffee.'

His head darted to the outdoor dining table in the courtyard. His fine china and cut glass sat on top of a white linen tablecloth. A jug of freshly squeezed orange juice sat next to silver salt and pepper pots. The courtyard was filled with an abundance of springtime flowers and the whole setting looked like a magazine feature on the ultimate romantic breakfast.

'Thanks, but I'll stay in here. I have to leave for work soon.'

At the kitchen table he clicked on to his usual newsfeed, using his tablet. He tried to concentrate on the various market analysts' commentary on his acquisition but she'd switched on the kitchen music system to an upbeat radio breakfast show. The DJs spoke in rapid French, sounding like children who had overdosed on a breakfast of sugary cereal.

And as if that wasn't bad enough she then proceeded to chat away herself, over their manic laughter. 'What a beautiful morning! Going to the *boulangerie* this morning reminded me of the summer I spent here as a student. I had an internship in a design house and I was penniless. I ate baguettes for the entire summer. I used to stare longingly at the patisserie stands, wishing I could afford to buy an éclair or, my favourite, a millefeuille.'

She continued this monologue while fiddling with the coffee machine's controls.

'Do you want some help?'

'No, I'm fine. I'll work it out.'

As she fiddled and twisted Patrick stared at the financial reports, very little detail actually registering. What *was* registering was the round swell of her bottom, the long length of her legs in skinny faded denim. Which only added to his growing annoyance.

Was it because he hadn't been with a woman for more than two years that he sometimes caught himself thinking that she was the most beautiful woman he had ever met? It wasn't just her prettiness, the seductive curves of her long-limbed body. Something shone through in her personality—a happiness, a strength of will that was beguiling.

He almost sighed in relief when she eventually popped a mug of coffee before him.

'Milk or sugar?'

'Neither, thanks.'

Sweet Lord, it was the strongest coffee he had ever tasted.

'I've messed up the coffee, haven't I?'

A crestfallen expression on her face, she waited for his answer.

He leant back in his chair and raised an eyebrow. 'I could probably stand on it.'

She moved to take the mug. 'I'll try again.'

'No!' That poor machine couldn't take it.

She planted her hands firmly on her hips. 'I take it you're not a morning person?'

'Correct in one. I like good coffee, silence, and preferably a tidy kitchen—not Armageddon.'

For a brief second a mixture of hurt and anger sparked in her eyes before she turned away.

She switched off the radio and then quickly cleared the countertops. She wiped them down and then filled the sink with a gush of steaming water in readiness to wash the used pots and pans piled high next to it.

A small part of him wanted to relent, to give in to his hungry stomach and her chatter. To start off the day in something other than the usual silence. A silence he now realised was somewhat lonely.

But if this was to work he needed to stand firm. Start as they meant to go along. Better to upset her than to give her any unrealistic expectations of what their time together would be like.

'I'm going for a shower.'

She didn't turn around at his call, just nodded her head in acknowledgement. But when he reached the door she said, 'I was only trying to show my thanks, you know.'

She turned from the kitchen counter and stared at him defiantly.

When he didn't speak she reddened a little and crossed her arms. 'I went to a lot of effort.'

He retraced his steps back across the room to where she stood. Her gaze rose up to meet his. 'Firstly, I don't eat breakfast. Secondly, I think we need to have some clear boundaries if this is going to work.'

She gave a tight laugh. 'What on earth do you mean by "boundaries"?'

Her laugh rightly mocked his stuffiness, and although he knew he deserved it he was in no mood to defend himself. 'Aideen, I want to help you in re-establishing your business. Nothing else.'

Her blush deepened, but her hands clenched tight at her sides. 'I was making you breakfast. That's all. What's the big deal?'

'I don't want you getting any ideas.'

She drew herself up to her full height and plopped a hand on her hip. 'Trust me—I won't. A workaholic, taciturn, controlling man is the last thing I'm looking for in my life.'

Workaholic, he would admit. But taciturn and controlling? What on earth was she talking about?

'Right—explain to me how I'm taciturn and controlling?'

'You had the next month of my life all planned out before you even spoke to me the morning after the storm.'

'So? It was the most logical plan. Even you agreed with it.'

'Yes, I agreed with it. But not once did you stop to understand just how difficult it was for me to accept it.'

Baffled, he asked, 'What do you mean?'

'I mean I lost not only my business last year. I also lost my pride and self-respect. Having to accept help from you made me feel like I was failing again.'

'That wasn't my intention.'

'I know. But maybe if you'd stopped and thought about how I might possibly feel—if you'd asked me my opinion—then you might have understood.'

She had a point, but he wasn't going to admit it. So instead he challenged her. 'And taciturn?'

'Do you really need to ask? You have barely spoken to me in the past two days.' Biting her lip, she studied him before she added, 'If you don't want me around why did you invite me to stay with you?'

Her bluntness left him for the first time in his life slightly speechless. But then anger rose up in him. 'I don't *do* breakfast…or small talk. I'm not going to be your friend. Now, if you will excuse me, I have to get ready for work.'

He marched away, down the long corridor and up the stairs to the master bedroom, yanking off his tee shirt as he went. Irritation ate into his bones.

As he stood in the shower he scrubbed his hair and defended himself against what she'd said. He wasn't controlling…or taciturn. She was exaggerating. She was saying he was wrong for being decisive. Well, 'decisive' had got him where he was today.

But as the water pounded down on his scalp the uncomfortable realisation that her words might have some truth began to creep into his consciousness.

Had focusing solely on work for so long numbed him to others' feelings? Yes, he was decisive and logical… but did he sometimes steamroller over others?

And as he dressed he began to grasp why he had been

so disturbed by her attempts to make him breakfast. Why it had irked him so much.

It had unsettled him just how good it was to arrive home to activity, to the comfort of having another person in the house. Of course the fact that it was Aideen, looking so happy and gorgeous, added to that uncomfortable realisation. Because it would be so easy to fall into the trap of enjoying her company, of wanting more with this woman.

Aideen emitted a low groan and dropped her head down on to the smooth mahogany wood of the library desk.

Could this day get any worse? First she had messed up with Patrick at breakfast. What was supposed to have been a small gesture of thanks had blown up in her face. Why hadn't she just let him walk away? Did it really matter that he hadn't wanted to accept her gesture of thanks?

He had left for meetings soon after, with a curt goodbye, and she had spent the day alone in this breathtakingly beautiful chateau, on a hill overlooking the Seine, annoyed about their argument but having to be cheery as she made phone calls to organise her own meetings for the coming days.

Several times with prospective new clients she hadn't even got past the receptionist. But she had eventually managed to organise enough meetings to make the trip worthwhile—some with colleagues she hadn't seen since she'd lost her old business.

Just now she had ended another call to an ex-client. The entire call had been a tense mixture of arduous questioning and awkward silences that had left her feeling completely flustered.

'Tough call?'

Her head jerked up and her stomach lurched as she saw Patrick standing in the doorway.

'The usual.'

She was cross with him—and hurt, and embarrassed. And she couldn't bring herself to look at him. But when he came and sat on the table she was working at she couldn't help but glance in his direction.

'I'm sorry for not being tidy…for taking over the kitchen. I just wanted to say thank you for everything you have done by making you breakfast… I guess it backfired.'

'You don't need to thank me. I suppose I'm finding it a little strange to be sharing my home with someone else.'

She'd only been here a day and he was regretting it already. She shuffled some books and placed fistfuls of marker pens and pencils into canisters, glad that her hair had fallen forward and blocked his view of her face. Which was burning in embarrassment.

'I can move out, if this isn't working for you.'

The touch of his hand on her arm had her jerking back in surprise. Her stomach flipped and her throat tightened when she looked at him, her eyes transfixed by the perfection of his thick dark eyebrows, now drawn into a frown, and by the length of his fingers when he drew a hand over his cheek in a gesture of exasperation.

'No. That's not what I mean. I think we need to give each other space, but also adapt to the other person's way of doing things. I've been under time pressure recently, with the demands of my work. I might have rushed to make decisions without taking how you would feel into consideration.'

She felt stupidly relieved by his words, and without

much thought said teasingly, 'Are you apologising to me in a very roundabout way?'

His lips quirked a fraction. 'I suppose I am.'

'So, basically, I need to stop making a mess of your kitchen and you'll try not to be so grumpy?'

His gaze challenged hers playfully. 'And I'll try to eat some breakfast.'

'You have a deal.'

He pushed himself back a little further along the table, creating more distance between them. 'Now, do you want to talk about that call? Who's Ed?'

Her stomach flipped over. The designer had asked her bluntly why she should use her consultancy over Ed's—her ex. She had put forward her track record in designing, her competitive price points, but she knew the designer was still unconvinced.

As she knew to her cost, Ed could be very persuasive and economical with the truth. There had been little point in protesting that a lot of the designs Ed claimed as his own were in fact hers. The designer wasn't likely to believe her. Of course she could take Ed to the courts as a way to claim her rightful ownership, but she didn't have the financial resources to do so.

And Patrick had heard her conversation.

Embarrassment flamed on her cheeks. She had only told her friends and family some of the details, too hurt and humiliated to tell them everything. So how on earth could she be expected to tell a billionaire that she had been so naïve and trusting? This stunning chateau alone told the story of his incredible success and obvious business acumen.

Also, as stupid as she knew it was, it still hurt that he hadn't wanted her breakfast. And every time she saw him she fancied him even more, which was starting to drive her a little crazy.

She lifted a box on to the table. She couldn't speak. Hurt, attraction, embarrassment all swirled away inside her, turning her brain to mush and catching hold of her tongue.

She worked with her back to him, but Patrick could still see how her fingers trembled as she scattered folders and loose cuts of material on to the desk. It was clear that she was going to pretend not to have heard his question. The surface of the desk was quickly disappearing under a mountain of her belongings.

Who was Ed and what hold did he have over her to cause this unease? Something that felt suspiciously like jealousy twisted in his stomach. He breathed it out. He wasn't going there. This was about helping her professionally. Nothing more. And although he was curious about this he would hold off asking her about him again… for now.

As she fought with the now empty cardboard box a low sigh of exasperation sang from her lips. Strangely compelled to ease her upset, to see her smile again, he stepped towards her and took the box, twisting it flat. A quick glance at the messy desk had him saying, 'This won't do. This room is all wrong. Come with me.'

He grasped her hand in his and almost at a run led her down the corridors of the vast chateau.

'Where are we going?'

'You'll see.'

What on earth was he doing? She should be protesting, should be working. But it felt so good to be chasing down corridors with him, to have his hand holding hers.

He brought her to a vast empty room, bathed in evening sunshine, with the warmth of the sun bouncing off the parquet flooring. White wooden doors and windows formed the entire length of the garden-facing walls.

'This is the orangery, but while you're here you can use it as your studio. The library is too dark and small—especially for someone like you, who likes to...' His mouth lifted ever so slightly and after some thought he said, 'Who likes to spread their work around. This is a better space for you to work in. There are some trestle tables stored in an outside storage room. There's other pieces of furniture stored there, too, that you can use. I can get my staff to move them in here tomorrow morning, when they start work, or if you want we could go and get them now ourselves.'

She was completely thrown, and moved by his suggestion. The room would be perfect to work in. She had two options: thank him and run the risk of the emotion in her chest leaking out in gushing thanks, or brazen it out and tease him back.

It was an easy decision. 'Are you saying I'm messy?'

'Based on the evidence of the papers scattered around the library just now...and the kitchen this morning... then, yes, I'd say pretty confidently that you're messy.'

She gave him a mock withering look. Once again she felt completely disarmed by his thoughtfulness. 'This would be perfect. The light and space in here is incredible. Thank you.'

'Good. Now, how about we go and get those tables?'

A little while later, as he helped to unpack a box, he gestured towards her company's logo.

'Where did you get the idea for your business name? Little Fire?'

'It's what Aideen means in Gaelic.'

'I didn't know that.'

'It also felt like a very apt name for the type of business I want. I want to create a small bespoke design consultancy—to be an innovator in the industry. A consultancy that is respected for its passion.'

'It suits your personality, too.' He said it in a deadpan voice, but once again there was a faint hint of humour sparking in his eyes.

Taken aback, she looked away. When she eventually glanced back the humour was gone.

'Are you going to tell me who Ed is?'

She didn't want to. She wanted to bury him in the past. But she needed to answer his question in some form.

'He was my business partner. I set up the company by myself and he joined me a few years later. I was having cash flow problems and he was able to inject capital into the business. We had been to university together and it felt like a good fit for him to come on board.'

'I'm hearing a big *but* here.'

'A very big "but", unfortunately. He insisted on taking a majority share in the business. After that we expanded too rapidly—spent capital on projects we shouldn't have. I shouldn't have agreed to him having a majority share—it led to an inequality in our partnership and gave him the leeway to overrule me. We started arguing. Eventually it became clear that he wanted me out of the business and he made life difficult for me. I tried hanging in there, but in the end I knew I had to go.'

Perched on a trestle table opposite her, he looked at her sombrely. 'What did he do?'

She pulled a wooden bistro chair to the trestle table she'd been working at and sat. She needed to do something while she spoke to avoid having to look at him. To pretend this was an inconsequential conversation. So she started to order by colour the pile of swatches she would take to her meetings in the coming days.

'He overruled all my decisions. He belittled me in front of clients. He dropped heavy rumours that I was difficult to work with.'

'Is that why you're so hesitant about visiting clients?'

'Yes. It's embarrassing. I don't really know how much he said to our clients and whether they believed him. I'm hoping not… But I'm going to do everything I can to make this a success. I love my job. Adore the creativity involved and all the opportunities I get to work with different designers. No two days are the same. I just have to make sure I build up my client base quickly to meet my overheads.'

She glanced up and caught his eye.

'And you know what? I want to prove Ed wrong, too. He said I would never make it on my own.'

'That's understandable, but be careful that proving him wrong doesn't distract from your energy, from your focus.'

She wasn't quite certain what his point was…and she wasn't sure she wanted to fully understand…so she shrugged it off. 'It won't.'

And he knew she had, because without missing a beat he said, 'Okay, tell me what you're going to do differently with this business.'

It was a good question. She knew instinctively a lot of things she would do differently, but hadn't consciously addressed them. She had been in too much of a rush to start again.

For a few minutes she thought about it, her fingers

flicking against the edges of a blue cotton swatch. What *would* she do differently?

'I need to manage my cash flow better—not expand too quickly. Meet with my clients on a more regular basis...communicate with them.'

He nodded at her answer, but fired another question at her immediately. 'Fine, but at a strategic level what are you going to do differently?'

For a while she was lost as to how to answer him. And then she thought about her client base. 'I need to think through what my target market is... Perhaps I'm too diversified at the moment.'

'Spend time thinking about those issues—those are what matter. Not Ed. Don't waste any more time on him. He's not worth it. You lost that business, which was tough. But it's in the past now. Your focus must be on the future.'

Her pulse raced at his words but she forced herself to smile. 'I know. You're right. I need to go and get some more files from the library.'

She practically ran from the room. She heard him call her name but she didn't turn back. Of course he was right. But the hurt of losing the business lingered stubbornly inside her and it was hard to move on from it. To just push it aside. Everything he said was true and right, but she wasn't ready to hear it yet...especially from a billionaire.

His assistants in Dublin and Berlin had long gone home, but after finishing a conference call with his development team in Shanghai later that evening Patrick checked in with his assistant in Palo Alto. He updated his calendar with her for the coming days and ended the call.

He spent the next hour reading the daily reports he

expected each of the managing directors of his subsidiaries to file.

The projected revenue for a new construction industry project management database was not performing as expected. He emailed the management team responsible and listed the new sales strategy he wanted them to follow.

When that was done he checked the time on his monitor. It was not yet nine. In recent months he had frequently worked until twelve. It felt a little strange to have all this spare time. He switched off the bank of monitors on his desk and walked over to the windows overlooking a dense copse of trees. In the dusk, flocks of birds swirled above the treetops, a pink-tinged sky behind them.

How was Orla doing? Should he call her? One of them would have to end this impasse between them. But it was she who had caused it. It was up to her to call.

From the corner of the window he caught a glimpse of Aideen working in the orangery. She was sitting at a trestle table, staring out towards the garden, lost in thought.

Anger bubbled in his stomach at the treachery of her former business partner. He could understand her desire to prove him wrong. If it was him he would exact revenge. But the guy wasn't worth it. She needed to focus on the future and not on the past.

He was tempted to go and speak to her. What was it about her that drew him to her? He certainly admired her tenacity and her determination to start again. And the moment he was in the same room as her, he was sidetracked by her radiance and beauty. By her positive outlook on life. By her smile. By the thick curtain of hair that seemed to change colour according to the light—chocolate-brown at times, filled with highlights of cinnamon and caramel at other times. By her body, which called to the most elemental parts of him…

Yes, she talked too much, and was way too messy… but after two years of silence part of him yearned for her chatter, for her warmth, for her positive outlook on life.

Another part of him wanted to shut it all out. At least that way he wouldn't be able to mess up a relationship again.

And at times her honesty and openness left him floundering. This morning and this evening she had spoken with an emotional honesty that had made him stop and think. And he wasn't sure if he liked that. She spoke about the past while he preferred to ignore it.

Knowing now, though, what she had gone through with her business collapse, made him want to protect and help her even more. He wanted her business to succeed and he would give her all the support that she required.

He just needed to ensure that he kept it strictly professional.

CHAPTER FIVE

WEARING FOUR-INCH HEELS on a day when she had to race from meeting to meeting using the Paris Métro hadn't been one of her best ideas.

At least her short-sleeved silk button-down dress, which she had designed and created using one of her new range of textiles, was comfortable. And thankfully it had also proved to be a major hit with many of the designers she had met with today. They had commented on the dress the moment she had walked into their studios, and it had been the perfect icebreaker for her to introduce the rest of her range.

Her toes were pinched, though, in her never-before-worn shoes, as she walked out of the headquarters of one of Europe's leading online luxury fashion retailers. But she still didn't regret her refusal to use Patrick's chauffeur for the day.

It was bad enough that they had travelled to Paris on his private jet. That they were staying in his unbelievably beautiful chateau. She couldn't accept any further help from him.

This morning they had travelled together into the centre of Paris and he'd had his chauffeur, Bernard, drop her at her first meeting. She had been too nervous to chat, and for once had been grateful for Patrick's silence.

But as she had been about to leave the car he had looked at her with a gentle kindness that had almost floored her and said, 'Believe in yourself.'

She stepped through the automatic sliding doors out on to the street and paused. The building was at the corner of an intersection of five boulevards. Which way was the Métro again? And would it look odd if she walked barefoot?

And then, a little further down the street, she spotted him—leaning against a lamppost, watching her. She faltered at the intensity of his gaze. And then his mouth curled into a smile and she came to a complete stop. He'd smiled at her. He'd actually *smiled* at her.

She knew she was staring at him in shock but she couldn't help it. He was smiling at her! And it felt like the best thing ever.

She smiled back, beyond caring that she probably looked really goofy. And for a joyous few seconds they simply smiled at each other.

Her heart was beating crazily, and her stomach felt as though it was an express elevator on a busy day.

He was so gorgeous when he smiled. Dressed in a bespoke dark navy suit and a crisp white shirt open at the collar, he wore no tie. Other pedestrians did a double take as they passed him by. And if she'd been in their shoes she, too, would have walked by with her mouth open at the sight of the extraordinarily handsome man standing on the pavement, his eyes an astonishing translucent blue, a smile on his delicious mouth.

Heat rushed through her body, quickly followed by a sharp physical stab of attraction.

As she walked to him she tried to disguise the blush that burnt on her cheeks by fussing with the laptop and samples bags in her hands.

'Hi. What are you doing here?'

'You told me your last meeting of the day was here, so I thought I'd come and see how your day went.'

He said it with such sincerity the air whooshed out of her lungs and she could only stand there, looking at him with a big soppy grin.

This was all so crazy. How on earth had she ended up in the city of love with the most incredible and gorgeous guy in the world smiling down at her?

'You look very happy.'

'I'm working on not being taciturn.'

She had to swallow a laugh as she eyed him suspiciously. 'Are you mocking me?'

'Possibly. How does a martini sound?'

She should say no. Pretend to have some work she needed to do back in his chateau. Keep her distance.

But instead she said, 'That sounds like heaven.'

He signalled down the boulevard. Within seconds a dark saloon had pulled up beside them.

His chauffeur had dropped them at his favourite bar in Paris. It had been a while since he had been to the sleek hotel opposite the Jardin du Luxembourg, but it was still as fun and lively as he remembered. And it served the best martinis in the city.

They had spoken little during the journey. The minute she had sat in the car she had slipped off her shoes, leant her head back on the headrest with a sigh and looked out at the familiar Parisian sights as Bernard took them down the Champs-élysées, then Place de la Concorde, and crossed the river at Pont de la Concorde.

'Are your feet still hurting?'

She had looked at him warily. 'Kind of.' Then, with a rueful smile, she'd added, 'Okay—I admit they're killing me. Lord, I miss my old shoes. Stupid flood.'

When she had earlier refused to use his car for the day, at first he'd been irritated at her stubbornness, but then he'd had to admit to himself a grudging admiration for her determination to be independent. But it did still irk him a little. Using his car would have been no big deal.

The lighting in the bar was low, and light jazz music played in the background. Her eyes lit up when the waiter placed their drinks on the table with a flourish. A kick of awareness at just how beautiful, how sexy she was, caught him with a left hook again.

Earlier that left hook had caught him right in the solar plexus when she had walked out on to the street from her meeting. Her black dress with its splatters of blue-and-cream print stopped at mid-thigh. And long, long legs ended in the sexiest pair of red shoes he'd ever seen. Red shoes that matched the red gloss on her lips. Lips he wanted to kiss clean, jealous of the effect they would have on any other man.

Despite himself he hadn't been able to stop smiling at her. And when she'd smiled back, for the first time in a long time, life had felt good.

'So, how was *your* day?'

It had been so long since anyone had asked him that question he was taken aback for a few seconds. She leant further across the table and looked at him expectantly, with genuine interest. Tightness gripped his chest. He had pushed so many people away in the past two years. And now this warm, funny and vibrant woman made him realise two things: how alone he had been and how much he must have hurt those he had pushed away.

Would the same thing happen to her?

He felt as though he was being pulled by two opposing forces: the need to connect with her versus the guilt of knowing that by doing so he was increasing the likelihood of hurting her when it was time for her to return to her cottage.

But once again the need to connect won out.

'It went well. I finalised my negotiations to buy out a mobile software application for hospital consultants.'

'That's brilliant. Congratulations.'

She lifted her martini glass and together they toasted the negotiations. It felt good to celebrate an acquisition with someone after all this time.

Her head tilted in curiosity. 'What are you smiling about?'

He scratched his neck and looked at her doubtfully. *Oh, what the heck?* He would tell her. 'I was just thinking that sitting in a bar with you, toasting an acquisition, sure beats my attempts to train the dogs to high-five my acquisitions.'

Her laughter was infectious, and they both sat and grinned at each other for a long while.

'You can always pop down to my cottage to celebrate in future.'

Instantly a bittersweet sadness reverberated in the air between them. Across the table her smile faded, and he could see her own doubt as to whether they could ever have such an easy relationship.

He needed to get this conversation back on neutral ground. 'Tell me about your day.'

She gave a groan. 'My first meeting was a disaster. It was with an ex-client who grilled me on the stability of my business and how I was going to deliver on projects now that I didn't have a team behind me.'

Her hand played with her glass and her chest rose heavily as she exhaled.

'To be honest, after that meeting I was ready to give up and head home.' A smile formed on her mouth. 'But on the Métro I thought about what you said to me this morning—to believe in myself.' She paused and ducked her head for a moment. When she looked up, there was a blush on her cheeks, but resolve fired in her eyes. 'I decided you were right. So I dusted myself down and got on with the next meeting.'

This morning she had been visibly nervous about her meetings, but he had deliberately not asked too many questions, nor overwhelmed her with his ideas on how she should approach things. He knew he needed to give her some space. Allow her to face this on her own.

Her comments about him being controlling had hit home and he was consciously trying to curtail his perhaps, at times, overzealous attempts to help her. He would help—but at the pace she needed. That hadn't stopped him from thinking about her all day. Or from leaving his meeting in the eighteenth arrondissement early to ensure he was there when she left her last meeting.

'The rest of the day went much better, thankfully. At lunchtime I met up with a designer friend, Nadine, who is over here from London on business, too. She has just received a major order from a chain of exclusive US boutiques—it will completely transform her business. And she wants me involved, which is really exciting.'

She smiled with such enthusiasm he was sorely tempted to lean across and kiss those full, happy lips.

She scanned the room and gave a nod of approval. 'Great choice of bar, by the way.'

He had to lean towards her to be heard properly above the chatter and music surrounding them. 'I used to live in St Germain before I moved to the chateau.'

'You *lived* in St Germain! I've always dreamt of living in the centre of Paris. Oh, you were so lucky. No offence—your chateau is lovely and everything—but why did you move?'

He wasn't sure he liked the direction this conversation was going in, so he gave a noncommittal answer. 'I like the space and peace of the chateau.'

A shake of her head told him she wasn't going to let it go. 'But you have that already, with Ashbrooke. Why would you want to live outside Paris when you have this incredible city to explore?'

He took a sip of his martini. 'I was tired of city life. And, like at Ashbrooke, I wanted peace and quietness in which to focus on my work.'

She shook her head in bewilderment before saying, 'Just for me, describe your apartment here.'

He was about to say no, but she looked at him so keenly, so hungry for detail, that despite his better judgement he gave her a brief outline. 'It was a two-storey penthouse in a Haussmann building overlooking Île de la Cité.'

'So you had views of Notre-Dame and Sainte-Chapelle? Remind me again why you gave *that* up.'

'For the peace of the countryside—for the space.'

'But why do you have all that space if you have no one to share it with?'

Taken aback by the bluntness of her question, and because it was too close to the bone, he speared her with a look. 'You really don't hold back, do you?'

Her head tilted for a moment and then she said in a more conciliatory voice, 'Not really… But why do you live in such isolated spots? What's the attraction?'

'I spent most of my twenties travelling the world to meet work demands. In recent years I've wanted more stability, a less chaotic and frantic pace. So I've opted to work out of Ashbrooke predominantly and travel only when necessary. And, anyway, I like the countryside. Who *wouldn't* want the ocean views that are at Ashbrooke?'

'I love the countryside, too… But you live behind tall walls, away from the rest of the surrounding communities. Do you never feel alone?'

Lord, she was like a dog with a bone. With someone else he would have cut them off a long time ago, but she asked these questions with such genuine curiosity he found himself reluctantly answering them.

'I don't have time to even *think* of being alone, never mind feel it. Trust me—it's not an issue in my life.'

'What about friends and family? Do you see them often?'

Right—he'd had enough of this. Time to change the subject. 'I see them occasionally.' He nodded at their now empty glasses and said, 'Would you like to walk in the Jardin du Luxembourg before we head back home?'

She nodded enthusiastically, and as they walked out of the bar together his attention was hijacked by the sensual sway of her hips in the high heels. Bewildered, he shook his head, trying to figure out just what was so hypnotic about her walk—and also how she'd managed to get him to talk about personal issues he had never discussed with a single other person before.

The martini and the relief of having survived the hurdle of visiting clients for the first time had combined to make her a little light-headed. So she had happily accepted his suggestion that they stroll through the park.

The paths were busy with joggers and families. A few times she caught Patrick smiling at the antics of careening toddlers and something pulled tight in her chest.

Did he ever want a family of his own? The question was on the tip of her tongue a number of times but she didn't dare ask.

They passed by a bandstand, where a brass band played happy, toe-tapping tunes to a smiling and swaying audience.

'I spoke to William today. The renovations are going well. You'll be glad to hear I will be out of your hair in less than a month after all. It might be three weeks, tops.'

He glanced across at her and then away. 'That's good news.'

A dart of disappointment had her asking, 'That I'll be gone soon?'

He came to a stop and folded his arms. He looked down with good-humoured sternness. 'No. That the renovations are going well.'

Emotion swirled in her chest. She shuffled her feet on the gravel path and she, too, crossed her arms. 'I'm really grateful for everything you have done.'

He looked beyond her, towards a group of children sailing model wooden sailboats on a pond. 'It's not a big deal.'

Of course it was a big deal. But he clearly didn't want to make out that it was.

Evening stubble lined his jaw, adding a rugged masculinity to his already breathtaking looks. How incredible it would be to feel free to run a hand against that razor-sharp jawline and to look into the eyes of this strong, honourable man. Her heart hammered at the thought that in the future some other woman might get close enough to him, might feel free to do exactly that. And he might welcome it.

She pushed away the jealousy that twisted in her stomach. Instead she nodded towards the children he was looking at and said, 'My dad's hobby is model boats. As a child I spent a lot of my Sundays standing in the freezing cold in Herbert Park in Dublin, wishing his boat would sink so that I could go home.'

He gave a bark of laughter and shook his head. 'You sound like you were a wicked child.'

'I used to get into a fair share of trouble, all right. I always blamed my two older brothers, though! Did Orla do that with you?'

He gave a heavy sigh. 'Don't get me started. She used to insist on coming everywhere with myself and my friends. Half the time she would cause mischief—running through people's gardens as a shortcut, helping herself to something from their fruit trees along the way. But when neighbours rang to complain it was always me they mentioned, never Orla. She was so small they couldn't see her.'

For the first time since they'd met he was speaking with genuine ease and affection about someone close to him. He was so animated and relaxed she longed for it to continue for a while.

'What was the village you grew up in like?'

'Everyone knew everyone. I went to the local school and spent my weekends with my friends—either on the beach or playing at our local Gaelic football club.'

Referring to the two traditional Gaelic sports played in most clubs, she asked, 'Hurling or football?'

'Both, of course.' For a while he paused, and then he said, 'I still remember my first day going to the club. My mum took me down and I was so excited to be wearing the club jersey. All the other boys on the street wore it all the time.'

Her chest tightened. 'Do you remember a lot about your mum?'

His voice was sad when he said, 'Just snapshots like that.'

And then he began to walk away.

She had lost him. To that silence he often fell into. She wanted to bring him back.

She followed him and after a while said, 'So, do you get your good looks from her or your dad?'

That elicited a smile. 'So you think I'm good-looking?'

'You know you are. I bet you were the heart-throb in school.'

He laughed at that. 'To answer your question—I take after my dad. Orla's more like my mum.'

'What was your dad like?'

'Hard-working, loving, supportive. A family man and a good neighbour. Orla and I were the centre of his world. He worked several part-time jobs to ensure he was at home when we were. Money was pretty scarce. It used to worry me, but he would just shrug and say that as long as we had one another that was all that mattered. When Mum died he was determined we wouldn't miss out. He even learned how to sew so that he could make us costumes for school plays.'

A lump formed in her throat at hearing the love for his father in his words. In a quiet voice she said, 'He sounds like he was a really good man.'

His eyes met hers for a moment. She felt her breath catch to see the soft gratitude there.

'He was. Each Christmas he would leave us both a memory chest under the tree, filled with little mementos he had collected for us during the year: our sporting medals, awful paintings and poems we'd created in school that only a parent could love, photos of our holidays.'

He paused as a catch formed in his throat. It was a while before he continued.

'In the chests he would also leave a handwritten list with all the reasons why he loved us.'

Her own throat felt pretty tight, but she forced herself to speak. 'What a lovely idea.'

He nodded to that.

They walked beside the urn-lined Medici Fountain and paused where Acis and Galatea, the lovers from Greek mythology, carved in white marble, lay reclined in a lovers' embrace. Their embrace was so intimate she had to look away.

'You said you used to worry about money when you were younger? Is that what motivates you now?' she asked.

'Partially. But it's also the challenge, and knowing that my products are making a difference in people's lives. Especially in the medical field, where they can have a huge impact on how services are delivered to patients. I also like to know that I can provide for others, too.'

She wondered if he meant Orla, but something in the look on his face kept her from asking.

They continued walking, and she said after a while, 'I'm sorry you lost your mum and dad…Patrick. It must have been very difficult.'

'You just get on with it, don't you? There's no other choice.'

'How old were you when you lost them?'

He inhaled deeply before he spoke. 'Seven with my mum…twenty-two with my dad.'

He'd been so young. To lose your mum at seven… She couldn't even begin to think about losing her parents, never mind at that age. 'What age was Orla?'

'She was just a baby with my mum—sixteen when my dad died.'

'Oh, the poor thing.'

He glanced towards her, and then away again quickly, but not before she saw the pain in his eyes. 'Orla found my dad when she came home from school one day. He had died from an abdominal aneurysm.'

For a while she was lost for words. What could she say about such a terrible loss? 'I'm so sorry. It must have been a terrible shock for you both.'

'It was.'

'I bet you were a great older brother, though, which must have helped her a lot.'

Instantly he stiffened and a coolness entered his voice. 'I tried to be.' He gave his watch a quick glance. 'We'd better get back. I have a conference call with Palo Alto in less than an hour.'

Thrown by the sudden change in conversation, and knowing instinctively that he deliberately wanted to end their chat, she looked at her mobile phone. It was almost eight.

'Do you have to take that call? You never seem to stop working.'

He gave a quick shrug. 'I have a problem with a system roll-out over there.'

'But you must have endless directors. Do you really need to have such a hands-on role?'

They exited the park and walked towards Bernard, who was waiting at the kerb.

Patrick answered. 'I like to be involved.'

As they approached the car she said, 'More like you like being in control.'

He looked at her unhappily. 'It's not that simple.'

About to slip into the car, she asked, 'Are you sure?'

He sat beside her and his rigid jaw and thinned mouth told her he was in no way happy with her comment.

He turned and fixed her with a lancing stare. 'It's my *responsibility* to be in control. I will not let down those who are dependent on me—in the workplace or otherwise. I will not apologise to anyone for doing my job.'

She was taken aback by the cold fury in his voice, but he had his mobile out and was speaking rapidly to someone before she could even respond.

CHAPTER SIX

A SET OF preliminary moss-green and off-white designs stared back at her from the laptop screen, as though willing her to make a decision.

Ever since Patrick had asked her what she was going to do differently with her business the question had constantly played on her mind. Time and time again she came back to the one major decision she had to make. Would she stop designing for the upholstery market in favour of specialising exclusively in fashion textile design—her true love?

And now she had to decide whether to submit these designs to Dlexa, a world-renowned upholstery textile manufacturer. Would she be crazy *not* to? It was a huge gamble to take. The upholstery business had often seen her through lean times. But it was also a distraction that ate into time she could be devoting to the fashion market.

So many times during the past few days she had been tempted to go and talk it through with Patrick, to get his advice. So much for her resolve to do this on her own…

Not that she had seen enough of him during the past few days to have such a conversation anyway. Their paths seldom crossed…and she had a sneaking suspicion that he had engineered it that way. Yes, they were both working incredibly long hours. And he was either out at meetings or locked away in his office at the chateau. Once or twice he had appeared in the kitchen while she was preparing a meal. But he'd always had an excuse to leave—something needing his attention elsewhere.

She tried not to let it get to her. Tried not to dwell on the fact that it was probably because she had said too much the other night. Asked too many questions. Tried to get to know him a little better.

At times she'd got a glimpse of a different man from the work-obsessed CEO the world saw. But as quickly as he opened up that fun and playful side he would shut it down again.

What did she expect, anyway? The man ran countless multimillion-pound companies. He wasn't going to have time to chat to her over a coffee.

She constantly felt as though she was waiting for him to appear, with a low-lying nervous anticipation she couldn't dispel. Each night disappointment sat heavily in her chest as she walked to her bedroom, knowing that yet another day had gone by without her seeing him for more than a few minutes. And in the mornings that disappointment was transformed into equally inexplicable excitement at the prospect of seeing him.

The designs for Dlexa would take at least another twenty to thirty hours of work to complete. Would it be worth the investment of her time? Her gut was telling her to specialise, to follow her dreams. But flashing in neon lights in her mind's eye was the total sum in her bank account, which had made her blanch when she'd checked it earlier today.

She needed a coffee.

His housekeeping staff had left for the day, leaving

behind, along the chateau's corridors, the smell of beeswax and the air of contentment that settled on a newly cleaned and polished space.

In the kitchen she tackled the beast of a coffee machine. It still made her nervous. There were way too many knobs and buttons for her liking. But she was slowly getting the hang of it and its temperamental nature. Thankfully so, because it produced the best coffee she had ever tasted.

She was about to head back to the studio when she spotted a parcel on the kitchen table, wrapped in luxurious cream paper and thick gold ribbon. The card on top was addressed to her.

Intrigued, she opened the card.

Aideen,
We are sorry the sea ate your shoes. We gathered all our treat money together to buy you a new pair.
Love, Mustard and Mayo
PS: We promise not to chew them when you return to Ashbrooke. We hope you are enjoying Paris.

Inside the parcel, wrapped in individual silk pouches, she found the most exquisite ivory ankle-strap sandals. High enough to make her feel a million dollars, low enough for her to actually be able to walk in them.

They were stunning; if she had seen them in a store she would have fallen over herself to hold them just for a little while. But she couldn't accept them. Her pride had already taken a severe dent at the amount of help she'd had to accept from Patrick. It was humiliating to take so much and give so little in return.

And, given his remoteness in recent days, she didn't even understand why he was giving them to her.

She needed to go and speak to him—figure out why he was giving them to her and then somehow explain why she couldn't accept the gift.

She knocked and waited at the partially open door of his office. He opened the door with a phone to his ear and gestured for her to come inside.

He sat down behind his desk, his eyes moving speculatively to the package in her hand.

Her belly tightened and she turned away, inspecting the modern paintings hanging on the French Grey walls, failing to convince herself that his deep, authoritative and decisive voice had no effect on her. She tried not to listen to his conversation but was intrigued by the way he was able to quickly fire out the pros and cons of purchasing an office block in Rio de Janeiro. He ended the call with an order to proceed with the sale.

Her chest swelled with admiration. She wanted to be like that. Certain and unwavering in her decision-making.

His office was incredibly neat. The desk contained four different monitors, a keyboard, a ream of paperwork neatly stacked into a pile and nothing else. No empty cups, pens askew, or sticky notes scattered with random thoughts like on her own desk. No wonder he thought her messy. The guy was a perfectionist. Perhaps, to achieve what he had, he'd had to be.

'Take a seat.' He gestured over to two silver-green velvet-upholstered sofas that sat before the fireplace. He replaced the handset in its cradle before he moved over to sit on one himself.

She sat, and placed the parcel on her lap. For a moment she stared down at it, the shoe-lover in her reluctant to give it up. But then she placed it on the coffee table between them and pushed it towards him.

'Thank you for the shoes but I can't accept them.'

To that he simply raised an eyebrow.

A knot of tension grew in her belly.

'Giving me accommodation and a place to work for a month, flying me to Paris… You've been more than generous. I can't accept anything else from you—it wouldn't be right.'

'They're just a token from Mustard and Mayo.'

She couldn't help but say in amusement, 'Dogs who internet-shop? Now, *that's* clever.'

For a moment he looked as if he was going to insist, but then he leant towards her. 'Why don't you tell me why you can't accept them?' When she smiled, he held his hands up in admission and said, 'See? I *do* listen to you. This time I'm going to try and understand why before I try to persuade you otherwise.'

'It's not that I don't like them…they're beautiful…or that I'm not grateful.' She came to a stop and her heart was beating so wildly she felt light-headed.

She bent her head and inhaled deeply, clasping her hands. She squeezed her fingers extra-hard.

'I think I should explain…'

Was she crazy, telling him this? But she wanted him to know. So that he would stop ruining all her plans to be independent by giving her so much.

She glanced at him quickly, and then looked away from his frown and stared out of his office window, seeing the tips of the trees blowing in the light breeze.

'After I lost my business I swore I would never be dependent on or beholden to another person again.'

'What do you mean by "beholden"?' His tone was sharp.

She struggled to find the right words to explain what she meant. 'I mean…not indebted to another person. I don't want to feel that I always have to be grateful—that I owe someone else. That I have no right to voice my opinions. But it's not just that… I have to prove to myself that I'm not a failure. And accepting all your help feels like I'm cheating, somehow.'

He looked taken aback, and then he argued, 'You're not a failure if a business deal goes wrong. It happens to a lot of people. At least you had the guts to risk everything in creating a business in the first place. Not everyone could do that. And accepting the help of a neighbour is not cheating.'

He stood and paced the room, his jaw working.

'And I certainly will never—and I mean *never*—make you feel obliged or indebted. I am not that type of person.'

She flinched at the annoyance in his voice. She was making a mess of this. She needed to tell him everything. Then maybe he would understand.

'I'm trying to be honest with you. I want you to understand and I'm sorry if I'm offending you. Let me try and explain…then you might understand. My business partner…Ed. He was my boyfriend, too.'

Heat rose in her cheeks and she stopped as humiliation gripped her throat. She bit the inside of her cheek.

'Not only did he manoeuvre it so that I had no option but to walk away from the business, but he was also having an affair with our finance director.'

She jumped when she heard him utter a low expletive, and was taken aback by the dark anger that flared in his eyes.

'What an idiot.'

'I know. Him…and me.'

'No! The guy's despicable. Don't for one second think you were in anyway responsible.'

'But that's the problem. I was. I shouldn't have agreed to him owning a higher percentage share in the business. I shouldn't have believed all the lies he told me. I honestly can't believe I was so stupid. That's what I hate most—I'm now so wary of others. It's one of the reasons why I can't even accept the shoes. It's not just that they're way too expensive, but I keep wondering *why* you're being so kind and generous.'

He stopped pacing and looked at her with breath-stealing intensity. 'Because just maybe we are not all jerks. Some of us might actually have a heart and want to do the right thing.'

'I'm finding that hard to believe.'

'Don't let him have the power to change you, to make you unhappy.'

'I know… In my heart I know all that. But I can't stop these feelings.'

Across from her he folded his arms on his chest. A look of frustration joined his anger. 'You don't trust me, do you?'

Completely taken aback she gabbled nonsensically. 'No! Yes…I'm not sure… We don't really know one another. Oh, God, I'm sounding really rude. I didn't come here to insult you, and I'm sorry if I have. I just want you to understand why I can't accept anything else from you. It's not that I'm not grateful…call it pride, self-respect… I just can't. I hope you can understand?'

With a raised eyebrow and a quick shrug he said, 'I'm trying to.'

Part of her wanted to turn and run. This conversation had not been a success by any stretch of the imagination. She had insulted him and annoyed him and possibly even hurt him. She needed to try to make amends. Starting with showing some trust in him.

She inhaled a deep breath and began to talk. 'I'm sorry. I honestly didn't come here to insult you. I wanted to explain about the shoes. But I also came in the hope of some advice.'

His brow had creased with doubt but she forced herself not to stop.

'I'll keep it short. You said I should think about my business strategy. Well, there's an area of my business that brings guaranteed revenue, but it's time-intensive work and it's in an area I don't particularly want to specialise in. I'm thinking of not submitting work in that area again, but I'm worried about the revenue.'

'What's the worst-case scenario?'

'I lose revenue for a few months.'

With a quick nod he fired another question at her. 'Can you absorb that loss?'

'Just about.'

'And if the drop in revenue continues for longer?'

'I can always re-enter that market… It will take time to build my portfolio back up, but it's doable.'

He didn't ask any more questions, but instead walked back to his desk. After a while she realised he was waiting for her to speak. And she also realised she had her answer.

With a light shrug, she smiled. 'I think I know what I should do.'

He nodded. 'I think you do.'

As she went to leave the room he called after her.

'Are you certain about the shoes?'

Her hand on the door, she paused, and it was a while before she could turn around. After all she had said he was still being kind. But maybe he was also indirectly asking if she still didn't trust him.

Her heart turning over, she faced him. 'Maybe some time in the future?'

His eyes narrowed at that, and she fled down the corridor before either of them had a chance to say anything further.

Standing at his office window later that evening, Patrick spoke to his chief financial officer while staring out at yet another incredible dusk sky. This evening it was a riot of pink, lilac and lavender, with faint wisps of cloud to the forefront.

A movement on the terrace caught his attention. Aideen was out there, photographing the sunset. Wearing jeans and a silver and grey top, she had her hair pulled back into a high ponytail, exposing the delicate angles of her face, her full lips, the smooth jawline and long, slim neck.

Too distracted to concentrate, he ended the call early and stood watching her.

Their earlier conversation had been difficult. The shoes had been his way of saying he was sorry about everything she had lost in the flood…and for being so tetchy in recent days.

After their walk in the park the other night he had opted to keep his distance from her. He had revealed too much of himself. And he didn't like how good it had felt to be in her company. Her comment about being a good brother to Orla had only reminded him of how he had failed, and of all the reasons why he needed to keep his distance from Aideen.

But the shoes had unwittingly hit a raw nerve with her.

He cursed out loud when he remembered the raw pain etched on her face when she had described her ex's betrayal. No wonder she was slow to trust him. Not that it hadn't stung to hear her admit it.

But knowing what she had gone through strengthened his resolve that nothing could happen between them. He had to suppress his attraction to her. She had just come out of a destructive relationship. The last thing she needed was to be hurt again. And a messy relationship with him was a sure way for her to get hurt.

She needed practical support right now—not a lover. Not all the complications and misunderstandings and raw emotions and intimacy that went with that.

He opened the door from his office out on to the terrace and walked to where she was now sitting, on a wooden bench on the first tier of the terraced garden. The grass muffled his footsteps and when he called her name she looked up in surprise.

'I saw you taking some photos.'

Angling the camera towards him, she asked, 'Would you like to see them?'

He sat beside her and watched the images as she flicked through them on the viewfinder.

'They're beautiful. Will you use them in your work?'

'Probably. They will look great in silk.'

As she kept on flicking the pictures of the sky disappeared and a family portrait appeared in the viewfinder.

With a fond laugh she said, 'Welcome to my family.' She zoomed in closer. 'That's my mum and dad. My brother Fionn.' Then she flicked through another few photos until she found a close-up of a family of three. 'And this is my brother Gavin and his wife Tara, with their little girl, Milly.'

In the photo Gavin and Tara gazed down at their baby with utter devotion. Something kicked solidly against his gut. And kicked even harder when Aideen flicked on to a close-up of Milly.

'Isn't she so beautiful? I never realised just how much I would fall in love with her. The day Gavin rang to say she had been born…' She paused and shook her head in wonder. 'I honestly have never been so happy. You might even have heard my screams of excitement all the way up in Ashbrooke!'

Aideen's enthusiasm and love for Milly slammed home just what he was going to miss. He was never going to get to know Orla's baby. He coughed as a sharp pain pierced his heart.

She looked at him in concern and said, 'Are you okay?'

What was it about her that made him want to tell her? Was it that he was tired of holding in all the hurt and anger inside himself? Was it that she was so open herself?

'My sister Orla is expecting a baby. Next month, in fact.'

Her mouth dropped open in surprise. 'Really? That's fantastic. You must be so excited. Oh, wait until it's born. It really is the best feeling in the world. You wi—'

He cut across her. 'It's not that straightforward.'

'What do you mean?'

'Orla and I haven't been getting on.'

'Oh, listen—I argue with my brothers all the time. You'll be fine.'

Her exuberance and happiness were too much. How could he explain to her just how bad things were between him and Orla? How he had failed her? How she didn't trust in him? How she threw everything he did for her back in his face? It was easier to pretend that she was right.

He answered without looking at her. 'Perhaps.'

'Have you bought anything for the baby yet? I went on a crazy spurge before Milly was born. I bought her the most exquisite hand-knitted blanket in a shop in Mooncoyne. You could buy Orla's baby one, too.'

'I transfer money to Orla every month. She can buy whatever she needs.'

She swung forward on the bench to catch his eyes, horror in her own. 'Please tell me you're joking. You're Orla's only family. You *have* to buy her a present.'

He gave her blistering look. 'Now who's being dictatorial?'

She backed off, hands raised. 'Okay. Fair enough.' She paused for a whole five seconds. 'But still—you have to buy something for your… Is it a boy or a girl?'

Frustration ate into his stomach at her question. He didn't know, and it was humiliating and painful all at once. 'I don't know.'

'Oh. Does Orla know?'

He had no idea. To avoid answering her he looked at his watch. 'I have some calls to make.'

As he stood up she said with concern, 'It's gone eight thirty at night—do you really have to make calls now?'

He simply nodded, indicating that he did, but as he went to move away her hand reached out and stalled him.

'Will you just wait for a minute? There's something I want to say to you.'

He was about to argue, but there was a warmth to her eyes that had him sitting down beside her again.

He looked at her suspiciously and she knew she just had to come out and say what was on her mind. 'Can I be a nag for a few minutes?'

He asked warily, 'Can I stop you?'

'The crazy hours you work…'

Something shuttered in his eyes and tension grew in his jawline.

For a moment she was about to apologise for overstepping the mark, but she stopped herself in time. Maybe he needed to hear some of this.

'I know I annoyed you the other night, when I said you just wanted to be in control of everything. It wasn't a fair comment. I understand you have a lot of responsibilities, and I admire how hard you work and everything you have achieved. What I was trying to say was that I reckon you really need more of a balance in your life.'

He crossed his arms on his chest. 'Pot…kettle…black.'

He had a point, but that wasn't going to stop her. 'You're right. We both need to get a life. Stop working such crazy hours and start having a bit more fun.'

His jaw worked and he fixed her with a cool gaze. 'I have a life. One that I'm happy with.'

'But your life revolves around just work. You *must* need downtime. A way of relaxing, blowing off steam. Answer me this—have you dated recently?'

His answer was curt. 'No, I've been too busy with work.'

She rose a sceptical eyebrow.

'What about friends and family? Do you get time to see them?'

'Occasionally.'

'So basically your life is just work? That can't continue. You seem to be very hands-on with all your different subsidiaries—perhaps you should delegate more? That would free up your time and allow you to have a better balance. Time you could spend with those close to you.'

'Are you trying to tell me *again* how to run my businesses?'

His voice was ice-cold, and it stung to be on the receiving end of his displeasure. Who was she, anyway, to tell a successful billionaire that he needed more in his life?

It would be so easy to change the topic. But she was the only person in his life right now, and someone needed to say these things. And she cared for him—possibly more than she should.

Her heart thumped in her chest at his obvious irritation but she ploughed on. 'No, I'm not telling you. I'm just suggesting. Look, I know that you are super-successful, and that I lost my business last year, but that doesn't mean I can't have an opinion. I admit I might be wrong, but at least give it some thought.'

His gaze, rather astonishingly, slowly turned from furious to quizzical to mild amusement. 'I have to give it to you, Aideen. You're pretty tough underneath all that beauty and happiness. I have managing directors of multinational companies who would probably agree with you but wouldn't have the nerve to say so.'

She threw her eyes heavenwards, trying to ignore the pulse of pleasure his words evoked, telling herself he was only joking. 'Well, I can't see how pretending it's otherwise will help you.'

'You think I need *help*?'

He sounded incredulous. What did he think? That he was the only one who could help others? That he was the only one capable of being a knight in shining armour?

'You say you're happy, but my guess is that you could be happier…God knows, I know I could be.'

He looked at her quizzically. 'What do you mean?'

How could she tell him that she was sometimes lonely…sometimes scared about facing life on her own? It would sound so needy. And it would probably set off all types of alarm bells in his brain.

So instead she leant back into the bench and said, 'I miss being spontaneous—living life for the moment. I have been so bogged down in my business for the past five years I think I've stopped knowing how to have fun.'

Giddy relief ran through her body when he gave her a rueful smile. 'Spontaneity? I haven't had a lot of that in my life in a while.'

Something in his smile freed her. 'Let's do something *now*!'

'It's getting late…'

She laughed at the incredulous look on his face. 'Let's go clubbing.'

'I don't think there are many clubs in the village,' he pointed out with a laugh.

'We could go into Paris.'

'Yes, but I have calls I need to make…I won't be finished before midnight.'

'Cancel them.'

'I can't.'

She folded her arms primly and said, 'I told you that you don't know how to have fun.'

For a while he considered her with a smile. But in the

silence a tense awareness blossomed between them. His smile faded and darkness entered his eyes. He leant closer and her heart began to thunder again. She looked up into his eyes, barely able to breathe. He came even closer and his whole body seemed to eclipse hers.

His head slowed, moved down towards hers, and when his mouth was level with her ear he whispered in a lilting, sexy voice, 'You want spontaneity…?'

A deep shiver of desire ran through her. Every pulse-point in her body felt as though it was thudding against her skin. Her body swayed closer to him, desperate to feel his strength and warmth.

Her throat had closed over. She barely managed to whisper, 'Yes…'

His hand lay against her cheek and with gentle pressure he turned her mouth towards his. Their mouths aligned and almost touched. She closed her eyes, suddenly dizzy with wonder. She squeezed her hands into tight balls. She couldn't touch him. Because if she did she was worried she would never be able to let go.

And then his lips were on hers and her entire body turned to jelly. His warm, firm lips teased hers with butterfly kisses and she gave a little sigh. He deepened the kiss. Her arms of their own volition snaked up to grasp the material of his sweater. Beneath her fingers his chest was hard and uncompromisingly male.

Her head swam. She swayed against him. His hard body was like a magnet. She longed to touch every part of him. She wanted more.

When he eventually released his hold on her and pulled away she looked at him, dazed, her senses overloaded.

With a lazy, sexy grin he asked, 'How's that for spontaneity?'

Without thinking, she breathed out in a husky whisper, ‘Pretty spectacular, really.’

Her already flushed skin flamed at his obvious amusement at her answer.

Flustered, she added, ‘And enough spontaneity for one night, I reckon. I think it’s time I went inside.’

She got up to leave, but he placed a hand on her arm. His eyes were soft pools of kind amusement.

‘Thank you for tonight…’ For a moment he looked down, a hand rising to rub the base of his neck. When he looked up again he said with wry amusement, ‘Thank you for the life coaching… You can pop the bill in the post.’ And then, with his eyes sparkling, he added, ‘And thank you for the kiss.’

It had been the most incredible kiss of her life. But this thing between them was going nowhere.

She gave what she hoped appeared to be a casual shrug, said, ‘Goodnight!’ and hightailed it up the steps to the terrace.

She walked briskly—first to the orangery, to return her camera, and then to her bedroom with a confusing mix of elation and worry.

It had been the most incredible, tender and emotional kiss she had ever experienced. But neighbours didn’t kiss like that…and certainly not with such underlying passion and poignancy.

She lay awake for hours later, their kiss swirling in her brain.

They were only supposed to be neighbours—nothing more.

But they already knew more about each other than many close friends did. She had revealed more about herself than she'd ever done before. And slowly, bit by bit, he was confiding in her.

And, even though she knew they had no future, time and time again her brain wandered off topic and she dreamt of him kissing her. And of that kiss leading to a lot more…

CHAPTER SEVEN

DESPITE BEING ON a teleconference with his Northern Europe management team Patrick found himself zoning out of the conversation about a project delay and losing himself in memories of how good it had been to kiss Aideen last night. The soft fullness of her lips, the press of her breast against his biceps, the low purr of frustration when he had forced himself to pull away…

It had been a stupid and reckless kiss…but a large part of him didn't care. How could he regret something that had felt so good?

But how was he going to play it with her now? In truth, he wanted to throw caution to the winds and kiss her again. And possibly even more. But what of all the messy awkwardness that doing so would cause?

A movement at his office door had him looking away from his screen.

Dressed in navy jersey shorts and a white tee shirt, a pair of white trainers on her feet, Aideen smiled at him cheekily and waved two tennis rackets in the air.

Her long legs were toned, as was the rest of her tall, strong but curvy body. She brimmed with fresh vitality and health. She stepped into the room and he was unable to look away. An image of her brown eyes heavy with pleasure, the heat of her mouth last night, popped into his brain.

The sound of someone coughing had him looking back at the screen. Seven pairs of eyes were looking at him speculatively, no doubt wondering what had caught his attention.

He looked at his team, and then back at her.

He shouldn't. He really needed to finish this call.

'Elsa, take over for me.' He looked towards Aideen and raised an eyebrow, challenging her. 'And, Elsa? Please decide and implement whatever strategy you deem appropriate to get the project back on track. Update me only if there are any issues.'

Aideen was right. It was time he had some fun in his life.

He cut the connection on seven even more stunned looking execs and leant back in his chair. 'I was in the middle of a conference call.'

'You've been in this office since six this morning. You know what they say—all work and no play…'

He stood and walked towards her, doing his best not to allow the threatening smile to break on his lips. 'Are you saying I'm dull?'

He took unexpected pleasure from the blush that blossomed on her cheeks.

She swallowed hard before she spoke. 'No. Never, ever dull.' There was a hint of breathlessness in her voice and she blushed even harder.

'So what's with the rackets?'

'Well, as there's a tennis court worthy of Wimbledon sitting unused outside, I thought we should use it.'

He placed his hands in his pockets and looked at her

with playful sternness. 'Is this a not too subtle way of making me "get a life"?'

'You have me rumbled.' She grinned back cheekily. 'So, are you up to the challenge or are you too scared?'

When she put it like that there was no way he was saying no. 'Give me ten minutes.'

As she turned to leave she said, 'I must warn you, though. I was under-thirteen champion at my tennis club.'

He caught up with her out in the corridor. 'So you think you might be able to beat me?'

'I'll certainly try.'

'How do I put this nicely…? You don't have a hope.'

To that she playfully threw back her head in a gesture that said she wasn't going to listen to him and walked away. About to turn the corner, she turned around. 'Nice delegation, by the way.'

'And I did it without even flinching.'

She gave him a wicked grin and turned away.

She was right. He did need to delegate more. He had a talented and ambitious team surrounding him. And he was starting to suspect that he was holding them back by insisting on such centralised decision-making. He needed to empower his subsidiaries more.

He had once. When he had started out he had given them plenty of autonomy. But in the past few years, as the business had exploded in size, he had reigned them in. The truth was as his home life with Orla had become more fraught he had used work as a way of feeling in control, driven by the thinking that if he couldn't support her emotionally he would at least do so financially. By pulling the businesses back under his control he'd felt as though he was achieving something and he'd been able to bury the feelings that went with failure.

But centralised control wasn't sustainable. It had to change. But relinquishing that control wasn't going to be easy.

Two hours later he threw his racket up in the air in elation. Aideen stood at the opposite end of the court wearing a deep scowl.

'That was *not* out.'

'It was out by a mile. I told you I would win.'

'You didn't give me as much as an inch.'

'Like you did *me* any favours!'

She shook her head and stomped down towards the net. 'I didn't realise you were so competitive.'

'Aideen, in comparison to you I reckon I'm almost comatose.'

With a laugh she conceded, 'I hate losing.'

'So I gathered. Come on. I think we could both do with a drink.'

They walked to the kitchen and he prepared them each a large glass of sparkling water mixed with fresh orange juice. They took them out on to the terrace to drink, a light breeze cooling them down.

Across the table from him she stretched her arm in and out a number of times.

'Cramp?'

'I think I might have pulled a muscle on a return volley.'

'You *did* throw yourself about the court.'

At that she gave a sheepish shrug. 'I admit I can get carried away sometimes. I spent my childhood trying to keep up with my two older brothers. I couldn't help but develop a competitive streak.'

'Your competitiveness…hating to lose…was that one of the reasons why losing the business was so hard for you?'

'I guess. Despite my less than tidy ways, I've always pushed myself hard. I suppose my pride did take a dent. It was the first time in my life I failed at anything.'

Her words immediately resonated with him. His business success highlighted just how badly he had messed up with Orla. It made the success seem somewhat hollow when you didn't have someone to share it with.

She flexed her arm again, and said, in a thoughtful almost sad voice, 'I know I have to think about the future and move on. But it's really not that easy to just wipe away the past. To ignore everything that happened. To bury the pain. I can't help but wish that things had turned out differently.'

Something sharp pierced into him and he practically growled out, 'Were you in love with Ed?'

She blinked rapidly and her mouth fell open. Eventually she answered, 'I thought I was.'

A strange sensation of jealousy seeped into his bones and he had the sudden urge to punch something. He had never felt so possessive of a woman in his life. He needed to change the subject quickly—to distract them both.

'Try to forget him—and everything that happened. I appreciate it's hard, but it's vital you focus on the future. Tell me about your dreams, what you personally want to do in the coming years.'

She eyed him with a mixture of surprise and suspicion. But then she shrugged and said, 'Well, that's a big question.' For the longest while she paused, her brows knitted together in concentration. 'Nothing extraordinary, really. I've always wanted to visit St Petersburg. And travel to Dharamsala in India. Where the most incredible mulberry silk is woven. Afternoon tea in Vienna has always sounded like fun. Oh, and I want to learn how to bake a soufflé.'

'A soufflé?'

'They always sink on me—it drives me crazy.'

Curiosity got the better of him and he couldn't help but ask, even though he wasn't certain what answer he wanted. 'And family and relationships?'

She eyed him warily and it was a while before she answered. 'Check back in with me in a few years' time. Right now I'm not exactly in the mood to be in a relationship. All you men have a black mark against your names.'

'All three and a half billion of us?'

'Yes, every single one. Well, apart from my dad and my brothers.' She hesitated, glanced at him briefly, and then said in a rush, 'And possibly you if you continue being such a good neighbour.'

Trying but failing to ignore the reality check her words had caused, he answered drily, 'Glad to hear that.'

'So what about you? What's on *your* list?'

Like her, it wasn't something he had overly thought about. And yet it was a question that filled him with unexpected excitement. 'I want to continue on with the restoration of Ashbrooke. The east wing in particular needs conservation work. And there's an old bathing house on the grounds I want to restore, as well.'

'You really love Ashbrooke, don't you?'

'Yes, I do. I suppose I have a lot of emotional attachment to it because of Lord Balfe. His family owned the estate for generations and it was a huge honour that he was happy to sell it to me. There were several other interested parties, but he chose me. He spends most of his time in the Caribbean now—growing old disgracefully, by all accounts.'

'Do you see him often?'

'Unfortunately, no. Maybe I should buy a business in the Caribbean so I'd have an excuse to go there.'

'Or…an easier solution…you just take a holiday and go and visit him.'

She smiled cheekily at him and he couldn't help but laugh.

For a while they just looked at each other, the warmth and understanding in her eyes causing his heart to thump in his chest. A deep connection reverberated between them.

A slow blush formed on her cheeks and she leant into the table, her fingers drawing down over the grain of the wooden tabletop. 'What else is on your list?' she asked quietly.

His blood thundered in his ears at the strength of the connection he felt with her. He wanted to tell her about Orla and his dreams of them being close once again. But where would he even start to explain the jumbled up, contradictory one hundred and one emotions he felt for his sister?

Instead he said, 'I want to take part in the Isklar Norseman Xtreme Triathlon in Norway.'

'Now, *that* sounds impressive.' Her eyes sparkled with admiration, but the sparkle slowly faded. 'And relationships?'

What would she say if he told her he could never be in a permanent relationship? That he wasn't interested in being in one? That he was no good in relationships?

That he had lost everyone he had ever loved and never wanted to expose himself to that again?

It was easier to be non-committal rather than get into a debate about it. 'Some day, perhaps.'

She moved forward in her chair, a familiar look of determination growing. 'You won't meet anyone if you're stuck in your office twenty-four-seven.' When he didn't respond, she asked bluntly, 'Are you going to sacrifice the rest of your life to work for *ever*? Are you *so* determined not to let other people in?'

He gave a disbelieving laugh. 'I spend my days speaking to people on the phone. I travel. I speak to my staff.'

'Okay, let's call a spade a spade, here. Work conversations and travel don't count. You don't *really* have people in your life—meaningful relationships. And you want it that way. Plus, you've stopped knowing how to have fun.'

Thrown by the uncomfortable truth of her words, he chose to answer only her latter accusations. 'No, I haven't.'

'Prove it.'

'And if I don't?'

'I'll cook dinner for you tonight.'

'Am I supposed to be scared of that prospect?'

'Just imagine the mess I'd make of your kitchen.'

Despite his best efforts he winced. 'Fine. If you want fun, we'll go out tonight. I'll take you to dinner at one of my favourite restaurants.'

'You're on. But I'm paying.'

'No. It's my idea. I'll pay.'

She threw him a stern look. 'I'm sure you appreciate why I would want to pay.'

He breathed out in exasperation. 'I wish you would just accept my help.'

She looked at him with quiet dignity. 'I don't want to feel like a freeloader.'

Something pulled in his chest and he said in a conciliatory voice, 'Let's just go out and enjoy ourselves. By all means you can pay.'

Though she had insisted she would be paying for the meal, the moment she got back to her bedroom, fretting at the likelihood of jaw-dropping décor with matching prices at his favourite restaurant, she checked her online bank account's balance. Thankfully she wasn't yet in the red.

But it turned out that the restaurant was a traditional bistro, located in the back streets of St Germain. The menu proudly announced that it had been established in 1912. She guessed that the décor—Bakelite lights, simple wooden tables and chairs, tiled floors—hadn't changed a whole lot in all that time. It was utterly charming.

After they'd been shown to their seats by the maître d' she continued to look around. 'It's really lovely here.'

'This is one of my favourite restaurants in Paris. The cooking is excellent and the service friendly.'

Yes, and it was also very romantic, with its low lighting and small, intimate tables with a single candle on each. In fact they were surrounded by fellow diners who were totally engrossed in one another.

This was awkward.

She shuffled in her seat and looked away from the amused glance he threw in her direction.

She was saved from further embarrassment by the arrival of their waiter, who brought them a glass of champagne along with their menus.

Holding his glass up towards her, Patrick said, 'Here's to the success of Little Fire.'

Taken aback by the sincerity in his voice, and his support of her cherished dreams, she felt unexpected tears form at the backs of her eyes. She blinked them away rapidly and took a sip of her champagne.

She read the menu with both relief—she could afford the prices—and growing excitement. Every item on the menu was a mouthwatering classic of French cuisine.

'They have Grand Marnier soufflé for dessert—I'm going to *have* to order that.'

'Why don't you order dinner for both of us?'

She looked from him back to the menu and then back at him, taken aback and slightly horrified. 'But I have no idea what you like.'

He shrugged with amusement. 'I don't care.'

Ed would have walked over hot coals rather than allow her to order for him.

'Are you sure?'

He watched her with an assuredness and yet an intimacy that had her looking back down at the menu with a ricocheting heart.

'Absolutely.'

As she ordered she couldn't stop fretting that he wouldn't like her choices. She exhaled in relief when he proclaimed the Pinot Noir she had chosen perfect. But when his starter of rillettes and her warm artichoke salad arrived she pushed the food around her plate nervously.

'Aideen.'

She looked up at the command in his voice and her breath stalled when she looked into his formidable serious eyes.

'My food is delicious… Why are you so nervous?'

Giddy relief mixed with her trepidation, causing nervous energy to flow through her veins. She inhaled a shaky breath. 'I guess I'm waiting for an argument.'

'Is that what would have happened with your ex?'

'Yes.'

A tense silence settled between them. A quick glance told her that he was still studying her.

'How about we leave him in the past and you assume that I'm an okay guy?'

He said it with such quiet forcefulness that her stomach and heart did a simultaneous flip. God, he was right.

She lifted her head and met his gaze. 'You're right. And you're more than an okay guy.'

He gave a wry smile. 'I guess I don't have to worry about getting a big ego around you.'

With a cheeky grin she said, 'I compliment where it's deserved.'

'Are you telling me I have to work harder to earn your compliments?'

'Possibly.'

His eyebrow rose slowly and sexily and at the same time his eyes darkened. In a low, suggestive voice he said, 'I'll have to remember that.'

No! That wasn't what she'd meant! And why was she blushing? And why was her heart hammering in her chest? And did the couple next to them *have* to look so in love?

They spent the rest of the meal chatting about the countries they had visited, the movies they loved, the books they adored, but beneath all that civility a spiralling web of deep attraction was growing between them all the time. In every look, in every smile.

And the intimacy was only added to by her excitement at the amount of new books and places she had to try, based on his enthusiastic descriptions. It was as though a whole new and exciting world was opening up to her because of him.

'*Mademoiselle*, would you care to follow me to the kitchen?'

Confused, Aideen looked at their waiter. She'd only just noticed he was standing there, and said, 'Sorry…?'

'The chef is waiting for you.'

Perplexed, she looked towards Patrick, in the hope that he might understand what was going on.

With a sexy grin, his eyes alight with mischief, he said, 'Remember how you said you wanted to learn how to make a soufflé? Well, this restaurant is world-famous for them. You'll find no better place to learn.'

Dumbstruck, she stared at him. She leant towards him and whispered, 'What if I mess up? You've seen the way I work in the kitchen. This is a professional kitchen, for crying out loud. I might set off the fire alarm or something like that.'

'Maybe the chef will teach you how to work tidily as a bonus?'

She gave the waiter a quick smile and whispered impatiently, 'Patrick, I'm serious.'

He shook his head, amused. 'Go and have some fun. You're the one saying all the time that we both need to be spontaneous. Well, now's your chance.'

She sat back and took a deep breath. 'You're right.'

The waiter held her chair as she stood. She moved to the side of the table and leant over and kissed Patrick's cheek. 'This is the best surprise ever. Thank you.'

A while later Aideen returned to their table, triumphantly holding the biggest soufflé Patrick had ever seen, and smiling so brightly that the people at the tables around them burst into spontaneous applause. She took a playful bow, then sat and looked at the dessert, enraptured. The woman at the next table leant across and admired the creation, and Aideen enthusiastically described her experience in the kitchen.

He could not stop watching the delight dancing in her eyes, the warmth and humour with which she spoke to the other woman.

Two things hit him at once. First, the realisation that tonight wasn't just about helping Aideen and giving her support. He genuinely wanted to be in her company. He wanted to get to know her better. For the first time in years he had met someone he could talk to—a woman he deeply admired for her optimistic and determined take on life. And secondly the realisation came that he wanted her in his life as he'd never wanted a woman before.

Both things left him absolutely confounded.

CHAPTER EIGHT

ALL THE WAY home in the car they had chatted, and Patrick had teased her when she'd got Bernard to switch on the radio and then sang along to the old-time hits playing. He had declined her dare to join in, but Bernard had been a more willing singing partner, and by the end even Patrick had been humming along.

But now they were home that ease had vanished, and tension filled the air as they stood in the chateau's marble-floored entrance hall.

Silence wrapped around them and her stomach did a frenzy of flips when she looked up into the bright blue of his penetrating gaze. Dressed in a slim charcoal-grey suit and white shirt, he looked impossibly big and imposing.

Her insides went into freefall when his hand reached out and a finger trailed lightly against her forearm.

'I enjoyed tonight.'

Her body ached to fall against the hard muscle of his. To feel the crush of his mouth. But she didn't want to ruin what they had. Their blossoming…dared she say it?… *relationship* felt so fragile she was worried that taking it any further, complicating it, might pull it down like a house of cards.

So instead she gave him a big smile and said, 'It was fun. I don't think I've laughed so much in a long time.'

'Would you like a nightcap?'

She should just go to bed. They were on dangerous territory. She could see it in his blistering stare. This need for one another was a two-way street. Much as it pained her to do so, she needed to create a diversion—to call a halt to the chemistry fizzling between them.

'A nightcap sounds good. And I have a surprise I want to show you. I'll go and fetch it from my studio.'

'Now I'm intrigued. I'll fix us some drinks in the lounge.'

Walking towards the orangery, Aideen marvelled once again at the sheer scale of the chateau. What Patrick casually called 'the lounge' was a room at least five hundred feet square, with priceless parquet on the floor, littered with modern designer sofas and rugs, and with work from world-famous artists on the light grey walls.

As she reached for the surprise she had made for him on the trestle table, she hesitated and looked at it warily. Would he even like it? He could afford something encrusted in priceless jewels. Would he think this was laughable? Would he hate it? Her ex would have made some barbed comment that would have made her feel small and insignificant.

What was she thinking? She knew Patrick wasn't like that. He never intentionally hurt people. He was a kind man, with integrity. She had to stop letting her ex colour her judgement.

He watched her over the rim of his glass, desire flooding his veins, as she walked across the lounge floor to where he was sitting on a sofa; she looked incredibly beautiful.

Over cream wide-legged trousers she wore a vibrant lilac blouse, tucked into a thick band that displayed the narrow width of her waist.

Her hair was pulled back and twisted into a low coil at the back of her head, and he had spent the entire meal wondering what it would be like to press his lips to the pale column of her throat.

It was only as she drew nearer that he realised she was carrying something.

She stopped before him and gave him an uncertain smile before holding out a rectangular box. Then with a nervous frown she changed her mind and placed it on the beaten bronze coffee table in front of him before sitting opposite.

Covered in a pale blue and dark green silk fabric, in which the two colours ran into one another in layers, and the size of a shoe box, the box was too tempting not to open.

He sat forward and placed it on his lap. What could possibly be inside? He opened it up, fascinated. Inside it was lined in a rich dark navy velvet. And it was empty.

Confused he asked, 'What is it?'

'A memory chest for Orla's baby.'

He pulled the chest closer and made a pretence of inspecting it, his heart twisting at the reminder that he wouldn't be part of their lives.

In the periphery of his vision he could see Aideen's hands clasp her knees, her knuckles growing whiter and whiter.

'I was down in the village today and I saw the box in the little antique shop. It was originally lacquered on the outside, but I reckon too much handling and love over the years had damaged it beyond repair. When I saw it I thought it would be the perfect size for a memory chest for a baby. And it felt fitting to use a box that had been loved by someone before. The material I used to cover it was inspired by the sea and the land around Mooncoyne. I thought you might like to give it to Orla's baby…as a reminder of Mooncoyne, but also to keep up the tradition your dad started.'

He winced at her words, and she must have seen it, because at once she said with dismay, 'You don't like it.'

Seeing the chest had brought home just how much he hated the prospect of not being a part of his nephew's or niece's life. Anger towards Orla, and anger that they had lost their parents so young, had him saying crossly, 'It's not that. You shouldn't have bothered. It was a waste of your time. Orla will never accept it.'

'Why not?'

He put the chest back on the coffee table and reached for his brandy. 'It's too complicated to explain.'

She shuffled in her seat and he glanced at her. He looked away from the disappointment in her face.

She cleared her throat before she spoke. 'I know we're still getting to know one another…but I do want to help.'

He picked up the chest again and twisted it in his hands. Beneath the silk there was a thick layer of padding. No sharp corners that might hurt a baby.

'I'm guessing you spent hours making this?'

She tried to shrug it off. 'Not too long—just this afternoon. It was fun to do. But if you don't like it…'

His gaze shot up at the despondency in her voice. A wounded look clouded her eyes, but she gave him a resigned shrug. As though to say, *never mind.*

She had gone to a lot of effort. He wished she hadn't. But she deserved an explanation.

His throat felt peculiarly dry, and he wanted nothing but to get up and pace. But he forced himself to sit and talk to her, face to face.

'When my dad died Orla went from being outgoing and happy to an angry, rebellious teenager overnight. I was in my final year of university. I had already started a few companies on campus, and when I graduated—a few months after my dad died—I took them off campus and into my own headquarters. Orla moved to Dublin to live with me. We had no other family. From day one she fought me. She didn't like the school I selected for her. Some days I couldn't even get her to go. When she went out with friends she was constantly home late. Just to rile me, she started to date a series of unsuitable guys. Her school reports were appalling. When I tackled her about them she said she didn't care.'

Even remembering those days caused his pulse to quicken. He gritted his teeth and tried to inhale a calming breath.

'She had just lost her dad. School reports were probably way down on her agenda.'

His pulse spiked again. 'Do you think I didn't *know* that?'

She visibly jumped at his curt tone and he closed his eyes in exasperation.

'I'm sorry. That was uncalled for.'

She nodded her acceptance of his apology and waited for him to continue.

'I could see that she was hurting, but I knew her behaviour was going to hurt her even more in the long run. I had to stop her. I was, in effect, her parent. It was my duty to protect her, and I couldn't even get her out of bed in the morning.'

'But you told me before that you were only twenty-two.'

'That didn't matter.' He had been so full of dreams and ambitions that didn't involve a stroppy teenager. But he'd loved Orla, they'd had only one another, and he had given everything to trying to sort her out. Not that it had worked.

'Of course it mattered. How many twenty-two-year-olds are equipped to parent a teenager? It was a huge responsibility to take on.'

'What other choice did I have?'

She gave him a sympathetic look. 'I know. But don't downplay what you had to face. It was *huge*. Most people that age would have struggled. Many wouldn't have taken it on.' She paused for a minute, and then said in a quiet voice, 'It must have been a really difficult time for you both.'

'Yes, it was. I was getting pressure from her school. Work was crazy. I had to travel, so I employed a housekeeper—in truth she was a trained nanny, but I couldn't tell Orla that. She, too, constantly struggled with Orla. I used to come home from travelling, exhausted, to a sister who used to yell at me that she hated me. That I wasn't her dad and I should stop trying to act like it.'

'What did you argue about?'

'Everything. Her clothes, her going out, her curfew, the housekeeper… But the biggest thing was her refusal to go to school.'

'Did you consider moving her to a different school? Maybe she wasn't happy there?'

'After the fight I'd had to get her into that school there was no way I was moving her. It was the best school in Dublin. And she wouldn't even give it a chance. I told her she had to give it a year, but she wouldn't listen.'

'What do you mean, it was the best school in Dublin?'

'It was consistently in the top three for academic results in the entire country.'

'Was Orla academic? Are you certain the school suited her?'

He looked skywards. 'She would have been academic if she had applied herself. Instead she spent her days stockpiling make-up and texting on her phone. In the end I even moved us to a different part of the city, where she didn't have as many distractions. I confiscated her phone and stopped her allowance, but she still fought me all the way.'

'Maybe you should have given her some say in what school she went to. Included her in the decision-making. She had lost her dad, moved away from her friends…my guess is she was feeling pretty confused. Did you both talk through all that?'

'I was up to my eyes with work. And any time we spoke she ended up storming off, refusing to speak to me.'

'When I was that age most sixteen-year-olds I knew were pretty good at looking after themselves and knowing what they needed.'

She paused and rubbed her hands up and down the soft cream wool material of her trousers before giving him a tentative smile.

'I know this is easy for me to say, standing on the outside… Heaven knows, I'm only too aware how easy it is to get caught up in the messy dynamics of a relationship… how acute the hurt can be when it's someone we really care about… It can be hard to think objectively, to understand where we went wrong, how we could do things differently in the future.'

Again she paused, and gave him an apologetic smile, as though to forewarn him that he wasn't going to like what she was about to say.

She inhaled a deep breath. 'But maybe you should have allowed her to make some of the decisions herself… or made a joint decision. Not you deciding everything, controlling everything.'

His spine arched defensively at her words. 'I had to protect her.'

'Maybe she needed her big brother more than she needed a father figure… She was grieving for her dad. She would probably have resisted anyone who tried taking his place. I know I would.'

Some of what she'd said was starting to make him feel really uncomfortable. He hated remembering that time—how he'd floundered, the frustration of knowing he was losing Orla day by day.

As much to her as himself, he said, 'So it was all my fault?'

She moved to the edge of the sofa. 'No. Not at all. You were worried about her, and understandably wanted to do right by her. Protect her. But maybe you should have stopped and tried to understand what she needed, rather than what you *thought* she needed.'

'Well, she has made it pretty clear that now she needs me out of her life. Two years ago she left for Madrid, and now she rarely answers my calls. Before our dad died we were so close—she used to tell me everything. Now we have nothing.'

'Maybe the baby will bring you both closer?'

He gave a sharp laugh. 'I don't think so. She was over five months pregnant before I found out. And that was only because I flew over to see her. She admitted she hadn't planned on telling me. And she wouldn't tell me who the father is.'

'Why is that of any importance?'

She *had* to be kidding. 'Because he left her—the coward. And I would like to have a word with him and set him straight on parental responsibility.'

At that she smiled, and then her smile broke into laughter. He watched her, bewildered. And then he got it. He sounded like an old-fashioned controlling father.

He rolled his eyes. 'Next thing I'll be marching them both up the aisle, a shotgun in my arms.'

This only made her laugh even more. It lifted the whole mood in the room and gave him a little perspective.

'Okay, tracking down the father isn't going to be on my list of priorities.'

'Glad to hear it.' Her head tilted and she gave him a small smile. 'I really admire how you took on the responsibility of caring for Orla. You did your best in very difficult circumstances. My take on it, for what it's worth, is that if you stop pushing she'll come back to you. We all need and want family support. It's not something we naturally walk away from. And now that Orla is having a baby she needs your support more than ever before.'

He had to admire her optimism. 'I think things are too fractured for that.'

'You were the one who said you admired me for restarting my business. How about you try to restart your relationship with Orla? Think about what you would do differently so that you can have a better relationship with her.'

She made it sound so simple. 'I don't know...I don't want to upset her at this late stage of her pregnancy.'

'I understand that, but she needs you.'

'Orla wouldn't agree with you, I'm afraid.'

Even he heard the exhaustion in his own voice. He stared up at the ceiling. His little sister…pregnant. He just couldn't get his head around it. How would their dad have reacted? He would have worried, but supported Orla one hundred per cent. His dad had had unconditional love down to an art form.

Across from him, Aideen sighed. 'Patrick, I really think you need to cut yourself some slack. You were only in your early twenties. You were running several rapidly expanding multimillion-pound businesses and trying to parent a teenage girl. You did your best. Sure, you made mistakes. Haven't we all? But, as you've said to me, that's in the past. Focus on the future now. You have to think about the next generation in your family. Your nephew or niece will need you. Orla's baby deserves to have you in its life.'

His gut tightened. She was right. But what if he caused Orla more upset? What if they had yet another bitter argument? He would never forgive himself if something happened to her or the baby because of him.

He picked up the chest, the material smooth against his skin. 'I would like to keep this, if that's okay with you. Hopefully some day I'll get the chance to give it to Orla and her baby. It's beautifully made.'

He genuinely looked as though he loved the chest, and Aideen prayed that a time would come when he could give it to Orla. She could see how much the rift was hurting him.

'Were the arguments with Orla one of the reasons why you moved to Ashbrooke?'

'Partially… And in truth they prompted my move here to the chateau, as well. I love both houses, and I'm proud of the restoration I've carried out at Ashbrooke. It would have been terrible to see it fall into further decay when it's of such historic importance. At the same time, I *did* need to retreat and focus on my businesses. They were growing at a rate even I hadn't anticipated. But I also needed some head space after years of arguing with Orla. My apartments both in Dublin and in Paris held too many memories. Orla moved to Paris and lived in my apartment when she was expelled from school. It was pretty tense, to say the least—especially when I arrived to find she had moved two friends in with her.'

'You didn't tell me that she was expelled.'

'Amongst other things. She came to Paris to attend a language school, but she dropped out of there, too. She said she'd learn French faster working in a bar.'

She didn't understand why he sounded so exasperated. 'But that was *good*—she was taking on responsibility for herself and learning to be independent.'

'You didn't see the bar she was working in.'

'Am I right in guessing you didn't allow her to keep working there?'

'Too right. She was on the first plane back to Ireland.'

'How old was she?'

'Eighteen.'

She inhaled a deep breath. 'Were there any other options other than sending her home? She was an adult, after all.'

'She certainly wasn't *acting* like an adult.'

'Did sending her back to Ireland work? Did it help your relationship?'

He glanced at her briefly and then looked away. 'No.'

'Would you do anything differently if you had that time again?'

He looked thrown by her question. For a good few minutes they sat in silence, his gaze trained on a spot in the far distance.

'I would do a lot of things differently.'

His thumb travelled again over the silk of the chest, and when he looked up she realised the pale blue of the material was a close match to the colour of his eyes.

He held her gaze and said, 'You're the first person I've ever told any of this to.'

'What do you mean?'

'Exactly that. I never told anyone about the problems we were having.'

'Not the school or your friends?'

'No.'

'You mean you carried all of this on your own?'

'Orla and I only had one another. It didn't seem right to tell anyone else what was happening. It was private—between the two of us. Family problems should stay within the walls of a home.'

'But not something as big as this, Patrick. Not when you're on your own, with no one to ask for advice or just talk it through with. It must have been so tough for you.'

Bittersweet sadness caught in her chest. She was honoured and moved that he had told her. But she also felt a heavy sadness that he had been burdened with this for so long.

'You shouldn't have carried it on your own.'

A solemn, serious gaze met hers. 'I could level the same accusation at you.'

Emotion took a firm grip of her throat. 'You're right… It's hard to speak when you're hurting, when you're embarrassed and loaded down with guilt.'

'I'm glad I did tell you.' A smile played at the corner

of his mouth and he added, 'I never thought I would say this, but it's actually a relief to talk about it.'

It felt so good to see him smile. 'I'm glad, too.'

He considered her for a while, and her cheeks began to flame at the way his eyes darkened. An emotional connection pinged between them and her heart slowed to a solid throb.

In a low voice he said, 'I've been thinking over what you said about having more fun, and I've lined up a surprise for you tomorrow.'

Her heart began to race again, and to cover the wide smile of excitement that threatened to break on her mouth at any second she eyed him suspiciously. 'I hope it's not a triathlon, or something crazy like that.'

He shook his head with amusement, 'No, but I reckon you'd be pretty lethal in a triathlon—if the competitive way you play tennis is anything to go by.'

'You might be right, but I'm not the best of swimmers.'

'Really? You can't live by the sea and not be able to swim! When we get back to Ashbrooke I'll give you some lessons in the lough.'

Was he serious? He seemed to be. Mixed emotions assailed her at once, and a crazy excitement to know that he would want to do something like that. That there might be some type of future for them beyond Paris.

But what if she was wrong? Was she reading way too much into this? Was she crazy to believe and trust in a man enough to even *contemplate* the possibility of some type of future with him?

Her doubts and fears won out and she dismissed his suggestion with a laugh, praying it would mask the embarrassing frozen expression of hope on her face. 'Only if I can wear a wetsuit. The water is pretty cold in the lough.'

'Wimp!'

'I am not. Anyway, I have meetings tomorrow until four. Can the surprise wait until then?'

'Perfect. I'll collect you.'

She stood up and said happily, 'It's a date. Now I'm going to bed.'

Only as she went to walk away did she realise what she had said.

'Not that it's really a date or anything like that… You know what I mean.'

He, too, stood, and looked at her fondly, laughter in his eyes. 'Aideen…relax. And I would *like* it to be a date.'

'Would you?'

He pinned her with his gaze. 'Yes.'

His answer was such a low, sexy drawl that goose-bumps popped up on her skin. She gave him a skittish grin and before she embarrassed herself any further decided to make a hasty retreat. But not before she threw him another goofy smile.

As she walked out of the room she heard him say in the same sexy tone, 'Goodnight, Aideen. Sleep well.'

A delicious, deep shiver of anticipation ran the length of her body.

CHAPTER NINE

THE FOLLOWING EVENING at Issy-les-Moulineaux heliport, close to the Eiffel Tower, a helicopter stood awaiting their arrival.

As Bernard brought the car to a halt beside the impressive machine excitement bubbled in Aideen's veins. 'Where are we going?'

Patrick considered her mischievously as he contemplated her question. 'Now, if I told you that it wouldn't be much of a surprise, would it?'

'The helicopter is enough of a surprise for me… Oh, please tell me! I hate being kept in suspense.'

'No can do, I'm afraid. The good things in life come to those who wait.'

Bernard was waiting patiently at the door for her to exit, so she stepped out of the car. When Patrick joined her and they walked towards the helicopter she asked playfully, 'So is that your philosophy on life?'

He brought them both to a stop and stepped closer. He leant down. His breath was warm against her ear when he spoke and her heart did a triple flip.

'Sometimes the anticipation and the wait can be thrilling, don't you agree?'

Heat erupted in her body and she drew back to meet

his eyes, which blistered into hers. When she finally managed to speak it was in an embarrassingly squeaky voice. 'I guess…'

His gaze changed to a look of amusement and, taking her hand in his, he led her to the helicopter, where the pilot was waiting for them with the rear door open.

As the pilot made the final checks for take-off her mind raced. Was he confirming what she suspected… that he would like more with her? She had read signals so wrongly in the past. Was she getting this wrong, too? But the way he looked at her said she wasn't getting anything wrong. He looked at her as though he would like to bed her then and there.

For the entire forty-five-minute journey they played a game of 'yes and no' in which she tried to guess their destination. She was wrong on every count, and was rapidly running out of names. It was a good job she had listened in her geography lessons in school.

But when a baroque castle appeared in the distance, with its raked roof and tall chimney stacks, she whispered, 'Oh, my…it's Château de Chalant.'

Privately owned by the Forbin family, Château de Chalant was considered one of the most beautiful castles in France. It was never open to the public.

'What are we doing here?'

'Frédéric Forbin is a friend and business associate. I called him and arranged for us to visit the chateau.'

Flabbergasted, she could only stare at him, and then down at the manicured elegant grounds as the helicopter swept towards the chateau. As the helicopter landed, she saw a man waiting for them at the bottom of the steps leading up to a terrace that then led to double wooden front door.

'Is that Frédéric?'

'No, it's the chateau director, who is expecting us. Frédéric is away travelling. The chateau is of such historical and architectural importance Frédéric employs a conservation team, headed by the director.'

As they exited the helicopter she tried to dampen down the enthusiasm fizzing in her blood. She had studied the historic textiles of Château de Chalant while at university. Now she was going to see them first-hand! She wanted to babble with excitement, but forced herself to shake the director's hand calmly.

Then both men shook hands.

'Monsieur Fitzsimon, it is a pleasure to have you back at Château de Chalant. It's been a long time.'

'Good to see you, too, Edouard.'

There was a slight catch to his voice, but despite that Patrick looked totally at ease and in no way fazed, as she was by the grandeur of the chateau. Once again she was struck by how different his life was from hers—how used he was to mixing in the world of wealth and power.

Edouard led them into the vast entrance hall of the chateau, where two sweeping marble stone staircases, one at either side, led up to a wooden gallery that encircled the hall. Historic tapestries hung from the walls.

Unable to help herself, she walked to a sixteenth-century oak chair and exclaimed, 'Oh, wow! That chair is upholstered in Avalan fabric. I've never seen it in real life before; only in textbooks.'

The director looked at her in surprise. 'Not many people would recognise this fabric—are you a historian?'

'No, I'm a textile designer, but I have a passion for historical fabrics. I love how designs and patterns tell us so much about the period of history they were produced in, about the social norms and conditions.'

'Well, you're in for a treat this evening.' The director turned to Patrick. 'I will leave you and Mademoiselle Ryan to tour the chateau alone. If you need anything I shall be in my office.'

As they walked away from the entrance hall she asked, intrigued, 'Why did you bring me here?'

'This is the most beautiful building I have ever visited. I thought you would enjoy it. But now I'm especially glad that I organised the trip. I hadn't realised you were so passionate and knowledgeable about historical textiles.'

'I have a lot of hidden talents you don't know about.'

With a glint in his eye he said, 'Is that right?'

She mumbled, 'Yes…' and turned away, heat flooding her cheeks. She felt as though she was floating on air between the excitement of being here and her desperation to feel his lips on hers again, to be encompassed by his size and strength.

He was right. Anticipation was thrilling. But what if that anticipation led to nothing?

The first room he took her to was the print room. As Aideen looked around the room in astonishment he explained, 'It was a tradition for royalty and the gentry to collect expensive prints and paste them directly on to the walls.'

Some of the black and white prints illustrated faraway picturesque locations—the lakes of Northern Italy, Bavarian forests… Animal prints showed farmyard scenes of cows and sheep; another was of a spaniel, standing before a raging river.

She was blown away by the sheer extravagance of the room. Priceless print after print covered the entirety of the four walls. 'They're beautiful—what incredible detail.'

'This room was created by Princess Isabella—it's said Prince Henri of Chalant built this chateau as a symbol of his love for her, before they married.'

'That's so romantic.'

He didn't respond, and when she turned to him the air was compressed in her lungs. He stood in the middle of the room, his hands in his pockets, gazing at her intently. He wore navy chinos and a white polo shirt. His bare arms were beautifully carved with taut muscle, the skin lightly tanned with a dusting of dark hair.

She even fancied his arms. Was there any hope for her?

An awareness passed between them and she suddenly grew shy, giving him a quick smile before walking away to inspect other prints.

But he made for the door and gestured her to follow. 'If you think that's romantic let me show you something else.'

She followed him down the corridor until he stopped at a closed door.

'Close your eyes and I'll lead you in.'

She eyed him suspiciously. 'You're not going to play a trick on me, are you? Lead me down into the dungeon or something like that?'

His head tilted and he gave her a sexy grin that sent her pulse into orbit. 'As intriguing as that suggestion sounds… no, I'm not going to take you to the dungeon.' Then he gave her an admonishing look and said, 'Now, for once will you please try and trust me and close your eyes?'

She held her breath as his hand took hers. She heard the door open and then he slowly led her forward for about ten paces. She felt oddly vulnerable, and her hand tightened on his of its own accord.

All her senses were attuned to the solid strength of his hand, the smooth warmth of his skin, the torturous pleasure of being so physically close to him…

'Open your eyes.'

She gasped in astonishment. It was the most dazzling room she'd ever seen. It was like something out of a fairytale. Or a room she imagined might have been in a Russian royal palace.

She twisted around in amazement, shaking her head. The double-height rectangular room was a feast of gilded Baroque plasterwork. It was opulent and outrageous in its beauty. And so much fun she couldn't help but laugh.

'It's absolutely stunning! It's like standing in the middle of an exquisite piece of twenty-four-carat gold jewellery'

'It's called the Gold Room. Prince Henri commissioned it to celebrate Isabella's fiftieth birthday.'

She gave him a wistful smile. 'He really was romantic, wasn't he?'

He gave a light shrug and looked up at the intricate gilt stucco work on the ceiling. 'I guess when you find the love of your life you just want to celebrate it.'

A rush of emotion tore through her body. 'It must be nice to feel so loved.'

Their eyes met briefly and they both looked away at the same time.

She moved through the silent room, unexpected tears clouding her vision. The past year might have made her wary of others, but at the same time there was an emptiness in her heart. She wanted to be in love. Desperately.

With each passing day, as they got to know each other,

things were changing between her and Patrick. They now shared an intimacy, an ease with one another that had her thinking maybe they had something between them… something significant. Patrick telling her last night about Orla had been particularly moving, and also momentous. It was as though he had finally allowed her to step fully into his life.

Behind her, he called, 'Are you ready to see some more rooms?'

She nodded, but was slow to turn around. Was he feeling the same intensity she was? This need to connect on a different level?

An hour later her head swam as she tried once again to orientate herself in the vastness of the chateau. They had passed through room after room, all full of sumptuous furniture and historically significant textiles and antiques. And yet, somewhat miraculously, Château Chalant retained an air of intimacy. Was it because it had been built to celebrate love?

Eventually they found themselves back in the entrance hall. For some reason she didn't want their time here to end. She wanted to stay here with him a little longer.

With a heavy heart she said, as brightly as she could, 'Thank you for bringing me here—it really is a magical place.'

'The tour isn't over yet. I have kept the best room for last.'

Intrigued, she followed him into a vast, empty room with marble flooring. A bow window overlooked the gardens to the rear of the chateau.

She looked around, perplexed, taking in the ornate plasterwork on the domed ceilings and alcoves. Painted a silvery white, the sunlit room was a sleeping silent oasis, even in the tranquillity of the chateau.

'Why is there no furniture?' She jumped to hear her own voice echoing noisily around the room.

He had remained standing close to the doorway, while she was now perched on the sill of the bow window.

'It helps with the acoustics.'

What had been a whisper from Patrick echoed loudly across the room.

Trying it herself, she whispered, 'This is amazing.'

Again her voice barrelled across the room in a loud echo.

'It's called the Whispering Room. In days gone by apparently it wasn't accepted for courting couples to stand too close to one another, so young lovers would use this room to whisper messages to one another.'

'That's so sweet.'

'I sometimes wonder what they would have said.'

As he stood and watched her something broke inside her, and she whispered from her heart. 'They wished they could be together...they longed for the day they could be.'

For the longest while he stared at her. Had he heard her whisper? Maybe it would be better if he hadn't.

But then he whispered back, 'You're lovely.'

He said it so gently and with such sincerity she thought her heart was going to break in two. 'You're pretty special, too.'

'I like you, Aideen Ryan.'

Had she heard right? Had she imagined it? His smile said otherwise.

Through a throat thick with bittersweet happiness she whispered, 'I like you, too, Patrick Fitzsimon.'

He walked slowly to her, and although she was leaning against the windowsill her legs began to wobble.

He came to a stop before her and she looked up into his dazzling blue eyes. His body shifted towards her. His hand twitched at his side and at the same time her body ached with the need for his touch.

His head moved slowly down, her heart speeding up with every inch closer he came, until his lips landed gently on hers. His mouth moved against hers, slowly and lightly, and she thought she might faint because it was so tender and right.

When he pulled away from the kiss he brought his forehead to lie against hers. His incredible blue gaze held hers. It felt as though he was spearing her heart with the silent communication of the need of a man for a woman.

'Would you like a tour of the grounds?'

Dazed, she whispered, 'Yes, please.'

They made their way through the extensive gardens surrounding the chateau and a silence fell between them. She tried to keep her distance from him, but invariably found herself swaying towards him. As she walked along the gravelled paths, the late-evening sun warm on her skin, she bumped against him and he pulled her towards him, wrapping his arm about her waist. They shared a quick look and her insides tumbled to see the desire in his hooded eyes.

She felt drunk with happiness just being there...being with him. And every cell in her body was electrified by being so close to him. A lazy, intoxicating tendril of physical desire coiled around her body. Her skin felt flushed and a deep pulse resonated in her lips.

But that nagging thought that this was not reality, that

she did not belong here, continued to rumble at the back of her brain. Even as she tried her best to ignore it.

They didn't stop walking until they reached an extensive lake with a small island in the centre. They stopped on the pebbled beach, where a rowing boat lay beached to one side.

He went immediately to it and pulled it towards the lake. Holding it in the water, he called, 'Come on—what are you waiting for?'

She looked around doubtfully, wondering for a moment if it would be allowed. But then she rushed towards the water. She pulled off her ballet flats, held up her midi-skirt and jumped on board, giving a cry of laughter when the boat wobbled.

Patrick strengthened his grip on her elbow, and as she sat down he pushed the boat out further and in one fluid motion jumped on board himself. The boat wobbled even more, but as soon as he sat opposite her it steadied.

His oar strokes were long and even and they were quickly out in the middle of the lake. Other than evening birdsong and the swoosh of the oars in the water there wasn't another sound.

'This is my first time ever being out in a rowing boat.'

He looked at her incredulously. 'Seriously? How did you get to be...?'

'Twenty-eight.'

'How did you get to be twenty-eight without ever being out in a rowing boat?'

'Beats me.'

He continued to row and she tried not to stare at the way his biceps flexed with each pull of the oar.

'You'll have to have a go at rowing.'

'Really?'

'Climb over here into the centre. Try not to wobble the boat too much. I'll move to your seat.'

As she moved down the boat it began to bob precariously. She gave a little shout of alarm and gratefully grabbed on to his outstretched arm. As she fell forward she twisted, and ended up landing in his arms, her bottom firmly wedged in his lap.

His hand came to rest just above her waist, its heat on the thin cotton of her blouse sending a shiver of pleasure through her. His thighs, his chest, as they pressed against her, felt as though they were made of steel. Electric blue eyes met hers. Her pulse leapt. It would be so easy to lean forward, to kiss those firm lips again. To inhale his scent.

He gave a low growl. 'If you don't climb off me in the next five seconds I won't be responsible for what I do next.'

She leapt away—and instantly regretted doing so.

After he had moved to the stern of the boat she started rowing. The boat moved with ease and she thought with unjustified satisfaction that she had this rowing lark immediately sussed. But then they started going in circles, and she couldn't get the boat to go in a straight line. The fits of giggles that accompanied her attempts weren't much help.

Opposite her, he threw his head into his hands and then looked at her with amusement.

Time and time again he demonstrated the motion she should be using, but the boat still twisted. He suggested they swop places again but, determined, she refused to give up.

And finally she did it. The boat went in one direction. Straight back to shore. She didn't try to alter their course in case she started circling again.

As they neared the small beach he moved confidently to the bow and jumped ashore. Then he hoisted the boat on to the stones. He held her hand as she leapt off. She knew she was grinning at him like a fool but couldn't stop herself. She hadn't laughed so much in a very long time.

He watched her with a smile, and for a while she looked at him happily, but her smile finally faded as his stare grew darker. He took a step closer. Shots of awareness flew through her.

An intensity swirled in the air between them. Everything had changed since Patrick had opened up to her last night. She felt trusted. Her heart drummed a slow beat of deep appreciation, wonder, and attraction to this man.

Closer and closer he came, his intense blue eyes transfixing her. Her breath grew more rapid. Her lips pulsed with the need to feel his mouth on hers again. Her legs grew weak.

When he was no more than an inch from her, she was the first to give in. Her body swayed and she fell against his hardness. Her hands curled around his biceps. Against her thumb, which rested at the side of his chest, she could feel his heartbeat, which was pounding even faster than hers.

'I didn't ask before, so I should this time round. Can I kiss you?'

Her heart stuttered at his question. It was the sweetest thing anyone had ever said to her. Even if she'd wanted to there was no way she could pull away from him—from his warm breath, the overwhelming pull of his hard body, the dizzying inhalation of his scent.

She placed her hands on his shoulders, closed her eyes, and gave a small sigh of assent as she pulled his lips down to hers.

Whereas their earlier kiss had been slow and sweet, tentative and testing, this kiss was instantly intense, wild. Their hands explored each other's bodies with hunger. It was a kiss that might easily become a lot more.

She was quickly losing herself.

As one, they pulled away at the same time. As though they both knew it might quickly spiral into something neither wanted...*yet*.

She pressed a hand to her swollen lips and blushed. She had to hide how much he affected her. Because in truth she was close to tears...of happiness and despair.

'I'll tell you this much, Patrick Fitzsimon, you certainly haven't forgotten how to kiss in all that time you've been locked away in your office.'

He looked at her with amusement. 'Glad to hear it.'

But then dark need flared in his eyes and her insides melted.

'I want you, Aideen.'

Her heart felt as if it was going to burst right out of her chest. She so desperately wanted to say *Yes, please* and not give a thought to the consequences. But it wasn't that simple.

'Are you sure? Won't it...complicate things?'

His hand came to rest on her cheek and he gazed at her solemnly while his thumb stroked her skin. 'I like you. A lot. It doesn't have to be complicated. I promise you, no game playing. But if this is not right for you I'll back off.'

No! She didn't want that.

His touch, his scent, the magnetic pull of his body might be making her head reel so much that she could barely formulate a thought, but she knew that much. She didn't want this to end.

When he had whispered 'I like you' in the Whispering Room, he had looked at her with such intense integrity and honour it had been like a bomb detonating in her brain. And just like that she'd realised she was in love with this kind, generous, strong man. And, God help her, she knew she would happily take a few days in his arms over the alternative: never knowing what it would be like to be held by him.

Right now, to have loved and lost was definitely better than never to have loved at all. She didn't want to think about the future. Living in the present was all that mattered.

She scrunched her eyes shut for a moment, and when she opened them again she said, with a huge smile, 'Okay.'

It was as though a weight had been lifted off her shoulders. She had never felt so exhilarated in her entire life. To feel this good it must mean it was the right decision. Mustn't it?

All the way back to Paris she regaled him with stories of her encounters with fashion designers. He held her hand throughout, his thumb caressing the soft smoothness of her palm, and every now and again she would stutter and lose her train of thought as his fingers lightly traced along her inner arm.

Each time she shivered and her eyes grew heavy he wondered if her entire body was that sensitive. And his pulse moved up another notch.

When the helicopter landed Bernard was waiting to take them to his private club, close to the Eiffel Tower.

She gasped beside him when the maître d' of the club's restaurant directed them to their table in the rooftop terrace restaurant. And he totally understood why. Because, no matter how many times he came here himself, the sheer size and beauty of the Eiffel Tower this close up was truly impressive.

Their table, as he'd requested, was beside the low-level redbrick wall of the terrace, with her chair facing out towards the tower, he sitting to her side.

Once the maître d' had gone she stared at him, her huge chocolate eyes dancing in merriment, and then she put a hand over her mouth in disbelief. 'Oh, my God, I can't believe this place. It's incredible.'

'The club is one of the closest buildings to the tower.'

Their waiter arrived with the champagne he had preordered and opened the bottle with a satisfying pop. He filled the flute glasses that already sat on the white-linen-topped table and retreated once he had placed the bottle in an ice bucket to the side.

She took a sip of champagne. And then another. 'Wow! That's the nicest champagne I have ever tasted. It's sharp, but with a gorgeous biscuit undertone.' She turned again to the tower and reached her hand out towards it. 'I feel like I can almost touch it.'

Then, as she looked around the rest of the terrace, he saw her expression grow even more radiant.

'This club is so impressive—' She stopped and blushed, and dropped her chin on to her cupped hand. 'Oh, dear. I must sound like the most uncultured date you've ever had.'

'You make a refreshing change from some of the jaded dates I've had in the past.'

She gave him a suspicious look. 'That's good...I think.'

If only she knew how many times in the past he had been left speechless by the cynicism and sense of entitlement of some of his previous conquests. 'That's *very* good.'

As they both leant forward to place their glasses on the table their arms touched and a silent energy bound them together. He moved closer and her lips parted ever so slightly. Hunger powered through him. He inhaled her scent. The scent that now lingered in the air of the chateau and one he looked forward to inhaling each day when he returned from his meetings.

Slowly their heads moved towards one another. Her head tilted to the side and passion flared in her eyes. Inch by inch they drew closer, and he had to stifle a groan when his lips met the soft fullness of hers.

When he pulled away he was amused by how dazed she looked, and said, 'You're the best date I've ever had.'

She blushed furiously and waved away his words, but her wide smile told of her delight.

A group of waiters arrived with the food he had also pre-ordered, earlier in the day. The surprise and glee with which she eyed the food had him smiling to himself in pleasure.

Once the waiters had departed she looked mischievously from the tiers of mouth-watering cakes to him. 'It's a bit late in the evening for afternoon tea, I would have thought.'

'You said you loved millefeuille.'

Shaking her head, she bent to inspect the three-tier stand. 'All the cakes I used to dream of when I was a student: opera cake, éclairs, *macarons*…even miniature tarte Tatin.' She looked at him, her throat working. 'Thank you.' She stopped as tears filled her eyes. 'This is so considerate of you…' And then she laughed. 'I'm actually lost for words.'

He gave her a smile. 'Then don't speak. Just eat.'

He poured her some tea while she selected a millefeuille. He chose a raspberry *macaron*, filled with fresh raspberries and raspberry cream.

She closed her eyes as she ate the first forkful of millefeuille. And he almost choked on his *macaron*. She looked incredibly sensual, with her head tilted back, pleasure written all over her face. He glared at a man sitting at a nearby table who was also captivated by her, a powerful surge of possessiveness taking him by surprise.

Her happiness was increasingly becoming everything to him. It was as though he was plugged into her emotions and felt them as keenly as she did. When she was happy he was elated. When she was sad or upset his heart plummeted. He had never before felt so attuned to another person.

It was both incredible and awful at the same time. Incredible that he could be so close to another person that he felt her emotions. Awful because it would make saying goodbye all the more difficult.

As they ate they spoke about their past experiences in Paris, with the tower lighting up before them as the sun set. They both looked towards its graceful night-time beauty, but he quickly looked back at her.

Her eyes shone with happiness. She was curled into her seat so that her body was directed towards him, even though her gaze was still on the tower. Her lipstick had faded from brilliant red to a faint blush.

Unable to stop himself, he leant towards her and said her name gently. She turned to face him fully with a smile and his hand reached forward to brush a flake of pastry from her lips. At least that was what he intended to do.

He removed the pastry, all right, but his finger lingered on her lips, desire coiling in his stomach.

At first she stared at him in surprise, but then her gaze darkened. He lowered his finger but moved forward in his chair, wanting to be closer to her…

Awareness of his masculinity, of his raw power, flooded Aideen's body and her head began to swim at the heat and scent of his skin.

'I want you.'

It was the barest of whispers and she drew back a little, needing to search his eyes, to see if she had heard right. The hooded intensity there told her she had heard correctly.

Her throat was too dry to speak so she mouthed the words *me, too.*

His eyes darkened even more as they traced the movement of her lips.

Immediately he stood and held out his hand to her. Her insides had gone all funny and she worried that her legs wouldn't carry her.

Just as they were about to leave, the tower started its hourly light show, and as she stood watching the twinkling lights, enraptured, he held her from behind, his hands encircling her waist, his thumbs drawing lazy sensual patterns up and over her ribs.

In the back of the car she tried not to tremble as he held her hand. Silent, powerful restraint pulsated from his rigid body.

Once home, he threw open the front door and pulled her into the darkness, backed her against the wall.

He stood so close the heat from his body curled around her, and she gasped when his fingers moved to undo the top buttons of her blouse. Once open, he pulled it down to expose both shoulders. Slowly he left a trail of soft, knee-weakening kisses along her collarbone and the sensitive ridge of her neck, his fingers dragging down the apricot-coloured lace straps of her bra, leaving a burning trail of heat on her skin.

A deep moan of pleasure ricocheted from deep inside her. Her fingers scratched against the cool wall at her back, desperate to cling to anything.

'I want to make love to you.'

For the longest while she fought to answer him, her mind distracted as he continued to caress her earlobe, her neck.

The absolute gorgeousness of inhaling him… The bone-melting thrill of his large, muscular body being so close… The desperate need to touch every inch of him… To have his body crushed against hers. To have him make love to her.

Her hands clasped his face and drew him up to face her. Her breath hitched as his burning gaze met hers.

'I want you, too.'

CHAPTER TEN

A BUBBLE OF happiness and excitement burst in Aideen's heart and spread little beads of serenity throughout her body.

Beside her, twisted on to his side and facing away from her, Patrick slept, his breathing a slow and steady rhythm. The top sheet rested below his waist, and the beautiful, muscular expanse of his back was only inches away.

In the pre-dawn light she could just about make out the faint scar that ran for a few inches just below his shoulderblade. What had caused it? There was so much she wanted to know about him. So much more to fall in love with. Simple everyday events like him brushing his teeth, the order in which he dressed, shaved.

She moved closer and lowered her head against the hard muscles of his back, inhaling the musky, salty notes of his scent which always made her light-headed with desire.

Last night had been more exhilarating and tender than she'd ever thought possible. They had made love slowly and gently, with an intensity that had had her fearing her heart would split in two. With each kiss and touch she had tried to show him what he meant to her, hoping he would see just how much she loved his strength and dignity, loved his kindness and integrity.

Throughout he had whispered words of endearment to her, his eyes dark with passion…and also with the same amazement and wonder that had had her reeling, too.

And as she fell back to sleep, as she fell into a contented, exhausted pit of happiness, she wished she could stay there, in his bed, at his side, for eternity.

Two hours later the morning sun bathed the bedroom in a golden light. In their haste they had not got around to pulling the curtains last night.

Lying on her stomach, Aideen was sleeping, her skin still flushed from their lovemaking. He leant forward and touched his mouth against hers. Her lips broke into a smile and her eyes opened, drowsy and lazy with happiness.

She gave him a contented sexy sigh. 'Good morning.'

The huskiness of her voice evoked startling images of their lovemaking last night. Images that left him reeling in disbelief and with the desire to experience it time and time again. He lowered his head and kissed the warm skin of her shoulderblade. A ribbon of pleasure unfurled in him when he inhaled the fresh vanilla and floral scent that seemed innate to her very being.

Against the sweet scent of her skin he whispered, 'Good morning to you, too.'

She edged her hip closer to him as his hand ran over her back. Her eyes met his and they shared a look so intimate it felt as though the world had stopped turning.

Eventually he found his voice. 'Did you enjoy last night?'

She looked at him innocently. 'Best night's sleep I've had in a long time.'

For that, he kissed her hard, and he didn't stop until he heard her whimper with need. When he pulled away she protested, and then nudged even closer to him, the length of her body tucking into his.

A sexy wickedness flashed on her face. 'Okay, I'll admit that it was pretty mind-blowing.'

A deep groan erupted from the core of him. He pressed his mouth against the side of her throat. He ran his hand down over her back, his thumb bumping along her spine so that she wriggled, and she wriggled even more when the entire span of his hand moved down over the firm roundness of her bottom.

'Have I ever told you that you have an incredible body?'

Her giggle echoed off the mattress and her body shimmied beneath his fingers.

'As I recall, you said something to that effect several times last night.'

'Well, you'd better get used to it, because I reckon I'm going to keep you in this bed for a very long time.'

She gave a heavy sigh and smiled. 'That sounds like heaven. Being with you is incredible. I never want it to end.'

His hand stilled and his heart sank. He'd thought this was nothing but banter and teasing. But now her words echoed in his brain. They both knew this was never going to last. Didn't they?

He glanced at her again and the joy in her eyes had turned to disquiet. Her brow drew into a frown. She twisted on to her back, pulling the sheet up around her as she did so.

'What's the matter?'

He collapsed on to his back, too, and stared up to the ceiling. 'You know this has to end… I thought we were agreed on that?'

He felt her yank the sheet a little tighter about her. 'I know. But after last night…'

After last night? Panic and disbelief had him sitting up on the side of the bed.

Without turning to face her, he said, 'I have a conference call in ten minutes. I need to get ready.'

She didn't respond, and he walked rapidly to the ensuite bathroom. He flicked on the shower and immediately stood under the stream of as yet cold water, his mind too agitated to care that his body was protesting.

As the water pounded his scalp he closed his eyes and cursed silently. He felt as though he was drowning in emotions. Drowning in feelings he didn't want to have. Drowning in how mind-blowing last night had been. And not just physically.

Making love to Aideen had been different from anything he had ever experienced. At once he'd wanted to cherish her, protect her, possess her. In the act of lovemaking last night he had wanted their hearts and minds to fuse together as much as he had wanted their bodies to join. He had felt emotionally wrecked after it. As though he had exposed every part of himself to her.

Had he just made the biggest mistake of his life? He had never opened himself up to another person so much. He wasn't sure how to manage the vulnerability of that. And now she was saying she wanted it never to end.

Part of him understood that. God knew it felt so good, so right, to have her by his side. He drew strength from her. From her enthusiasm, from her sense of fun, and also from her quiet compassion.

But he couldn't ever commit to a relationship. Not with its demands and hurts and misunderstandings. Not when he already lost all those he had loved. What if he messed up in years to come and lost her? Just as he'd messed up with Orla? What if he failed her as he'd failed his mum and dad?

He was no good at relationships. In the end he would only hurt her. He didn't even know what to say to her now.

When she heard the bathroom door close Aideen looked down at her trembling hands and drew in a shaky breath. What had just happened?

She had spoken the truth—that was what had happened. And she had got it all wrong.

After last night she'd thought he might feel the same way. Even this morning, when he had looked at her with such affection, she'd thought there was more to this for him than just a casual affair.

Oh, God, she was so bad at reading men. First Ed. Now Patrick. How could she have got it so wrong?

He had looked horrified when she'd said she wanted it to last for ever. She had said it unconsciously. But it had been the truth.

Humiliation burnt deep in her stomach and her heart pounded in her chest. She needed to get out of here before he returned to the bedroom.

She wrapped the sheet about her and frantically picked her clothes off the bedroom floor. And then she ran down the ornate corridor to her own bedroom.

There, she collapsed on to the bed, her pulse pounding, her entire body trembling. Her skin was burning with embarrassment, but ice was flowing through her veins.

What was she going to do? She had sworn she would never fall for a man again, and here she was in love with a billionaire who was completely out of her league. A man who had run at the first notion of her wanting more from their relationship.

What had she been *thinking*? Talk about messing up on a spectacular scale.

She needed to get away. The humiliation was too much. She couldn't stay here. She couldn't pretend not to have feelings for him.

She winced at the thought of walking away. It might mean never seeing him again. Was she really ready for that? No. But there was no alternative.

An hour later, after an extra-long shower and generally delaying as long as she could, she walked downstairs. Patrick was nowhere to be seen, so she grabbed a cup of coffee, wrestling once again with the machine, and sat at the island unit, all the while rehearsing what she was going to say to him.

Not long afterwards he arrived in the kitchen, dressed in a slim-fitting navy suit. It showed the contours of his broad-shouldered, narrow-hipped frame to perfection, and for a crazy moment she longed to go to him, to wrap her arms about his waist, lower her forehead to that impregnable masculine strength and the power of his chest. Longed to inhale him. Soap… The sweet, musky tang of his skin…

He had no right to look so gorgeous and calm when she felt so distraught. But his calmness strengthened her conviction that she was going to leave here with her dignity intact.

He glanced at his watch. 'I have another conference call in ten minutes and then some meetings in Paris later. When I get back I think we should speak.'

His tone, his words, his stance were all shutting her out. He barely looked at her. Where had the warm and kind man of last night gone? Had it all been an act?

Horrible tension filled the room. Unsaid words, hurt and humiliation were thick in the air.

She wanted things to go back to where they'd been when they had woken, or to last night. To that carefree existence where reality had been suspended.

She didn't know what he was thinking. And the vulnerability that came with that cut her to the core.

Did he regret their relationship? Did he even regret answering the door to her that night of the storm? Did he wish she had never come into his life?

He was waiting for her to say something, but her throat was closed over and she was struggling to tell him what she had rehearsed. It was as though her heart was physically preventing her from saying the words logic said she had to speak.

He came a little closer and leant a hand against the island unit, his voice less brisk now, almost sad. 'I've always told you that I never want to be in a permanent relationship. I've never lied to you, Aideen.'

First Ed had cheated on her. Now Patrick looked as though he wanted to head for the hills. She had to understand why she wasn't good enough…why she kept getting relationships wrong.

'Why don't you want to be in a relationship?'

He looked totally taken aback by her question for a while, and then frustration flared on his face. 'I'm not interested…I don't want to be tied down. I want to be able to focus on work. It's not something I've ever wanted in life.'

Was it really that simple for him? Maybe it was. Maybe he didn't need love or affection.

She couldn't think straight.

Swallowing deeply, she said in a strained voice, 'I think we should call a stop to it all…it's becoming too complicated.'

A slash of red appeared on his cheeks and his voice was cool when he spoke. 'I don't want it to end, but if that's what you wish…'

Why couldn't he fight her a little? Had last night been nothing but a figment of her imagination?

She had to pull herself together.

All along she had said this would never work, and yet after just one night in his bed she had become delusional.

Now she knew for certain that this was never going to work. That this had been nothing but a brief interlude in her life. A magical, unbelievable interlude, but one that had to end. This wasn't her world. She didn't belong here.

She stood up and placed her cup in the dishwasher before turning to him. 'I think it would be best if I leave now.'

He moved closer to her, his hands landing on his hips. 'Oh, come on, Aideen. There's no need for this. Stay. I don't want you to go. Why can't we just enjoy each other's company for a while?'

'I'm not up for a casual relationship, Patrick.'

He looked at her in exasperation. 'Fine. I'll respect that. Nothing needs to happen between us again. You don't even have a home to go to. The cottage isn't ready.'

'I'll sort something out.'

'Stay at Ashbrooke.'

'You're not getting it, are you?'

'What do you mean?'

The sheer overwhelming impact of standing so close to his powerful, addictive frame but being so adrift from him emotionally had her blurting out, 'I can't stay in Ashbrooke. I can't be around you, Patrick.'

Heat fired through her body. Her cheeks were red-hot and tears burnt at the back of her eyes. She had said too much already, but she couldn't hold back the truth. The weight of it was physically hurting her chest.

'For the simple reason that I've fallen in love with you.'

Without meaning to do so he stepped back from her.

This was all going wrong.

She wasn't supposed to be telling him she loved him.

He didn't know what to say.

And in that moment he regretted ever opening up to Aideen. He should have kept his distance. He shouldn't have let her in. Look at what had happened as a result. He'd said he didn't want to hurt her. Judging by the pained expression on her face, he had done exactly that.

'I never wanted to hurt you.'

She gave a little laugh. 'I'm sure I'll get over it.' She paused and then stood up a little straighter, looked him in the eye. 'It was never going to work anyway. I always knew that. We are from different worlds. I don't belong in this world of wealth. I want a relationship of equals—one where I bring the same as the other person. That was never going to be the case with us.'

Though she looked as though she might crumble, she gave him a wobbly smile, her eyes brimming with tears again.

With a light shrug she added, 'This was never going

to be anything more than a brief interlude of happy madness. And even though I can barely breathe right now, knowing it's over, in my heart I know I will always cherish these weeks together. I'm glad I met you. And a part of me will always love you.'

Pain and shock had him sitting there and watching her walk away. He couldn't take it in, process all that she had said.

Both of them were agreeing that being together wouldn't work.

But if that was the case why did it feel as though he was being torn apart?

Less than ten minutes later he was still trying to process all that had happened when she reappeared in the kitchen, her suitcase beside her.

'I've booked a flight back to Ireland. When you return to Ashbrooke can you bring my files and paperwork from the orangery? I haven't had time to pack them. Perhaps you can ask one of your staff to do so?'

'I'll ask William to drop them off at the cottage.'

Part of him wanted to plead with her to stay. But this was for the best. Everything had spiralled out of control. He couldn't give Aideen the type of relationship she needed and deserved.

'I'll organise for my plane to take you.'

'No! Absolutely not.'

He was about to fight her, but then he realised why she would feel the need to pay for her own transport home.

With a resigned shrug of acceptance he said, 'I'll drop you to the airport.'

'I've already asked Bernard to take me.'

Fury shot through him and he said abruptly, 'No. *I'm* taking you.'

He had hurt her and let her down. The least he could do was see her safely to the airport. Say goodbye somewhere other than in the house where they had made love.

She looked away for a few seconds, and when she spoke again, he was taken aback by the pain in her voice.

'No. Bernard is taking me.' Tears shone in her eyes. 'I just want to go.'

'Aideen…'

Angry eyes flicked to his, and her voice was raw with emotion. 'I don't understand why you're fighting me on this. I can see that deep down you want me to go.'

'That's not true.'

'Yes, it is. You fled from our bed this morning. You're distancing yourself from me—burying yourself in work. Admit it, Patrick, you're pushing me away. Like you push everyone away.'

'I have never pretended that my work doesn't come first. It has to.'

'Oh, *please*… No, it doesn't. You just want it that way. At least admit that much to yourself.' She stopped and closed her eyes for a few seconds. When she reopened them they were filled with pain. 'Bernard will drive me to the airport.'

'I want to—'

She cut across him. 'Please don't make this any harder for me. I'm humiliated enough.'

He reached for her. Anger at his own bungling of this situation had him saying sharply, 'You have no reason to feel humiliated. I should never have suggested you come to Paris. This was all a mistake on my part. I'm sorry that I hurt you. That you have these feelings for me. But

I can't reciprocate them. Not with you. Not with anyone. I don't deserve your love, Aideen. Please remember that.'

She yanked her arm free and strode away from him.

He followed her out to the front steps, but she was already getting into the waiting car. Not once did she look back towards him.

CHAPTER ELEVEN

CYCLING HOME FROM MOONCOYNE, her front basket sparsely filled with the few food items she had forced herself to buy at the weekly farmers' market in the hope that they might kick-start her appetite again, Aideen heard the low cooing of a wood pigeon. Something about its regular familiar call reassured her. It told her that the world went on spinning even though it felt as though hers had ground to a halt.

Spring was in full bloom. The trees that lined the road were no longer stark grey-brown statues, reaching up to the sky, but lush green flowing bodies of movement and life. Waves of white cow parsley littered the hedgerows on either side of her, yellow buttercup flowers popping through at intervals.

Everything was changing.

It had been a week since she had returned from Paris. She had moved back into Fuchsia Cottage immediately, not caring about the dust or the noise as the builders carried out the renovations. It wasn't as if she was getting a lot of work done anyway. Thankfully their work was due to be completed by the end of next week. Hopefully then she would be able to give her work one hundred per cent of her concentration.

She had neither seen nor heard from Patrick since she'd returned. A part of her had hoped he might contact her. See how she was doing. Which was pretty crazy, really. He was probably just relieved to move on from what had been a disastrous scenario from his point of view.

He had visibly paled when she'd said she loved him. The panic in his eyes had told her everything she needed to know. Even now her cheeks glowed bright red at that memory.

In her first days at home she had wondered if she had made the worst decision of her life, becoming so involved, so intimate with him. In those long days and sleepless nights she had lived with numbing pain and an overwhelming sense of loss. And the haunting question as to whether her judgement had been all wrong once again.

But in the days that had followed, as her initial shock and gruelling pain had subsided a little, she'd found a clarity of thinking that had evaded her all the time she was with him.

She had been so overpowered, intrigued, in love with him, that when they'd been together she hadn't been able to think straight, think objectively.

Being with him had been like being awash with emotions that left no room for perspective. A perspective that now told her that it could never have lasted. He had said from the outset that he didn't want to be in a relationship. And she knew only too well that they were from different worlds. But when she had been with him all she had known was desire, longing, excitement, happiness. An itch to bury herself into his very soul, to know him better than she even knew herself.

Now that she was away from him, those emotions had lessened and she had finally got that perspective. Though her heart was physically sore, though she could barely eat or sleep, and though she sometimes thought she was going mad with her frustration, her wanting to be near him again, she didn't regret anything.

How could she when she had experienced such intense love and passion for another person?

Yes, she had wanted it to be for ever. She hadn't wanted it to end. But better that than never to have experienced it at all. How incredibly sad it would be to live a life never knowing such love existed.

In her heart she knew he had loved her in his own way. She had seen it shining in his eyes when they had made love. In the things he had whispered to her. But he hadn't loved her enough. And that was a fact she would have to learn to live with.

Now she had to start focusing on her work again. And hope that with time the pain would subside.

She neared the junction for the turning down to the road that led to her cottage and her pulse speeded up as she passed the wide entrance to his estate. But then she brought her bike to a sudden wobbly stop.

She dismounted, turned, and stared back at the board that had appeared on the wall. A sales board, to be precise, for a prestigious Dublin firm of auctioneers. And written on it, in giant capital letters, were the words FOR SALE: Historic House and Thousand-Acre Estate.

He was selling Ashbrooke!

What was he thinking?

She knew how much he loved this estate. Was he so desperate to put distance between himself and her?

She wheeled her bike over to the imposing twenty-foot wrought-iron double gates. For a minute she considered the intercom. Should she just leave it? It was none of her business, after all. But she could not shake off the feeling that he was selling for all the wrong reasons.

She pressed down on the buzzer and jumped when it was quickly answered. She instantly recognised his housekeeper's voice.

'Hi, Maureen, it's Aideen Ryan. I want to have a word with Patrick.'

'Aideen? Of course—come on in. I'll give Patrick a call to let him know you're here.'

The gates opened slowly and Aideen drew in a deep breath before she jumped back on her bike and started to cycle up the drive.

When she caught her first glimpse of the house, in all its magnificent grandeur, her chest tightened with a heaviness that barely allowed her to breathe. How could he walk away from this house which meant so much to him? She tried to imagine someone else living here but it seemed impossible.

The sound of fast-approaching horse's hooves on the drive behind her had her wobbling on her bike once again, and she came to an ungraceful stop when she hit the grass verge.

She twisted around to see Patrick, heading in her direction riding a horse. He was a natural horseman, confident and assured. Totally in control. And heartbreakingly gorgeous.

He pulled the horse to a stop a few feet away.

Heat and desire instantly coiled between them. Her heart thumped wildly against her chest as his eyes held her captive.

Memory snapshots of him making love to her had her almost crying out in pain, and she gripped the handlebars of the bike tighter against the tremble in her legs.

He dismounted and led his horse towards her. He was wearing a loose blue shirt over his jodhpurs. His eyes matched the blue of the sky behind him, but gave nothing away as to what he was thinking.

'Maureen rang to say you wanted to speak to me.'

No, *How are you? How have you been?* Instead this bleak, unwelcoming comment. It made her feel as though all the closeness and warmth they had once shared had been nothing but a mirage.

She couldn't show him how upset she felt, so she took a deep breath and tried to control her voice. 'I saw the for-sale sign.'

He frowned slightly and shrugged. 'And?'

'Why are you selling?'

'I listened to what you said. You're right. I *am* isolated here in Ashbrooke.'

She didn't understand. Bewildered, she asked, 'Where are you going to go?'

'Wherever my work takes me. I have property throughout the world. I'll move around as necessary.'

'But you *love* Ashbrooke, Patrick. I know you do. You love this house and this land as though you were born into it.'

His mouth twisted unhappily and he fixed her with a lancing glare. 'I thought you would be pleased. It was you who put the idea in my head.'

'No. My point was that you deliberately choose houses that enable you to be isolated. But you can be isolated in the middle of Manhattan if you really want to. I didn't mean for you to sell Ashbrooke. This is crazy.'

'I need to move on. It's nothing more complicated than that.'

'Isn't it? Are you sure our relationship hasn't anything

to do with it? Are you worried I might still hope something can happen between us? Because if that's the case, please believe me—I have absolutely no expectations. I know it's over. And I accept it's for the best. Never the twain shall meet, after all.'

He shook his head angrily and uttered a low curse. In that moment he looked exhausted. 'Aideen, I wish I could explain…but I can't.'

What did he mean? For a moment she considered him, wanting to ask what there was to explain. It was all pretty simple, after all. He didn't love her. End of story.

'Please reconsider selling Ashbrooke. Moving from here won't change anything. Selling a house won't stop you being isolated. You need to open your heart to others. My fear is that you won't, and you'll be alone for the rest of your life. And you deserve more than that.'

He threw her a furious look. 'Do I really, though? I hurt Orla. I hurt you. Why on earth are you saying that I deserve more?'

'Because you're a good man, Patrick.'

His hands tightened on the reins. 'And you're too kind-hearted and generous.'

She lifted her chin and glared at him. 'Don't patronise me. I know what I'm talking about. And maybe you should listen to your own advice sometimes. You told me once that I should believe in myself. Well, maybe you should do the same.'

His jaw clenched. 'I can't give you what you need, Aideen.'

'This isn't about me. Trust me—I wouldn't be here if I hadn't seen the for-sale sign. I want nothing from you. But I'm not going to let you make the mistake of selling the house you love because for once you actually allowed someone into your life.'

His eyes were sharp, angry shards of blue ice. 'That has nothing to do with it.'

'Are you sure? Because I'm not convinced. Are you going to reconnect with Orla and your friends once you leave Ashbrooke? What changes are you going to make to your life?'

His mouth thinned and he threw her a blistering look. 'Frankly, that's none of your business.'

She gave a tight laugh of shock and took a step back. Her heart went into a freefall of despondency. 'Wow, you *really* know how to put a person in her place.' Her throat was tight, but she forced herself to speak. 'And it *is* my business because I care for you. I don't want to see you shutting more and more people out of your life. You deserve to be happy in life, Patrick. Remember that.'

There was nothing else she could say. She turned and picked up her bike. At the same time his phone rang.

He gave another low curse and muttered, 'This number has been calling me non-stop all morning.'

As she pushed away she heard him answer it.

She pedalled furiously.

Seeing him again had brought home just how much she missed him. Would she ever meet another man to whom she was so physically attracted? Just from standing close to him her body was on fire. And her heart felt as though it was in pieces. Because emotionally she missed him twice as much. She wanted him in her life. It was against all logic and reason. But there it was. She wanted his intelligence, his kindness, his strength.

The sound of his voice calling her and the thundering of hooves had her looking around, startled. Patrick was racing towards her. He yanked his horse to a stop, but didn't dismount. He looked aghast.

'That was a hospital in Dublin calling. Orla has gone into early labour.'

For a moment she wondered why he was telling her, but then she saw the fear in his eyes. He didn't know what to do.

She dropped her bike down on the grass verge. 'Are you going to go to Dublin to be with her?'

He looked pale and drawn. For a moment she thought he hadn't heard her question. But then he looked down at her beseechingly. 'I don't know what to do. I don't want to cause her any upset.'

'Did she tell the hospital to call you and ask you to come?'

'Yes.'

'Well, then, she needs you.' For a moment she looked at the horse warily, and then she held out her hand to Patrick. 'Pull me up. We need to get back to the house quickly. While you get changed I'll organise for your helicopter to come and collect you.'

He looked at her, taken aback, but then nodded his agreement. 'Put your leg in the stirrup and I'll pull you up.'

He drew her up and sat her in front of him. It was her first time on a horse, and it looked like a long, long way down, but she couldn't think of that. Instead she tried to think of the practical arrangements that needed to be sorted out in order to get Patrick to Dublin immediately. She tried to ignore how good it felt to be so physically close to him again.

At the stables, a groom helped her dismount. When Patrick jumped off he hesitated, so she held his hand in hers and tugged him forward. 'Come on—there's no time to waste.'

They entered the kitchen via the cloakroom. 'Is the number for your pilot stored on your phone?'

'Yes, but I'm not—'

'No, Patrick. You *have* to go. Orla has never needed you more than now. I know you feel you have failed her in the past. That there is a lot of hurt and misunderstanding. But right now none of that matters. Orla and her baby are the only things that matter. She needs her brother. She needs your strength and support.'

For a moment he blinked, but then, as her words finally registered, determination came back into his eyes. 'You're right. Call the helicopter. I'll be ready in ten minutes.'

Aideen immediately made the call, and the helicopter crew promised to be at Ashbrooke within twenty minutes. True to his word, Patrick was back in the kitchen within ten. Wearing a dark red polo shirt and faded denim jeans, his hair still wet from the shower, he looked gorgeous—if a little distracted. She could feel the pumped-up energy radiating from him. She needed to keep him calm, reassure him.

'The helicopter will be here in ten minutes. Do you want to call the hospital again for an update?'

Instantly he took the phone from the counter and dialled the number. He spoke looking out through the glass extension, down towards the sea, his polo shirt pulled tight across his wide shoulders, his jeans hugging his hips, and Aideen remembered her first night here. How in awe of him she'd been. How bowled over she'd been by his good looks.

Her heart dropped with a thud and she felt physical

pain in her chest. Would she ever stop missing him every single second of every single minute of every single hour?

'She's seven centimetres dilated…whatever that means. She's doing okay, but they're worried as she's a month early.' His jaw working, he added, 'She has nobody with her. Damn it, she shouldn't be alone at a time like this.'

She walked towards him and placed a hand on his arm. 'She's going to be okay. She's in good hands, but she'll be relieved to see you. I bet it's pretty lonely, going through something so big all on your own.'

He inhaled a deep breath at her words and felt some of the tension leave his body.

'You're right.'

And then it hit him just how much he wanted Aideen by his side today. He felt as though he had been struck by lightning, the realisation was so startling.

'Come to Dublin with me.'

'No, I can't…'

'I want you to come—please.' His throat worked. Could he actually say the words he needed to say? After so many years of going it alone, to ask for help felt alien. 'I need your support.'

Aideen looked totally taken aback. Out of the window he could see the helicopter approaching. He looked from it to her, beseechingly.

'Okay, I'll come.'

He was about to lead her out to the garden when he remembered something. 'Hold on for a minute. There's something I need to bring.'

He sprinted down to his office and then straight back to the kitchen.

Aideen looked at the memory chest and then up at

him. She said nothing, but there were tears in her eyes before she looked away from him.

As the helicopter took off his pilot gave them their estimated flight time. He inhaled a frustrated breath and shook his head.

Beside him, Aideen asked, 'Are you okay?'

'No. If Orla had told me she was back in Dublin I could have been there much earlier. I wouldn't have been ignoring my phone all morning.'

'I can understand your frustration, but Orla wasn't to know that she was going to go into early labour. And, anyway, that was *her* decision. She's a grown woman, Patrick, about to have her own child. You can't control everything in your life. Today you just need to be there for Orla. Be the brother she loves, and trust that that's enough.'

Thrown, he was about to argue. But then he realised she was right. He had to stop thinking that the only way he could show his love for Orla was by taking charge and forcing her to lead the life he thought she should.

With a small smile he lifted his hands in admission and said, 'You're right.'

She gave him a smile in return and then looked away, her gaze on the endless patchwork of green fields that appeared through the window as the pilot banked the helicopter.

He longed to reach out and touch her, to hold her hand in his. His heart felt as though it would pound right out of his chest at any moment. Being so near to her but not being able to touch her was torture. But the hurt in her eyes was even worse. You could cut the tension in the helicopter with a knife.

Though his teeth were clenched tight, he forced them apart in order to speak. 'How is your cottage?'

She glanced at him warily, as though questioning why he was asking. 'Dusty and noisy…' She paused and held his gaze. 'But that doesn't matter. It's just really good to be home.' Then her gaze flicked away.

Why was the silence between them making him feel so uncomfortable? Before, he'd never had an issue with silence, but now it felt as if his heart was being ripped out to fill the void that sat like a physical entity between them.

He had to speak. Anything but this mocking silence which drove home much too eloquently everything he had lost: her humour, her warmth, her spark and her love of life.

'William will bring down all your files and office equipment once the cottage is finished.'

She nodded to this, her face impassive. But then she looked towards him with a frown. 'What's going to happen to William and Maureen and the rest of the staff?'

'It's part of my sale conditions that all the existing staff are retained by the new owner.'

'They're going to miss you—they're really fond of you.'

Were they? He had never stopped to think about it. But now he realised just how much he would miss them, too.

What was he *doing*? Was anything making sense in his life any more?

He looked back at her when he heard her clear her throat. 'I really hope your time with Orla goes well today. Please be patient. I bet Orla misses you desperately, but can't say it. Maybe for the same reasons that you can't say it to her.'

His mind raced at her words. Did Orla fear losing him, too? Was that why she always pushed him away? No wonder the harder he tried, the harder she pushed back.

He looked at Aideen in amazement. 'You might be right. So I just need to be there for her?'

'Yes!' With a small laugh she added, 'And for goodness' sake don't go ordering the midwives and doctors about. I'm sure they know what they are doing.'

'I won't.' He gave her a rueful look and added, 'My managing directors have a lot to thank you for, by the way. I thought about what you said about delegating more control to them and I've started doing so.'

She gave a small satisfied smile. 'And I bet the world hasn't come crashing down, has it?'

He gave an eye-roll. 'It's actually a relief to not be bogged down in day-to-day operations. I now have more time to focus on a strategic level.'

He paused for a minute, uncertain of where to take the conversation. There was so much more he should say, but he couldn't find the right words.

'How about you? What are your plans?'

For a split second she winced, but then she sat up in her seat, her voice unwavering as she spoke. 'I've had a lot of orders since Paris, and more than ever I'm determined to make Little Fire the most exciting bespoke textile design business in the world. And I'm looking forward to getting to know the people of Mooncoyne, I want to become part of the community. Get involved. I want to establish roots, to belong.'

Fresh admiration for her determination to succeed washed over him. But then a kick of reality came when it dawned on him that he didn't feature in any of her plans.

Which was only to be expected. And yet it twisted in his gut that they would soon go their separate ways.

It was what he wanted. What they had to do. Wasn't it?

CHAPTER TWELVE

His helicopter landed on the hospital's helipad and within minutes they were rushing through the front doors of the hospital.

The receptionist at the front desk blushed furiously when she looked up to see Patrick, and garbled out directions to the delivery ward. As she left Aideen gave her an understanding smile. He had that effect on all women. Herself included.

He didn't wait for the lifts but instead took the steps up to the third floor two at a time. Aideen followed his frantic pace, glad she was fit from cycling around Mooncoyne.

Again there was a flutter of activity when he stopped at the nurses' desk. Then they were directed to a number of chairs dotted along the corridor outside the delivery rooms, while one of the nurses went into the delivery suite to enquire if Orla was able to see him.

She could feel Patrick's nervousness radiating off him. 'It's going to be okay.'

He looked at her for a long while and then nodded, the tension in his face easing a little.

The door of the delivery suite opened and the nurse came back out, beaming. 'They're ready for you,' she said.

Patrick looked at Aideen in amazement. 'Does that mean that…that the baby has been born already?'

Memories of holding her own niece for the first time, the tremendous wave of love that had speared her heart, caused a lump of happiness to form in Aideen's throat. 'Yes. You better get in there.'

'Will you come in with me?'

'No. This is *your* time with Orla and her baby.'

He hesitated for a moment. 'What if I say the wrong thing?'

'You won't. Just be yourself… And remember Orla is a mum now, well capable of looking after herself. She doesn't need you to make decisions for her—she just needs your support.' She paused and eyed him with amusement. 'And advice… But only if she asks for it.'

'Will you wait here for me? I'd like to introduce you to Orla.'

'I'll wait.'

He stood and moved to the door, but then turned and said, 'Thank you. For everything.'

She returned his smile, but after the door had swung closed after him it slowly faded.

From the delivery suite she could hear the murmur of voices. Earnest, but with no hint of argument. Maybe they would be okay. She willed them to be kind and patient with one another. To realise that they needed each other. She hoped they could forget the past and realise what a wonderful future they had before them.

Patrick would be a great uncle. He had so much generosity and integrity burning inside him. Along with strength and pride. He would be an incredible role model for Orla's baby.

The murmurs had given way to light laughter. Patrick now had a newly expanded family to fill his life.

It was time for her to move on.

She left a brief note for him on her chair, and then walked back down the stairs and out of the hospital. She would get a cab to the train station. In Cork, she would get a bus to Mooncoyne.

As she queued at the taxi rank she tried to ignore the excited families going in and out of the hospital. But when a young couple emerged, the dad proudly holding his newborn child, she had to turn away, tears filming her eyes. She could go and stay with her own family, here in Dublin, but knew that if she saw her mum she would instantly burst into tears.

She would go home and lose herself in her work.

The taxi rank was busy and the line shuffled along slowly. With growing impatience she willed the taxis to come. She needed to get home. She needed to be in Mooncoyne. She needed the silence and beauty of West Cork in order to heal her broken heart.

At last it was her turn. The taxi drew to a halt, but just as she stepped forward to open the rear door a hand clasped her arm.

Patrick.

She had been crying. He tried to draw in a deep breath, but his heart was pounding too loudly, his stomach flipping so frantically there simply wasn't enough room for his lungs to expand. He'd panicked when he had realised she had gone, and her note hadn't helped. She had said she wished him well, but would prefer it if he didn't contact her again.

This was going to be the most important conversation of his life.

What if he messed up?

What if he failed to convince her?

For a moment he hesitated, fearful of blowing this.

He had to pull himself together.

'Will you come for a walk with me?'

She looked back at the taxi and for a moment he thought she was going say no. But then her shoulders dropped and the wariness of her gaze lessened.

'Is this a good idea?'

He gave her a crooked smile and shrugged. 'I'm hoping it's the best idea I ever had.'

She stared at him in confusion, but then a faint hint of amusement shone in her eyes. 'Okay.'

He took her to a nearby park, where sunlight glimmered through the trees and cast dark dancing shadows on the grey tarmacadam paths.

He didn't know where to start, so he just blurted out everything that had been building in his chest, in his mind, in his heart, for the past week.

'I've missed you.'

She looked at him with surprise and hurt.

God, this was harder than he'd thought. He wanted her to understand but he couldn't find the words. He was usually articulate, forceful. But all of that was now lost to him.

Should he just take her into his arms and kiss her? Physically show her what he was trying to say?

That wasn't the answer.

He needed to start making things right.

'I'm sorry for what happened in Paris.'

Her head whipped round. In a rush, she said, 'No, *I*

should apologise. I said things that were too intense.' Pointing to the cute blush on her cheeks she added, 'As you can see, I'm pretty embarrassed about it all. I didn't mean to put you under any pressure. I guess I misread all the signs.'

He shook his head. 'No, you weren't to blame. Everything happened so quickly. The intensity of it all got to me. After focusing on nothing but work for so long I felt overwhelmed.'

Her mouth twisted ruefully. 'I guess what I said would have had most guys heading for the hills.'

A heavy sadness sat in his chest and his throat tightened with emotion. 'Not if they'd experienced what we had together. It was special… But I had believed for so long that I wasn't cut out to be in a relationship I couldn't see beyond that.'

She looked at him, bewildered. 'I don't know why you keep saying that you aren't suited to be in a relationship. Forget me, for one moment, and what we had. All I can see before me is a thoughtful, strong, honourable man who is deserving of love.' She shook her head in exasperation. 'You deserve to be loved, Patrick. I just hope in the future you can learn to let people into your life.'

He inhaled a steadying breath. He needed to let his heart speak and ignore the vulnerability and fear of exposing himself. The fear that she would say no.

'You asked me in Paris why I couldn't be in a relationship and I didn't answer you truthfully. It was a step I just couldn't take. Even now it feels like I'm about to yank out my heart and give it to you…which makes me feel pretty exposed.'

She looked at him, confused.

He took a deep breath.

'When Orla moved in with me I was frightened of losing her, like I'd lost my mum and dad. So I tried to protect her as best I could. But now, because of you, I understand that I took the wrong approach. I shouldn't have been so controlling, so protective. I should have included her in the decisions that had to be taken in the new life we were both suddenly facing.'

He inhaled a deep breath against the way his insides were tumbling.

'You were right about Orla. I have to let her decide what support she wants from me. I'll admit it will be hard to change, after years of trying to take charge, but I know I can no longer foist what I *think* she needs on her.'

His chest felt heavy with so many words still unsaid. He drew her away from the path and guided her to a bench under a giant chestnut tree. The wood was warm under his hands when he gripped the base of the seat tight. He glanced at her, and then away.

'That fear of losing someone is the reason why I swore I never wanted to be in love with a woman. In Paris, as we grew closer, that fear intensified. I was worried that if I fell in love with you I'd only end up losing you at some point in the future. And that thought terrified me.'

His jaw ached with tension and he had to work it loose before he continued.

'And rather than face that fear I refused to acknowledge what you meant to me. After we slept together all my feelings for you were exposed, and I panicked. I couldn't handle how I was feeling. How close I felt to you, how I wanted you in my life. And when you said you were leaving I didn't know how to ask you to stay.' Shaking his head, he added, 'At first I was angry at you for going. I wanted you not to love me.'

He gave a rueful laugh and looked towards the sky in disbclief.

'I was cross that you had fallen in love with me. As if somebody can opt in or out of falling in love. And then I tried to convince myself that perhaps you going was for the best. That if you stayed any longer I wouldn't be able to hide my feelings for you. And then I realised I was kidding myself—that I was lost without you. I missed you, Aideen, with every fibre of my being.'

He risked a quick glance in her direction and her look of compassion caught him off-guard. His throat tightened, but he forced himself to speak.

'For so long I thought I'd failed not only Orla but my mum and dad, too. That I had not faced up to my responsibilities. But now I realise I have to accept that I did the best I could in looking after Orla. That I couldn't do any more. I have to stop blaming myself.'

His heart raced in his chest and he squeezed his hands even tighter on the edge of the seat before he continued.

'Today, as Orla and I spoke, I could see for the first time in a very long time that we can have a relationship that works, one that's supportive and loving. And I realised that I have to stop worrying that I will mess up relationships… I have to let go of my fear of losing those I love. I also realised that if I let you go then I would really have failed. Failed you. And myself.'

Tears shone brightly in her eyes and his hand rose to capture her face. His thumb slowly stroked her skin. She was about to say something, but he spoke first.

'That first time I opened my door to you the night of the storm—when you fell into my arms and soaked me through—I looked into those startled brown eyes and deep inside myself I recognised you. Recognised that you are the one. But I was too wrapped up in feelings of guilt and fear to see it. The last thing I wanted to do was hurt you, so I kept telling myself not to fall for you. I hadn't reckoned on how you would worm your way into my heart. How my resilience would waver each time you smiled and laughed. I hadn't reckoned on the joy and fun you brought into my life. Just how mind-blowingly and crazily I would be physically attracted to you. How I'd lose my mind and my heart to you when we made love.'

His hand dropped from her cheek to hold hers. Blood pounded in his ears.

'I love you, Aideen. I don't know how, but in a matter of weeks you've turned my life upside down. I can't even pinpoint when I fell in love with you. Perhaps it was at every moment that you challenged me, whether it was on the tennis court or in how I chose to spend my life. Of course I didn't want to listen to you, but you loosened yet another chink in the armour I had wrapped around myself for years. Or maybe it was after I saw your delight went we ate at my club next to the Eiffel Tower. Until the day I die I will remember just how stunningly beautiful you looked that night.'

He watched her shocked expression, saw her hand pressed to her mouth. His stomach clenched.

He leant towards her and said in a low voice, 'Since Paris, all I can think of is our lovemaking...your soft whispers. I'm in love with you, Aideen Ryan.'

She said nothing, just shook her head, her hand still over her mouth. Didn't she believe him? Panic gripped him. Should he just stop? No. He had to tell her how much he loved her. How much he needed her in his life.

'I'm in love with your chocolate eyes, your smiling mouth, your messy chatterbox ways. There's so much I want to know about you. How you like to celebrate Halloween, Christmas, birthdays. What's your favourite flavour of ice cream? There's so much I want to experience with you. So much more I want to learn about you and fall in love with. To go along with how much I love your lips. The never-ending length of your eyelashes. Your constant daydreaming. The five tiny piercings in your right ear.'

That, at least, elicited a smile.

'In Paris I was convinced I couldn't give you the love you deserve. You had been hurt enough in the past without me adding to it. For so long I allowed my fear of losing those close to me to push people away. I was certain I wasn't capable of being in an effective relationship. I was terrified of taking that blind leap of faith—of telling someone you love them and all the vulnerabilities and uncertainties that go with that.'

He looked into her eyes, his heart thumping wildly.

'You helped bring Orla and her baby girl back into my life. My life was pretty empty until you arrived into it. My heart had shut down. I was tired of losing people I loved. But you kick-started it with a bang within hours of turning up in my life. That night of the storm I tried to shut you out, but you kept worming your way in with your warmth and humour.'

He shook his head and ran a hand through his hair.

'At first I thought helping you would be a good distraction from everything that was happening with Orla. But, in truth, now I realise that I wanted to make up for failing Orla so badly by helping you instead. I hadn't anticipated that it would actually be more about you helping me. As each day passed you became a bigger and bigger part of my life…until now I can't imagine a life with you. So much so that in the past week I couldn't settle to anything. I grew increasingly restless, and the only way I could think of distracting myself was by taking to the road again, by selling Ashbrooke. But the truth is I can't live without you. You have made me want to live life again—fully. You are the most beautiful, courageous, kind, funny, and tender woman I have ever met and I want you in my life…for ever.'

Her head swam with all his words. It would be so easy to give in to her heart, give in to the chemistry and attraction that drew her like a magnet to him. She wanted nothing more than to spend every second of the rest of her life with him, to know every single inch of him.

But they were from different worlds, and no amount of love would change that.

'I don't know what to say. Oh, Patrick… You know how I feel for you, but this is never going to work. We're too different. We're not equals. I don't want to be in an unbalanced relationship.'

The pull of his hand on hers forced her to look back up at him. Gentle eyes held her gaze.

'What are you afraid of?'

Her pulse pounded at his question and her throat dried. 'That you will have power over me. That I will spend my life feeling inadequate, unequal, that I didn't contribute my fair share.'

He pulled her closer until there was only an inch separating them. His beautiful gaze held hers with such compassion and warmth tears trickled down her cheeks in response.

'Have I ever done any of those things to you? Made you feel like you aren't my equal?'

'No…'

'Do you trust me?'

Her heart burst forth with the truth and she answered resoundingly. 'Yes, I trust you.'

'Will you trust me when I say that we *are* equals? That we are both bringing different but equally important things to this relationship? You are bringing empathy, joy, creativity…and you brought my family back together. What could be more important than that? You have a love for me that no one else can ever give me. How can any of those things be of less importance than wealth?' Before she could answer he said quickly, 'You *do* love me, don't you?'

She struggled to speak against the wave of emotions that churned in her body. She squeezed his hands, needing to clutch on to his strength in order to carry on. 'I love you with all my heart. You are kind and generous. More handsome than any man deserves to be. You make me feel like the most special person in the world. When we made love I felt an intimacy, a love for you, that was so intense, so real…it was almost frightening. I love you so much… But you have so much wealth, and I have practically nothing… It doesn't seem right. And I'm so confused.'

For a while he simply looked at her, deep in thought. His eyes grew sombre and determined. 'Are you saying that if I lost all my money in the morning you wouldn't love me?'

'No! Of course not!'

And then she stopped as a satisfied smile broke on his lips.

'So what *are* you saying?'

For the longest while she just stared at him, unsure. She trusted him. He had never tried to control or dominate her with his wealth and power. And if he was penniless it wouldn't change her love for him.

'I suppose I'm saying that I'm a little scared and daunted by all this.'

His head tilted to the side and he said gently, 'Being in love is a little scary…but I promise I will never hurt you.'

'Are you scared?'

'Of course! I'm scared of being hurt, too—of you not loving me as much as I love you.'

'But that would be impossible.'

'Would it? Are you willing to take the risk and be with me? I love you. I want you by my side always. I want to wake to your smile, sleep with you in my arms. I want to care for you, protect you, argue with you, grow old with you. I want to share everything I have with you. Because in giving, in sharing everything I have with you, I hope you'll see it as an indication of how much I love you. And in accepting me, and all that I have, you can show me how much you love and trust me. That you are willing to share my life.'

He dropped to his knees on the path before her and she could do nothing but gape at him, open-mouthed.

'Before this year is out I want to stand before our families and friends and ask you. Aideen Ryan, for richer or poorer, will you marry me?'

Dizzy, she closed her eyes for a moment. The sun warmed her face as she turned it upwards and her hand swept away the tears on her cheeks. A fiery intensity beat in her heart.

The sun danced beneath her eyelids and when she dropped her head she opened her eyes to the pale blue Irish sky. The same glorious colour as his eyes, which she then turned to. Eyes filled with love…and a little apprehension.

She could barely speak, her pulse was pounding so hard. 'I never thought I could ever love someone as much as I love you. With you I feel complete…I feel secure. I can be the best that I am with you. The world is more beautiful, more exciting, more intense with you in it. So, yes, I would be honoured to be your wife, to spend the rest of my life with you.'

His hands wrapped about her face and he gently drew her to him. Her breath caught at the power of the joy and love shining in his eyes.

He spoke in a low whisper. 'It has taken me so long to find you…to allow love into my life. I'm never letting you out of my sight again. Promise me that we will never sleep a night apart. That you will come with me wherever I go.'

Her thumb traced the lines of his lips and she spoke with light, teasing laughter. 'I promise… I will follow you to the ends of this world. But I'm warning you: I want lots of children, so you'll have a lot of uncomfortable nights in hospital chairs.'

At that he stood, and looked down at her with stunned joy. Then he pulled her up and, holding her by the waist, swung her around and around.

When he stopped they were both breathless with laughter. And then his gaze darkened. 'How about we start trying straight away?'

She inched forward and brushed her lips against his. 'Good idea.'

And then she was lost to his strength, his warmth. His love.

EPILOGUE

Eight months later

AS SHE STOOD outside the double doors to the entrance of Ashbrooke's ballroom Aideen's fingers trembled where she held on to her dad's arm.

Behind her, her cousin and bridesmaid Kate fussed with the train of her dress.

To one side of the hallway a huge fir tree from the estate was bedecked in twinkling white Christmas lights. Through the windows beyond, fat flakes of snow fluttered down to join the heavy carpet of snow that already covered the estate.

Tomorrow—Christmas Day—she would wake up beside her husband. Giddy excitement raced through her at the thought, and she smiled quietly to herself.

She ran a hand over the delicate lace of her dress, her trained eye once again inspecting it. But there was no need. It was perfect.

She had spent weeks deciding on the design, and it had been handcrafted by a group of lacemakers who lived locally. It was a traditional Bandon Lace design, but with personal touches added—the shields that represented valour and honour on the Fitzsimon family crest, the three griffins of the Ryan crest representing courage and bravery. A seashell to represent Ashbrooke House. The sailing boat from the Parisian coat of arms. Symbols from all the places where she had fallen deeper and deeper in love with Patrick.

And on her feet were the ivory ankle-strap sandals Mustard and Mayo had bought her all those months ago.

With a nod, she signalled to her dad that she was ready.

The doors opened and once again she was dazzled by the ornate heavy gilt mirrored walls, the cherub-filled frescoed ceiling of the ballroom, and her heart leapt at its spectacular beauty.

Her family and friends beamed back at her and her already bursting heart exploded with joy. Her mum openly cried, while her two brothers tried to pretend they weren't.

Orla, holding baby Evie in her arms, looked from Aideen to Patrick with love and pride.

Patrick's best man, Frédéric Forbin, whispered something to him and he nodded in response.

When was he going to turn to her?

The dogs sat patiently at his feet, both wearing pale pink bows to match the bridal party. Behind him stood his large group of friends, including Lord Balfe, all of whom had travelled from around the world to be here. Friends who were once again part of his life.

And then he turned to her.

She wanted to run to him but forced herself to take the slow bridal steps. His hair was shorn once again, highlighting the sharp masculine lines of his face, the brilliant blue of his eyes.

Step by step she moved closer to her best friend. To the

man who made her feel like the most beautiful woman in the world.

With him, she was complete.

Before him, she'd felt as though she was a feather—floating through the air, happy, but never quite belonging, never quite understanding.

And now, because of him, she understood. That this life was about love. Giving love. But also receiving it. That was all that really mattered.

And tonight, at the stroke of midnight, she would give him his Christmas present: the news that she was six weeks pregnant.

* * * * *